Cave of Bones

ALSO BY ANNE HILLERMAN

Song of the Lion

Rock with Wings

Spider Woman's Daughter

Tony Hillerman's Landscape:
On the Road with Chee and Leaphorn

Gardens of Santa Fe

Santa Fe Flavors: Best Restaurants and Recipes

Ride the Wind: USA to Africa

Cave of Bones

A Leaphorn, Chee & Manuelito Novel

Anne Hillerman

An Imprint of HarperCollinsPublishers

HarperCollins books may be purchased for educational, business, or sales promotional use. For information please e-mail the Special Markets Department at SPsales@harpercollins.com.

FIRST HARPERLUXE EDITION

ISBN: 978-0-06-279198-6

HarperLuxe™ is a trademark of HarperCollins Publishers.

Library of Congress Cataloging-in-Publication Data is available upon request.

18 19 20 21 22   ID/LSC   10 9 8 7 6 5 4 3 2 1

Cave of Bones is dedicated to the memory of
Navajo Police Officer Houston James Largo,
who was killed in the line of duty; and to my dear
brother and supportive fan Steve Hillerman,
who died of cancer August 23, 2017.

1

Annie Rainsong knew that today she would die. And that she deserved to.

She never should have left her vision site, but she was cold, restless, bored, hungry, and ready to be done with this outdoor stuff. She wanted a beer and a cigarette, or at least a shower and a sandwich. No, two sandwiches. She knew she should have been back at base camp by now. Leaving her vision site had been a bad, bad idea.

The stupid piles of rocks that marked the trail blended into the darkness now. Nothing looked familiar—or everything looked like something she had seen before. Nothing looked safe. Her head ached; her feet hurt from the ugly new hiking boots. She wanted to stop moving, be done with this. Her *shimásání* had always told her not to complain, only to be grateful.

She pictured her grandmother's face and remembered the warm smell of the blue corn cakes she fixed for breakfast. It made her feel like crying, so Annie swore out loud instead.

She saw what looked like a cave up ahead and directed the weak beam of her flashlight into the lava. She would climb there, she decided, and hope there weren't any dead bugs or bat poop to creep her out. The old ones had lived in caves, hadn't they? Maybe she'd be lucky enough to fall asleep and die. She'd heard of that happening.

She hiked toward it, relieved to have a destination even though the blister on the back of her left heel rubbed against the stiff boot every time she took a step. She felt less lost now. Maybe it would even be warmer in there. Mr. Cruz and Mrs. Cooper had told her to stay out of caves, because of hibernating bats and because the caves might have been used by the old ones and contain bones or gifts for the dead. She decided it didn't matter now. This whole stinking program was a farce, and she was as good as dead anyway.

When she got to the cave, she'd take the boots off. Who cared what Mr. Cruz said? He was a jerk. She never believed in this vision stuff anyway, but she played along. It was better than being on probation for a year and all the bull that went with that. At least, that's what she'd thought when she let her mother talk her into participating.

As she limped closer, she realized that there were big lava boulders around the mouth of the cave, making it hard to see at this angle. She was lucky she'd found it. Lucky? Cooper said the experience out here changed people, but if it actually gave her some luck, she'd be amazed. She started to climb, struggling against the angle of the hillside, slipping on patches of icy snow she hadn't seen in the cloud-covered night. Before she reached the top she was practically crawling, using numb fingers to help pull herself to the cave.

Annie made it to the crest of the slope and straightened up, catching her breath.

She remembered the pack-rat nest she'd seen at Grandma's place, out past the hogan, when life was better, before her *shimásání* died and her brother had his accident and everything changed. Would the cave be a good place for a pack rat? Or for *shash*, a bear snoozing off her fall fat and waiting to emerge in the spring, maybe with some cubs? She didn't like the idea of disturbing a sleeping bear.

The flashlight's beam reflected off the black rocks at the cave's mouth and illuminated wavy white lines and stick figures, before the beam disappeared into the darkness. The figures made her think of something a little kid would draw, simple light marks on the dark stone. Mrs. Cooper had mentioned that they might see something like this and told the girls not to touch them.

Annie ran her finger over a spiral. The image captured the moon's milky light. Cool, she thought. The pictures looked like something her brother might make. She could hear Mother telling him not to draw on the walls; maybe this little brat's mom told him the same thing.

To get the flashlight to shine inside the cave, she had to sink to her knees. The tremor in her hand made the faint beam dance against the blackness. She inched her way toward the entrance, the light preceding her like bad news. She saw nothing threatening. The light bounced off her wrist, and Annie Rainsong glanced at her forbidden tattoo, the skull her mother hated. She'd always thought it was cool, but now she looked away and used her light to search the cave, finding no rats or rat's nests or anything that looked bearlike.

She sat on the rock ledge at the entrance of the cave, put down her flashlight, pulled up the collar on her jacket, and shoved her hands in the pockets. She wasn't even hungry or thirsty anymore. Only bone-cold and scared and ready to die. Maybe there was a bear in the very back of the cave, where her light didn't go. Maybe the bear would find her and eat her or feed her to the cubs. That would be all right, she thought. Better than having her own mom yell at her for being a screwup. Better than having Mrs. Cooper tell her she'd messed up the whole trip for the group by not following the rules. Everyone cared about the rules. Nobody cared about her.

The cave would be a hard place for Mr. Cruz to find her, but it would be a safe place to die. She was glad those big rocks blocked most of the entrance. They would keep animals out, unless something was already inside; the cave smelled funny. She didn't like the thought of a coyote finding her. It was bad enough when she heard them howling, and she remembered that time when she was little and she and Grandmother had come across the sheep—or what was left of it—that the coyotes had just killed.

Annie started to relax. The cave was safer than that stupid flimsy tent they gave her. She was OK here, she told herself. She heard the sound of her own breathing and the beat of her heart pushing blood up to her ears. She leaned back, feeling the cold stone wall through her coat, staying close to the entrance. It bothered her that she couldn't see what was beyond the beam of her flashlight, but being outside bothered her even more. She would wait for the sunrise and as soon as it got light she'd start to yell for Mr. Cruz or go back to hiking, watching for those stupid towers of rocks, the Karens or something, to find the dumb campsite.

Annie Rainsong took pride in her toughness. Nobody in school, when she went to school, messed with her. Teachers left her alone except for some *bilagáana* do-gooders. If any adults looked at her with pity because of her brother, she gave them a hard glare that said *Hands off!* She'd sit in the cave and wait for a vision, or wait to die. Who cared about a stupid vision, anyway? She could make that up if she had to.

She readjusted her back against the sharp lava. It wouldn't be so bad to die out here, she thought. Kind of peaceful. She stretched her legs into the darkness. She had seen on TV that the cold made people sleepy, and then they died. Hydrophobia or something. She wouldn't mind that. Her mom would start to cry and beg forgiveness. Too late. Her *chindi* would hang about and bug her. Maybe they would leave her in the cave, wall up her body until it became a pile of bones. Or not find her at all. Then Mom would be really teed off.

Annie stretched a little more. Her right foot encountered something hard, probably a rock. She adjusted her position, wishing she'd brought her sleeping bag instead of leaving it in the tent. Even with the cold, she felt better here, out of the wind, without the noise of the tent straps and fabric flapping. She saw the sliver of a moon as it rose over a river of darkness separating the clouds. It was *hai*, winter, and the month of *nilch'itsoh*, a time when some creatures would rest and others would die. Either way, she thought, it's how my story plays out.

She must have closed her eyes, because when she opened them again the sky wore a tinge of pink. She remembered where she was and why in the next millisecond. On the next breath, she realized that her back and hips hurt, her stomach ached, and December's cold had seeped up through the little bones of her smallest toes all the way to her knees, her spine, and the very top of her head. Ever her hair was freezing cold. She shifted and wiggled her feet, glad that she had left her boots on because her stiff fingers would not have been able to deal with shoelaces.

She pushed herself to sitting and glanced down to see what she had pressed against in the dark.

Her screams echoed off the lava.

2

The trouble started simply enough, as many things do. Several weeks earlier, Captain Howard Largo had asked Officer Bernadette Manuelito if she would help the Ramah Navajo district with a little volunteer project. Officer Cheryl Jasper had signed up to do it, but then Jasper's daughter qualified for the finals in something at school and the family had an opportunity to go to Albuquerque to cheer her on.

Largo reminded Bernie that Officer Jasper had filled in at the Shiprock district three years before, when Bernie and Sergeant Jim Chee wanted time off together for their honeymoon. The Ramah Navajo were known for their independence, and if it hadn't been for clan ties traced back to Bernie's mother's mother, Cheryl Jasper might not have been as gracious about spending some of her precious vacation working in Shiprock. Bernie knew she owed her colleague a favor, and payback time had arrived.

"What do I have to do?"

"Oh, nothing much, and it will get you outside. Hiking is involved, and Officer Jasper especially asked for you." Largo's voice had a touch of the trickster in it. "I'm not making you do this, Manuelito, but I'm telling you it would be a darn good idea."

"Don't say it will build my character."

"You're already enough of a character."

That Largo hadn't volunteered the details seemed suspicious. "Sir, can you tell me more about what doing 'nothing much' means?"

"Don't worry, Manuelito. You like being out of the office. Officer Jasper will fill you in. Thanks."

He picked up his phone, indicating the conversation was done.

Chee planned to be away in Santa Fe for a few days, for intensive training at the New Mexico Law Enforcement Academy. Bernie's sister, Darleen, had been invited to attend a program for prospective students at the Institute of American Indian Arts, a college in Santa Fe. Even Mama would be gone. Her mother felt so well she planned to go to the Crownpoint rug auction with her weaving student, Mrs. Bigman.

So Bernie had agreed before she called Officer Jasper, and that was her first mistake.

The Ramah Navajo in many ways considered themselves and their schools, police force, and jail separate from the larger Navajo Nation. They were physically separated, too. Their territory, which didn't adjoin the rest of the Navajo Nation, encompassed some two hundred square miles of land interspersed with private holdings, creating what was known as the Checkerboard because of the pattern it made on a map. Some of this land not owned by the Navajo had been deeded to the Atchison, Topeka and Santa Fe Railway for a route to Needles, California, but it was never used. It was opened to anyone who could develop it under the Homestead Act of 1862—but somehow the government forgot to notify the Navajo families living in the area.

After Bernie told Largo yes, she phoned Officer Jasper. They talked about Jasper's daughter's award, about Chee, about Bernie's mother, and about Darleen. Then Jasper laid out the bad news. Before she learned her daughter had won the trip, she had agreed to go out to talk to a group of Navajo girls participating in an outdoor program.

"You mean, make a speech?" Bernie felt her heart beat faster.

"No. Nothing as serious as that. It's not a big deal."

Jasper's voice sounded calmly reassuring. "You could do it in your sleep."

"Where will the group be?"

"In the Malpais. They're camping at the Narrows. You'll like them, and the location is wonderful."

"When?"

Jasper gave her the time she was expected to speak— a few weeks in the future—and the phone number for the program's contact. "Can you call them and tell them I can't make it, but that you'll be substituting? They'll want to know a little about you so they can tell the girls. Thanks, Bernie. You're the best."

Bernie would rather face a rampaging three-hundred-pound drunk than gaze out at an audience. Every time she had to speak in public, become the center of attention, her mouth went dry, her palms started to sweat, and her stomach tied itself in a knot. Her heartbeat accelerated faster than when she was chasing a meth head. She could see Mama frowning at her, hear her chiding—in Navajo, of course. *It isn't good to puff yourself up. It isn't the Navajo way.*

Bernie immediately called the woman in charge of the program, a *bilagáana* named Rose Cooper, to tell her that Officer Jasper had been called away on family business and wouldn't be able to talk to the girls. She did not volunteer to take her place.

Cooper's disappointment resonated over the phone. "That's too bad. The girls look forward to her presentation each year. Do you know anything about our program?"

"I don't."

"Well, we're based in Shiprock, and we do sessions all over the Four Corners. We work mostly with young people referred by the court system or schools and sometimes parents at their wits' end. All of them are facing transitions and need some breathing room to figure out what comes next." Cooper segued to the group of Navajo girls Officer Jasper had promised to speak to. "Some of them have had a brush with the law— shoplifting, drinking, marijuana, fighting. Others were enrolled because their parents thought being outside, learning new skills, and testing themselves against nature would help them gain confidence. They are fine kids, full of ideas and energy. The program gives them a new way to view themselves and the world. We have a leader who talks to them extensively about *k'é*—you know, the importance of kinship, and about traditional Diné values as a way to find a path through the world."

Bernie had heard of such programs. She'd even suggested one to Mama for Darleen, as an antidote to beer and partying.

"I could go on talking, but the best way to learn what

we do is to come up and see for yourself. You'd be doing yourself a favor, and these girls need to see the police as the good guys, right?" Cooper didn't wait for her response. "Some of them might even want to go into law enforcement, and they have to stay out of trouble to do that. And besides, the place where we set up the base camp is lovely. Do you know the area very well?"

"No. I'm from Shiprock, too." Bernie remembered Cooper saying that was the program's headquarters. She waited to see what Cooper would come up with next.

"When you get to the Wings and Roots campsite, you can take a trail to the top of a gorgeous sandstone mesa and look down on all that lava. The view is spectacular, no kidding."

"I can't make it. I like to hike, and I'm all for helping girls grow into strong women. But speaking to groups isn't my strong suit."

Cooper chuckled. "So that's what it is. No problem. We're more like family than an audience. Just talk about what you do and how you got to be a cop, and then let the girls ask questions. Pretend they are your little relatives. That's what Cheryl, Officer Jasper . . . that's what she did last year. We're very casual here. No microphones or stuff like that."

"Well. Ah . . ." Bernie searched her mental library

for another excuse. "It's hard to make plans weeks ahead like this in police work. You never know when something might happen that you'll have to take care of as an officer."

Cooper injected her final argument. "We always grill hamburgers for lunch that last day of the course. Just come and eat with us. You don't have to say a word if we don't make you feel welcome. I imagine it will do you good to get out of that dang car. I know you officers are always driving around. You'll need to eat anyway."

"I'm not sure what my schedule will be." That sounded weak even to Bernie.

"Of course you aren't. But we'll count on you arriving late morning and figure out the details when you get here. See you soon." And with that, Cooper ended the call.

The woman reminded Bernie of a non-Navajo version of Mama, with the same will-of-iron attitude toward getting what she wanted. But the place sounded beautiful, and burgers on the grill were one of her favorite foods. And how hard could it be to talk to girls about why and how she became a cop? She'd already had the conversation with Mama, Darleen, and Mama's neighbor, Mrs. Darkwater.

Now, as she drove her green-and-white Navajo Police SUV from Grants toward the Narrows campground where Cooper told her the program had set up base camp, she was having second thoughts. She stopped at the visitor center, a sunlit building perched at the edge of the park, for a map and some brochures. She scanned the information, stalling as she read and hoping that some malfeasance—nothing serious, just any incident demanding her presence—might result in a call on her radio. But it remained frustratingly silent.

She drove southwest on New Mexico 117, one of two paved highways that skirted the acres of lava flow. NM 117 formed the border between El Malpais National Monument and the El Malpais National Conservation Area, threading its way between the lava and towering sandstone cliffs shaped by the forces of time. The conservation area abutted Acoma Indian Reservation land and, like ancient trails across the lava, was dotted with prayer sticks, shrines, and the sacred, unmentioned burials of Pueblo ancestors. This public land, administered by the Bureau of Land Management, also bordered the Ramah reservation and pockets of private land holdings. Most people driving through or stopping to hike simply called this whole area El Malpais—"the Badlands" in Spanish—leaving the changing jurisdictions as a matter of discussion for those who created the maps. But the checkerboard of state, federal, and tribal jurisdictions made law enforcement here complicated.

Bernie knew El Malpais as Yeiitssoh Bidil Niniyee-zhi, Navajo that translated to something like "Where Big God's Blood Coagulated." The name came from one of the legendary adventures of the Hero Twins as they made the world safe for the People. The families of the Laguna, Acoma, and Zuni pueblos had their own names and stories for the supernatural way in which this landscape came to be, wisdom that predated both the Spanish encounters and the American geological surveys. She'd read that scientists traced the lava to several different eruptions, including one of the most recent. The river of melted stone stretched forty miles long and from five to fifteen miles across, a landscape of craters, cones, lava falls, and ice caves. The lava also created what geologists called "tubes." As the molten lava flowed, the top layer started to harden, but the stone underneath remained liquid and flowed on. Over time the unsupported top layers collapsed in places, creating access to underground caves.

Bernie found this landscape both foreboding and beautiful, in the same way that she appreciated the good looks of a fearsomely strong bull in the chute at a rodeo.

The Narrows campsite sat at the spot where the lava and the sandstone might have met if it hadn't been for the ribbon of pavement. Bernie climbed out of her unit. As Cooper had suggested, it felt good just to stand in this expansive landscape, and the promise of hamburgers sweetened the morning. The early December sun shared the blue sky with a few clouds. She'd heard a snow storm was on the way, but she and the girls would be home before it hit.

She approached the red tent, which, from Cooper's description, served as headquarters for the Wings and Roots camp. Two girls sitting at a picnic table focused on her now instead of whatever they'd been talking about. Beyond them, a woman with reddish-brown braids was sitting in a camping chair with a book in her hands, next to a pile of backpacks, an orange water jug the size of a small barrel, and cloth bags stuffed with enough of whatever to let them stand straight.

The scene resembled a typical campsite in the process of closing down, but the vibe was wrong. The girls looked worried as she approached, different from the typical expressions of civilians interacting with a cop.

"Hi," Bernie said. "Can you tell me where to find Mrs. Cooper?"

"She's on the mesa, at the group campsite up there," said one of the girls at the picnic table, whose dark hair was pulled back in a ponytail. "Are you here because of Annie and Mr. Cruz?"

"I'm here because Mrs. Cooper invited me to talk to you guys."

The girl looked disappointed. A great way to start off with her audience, Bernie thought.

The woman with the book approached her. "Are you the officer who was giving the lecture?"

"That's me. Bernie Manuelito." A lecture? "Will I be speaking to the girls down here?"

"You better talk to Cooper about that." The woman had a touch of an accent, and there was a bit of attitude in her voice. "She's the one in charge of everything. I'll let her tell you what's going on. That's the way she likes it. I'm only the assistant. Lacy Mayfair."

"So Mrs. Cooper is up on the mesa?" Bernie looked up at the sandstone cliffs that provided a backdrop to the campsite.

"Yes. That's right. You'll see the tent, our head-quarters." Mayfair turned to the girls. "You two show her the way, then get back down here to help me. Understood?"

They nodded and headed off, Bernie following.

The trail started at the edge of the parking lot and, after a rather steep ascent, became a flat, sandy, serpentine path, sometimes meandering close enough to the mesa's edge to offer a fine view of the lava field just across the highway. The girls walked single file, and Bernie trailed behind. A raven soared, a glistening dark shape against the vivid blue sky. The cool morning air was invigorating. Too bad all speaking requests didn't include a half hour of walking on a brilliant December day. The hike calmed her, pushing aside the anxiety of the pending talk.

A woman with gray hair clustered in short, tight curls was pacing outside a tent as they approached the campsite. Bernie saw piles of equipment, neatly stacked, and the ring of rocks that surrounded a few pieces of blackened wood where a campfire had blazed. The woman glanced up and waved Bernie over. "Officer Manuelito? Rose Cooper. Good to see you. Thanks for coming." Cooper looked at the girls. "Get a drink and a snack if you'd like, and then wait up here for the closing circle."

"But Ms. Mayfair said—"

Cooper put a finger to her lips. "I'm in charge, remember?"

The girls smiled and bounced away to join the other campers.

The area seemed naturally intended for small group gatherings. A few girls stood in clusters or sat on rocks. Bernie counted nine, plus the two who had come up with her. All looked to be Navajo and in their early teens.

Cooper had dark half-moons beneath her eyes. "I'm glad you're here, Officer. We've got a big problem."

"What's going on?"

"A girl and the assistant program director are lost out there in the lava somewhere."

"Tell me what happened."

"A girl, Annie Rainsong, wasn't where she should have stayed for her solo. Mr. Cruz brought the other three girls he was responsible for to base camp and then went out for Annie. They haven't come back." Cooper's right hand made a pass through her curls. "He knows this area, and he's had a lot of experience outdoors, as a hiker and a guide. At first I didn't think much about it. But now I'm worried that something has happened to them."

"Tell me more about the girl and the solo."

"Each camper has a designated spot for her solo, her time alone to reflect on her life. We tell them to stay at that spot overnight, and at dawn Mr. Cruz, Ms. Mayfair, or I come to bring them back to base camp." Cooper shook her head. "Mr. Cruz saved Annie's spot for last, since she was closest to base camp."

"How long has he been gone?"

"Two hours." Cooper glanced toward the lava again, and when she turned back, Bernie saw the tears.

"Have you looked for them?"

"Yes. I sent Mayfair and the two girls you just saw—they are a bit older, more responsible—out to search. I told them to stay along the trail from here to Annie's solo site, the place she was supposed to wait. They saw Annie's tent and sleeping bag right where they should be, but they didn't find any trace of her, and no clue as to where she or Dom might have gone."

"Dom?"

"Domingo Cruz, the missing man." Cooper looked at her watch, then back at Bernie. "Annie has been trouble from the start of the trip. Her mother leaned on me to accept her as a camper, and I should have said no."

"Have you called the police?"

"No. I knew you were coming, and I figured . . . I should have called already, shouldn't I? But I know Dom can find his way out there. He's had so much experience. He'd be embarrassed if we made a big fuss for nothing. He's always taking pictures out there. I'm hoping he just got distracted, lost track of time."

"How far was Annie's solo site from the base camp?"

"You mean, how long would it take to get there?"

Cooper didn't wait for Bernie to respond. "Maybe a twenty-minute hike. Mr. Cruz mapped it out so each of our girls would get a flat place for her tent. We wanted Annie to have some solitude without being too far from help if she needed it, like all the girls."

Bernie did the math. Considering Cruz's experience, it wasn't too soon to notify the New Mexico State Police, the agency that activated operations to find people lost in the wilderness and bring then out safely. "You've done everything you can, Mrs. Cooper. It's time to put search and rescue on alert."

"Whatever you think, Officer."

"Call me Bernie."

"OK. Call me Rose."

"Rose, hike down with me to my unit, and we'll use the radio to call this in. The police will need information from you."

"Of course." She turned to where the girls were clustered, motioned them over, and explained the situation. "While Officer Bernie and I talk to the police, you all gather up your belongings, and make sure the campsite is spotless. Then finish your expedition journals. Any questions?"

The girls looked at her in stunned silence.

Cooper led the way, setting a rapid pace. The trail didn't seem quite as beautiful now, even though the sun warmed Bernie's face and the air smelled subtly of the vanilla essence of ponderosa pine.

The older woman spoke first. "What kind of information will they need to start the search? I figure they'll want a physical description, age, height, weight, what they both were wearing."

"That's right. They will need the location of the girl's campsite and where Mr. Cruz was last seen. They'll ask if either of them had any medical conditions, seizure disorders, things like that."

Cooper made a sound that resembled a laugh, but without the happiness. "Annie is disorder on two legs. That girl demanded more attention than the rest of the group put together. But no medical issues. Of course, she's also a chronic liar."

"Could she have disappeared on purpose?"

Cooper took a moment to respond. "I guess so, but Annie had the most fear about doing the solo of any of the girls in the group. I can't imagine her trotting out in the lava by herself. She and her mother don't get along, but that's true of a lot of these girls. Annie doesn't have a history of running away; that's one of the questions we always ask."

"You said Mr. Cruz is experienced out here."

"He knows this place better than Mayfair or I do. And he understands our protocol. He should have hiked in by now, even if he wasn't able to find her. I'm worried that he might be hurt."

"What did he have with him? Cell phone, water, food, first aid supplies?"

"Of course. I'm not sure about the phone. They don't work very well out in areas of the lava fields."

Bernie thought about how to best ask the next question and couldn't come up with a graceful way. "Do you have any reason to suspect that the two of them may have had a physical relationship? Some reason to run off, disappear together?"

"Never. Not at all." Bernie heard the flare of anger in Cooper's voice. "Dom is not that kind of man. He's not a pedophile, if that's what you're implying. I'd swear to that on my mother's grave. Some of these girls have been molested, traumatized, abused, you name it. How could you imply that I'd hire a person like that to work with them?"

"I'm not implying anything. I'm just asking a question."

They walked in silence.

Bernie had explored a little in the Malpais, and she knew that the lava could be treacherous. This time of year, the area might be hit by blizzards that buried the trails and their markers under snow. In the summer, the temperatures ratcheted to over a hundred degrees.

In all seasons, the dark rock was slippery, sharp, and filled with crevices and unexpected challenges. What looked like solid footing could turn out to be the thin dome of a lava bubble.

As she followed the trail off the mesa top, Bernie was glad she had stowed her hiking boots in the unit. Her work shoes had been fine so far, but she expected to be walking this route several more times and possibly climbing into the lava before the day was done. She would change after she radioed state police to tell them about the lost ones.

Bernie had worked with searches on the reservation, and she thought about them as she hiked. On Navajo land, she had searched for competent adults who had been gathering piñon nuts in the mountains or searching for missing livestock and lost their bearings. She had helped find older people with memory problems and children who had wandered away from home and disappeared. The Nation's four million acres on the Colorado Plateau encompassed terrain from the ponderosa-dotted slopes of the Lukachukai Mountains to the sprawling shale and sandstone emptiness of Monument Valley. It offered an abundance of places to get lost in.

The Navajo Nation's own search and rescue unit sometimes requested help from the states of New

Mexico or Arizona, depending on where the problem originated. Diné searchers reciprocated, working with teams in areas bordering the Navajo Nation.

In the parking lot, Mayfair stood when Bernie and Cooper approached. Bernie unlocked her unit and opened the door.

"Wait." Cooper touched her arm. "I see something."

3

Bernie followed Cooper's gaze and spotted a figure running toward them, long hair swaying back and forth as she moved.

"Annie!" The director's voice rang out, and she sprinted to meet the girl, enclosing her in outstretched arms. The embrace continued for a while, and then the sobbing stopped. Cooper led the girl toward the police car.

Annie looked pale and distraught, but she seemed uninjured.

Cooper had her arm over Annie's shoulders, but the girl shrugged it off. "Did you call the police on me?"

Cooper stepped back, and Bernie took charge.

"Mrs. Cooper invited me to talk to your group, and when I got here, I learned that you and Mr. Cruz hadn't come back from the lava. You aren't in any trouble with me."

"Where's Mr. Cruz? He's not here? Oh my god. I thought . . ."

"You thought what?" Bernie held the girl's gaze until Annie looked away.

"I thought he would be here. This is terrible." Annie leaned against the hood of Bernie's unit and closed her eyes.

Cooper moved next to the girl. She unhooked her water bottle, pressed it into Annie's hand. "Drink some of this now."

After the girl drank, Mayfair helped Annie off with her pack and made her sit down. Cooper gave her assistant a faint smile. "Keep an eye on this one while we notify the police about Mr. Cruz. When she feels better, walk up to base camp with her, and stay with the girls until I get done, and we can do our closing circle. They will be relieved to see that she is back and safe."

"I'm OK," Annie said. "I wanna go now."

Bernie took a step toward the girl. "Annie, do you know where Mr. Cruz is?"

"No. Why would I?" The girl stared at the ground.

"Because he went to look for you." Bernie kept her voice gentle. "We need to talk about what happened, but first, Mrs. Cooper and I need to get the search going."

Mayfair looked at Annie. "Let's go. We can stop whenever you need to, if you're tired."

"I'm not tired. I wanna see my friends."

After they left, Bernie made notes based on Cooper's description of Domingo Cruz: Navajo, six feet tall, about two hundred pounds, forty-two years old, black hair with a touch of gray at the temples, dark brown eyes, wearing a blue jacket with reflective trim.

"Anything else?"

Cooper straightened her shoulders. "Well, he has a black backpack with a bear bell he bought in Alaska to keep from surprising a grizzly, and hiking boots. He might have his red knit cap. It was below freezing this morning when he went out after Annie."

Bernie turned to Cooper and stared directly into the older woman's face, something she'd had to train herself to do in dealing with white people. "Was Mr. Cruz depressed, upset, worried about something?"

"Worried? Who doesn't worry?" She ran a hand through her curls. "We've got some budget issues, some staff changes in the works. He might have been a little preoccupied, you know? That's just part of life around here."

"Is there any reason you can think of he would have chosen not to return?"

Cooper's eyes widened. "He would never kill himself, if that's what you're asking."

Bernie knew that many times lost ones came back on their own as Annie had; she hoped this would be true with Mr. Cruz. Sometimes the people being sought failed to return on purpose, the weight of responsibility and unhappiness pushing them into a place of despair so deep and lonely they forgot that their relatives still cared about them.

"Did he have a weapon?"

"Yes. A knife and a gun."

Bernie felt her cell phone vibrate she approached her unit. Sandra, the Shiprock substation dispatcher and her friend, was on the line.

"Are you done out there? Captain Largo has something for you."

"Not yet. There's a new development." She explained.

Sandra's voice came in clear and strong. "Wow. I'm glad that girl is safe. I'll tell the captain. Will you be somewhere with phone reception for a few minutes so he can talk to you?"

"Sure. I'm calling for search and rescue now, and I'll give Largo an update after that."

In New Mexico, the state police resource officer, based in Albuquerque, is the person with whom official search and rescue operations begin. Bernie described the situation to the coordinator, gave directions to the group campsite, and asked him to inform law enforcement assigned to the Malpais National Monument and the BLM, who managed the conservation area.

"How long do you think it will be before the team gets here?" Bernie asked.

The voice on the phone was calm. "I think the quickest will be two or three hours. Can you or someone stay at the youth camp until the state police officer comes? Officer Manzanares will be dispatched from Grants."

Bernie repeated the question to Cooper. The director shook her head. "I'll stay as long as I can, but I have to get the other campers back to their families."

Bernie relayed Cooper's information to the coordinator. "If the program director has to leave, I'll wait here until the officer arrives. He'll see my unit in the parking area. I hope my captain doesn't give me any grief."

The coordinator chuckled. "I know Largo. Have him call me."

Bernie ended the call.

"Thank you for handling that," Cooper said. "What happens now?"

"We wait. The state police officer will talk to us and then launch the search." She explained how the officer would assess the situation and contact a regional incident commander to activate teams of trained volunteers who lived in the area. The teams would then put their everyday lives on pause, organize gear, load up, and head out with the goal of getting to the area to be searched and setting up a command center there as rapidly as possible.

Cooper nodded. "That gives Cruz more time to come back. He'd be embarrassed about causing a fuss. But it also means more time to suffer if he's hurt out there. I'm not going to think about that."

"They'll want to start the search at the last place Cruz was known to have been."

"That's up there at base camp where I saw him leave, hiking down the trail to the parking area. He planned to cross the highway and head out into the lava."

"Did you notice anything different about him today? Anything he said or did?"

"It's hard to explain. He's always professional. But it seemed like there was something on his mind all week that took away some of his focus."

"Did he say anything unusual?"

"Not really. As we were driving, he mentioned the political game all of us agencies have to play to get

money from the government. He said he enjoyed working with me and that he appreciated all the time and
energy I gave the program." Cooper zipped her jacket
against a gust of wind. "On the other end of the age
spectrum, there are twelve lively reasons in this camp
to be distracted, but Dom had dealt with it all before.
The Rainsong girl, for instance, the one he went to
find, is a hard case."

"I want to talk to her."

Cooper nodded once. "She's not much of a talker.
And now, besides the stress of getting lost, I think she's
still shaken from her vision state."

"Vision state?"

"That's part of the solo. The girls come here to
think about their future, their past, how to dismantle
or navigate the obstacles in the way of their happiness
and success, however they define it. We talk about all
that and do some outdoor-skills work in preparation
for the solo. The idea is to let them calm down, get
more introspective, be at peace when they are alone.
A staff member helps each girl find a special campsite
for herself, and she spends about twenty-four hours
alone. We make them leave cell phones, music players,
video games, all that in the van. Only a tent, a sleeping bag, water, a flashlight, some snacks, and their own
thoughts out there with them."

"Do they actually experience a vision?"

"If things go like we want them to, the kids have insights." Cooper shrugged. "Sometimes a spirit animal visits them as a guide. Sometimes they hear a voice giving them advice or hope. Like I said, when it gets light, Cruz or Mayfair or I come for them at the solo site. Then they pack up their tents and hike back here for our group breakfast and a circle of sharing."

Cooper put her pack back on. "I need to hike back to the campsite for our closing ritual. You're welcome to join us and say a few words. I'm sorry you didn't get to give your talk. And no hamburgers today. All this commotion has put us way behind schedule."

"No problem. I need to wait down here for the search team."

After Cooper headed off, Bernie called the Shiprock substation and learned that Largo had stepped out. She chatted a moment with her friend in dispatch.

"How did your talk go?" Sandra asked.

"Best talk ever. Because of all the commotion with the girl and Mr. Cruz, I didn't have to give it. I'd rather deal with a missing person any day."

"That poor man. And the young girl who was lost out there. She must have been scared, and now she's probably thinking this is all her fault."

After Sandra signed off, Bernie dialed Chee's cell

phone, surprised that she had service and disappointed when the call went to voice mail. She left a "call me" message and then changed into her hiking boots and locked the unit. She'd noticed the white van with a Wings and Roots logo on the side when she first pulled into the parking area, the only vehicle besides her own. Now she realized that the driver's-side door was slightly ajar. She closed it, hoping that the battery still had some juice. Cooper, Mayfair, and the girls didn't need any more complications.

Three girls were hiking down the trail toward the parking lot, carrying duffels. The last one of them was Annie. The girls set the bags by the truck, and then the other two headed back up the mesa as Annie stepped toward Bernie.

"Mrs. Cooper said I should talk to you." The girl looked as though she'd been crying.

"Let's go over there." Bernie walked toward an empty picnic table.

"Why do you want to talk to me? I didn't mean to get lost." Annie's voice trembled.

"It's about Mr. Cruz."

The girl was silent.

"Sit down with me a minute. You've had a rough morning."

Annie lowered herself onto the bench across from

Bernie and rested her head in her hands. The sunlight added a sheen to the girl's straight black hair. She had chipped purple polish on her nails, and silver and turquoise rings on various fingers. With her head bent, her hair created a curtain around her face that moved when she spoke. "I didn't do anything."

"You're not in trouble."

"Really?" Annie looked up. Gold balls paraded around her ear lobes, from small to larger. "Mrs. Cooper said Mr. Cruz got lost because of me."

"What do you think?"

"Cooper hates me. She's a witch, and I hate her more." Annie reached for a water bottle emblazoned with the program logo. "If I tell you something, will you have to tell her?"

"That depends on what it is."

Annie rolled the bottle between her hands, and when she put it down, Bernie noticed a tattoo of a skull on her wrist. She rose from the bench, graceful as a fawn, and paced for a moment. "I guess it doesn't matter if you tell her," she said as she came back. "The witch already thinks I'm a hopeless loser because I screwed up my solo. Did she tell you about it? I mean the rules, how it was supposed to work?"

"I'd like you to tell me." Build a little rapport, Bernie thought, and maybe Annie's story would offer a clue to finding Cruz.

Annie picked at a cuticle. "Well, OK. We all had our own vision site, and Ms. Mayfair—she's the one who does the work around here—she said we could walk around until it got dark, and then we had to stay put until it got light again. We could think about things, take a nap, sing to ourselves, whatever. In the morning, everyone would come back to talk about what happened. Then Mr. Cruz hiked out with me."

"So after Mr. Cruz left, you were out there alone."

"I thought it sounded lame, but it was all right at first. I heard ravens making those sounds, you know, kind of like voices. I saw a deer. I walked around a little and saw some prayer sticks, but I didn't touch them. I came back to the vision site, but I thought it was stupid.

"Then I was starving, and it was soooo boring and weird. I had a headache. I tried to sleep, but I felt all nervous, cramped up, you know? I hated the stupid little tent. It smelled like old feet. I took my sleeping bag outside, and that was better.

"Then it got dark, and I got cold. I started hearing crazy noises, and that freaked me out. And then the moon came up, and that was worse than the dark because there were all these bizarro shadows. Things would move out there, you know, like maybe trees or a hawk or something scary with shiny eyes. I didn't know if that was my vision, you know, or if all this stuff was really happening."

Bernie pictured the scene. Blessedly quiet except for *ma'ii*, the coyote, the quiet of a winter night broken by the call of the Trickster. Perhaps, if the wind were right, she'd hear the muted, faraway roar of a big truck on the highway. She imagined watching the sunset and then seeing the night sky alive with its winter banner of stars, stars you couldn't see in Farmington, Gallup, or even Shiprock. She pictured the moonrise. The hours of peaceful solitude sounded wonderful to her. No television, no cell phone, no police scanners. No reports to write.

"So how did you get lost?"

Annie stood again, paced, hugged herself. "They told us not to leave the vision site no matter what, but I had to get out of there, you know? I had to get back to base camp before I went crazy or got eaten by something or died from hunger. So what if the other girls or Mrs. Cooper thought I was a loser, a freak? So what? But now, well, but now I only wish . . ."

Bernie heard the girl's voice crack. "Let me say this back to you. You were frightened and hungry out there, so you decided to come back to base camp, right?"

Annie picked up her plastic bottle and took a long, slow drink. "I ran out of there as fast as I could. I didn't mean to get lost. I was . . ." Annie raised both hands, palms open. "I don't know how to say it."

"Is that how you got lost?"

The girl nodded. "I thought I could get to camp, but instead everything looked different than when I'd walked out there. I couldn't see the trail. Everything turned weird in the dark, even with my stupid flashlight. After a long time I stopped, and just stood there, bawling my eyes out. That's when I found the cave because the moon was brighter now and the light was, you know, like leading me up there. I thought maybe that was my vision, and if I died in there from hunger or something, at least my body wouldn't be out in the open for bugs and animals to eat."

Annie stood again and returned to pacing. "So I crawled in, just barely in, and waited. I didn't want to fall asleep, but when I opened my eyes, the sky had changed from black to gray. That's when . . ." Annie stopped moving and stared at her boots.

"That's when something else happened?"

Annie nodded.

Bernie could read fear in the way the girl's body tensed. "Take a breath."

Bernie took a breath, too, considering how to proceed. "Did Mr. Cruz find you out there and do something he shouldn't have?"

"No way. No bleepin' way." Annie yelled the words. "The dude is way chill, and that's too creepy. Besides that, he's gay. Has he come back yet?"

"No."

Annie pushed her hair out of her eyes. "I know he came to look for me because he promised that he would when he dropped me off. It's my fault that he got lost." The girl rose to her feet again. "Why don't you go out and look for him? I can't talk to you anymore."

"If he doesn't come back soon, a whole bunch of people will search for him." Bernie consciously slowed her rate of speaking. "You know, I've had experiences I don't like to talk about, things that scared me. Things I couldn't make sense of . . . like what happened to you in that cave." She softened her tone a bit more. "Discussing it helped me figure out what was going on. Why don't you tell me what scared you? Start at the beginning."

Annie squared her shoulders. "I'm not sure what it was."

Bernie waited.

"When I got to the cave, the moon let me see inside a little. I got on my knees to shine my flashlight into it in case there was a bear or something. I didn't see anything, but it smelled kinda funny. The cave had a little ledge, so when I thought it was safe to lie down, I kept my head on the ledge so I could see if there was something, you know, coming for me. And because of the stink. In the morning, as I was waking up, I noticed a big piñon tree, one with two trunks. I thought it might have nuts that I could eat to keep from dying because I already ate those dumb little snacks."

The girl grew quiet and then picked up the story, her tone changing. "I stretched out my legs, you know, from the ledge into the dark part of the cave. My foot pushed against a hard thing, and I pulled away. I looked in the cave again, and I felt a chill, you know, like there was something evil in there. I could see that the cave went back a lot farther than I realized. Then I saw an old rope. When I picked it up, it wasn't a rope, it was a beat-up sandal. You know, the kind woven out of yucca. I put it back, and that's when I saw the other thing."

Bernie waited for her to continue, but she sat frozen in place.

"What did you see?"

Annie put her hands on her cheeks and then over her mouth.

"Was it alive?"

Annie shook her head.

"Talk to me. Tell me about what you saw."

"I don't know how to say it." The girl's voice had an edge of hysteria now. "It looked like old bones. I was in a cave of bones."

Bernie knew the Malpais was dotted with lava caves. Despite what Mrs. Cooper had said about Annie's lying, this part of her story rang true."Could you find that cave again?"

"I don't want to go back there ever again. I don't want to talk about this anymore." Annie leaned away from her. "What if I hallucinated it? What if the bones were my stupid vision?"

"From the way you've described it, the experience really happened." Bernie pulled out her notebook and jotted down the sketchy details of Annie's cave of bones. If these were human bones, an ancestor of the Diné or Laguna or Acoma or Zuni people or even *bilagáana* settlers, they deserved respect. She hadn't heard of Navajo burials in the lava, but the Ramah Navajo land bordered the Malpais. The Big Rez, the major reservation for the Navajo Nation, was farther west and north. No matter. This wasn't the kind of thing people talked about anyway.

If Annie had stumbled upon an ancient native burial, the family would have interred the dead one with the traditional gifts. Annie hadn't mentioned seeing any-thing except the bones and the sandal.

"What happened next?"

"I ran out of there, away from those bones. But I knew that Mr. Cruz would be looking for me so I sat on a rock for a while, until it got light, so I could find a trail if I had to. And then I started moving and I saw some stuff, you know, that looked kinda familiar and made it back."

"One last question. Did Mr. Cruz go in that cave?"

"No." She emphasized it with a shake of her head. "Never. He told us how dangerous caves are. He would be so angry if he knew I'd been there."

Bernie put the notebook back in her pack. While she and Annie were talking, Cooper and Mayfair had returned with the girls behind them and enough gear to fill the van. The girls clustered together now. They seemed like the *dibé*, sheep huddling for warmth on this cold, sunny winter afternoon. Annie had noticed them, too. "Can I go?"

"Yes. I may need to talk to you again."

The girl glided off to join the flock and Mayfair, who was organizing the girls to create small piles of tents, sleeping bags, backpacks, and the rest.

Cooper took Annie's place on the bench.

Bernie summarized the interview. Sensing Cooper's unspoken skepticism when she reached the part about the cave, she didn't mention the bones.

"She's not the first girl to have issues during the solo," Cooper said. "Mr. Cruz and I designed the program to shake them up, to motivate them to reconsider their lives. We push their limits, but they are never in any serious danger. That Annie loves attention even more than the rest of this bunch. I wasn't surprised when she broke the rules. We specifically tell them to stay out of caves. She's probably elaborating on that story now, talking with the other campers, adding a bear, a treasure chest full of gold. Who knows?"

Bernie said, "I want to take a look at the place where she soloed and see if I can find the cave she mentioned."

"Really?"

"Really."

"Well, Mayfair needs to hike out to get the equipment Annie abandoned. She'll show you where the tent is. I doubt that you'll find a cave. What about the search and rescue people?"

"If a state police officer gets here before I come back, you can tell him about Mr. Cruz better than I can."

Cooper ran her hand through her curls. "That girl is a good liar. Why do you care about a cave?"

"I'll tell you later." Bernie gave her a smile, hoping it offered some reassurance. "I'll tell you if it's something that matters."

Mayfair wasn't happy about having company. She tapped a spot on a hand-drawn map with her index finger. "Why doesn't Cooper send wacko Annie back for her own things? Part of the experience is learning personal responsibility. Cooper is losing it. Thank goodness she's leaving the program before she embarrasses us and herself."

"What do you mean?"

"I guess you didn't hear. Cooper's retiring." Mayfair folded the map and put it in her pocket. "Why do you want to hike out there? We already searched that route for Cruz, and you won't find him there."

"I need to check on something Annie said."

"Seriously?"

Bernie nodded.

Mayfair gave Bernie a challenging look. "I hope you can keep up."

"Let's go. I want to get back before the state cop gets here."

Mayfair looked like she could walk the fifty miles to Grants and back without breaking a sweat and, with her long legs, she set a challenging pace. Bernie was breathing harder than usual when Mayfair stopped abruptly, after about fifteen minutes of serious hiking.

"Officer, if I knew what you were after, I could help. Tell me why you're coming with me. Did Cooper suggest this?"

Bernie welcomed Mayfair's change in attitude. "No, Cooper tried to talk me out of it. Annie told me she climbed into a cave and she saw something unusual inside. I'd like to find that place. Do you know this area well?"

"I've been working with Wings and Roots out here for the last two years. So, yes. Not as well as Cruz or Cooper, but a lot better than most people. We wouldn't be hiking out here otherwise, right?"

Mayfair's defensiveness puzzled Bernie, but she had dealt with this attitude before. "Based on where Annie's solo site was, can you help me find the cave? She mentioned a couple landmarks. I'd appreciate it."

Mayfair shrugged and started walking again, talking as she hiked, her long braids swinging behind her as she moved. "Well, to start with, Annie doesn't have much respect for the truth, and she likes attention. Next, this place is full of caves. What kind of *directions* did she give you?"

Bernie heard Mayfair's emphasis. "She said it took

her about forty minutes to hike back to base camp from there. She said the moon shone inside it, so that means it must open to the east. The cave had a ledge, large enough for her to sleep on, at least her upper body. And it was roomy enough for her to stretch her legs inside and not hit the wall. She said she could see a big piñon tree with two trunks from the opening

"Well, that narrows it down. Not a lot of trees get large out here. Not like back east." Mayfair laughed.

As Mayfair led the way, Bernie maneuvered over the lava, maintaining the energetic pace the taller woman set. Unlike most civilians Bernie encountered, Mayfair didn't bombard her with the usual questions: What was it like to be a cop? Did the men on the force treat her as an equal? Had anyone ever tried to shoot her? Had she killed anybody? And, her favorite: What were some dumb things bad guys did that got them arrested? She didn't even ask about the pending search operation.

They found Annie's one-person tent and sleeping bag after about fifteen minutes. Bernie took binoculars from her pack and scanned the lava surrounding them. She didn't see any caves.

"How far to an area with the caves?"

Mayfair put her hands in her pockets. "It depends on which way you go."

Bernie waited.

"The closest are about ten minutes. Well, fifteen for most people."

"I need to take a look because of what Annie said. Will you help me?"

Mayfair spoke quickly. "Like I told you, that girl was unhinged before the trip started, and then she got worse—sulky, uncooperative, acting out, argumentative. Cooper pushed us to include her, and Cruz eventually went along with it, like he always does. I don't trust most of what Annie says, and you shouldn't either."

Bernie weighed her words. "She mentioned that there might be a burial. Other old bones have been discovered out here, so even though her story might be suspect, I have to follow up."

Mayfair sighed. "You see that pile of rocks over there?"

"The trail marker?"

"Yes. I'll leave the equipment there and go with you and show you a cave area. There's been enough excitement for one day already. We'll stay together. You don't want to disappear out here."

The irregular surfaces made Bernie glad she'd kept up with her morning runs, worn her hiking boots, and brought the water in her backpack. They passed areas where it looked as though liquid rock had bubbled up from the earth's core and frozen at the surface like ropes of lava, and pitted black rocks that came to Bernie's waist. In some places the lava was dotted with white and bright yellow lichens. They passed caves, but none large enough to hold a person.

"Let's stop a minute." Bernie took binoculars from her backpack. She scanned the lava but saw nothing that matched Annie's description.

She offered the glasses to her companion, who declined.

"Manuelito. What kind of a name is that for a Navajo? It sounds Spanish."

Bernie thought about what to say, how much detail to go into. "Manuelito was one of the Diné leaders who signed the 1868 treaty with the United States that established the Navajo Indian Reservation. He pushed hard to get education for Navajo children, to help them be part of the new world. I could go on, but it's your turn. Mayfair—what kind of a name is that?"

"My own. I selected it after I left home, or got kicked out, depending on who's telling the story. My parents' last name is one that everyone on the East Coast who watches public television or goes to art museums recognizes. Mother and Father say they love the idea of my having this job. They've suggested that I stay out here indefinitely, working with Wings and Roots." Mayfair extracted a metal water bottle from her pack and took a sip. "They try to soft-pedal it, but I know it delights them to have their difficult daughter away from their friends, and that she gave herself a new last name."

Bernie knew there was more to the story, but Mayfair stopped talking.

"Many of us Navajos have several names," Bernie said. "Our Diné name, our English name, a bunch of nicknames."

"I kept telling Cooper she should change her name, but she reminded me that Cooper is a kind of hawk, and now we tell the girls that, too. We've even seen a Cooper's hawk out here. But Cruz? That seemed to fit. His name means 'cross' in Spanish, did you know that?"

"No. I don't speak much Spanish."

"You haven't been around girls like Annie much either, have you?"

Bernie heard the judgment in the woman's voice. "Actually, I have." She pictured Darleen, her little sister with a big attitude.

Mayfair waved the comment aside. "I told Dom that his name was appropriate because this program was a crossroads for these kids, and sometimes he has to lay down the law with them, get a little cross."

"Did anyone tease Cruz about just cruisin' along?"

Mayfair chuckled. "You got that right. I can't believe Cooper decided he was the one who should be director when she retires."

"Why can't you believe it?"

"He's our designated fund-raiser, you know? He's one of the reasons the program is in financial trouble. With all the good Wings and Roots does, it wouldn't be right for us to go away, but that's what could happen when Cruz takes over. And he's a man; the program deals with a lot of girls. They need a woman as a role model, not only here in the field but as the program's face, too."

They were hiking now up a narrow trail with lava boulders higher than Bernie's head on either side. They came to a crevice that the taller woman stepped across but Bernie had to jump.

"Stop a minute." Bernie scanned the lava again for a cave matching Annie's description and then put the binoculars back in the pack. Maybe the girl *had* made it up.

Mayfair watched as she stowed the glasses. "A few more minutes, and we have to go back. No cave that matches her description, right? Of course Annie would be the one to cause Mr. C to come back out here."

"I thought the whole point of the program was to help girls like that."

"You can't help somebody who doesn't want to be helped. The way I see it, Annie only wanted to get away from her mother. Cooper challenged her, told her she was a con artist, in one of the meetings out here. Annie resented that. I think she left her campsite to give us grief." She frowned and looked out over the lava bed. "Let's go. Ten more minutes, and we turn back."

Mayfair's braids bounced as she walked on. The trail kept climbing, offering views of a complicated landscape of boulders, ridges, and valleys, and of the sandstone mesas across the highway. Mount Taylor, pinned to the horizon by the Holy People with a stone knife, rose to the north. Bernie knew it as beautiful Tsoodził, Turquoise Mountain, its higher slopes frosted with early snow—one of the four sacred mountains marking the cardinal directions and the boundaries of the Dinétah, the People's homeland.

She stumbled, caught her balance, and focused on the challenge of the ever-changing terrain at Mayfair's ambitious pace. Had Annie really navigated these trails in the dark?

Mayfair broke the silence. "I've heard that you Navajos have a story that goes with this lava. Is that true?"

"Our grandparents tell us that this is the blood of a giant monster killed by the Hero Twins in their work to make the earth safe for us humans." Bernie didn't get into the complicated details of the *Diné Bahane'*, the Navajo equivalent to the book of Genesis.

"That's gruesome. I wish they'd done a better job getting rid of monsters. Lots of monsters still around. People who discriminate against women, for one."

The translation of the Diné word for monster that Bernie liked the most was *that which gets in the way of a successful life*. "The Zuni and the Acoma have their stories about this place, too," she said. "Their healers come here to collect the herbs and plants they need for their blessings."

"It's wonderful how plants adapt to this environment." For the first time, there was enthusiasm in Mayfair's voice. "In the spring I've seen ferns, Indian paintbrush, blanket flower, desert globe mallow, Apache plume. More kinds of lichens than I could count. I've seen islands of grass and places you find trees that normally don't grow together—aspen and juniper, for instance—because the environment is so unusual. That's what I like to share with these girls. I tell them, 'Put down the electronics and look around at this gorgeous world.'"

They walked in silence for a while. "It's tough finding a trail through this lava," Bernie said finally. "It's disorienting, and it would be easy to twist an ankle, get caught in one of these cracks, step on a lava crust that looks solid but isn't. I can picture Cruz getting lost out here."

"He's been here so many times, he knows this area like his own backyard. But I guess anything can happen. Cruz told me this was going to be his last trip."

Interesting, Bernie thought. "Did he say why?"

"He was headed for office work and the suit-and-tie circuit of fund-raising. I think he'd burned out as a group leader, probably from too many kids like wacko Annie."

"Hold on." Bernie had spotted a lone piñon that seemed to be growing out of the lava. She studied it with the binoculars before pointing it out to Mayfair. "That looks like Annie's tree."

The piñon was farther away than it seemed. Along the way, Bernie spotted more caves, all too small for even a slim girl to sleep in. When they got to the tree, Bernie scanned the lava, then handed her binoculars to Mayfair. "Up that way, it looks like a cave. You see it?"

Mayfair put the glasses to her eyes.

"That's a big one, but it's another hike away—Annie wouldn't have walked that far, especially by herself, in the dark." She handed the binoculars back to Bernie. "Let's go pick up her stuff and call it a day. With Cruz gone, I've got a lot more work to do."

"I want to stay," said Bernie, "look around, try to figure this out. Go get the equipment and meet me here."

Mayfair hesitated. "I'll be back by this tree in a few minutes. Be here. I don't want to have to look for you, too." She headed off at a trot.

Bernie examined the piñon again, surprised at how well it matched Annie's description: a lone, double-trunked tree with roots in the dark rock. She had been looking too high. Annie said she had climbed a rise and then knelt down to shine in the light.

Bernie took the binoculars from her pack again and focused on the waves of lava closest to the tree. Finally, she found what looked like a large, hollow depression in the lava. Next to it was something white. She adjusted the focus and realized that the white came from a spiral petroglyph.

She negotiated the rough ground toward the cave, concentrating on each step and letting the quiet part of her mind puzzle out her situation. She wanted nothing to do with the ancient dead. Why was she even here? As a Navajo Police officer, she was out of her jurisdiction. Her young informant was both a known liar and a participant in a program designed to alter consciousness. Not only was the girl's story vague, but the bones she mentioned had no immediate connection to the lost man.

But she was here, Bernie knew, because her gut said Annie was telling the truth, and her heart told her that if the bones were human, they deserved to rest in peace, away from the restless feet of teenagers on a self-improvement program or anyone else hiking in the lava.

Whatever that cave preserved had been there a long time. Whatever Annie had seen had terrified her. As a young Navajo girl, despite her purple nail polish and multiple ear piercings, she had heard stories about the evil that is freed with death. Annie had said she sensed something bad inside the cave. If a person was buried there, now, through no fault of his or her own, the grave was in a public place, a national monument or the adjoining wilderness and national conservation areas. Visitors could unintentionally come across the bones, and the idea that someone would stumble upon them again, as Annie had, bothered Bernie. It troubled her even more than the fact that she would have to expose herself to their power to find out whether Annie had told the truth.

As Bernie neared the depression, she found what might be an entrance, an opening partly obstructed by lava rocks, just as the girl described. She moved closer.

She had never understood the attraction of climbing into caves, especially little caves, just for fun. When she was with the US Border Patrol, she and the woman whose house she shared had driven to Carlsbad, New Mexico, to see the famous caverns there. That huge, chilly underground space naturally decorated with towering stalagmites stretching toward the ceiling like giant stone cacti captivated her. They went to the amphitheater at the cave entrance at dusk to watch the departure of thousands of Mexican brown bats on their way to gorge on an evening insect feast. She understood the appeal of a cave like that, a unique spot in the American Southwest. But why put yourself inside a small, dark space? She'd opt for the fresh air of open country any day.

The view from here was spectacular, at least. Tsoodził stood with its head in the clouds. The dark river of the lava contrasted with the deep blue of the western New Mexico sky. She turned her attention back to the cave, keeping the opening in her line of vision as she hiked, pushing herself to go faster. As she approached, she could see a small, flat ledge inside it, a shelf of rock she hadn't been aware of through the binoculars, just as Annie had described.

Maneuvering her way through the rocks that blocked the cave's entrance, Bernie carefully lowered herself to sit on the ledge. She caught her breath, pulled the flash-light off her duty belt, put on her gloves, and thought about what she had to do next. Maybe what Annie had seen was a hallucination or an animal's skeleton. Maybe a pack rat had a nest in there and had found some yucca somewhere that Annie took to be an old fiber sandal.

Maybe.

The flashlight felt solid in her hand as she turned it on and let the light penetrate the cave's secrets. There was a pungent smell in the air. Her eyes took a moment to adjust from the bright December day to the cave's total darkness. The beam bounced off rocks and shone into deep blackness. She scanned systematically, moving clockwise, the same direction she would go if physically entering a hogan. At about the half-way point, her light reflected off a long, amber-colored something on the cave floor. She crept forward into the cave to get closer, and then she realized what she was looking at: a human femur. She moved beyond and found the smaller bones of a human arm and then the aged remains of a yucca fiber sandal. She forced herself to continue the scan, her light discovering small yel-lowed bones that once were human fingers on the black stone. The cave's floor sloped away from her, and her light penetrated a space that seemed to grow larger in the rear.

"Mr. Cruz, are you back there?"

Bernie's voice bounced off the rock. She remembered Annie's strong assertion that Cruz was not in the cave, and Cooper's description of him as a man as large as Chee. The space she'd just crawled through would be too small for him. Still, she had a job to do. She inched forward, careful not to disturb the bones. Her light shone on more blackness, rough, sharp lava and then a section that looked smoother.

"Mr. Cruz?"

She stayed long enough to convince herself without a doubt that there was no sign of him and that the human bones had been in the cave much, much longer than Domingo Cruz had been missing.

Bernie climbed out of the cave, turning off the light and replacing it on her belt as she said a quick prayer for protection. She forced her thoughts away from what she'd seen. She'd call Largo so he could inform the tribal office that dealt with disturbed graves, the park service, and probably the office of the medical investigator. If this person had been buried with grave goods to help him or her move to the next world, all that was gone. The looters, at least as far as she could tell, had left nothing behind to identify themselves. The bones would remain silent about who had desecrated them.

She made her way back to the meeting place in time

to see Mayfair approaching, bringing a tent and sleeping bag.

"Did you find anything up there?"

"Only some old bones." Bernie ignored the question in Mayfair's eyes. "Let's go. I can help you with Annie's stuff."

Mayfair handed her the tent, compressed into a tubular shape with a sturdy handle.

"If you tell me more, I'll let you carry the sleeping bag. It's lighter."

"There's no more to say."

They hiked on in silence.

Back at the parking area, Cooper and the girls were nearly done with the packing. Bernie put Annie's tent with the others. Cooper sat in the sun on a picnic bench and motioned Bernie over.

"What did you see out there?"

"I found the cave that Annie mentioned. No sign of Mr. Cruz." Bernie could tell that Cooper wanted more, but there was nothing more she wanted to say.

Cooper handed her a sheet of paper. "While you were gone, I wrote up a more detailed description of him for the searchers. I'd like to stay until they come, or until Dom returns, but we'll cause a riot if we don't get back to Grants, and we're already an hour late."

Bernie looked at the sheet Cooper had prepared. "This will be helpful, but they still might want to talk you."

Cooper shook her head. "I have to get the girls out of here. They might be even more upset if they're around when the search starts. I'm glad you came, Bernie. You know how to deal with stuff like this."

"Can't Mayfair handle the trip? I can give you a ride in my unit once the—"

"She's not authorized to drive the van, only Cruz and I. And what can I do here anyway? Everything I know about him is on the sheet."

Bernie looked at the paper again. It contained most of the obvious information the searchers would need, including his coat with that reflective trim that makes it shine at night and the brand of his hiking boots: Merrell.

Cooper pointed to a black sleeping bag near the picnic table. "That belongs to Dom. He has his backpack with his other personal stuff with him."

Bernie said, "Leave it here in case they want to bring in a dog to help find him." In her search and rescue training, she'd learned enough to know that the teams used two kinds of dogs, air scenters and ground trackers, to search for missing people. When necessary, they also used cadaver dogs.

"I don't think dogs can work in the lava. Even when they wear those special boots—it still hurt their pads." Cooper turned to the girls, standing in anxious clusters. "Campers, make a final check of the area. We'll load the van in five minutes."

Bernie said, "I need a moment with Annie. We'll meet you at the van."

She found the girl by herself, her gear in front of her, staring into space. Bernie stood next to her, speaking softly. "I wanted you to know I found the cave."

Annie stood straighter. "You believed me."

"Yes. That's why I went out with Mayfair to bring in your equipment."

"I should have gone out to get my own stuff, but Cooper doesn't trust me. Did you see that thing in there?"

Bernie nodded.

Annie looked around. "Did you tell anybody?"

"I told Mayfair I saw some old bones. I didn't make a big deal of it."

"I don't want to talk about that ever again."

"I understand why that scared you. Are you a Navajo?"

Annie shrugged. "Yeah."

Bernie unzipped her backpack, got a business card, and then found a pen and wrote something on it. "This has my number at the station and my cell phone on the back. You can call me if you think of anything else. Please tell your parents to call me if they would like to talk to me about a ceremony."

Annie hadn't mentioned *chindis*, the restless spirits of the dead. Bernie wasn't going to bring it up, but because she would want a ceremony to cleanse herself of the residual evil in the cave, she'd mention it to Annie's parents if they called her. Maybe she and the girl could be healed together, reducing the cost of the ritual for each family.

Bernie saw the look of concern in Annie's face. "Girl, you did the right thing back there, and I'm glad you told me about the cave."

Annie nodded. "I don't have much family. My mom is . . . gone."

"Cooper told me your mother pushed to have you in the program."

Annie didn't miss a beat. "Yes. That was her last wish." She put Bernie's card in the front pocket of her backpack. Bernie followed her glance to the girls assembling near the van. "Can I stay and help look for Mr. Cruz? He got lost because of me."

"No. We don't know what happened to Mr. Cruz, but it's not your fault. We don't know why he hasn't come back, but he's an adult. He was responsible for keeping you safe, not vice versa."

Bernie heard footsteps and saw Cooper standing just out of earshot. She tapped her wristwatch.

"Time to go," Bernie zipped her pack's front pocket. "I'll walk to the van with you."

"You don't have to." Annie trudged off to join the other girls.

"Why is it taking so long for the searchers to get here?" Cooper said. "It's been a while since you called."

"I'm wondering the same thing. I thought the officer from Grants would have been here by now. I'll call again."

Outside the van, Cooper took the keys from her front pocket and went to open the driver's-side door. "I want to give you the topographic maps we used to plot the solo sites. That will make it easier for the searchers." She slid the key into the door lock, turned it, and paused, looking puzzled. "Mayfair, did you leave the vehicle unlocked?"

"Of course not. You know me better than that. It must have been you or Cruz."

Bernie walked closer to inspect the lock for signs of tampering. "When I went to my unit to call about the search, I noticed that the van door was ajar, so I closed it, but I left it unlocked. I couldn't see anything that looked messed up."

"It couldn't have been open." Cooper sounded convincing. "I know I locked it."

"Maybe you only forgot."

"No. But even if I did, Dom always double-checked everything. He wouldn't have let us hike off without making sure the van was secure. We never would have left the door open."

"You and Ms. Mayfair had better double-check in case there's been a break-in."

"How did the lock look?" Mayfair peeked in the window. "Jimmied or something?"

"Not that I could tell."

Cooper opened the driver's door, climbed in, and put her key in the ignition. She gave Bernie a report: the radio, a thief's usual target, was in place; the glove box and center console, other favorite spots to ransack for money, were untouched.

Mayfair joined the conversation. "Make sure it starts."

Cooper turned the key, and the old van's engine came to life almost immediately. "At least they didn't steal the battery or siphon the gas." She turned off the engine, studied the interior for a few minutes, grabbed the maps, and scooted out.

Mayfair climbed into the van and looked around, taking longer than Cooper had. "Everything is OK."

The campers were milling about, generating let's-get-out-of-here energy. Cooper gave the orders. "Girls, line up by the back door. Please load your packs and equipment neatly. Mayfair, you supervise. Then come over to me, and I will return your phones."

Bernie moved to stand between Cooper and the girls. "Let me know if anything is gone."

Cooper opened the van's double back doors.

"Backup first aid kit, extra blankets, water, energy bars, the box with the girls' electronics. All here. Nothing has been disturbed as far as I can tell."

Bernie could feel the girls' impatience. She turned to Mayfair. "Do you see anything missing?"

"The nylon bag that had some extra water bottles and energy bars is gone. Or did we bring it?"

"I think Cruz put it on the floor in the front seat."

Mayfair scrambled to look. "Not here. It's gone."

"What if somebody stole my phone?" a young voice yelled.

Bernie used the tone she'd found to be effective in getting the attention of drunks. "Girls, listen up. Mrs. Cooper needs to make sure all your electronics are here, and I'm going to stay at the van until everyone has whatever she came with or we know if anything has disappeared."

"After I give you your phone, climb up into the van," Cooper said, sliding the side door open for access to the seats while Mayfair began the loading process in the back. The girls waited expectantly as Cooper returned their possessions, but Annie, who had been standing at the back of the crowd, bypassed the phone line, headed to the van, and found a window seat.

Bernie climbed in beside her. "Don't you have a phone in the box?"

"Nope." Annie scrunched her eyes closed, and her chin started to tremble. "I wish I had one."

"Don't forget to tell your family I want to talk to them."

"Right."

But from the tone of Annie's voice, Bernie doubted that she'd hear from them. "Annie," she said, "think about what happened out there, and if you even caught a glimpse of Mr. Cruz after you ran from the cave. It could help find him."

She glanced at Cooper's cardboard box that had held the girls' phones. It was empty. "Anything else missing?"

"All the phones, iPods, and the rest are accounted for." Cooper hesitated. "I hate to ask you this, but can you loan me twenty dollars? I have to return the van to the rental company full of gas. I've got a little money, but not enough to fill it, and Mayfair is always broke. Dom had the company credit card."

Bernie had forty dollars. She gave Cooper four $5 bills.

"Thanks. I'll pay you back in Shiprock."

Bernie nodded. "What happened to Annie's mother?"

"What do you mean?"

"Annie told me she was dead. Maybe that's why she's been difficult on this trip."

Cooper put her hands on her hips. "Dead?"

"She said gone, actually, and I thought she meant dead."

"Annie's mom goes to a lot of meetings, but she's alive and—well, I could say more about her, but we better go."

After the van pulled away, Bernie walked to her unit and called the substation.

Sandra's voice sounded scratchy over the phone. "Anything new out there on the lost guy?"

"No. Still waiting for search and rescue."

"How's that girl who was lost?"

"Embarrassed but all right. I need to talk to the captain about something else."

"The captain wants to talk to you, too."

Largo's deep voice came on the cell phone. "I contacted our office in Ramah and the Cibola County Fire and Rescue Department about the situation there. The search teams are on alert, and they say they've got a good group of volunteers ready to go out there as soon as the state police give the OK. Anything else going on?"

"Yes, sir. I found what I think could be a burial in a cave in the lava."

"You're kidding."

Bernie stayed silent.

"Tell me."

She told him.

"Why were you in that place?"

"Remember the girl from Cruz's program who was lost but made her way back?"

"Go ahead."

"She told me that she climbed into a cave for shelter and that something scared her. I thought if she had found a burial site, it should be protected, especially with a crowd of searchers coming out there. It looked like someone sealed the cave at one point. I noticed the spiral petroglyph Annie described. I saw the sandal she mentioned, and bones. I'm sure they are human, sir, because the skull was there."

She could almost hear Largo thinking over the phone. Finally he said, "As far as you could tell, had Cruz been in the cave or near there?"

"No sign of him at all, sir. That's another thing I was looking for."

Largo said, "Based on what I know about the archaeology of the area, it's likely that the bones are those of a Pueblo person. But he's now on Navajo land or in a national monument, right?"

Otherwise, she knew, she and Largo had no reason to be involved with the cave of bones. "Sir, it's hard to tell where the boundaries are when you're hiking out here."

"Hold on." Another pause. She pictured Largo digesting the information.

"Sandra just confirmed that a state police officer from Grants is almost there. Make sure you tell him you've searched that cave and that it's off limits to the team because of the bones. Then get back here."

"Yes, sir." She paused. "You know, it might be a her."

"What?"

"The bones might be a woman."

Largo chuckled. "Noted. Speaking of that, I met the new FBI person, Cordova's replacement. Agent Sage Johnson. She's a she."

"Sage? Is she a Native?"

"Not from around here. I didn't ask her, and she didn't mention it. She's fresh out of training, first experience working on the Navajo Nation. Maybe her first trip to the Four Corners."

"Cordova said he thought a woman from California would be coming our way."

"She's from San Diego. You have anything else for me, Manuelito?"

"Well, maybe." She told him about the odd smell in the cave and then about the unlocked van and the potentially missing water and energy bars. "There was no damage, but Mrs. Cooper swears they wouldn't have left it unlocked. Except for the water and food, they didn't find anything missing, and there were jackets, flashlights, some change in the console untouched."

"Mention it to the state cop. And, Manuelito?"

"Yes, sir?"

"While you're waiting for the state cop to show up, keep thinking about what I asked you to consider."

They ended the call. Bernie climbed out of her unit and stood in the sunshine. She had been considering Captain Largo's request that she get some training to work with domestic violence victims. She agreed with him that having a woman investigator could make it easier for the victims. But the recent car bombing at Shiprock High School had stirred her interest in learning more about explosives, arson, and the profile of people who like to blow things up. She was sure someone offered courses in that, too. She had talked it over with Chee, but his only advice was "Follow your heart" and "You can always do something else if you don't like it."

The next class in responding to domestic violence would be starting soon. She needed to decide.

She considered using this break to call Darleen, but the silence seduced her. She studied the natural carving of wind and water on the cliff face, which reflected the color of warm desert sand. She watched a cloud form and scud across the immense and brilliant sky. The sharp, clear winter air smelled of possibilities. Was change in the air for her?

Three cars roared past on the highway, perhaps heading to Quemado or Fence Lake. A fourth, a black-and-white from the New Mexico State Police, pulled up next to Bernie's unit, and the driver, a uniformed officer, unfolded himself out of the big car. He was a small, slim man probably in his late forties. An out-of-uniform silver chain glinted at his neck.

"You must be Officer Manuelito." He extended a hand. "Cristóbal Manzanares. Call me Cris. So one of the grown-ups from Wings and Roots is missing? It's usually the kids who wander off."

"A girl was lost, but she came back on her own. The missing person is one of the leaders, Domingo Cruz, the man who went to look for her. The program director left a note with information about him and some maps for the searchers."

Manzanares slid back into the driver's seat of his unit, keeping the door open. "I'll get things moving. How long has he been gone?"

"Maybe five hours now."

"The guy is Dom Cruz, a big Navajo who likes to takes pictures, right?"

"You sound like you know him."

He fingered a silver chain around his neck. "A little. His sister, Merilee, married my cousin, and we met at the wedding reception. So how did you and the Navajo Police get involved in this? You think he's on Ramah land?"

"Who knows? Mrs. Cooper wanted a woman cop to come out to talk to the girls in Wings and Roots. When I arrived, Cruz was missing. The whole group was upset."

The radio squawked, and Manzanares began the relay of information. He confirmed that the situation was legitimate, the missing person had not been located, and the search could begin immediately.

While he spoke, Bernie spread Cooper's maps on the shiny black hood of the state police car. "The girl Dom went to find spent the night in a cave. I checked it out. It might have been an old burial site. No sign Cruz had been that way. I'll show you the area on the map so no one will have to waste time there." She pointed out the approximate site of the cave, the base camp, and the trails where Mayfair and the girls had done a quick search.

Manzanares studied the map. "I'll make sure it's off limits. Did you go inside?"

"Yes. It looked like it had been looted."

He ran his hand over the silver chain again. "These burials shouldn't be disturbed. Did you see any sign of who'd been in there?"

"Nothing. I think some animal must be living in the back. The cave had a stench."

"I bet you got out of there pretty quick. I know how you guys feel about dead people."

The insinuation that she hadn't done her job bothered her. "I bet you don't like corpses much either, do you?"

"That's another reason I'm glad I'm a short-timer. I retire in two weeks. I've seen enough car accidents, suicides, overdoses, all the rest, to last me a long, long time. I'm planning on doing some traveling. I just need to find my Saint Christopher medal. I always wear it along with Saint Michael around my neck inside my uniform for protection, but since I'm KMA, I can wear my chain anyway I want. What are they going to do to me? It will take them more than two weeks just to figure out how to discipline me for violating uniform standards!"

She raised an eyebrow.

"KMA as in Kiss My Ass. Saint Christopher is the guy upstairs who protects travelers. My patron saint."

Bernie mentioned the unlocked van and the missing food and water. "Nothing else was taken, not even the girls' cell phones, iPods, or headphones."

"My guess is that someone forgot to lock up and they didn't bring that stuff they say is missing. If it was a break-in, the van would have been ransacked. I'll make a note of it." He winked at her. "You did your job, Officer."

Manzanares took another look at the map and turned to Bernie. "Have you been to the base camp?"

"Yes. I met with Mrs. Cooper there."

"Good. Hold on to this map and show the incident commander both the location of the cave and the base camp, the place Cruz was last seen."

"Can you wait? My captain wants me back in Ship-rock."

He shook his head. "I would, but you can handle this. You're the one who talked to the program direc-tor, visited the base camp. That's where they will want to start the search. This is yours, Officer. Another ex-perience for your résumé. Beside, I'm KMA and I've got an appointment with HR."

"But—"

He interrupted. "The incident commander, the gal who directs all the volunteers, sets up logistics and the communication center, will be here in a few minutes. But just leave the note and map if you want, and I'll radio her. No skin off my nose."

Bernie was thinking about something else. "Are you going to call your cousin's wife, Cruz's sister, and tell her about the search? It might be easier to get the news from family."

Manzanares chuckled without humor. "My dad always said there were two kinds of family members—in-laws and outlaws. My cousin died—drowned, actually—before he could divorce her. The investigation determined his death was an accident, but I don't buy it. Merilee got everything he'd worked hard for. So, no, I'll let the incident commander—"

Bernie felt her pocket vibrate and held up a hand. "Hold on a minute." She reached for her phone.

But Manzanares walked away. "I'm outta here. Stay or go, your choice."

She heard him start his unit as she looked at the caller ID, hoping it was Chee, but instead read ROSE COOPER on the screen.

"Hello?"

"Bernie, are the searchers there?"

"Not yet. The state policeman called the incident commander and she will arrive in a few minutes. He asked me to wait to give her the basics, so I will."

"I knew I could count on you. I'm sorry you didn't get to give your talk. I know the girls would have loved it."

"I'm glad I could help in a different way." And she meant it.

4

When he agreed to go to the New Mexico Law Enforcement Academy in Santa Fe for the training, Jim Chee hadn't dwelled on the downside. He liked learning more about the work he loved. Even though it took about three and a half hours to drive from his home in Shiprock to New Mexico's state capital, he'd been eager to come for this class on the Amber and Silver Alert systems. The Navajo Nation had suffered a heartbreaking incident in which two children were abducted on their way home from school. The kidnapper freed the little boy, leaving him alone in the darkness far, far from home. But his eleven-year-old sister was raped and killed. The situation called attention to the lack of an Amber Alert system on the Navajo Nation, and since then, the tribe and the Arizona

Department of Public Safety had worked hard to put such a warning system in place.

The downside? First, he was away from Bernie because he had to be in Santa Fe by 8:00 a.m., and the department authorized a couple nights in a hotel. But then, because he was in Santa Fe anyway, the captain suggested that he spend some more time and take another course—the dreaded legal updates. Chee respectfully argued against the class to save the department a third night's lodging, but hierarchy prevailed. The extra night far from home did give him more time to check on Darleen and to see what he thought of the art school that seemed to be interested in her.

During a break in the first day's class, an officer he knew from Farmington came up to chat. "Hey, have you met our new FBI person?"

"Not yet," Chee said. "You?"

"No, but I heard it's a woman from California." The deputy rubbed his shaved head. "I wonder how bad she screwed up to get sent to the Four Corners."

Chee laughed. "Maybe she's a newbie."

"We'll get to show her how things work out here in cowboy-and-Indian country. I kinda miss Cordova, but no surprise that he left. The agency wanted him for bigger things. The guy had too much ambition to stay in the boonies. Not like us, huh?" He gave Chee a playful punch in the arm and went outside with an unlit cigarette.

It depends, Chee thought, on what you're after. He'd had offers to move away from Dinétah to places where he could earn a higher salary, even an invitation to apply to the FBI. But to live on the land between the four sacred mountains meant more to him than money. His relatives had survived the Long Walk, endured the hard days of incarceration and starvation at Hweeldi. They came back to start over with a few sheep and the deep relief of being in the place the Holy People had given them. For all its challenges, this harsh, breathtaking landscape would always be his home.

The vibration of his cell phone disrupted his thoughts. Captain Largo sounded slightly apologetic. "I have a little something I'd like you to check on. It's probably nothing, but Wilson Sam brought it up. I figured since you were already there in Santa Fe, you could help us out."

Wilson Sam was new on the Navajo police force. A rookie. "What's the story?"

"I want you to talk to a woman at Tesuque Pueblo, that's just north of there. Ask a couple questions. That's it. I don't have her exact address or phone number." Largo gave him the number of the pueblo governor's office, where Chee should be able to get her contact information. "The woman, Caitlyn Vigil, is married to a Navajo man, George Curley. George's mom hasn't heard from him for about two weeks. She assumes her son has gone back to his wife, but Curley's phone is disconnected. Could you tell the guy to call his mother, Mrs. Curley, before she heads to Tesuque herself and makes a big stink?"

Chee shifted his weight from toe to heel and back again. "I gather Mrs. Curley and Caitlyn Vigil don't get along."

"Right. It's the old conflict. Mothers wanting their son to marry a Navajo girl so their grandchildren will be raised the Navajo way. Since those two don't have any kids yet, George's mama thinks there's time for him to leave Caitlyn and find someone else. They separated last year, and George moved back to Navajoland. But they reconciled. He told Deborah, that's his mom, that he wanted Caitlyn to move out of the pueblo and into a house with him, but her mother, Mrs. Vigil, was giving them all kinds of grief." Largo stopped. "Yeah, that's more than you need to know, but it gives you some insight."

"So are Mrs. Curley and George related to the rookie? Is that why he's so interested in this?"

"No. Deborah Curley was Wilson Sam's math teacher in high school."

"Captain, I can drive out after lunch, but I'll have to miss the second part of that legal-update course."

Largo chuckled. "I don't think so, but good try. Go after class today or tomorrow. Let me know what you learn so I can pass it along to Sam."

"Tell the rookie he owes me a favor."

When the class recessed at noon, Chee joined some other cops for lunch at a restaurant known for its good barbecue. After he ordered the green chile brisket with corn bread and a salad, he headed to the men's room. Two men stood in the lobby, paying their bill.

"Yá'át'ééh," the heavy Navajo with a tattoo on his neck called to him. "They let you out of Shiprock, huh?" There was anger in the man's deep, gravelly voice. His companion, a younger Navajo, stared at the floor. Chee read embarrassment in his body language. Something about him was familiar, too.

"Yá'át'ééh." Chee remembered the older man, a person he had arrested for beating his wife with a vodka bottle and kicking her hard enough to crack her ribs. Last he'd heard, Clyde Herbert was in prison. "How are you doing?"

Herbert moved to block Chee's passage. "Real fine, boss." Chee smelled onions on his breath. "My old lady, too." He gave Chee a smirk. "I didn't see your green-and-white in the parking lot. You get fired or somethin'?"

"I'm here taking classes so I'll know how to deal better with people like you." The big man grunted and then moved away from Chee, pushing the restaurant's heavy exit door open. The younger man followed him, keeping his head down.

Chee called after him. "Hey there, aren't you Darleen's friend?"

The man ignored him. The guy had a funny name, BS or something like that. Chee remembered talking to him in Tuba City. And that he was with Darleen at the time.

A steaming cup of coffee had arrived when Chee returned to the group at the table. The waitress was delivering a basket of chips and a bowl of chile con queso to dip them in. "We like having you guys around, so this is on me." She gave them a smile. "Spread the word, OK?"

The Farmington officer turned to Chee. "You look like you ran into an angry old girlfriend, or a buddy you owe some money to. Or got confused by those unisex bathroom signs they use in Santa Fe."

The conversation turned to the class they were taking. An African American officer at the table, a classmate from the eastern part of the state, was especially enthusiastic.

"If I had realized how much interesting, complicated legal stuff I'd have to know as a cop, I would have gone to law school."

"I can't see you as a lawyer, buddy. You have a low tolerance for official bull."

"And people hate lawyers even more than cops," someone else chimed in.

"Go ahead and joke, but I'm considering it. I'm checking to see if I can find a grant or something to help with tuition. After some of the prosecution screw-ups I've seen, I think I could do better at getting these guys put away—even without going to school."

The man turned to Chee. "Hey, you're with the Navajo PD. Did you ever hear of a Lieutenant Staghorn? He was with that department for a long time. He knew a lot about the law."

Chee smiled. "You mean Lieutenant Joe Leaphorn?"

"That's him."

"I worked with him."

"What was that like?"

Chee paused. "He was one of the smartest cops I've ever met. He knows how to think his way around a problem, how to connect the dots. He's doing consulting work with the department now, and he's still as sharp as ever."

Another officer nodded. "He came up to consult with us on something when I was new on the force. I remember thinking he seemed like a bright guy, but someone who wouldn't be easy to work with. Is that right, Chee?"

"I respect the man, and he taught me a lot." And then, saving him from going into more details, the food arrived.

The banter continued while they ate. Like Chee, several of the officers were staying in Santa Fe for classes the next day, and they talked about getting together later for a beer and a burger and to watch football on TV.

"I might come by, but I promised my wife I'd look in on her sister. She's taking an art course up here this week."

The Farmington cop said, "You mean Darleen?"

"The one and only."

"How's that girl doing?"

Chee considered his answer. "Better. She'd stopped drinking last time I saw her. She's looking at a school here."

"Santa Fe is a lot bigger than Shiprock. Maybe that

would be a good thing. Get away from home, make some new friends, give her some confidence."

"She's got confidence." Chee reached for a chip. "What she's lacking is common sense."

The mention of Darleen's friends brought the rude young man into focus. Chee remembered his name, CS, short for Clayton Secody, the guy who said he made videos. His first impression, when they met in Tuba City, had been positive. Why had the man acted like a jerk today? Why was he hanging with a convicted felon?

The afternoon training session focused on changes in the law regarding stopping suspects for probable cause, search and seizure, and more. Chee took notes to reinforce the information and to help himself stay awake. He knew the material was important. Chee's responsibilities were influenced not only by the rules of the US Supreme Court but also by the Navajo Nation's own code and by the relationship of tribal law enforcement to the states of New Mexico and Arizona, the BIA, FBI, and an alphabet soup of other agencies.

When the class ended, he walked to the parking lot and stood by his truck. The cool air was clear and crisp. People complained about the changes growth had brought to Santa Fe, but he enjoyed the view of the Jemez Mountains, the Sangre de Cristos, and the

Sandias rising against the dome of blue sky. As long as people could see that, how bad could life here be?

Just when he had decided to drive to Tesuque, his phone buzzed with a text.

He had offered to pick up Darleen at the school campus after his training and take her to dinner. She was texting that she had to finish a project and would catch a ride to meet him at a restaurant she liked: CU @ 7?

OK, he typed back. The delay gave him a bit of extra time to follow up on the favor for the rookie.

No matter how good the class, being cooped up in a room with no windows for hours made him restless. He was glad to be free. He took the bypass to US 85 and got off at the exit for the pueblo. He didn't see the governor's office, so he stopped at the community center and spoke to the receptionist after showing her his credentials.

"Caitlyn Vigil?" The receptionist gave him a puzzled look. "She's never been one to get in trouble."

"She's not in trouble. Someone in my office back in Shiprock is friendly with an elderly lady who knows Caitlyn. He asked me to stop by to say hello while I'm in Santa Fe taking a class."

Despite a universe of differences, the Pueblo people and the Navajo share an attitude of respect for their elders.

"I'll tell you where she lives. Tell her hello from Vangie, too." The young woman's grin showed her braces.

The directions eventually led him to a sprawling house under a large cottonwood tree. None of the homes had numbers, and none of the streets had street signs. Not much different from the Nation, except that Tesuque Pueblo included about five hundred members, and the Navajo Nation spread over three states, with a population five hundred times larger.

A blue Volvo station wagon from the 1970s with a yellow daisy fastened to the antenna with duct tape was parked outside. He knocked on the front door, but there was no answer. He tried again, listening for someone stirring, and looked around to see if any curious neighbors had spotted him. The place seemed deserted except for some ravens sitting in the dormant trees. Even the birds looked cold.

He went back to his truck, found some paper, and wrote a note asking Caitlyn to call him on his cell phone. He added a line he thought might get her attention and slipped the sheet and his business card into a crack in the frame.

As he was leaving, he heard a door open toward the rear of the house, and an old woman called out in a language he didn't understand.

He turned toward her, and she studied his face. "I thought you were Curley. I thought that Navajo had finally gotten a real job. But you're too big. He's a pip-squeak." She spoke in English.

"I'm not Curley," Chee said, "but I'd like to talk to him. Or to his wife. Is this where they live?"

The woman said nothing.

"They aren't in trouble. No, ma'am. Not at all. A friendly visit."

"Then you got the right house."

"I left a note there." He indicated the front door with a twist of his head. "If you see them, could you tell them I'd like to talk to them for just a minute or two?"

"I can't."

Chee waited.

"I don't know your name. Whatsa matter with you?"

He introduced himself. Because she wasn't Navajo, he didn't name his clans. Because she was an elder and a Pueblo Indian person, he knew she would care more about where he came from than what he did. But, after talking about his family, he added that he had been in training as a *hataali* and mentioned his rank as a sergeant with the Navajo Police. He told her he lived in Shiprock and a little about Bernie.

"I am Mrs. Vigil. If you want to talk to my daughter, you can call her in Santa Fe. She works at the Land Office."

"What about her husband?"

"She never should have married him."

And before Chee could ask if she'd seen the man, Mrs. Vigil disappeared behind a closed door.

Knowing the offices at the state capitol had closed at 5:00 p.m., Chee decided to call later and drove to the restaurant Darleen had suggested. The Pantry, across the street and down a few blocks from the Indian Hospital, looked as welcoming, unpretentious, and well stocked as its name. He parked in the paved lot behind the building, and as he headed toward the entrance, he noticed the bus stop bench down the street. So Darleen had figured out how to take the Santa Fe buses. She hadn't had much practice doing that in Toadlena or Shiprock because there were no public buses except for the big yellow school buses and the Navajo Transportation line that took people to Window Rock if they didn't mind leaving around 5:00 a.m. Back home, everyone he knew drove, caught a ride, or walked.

It was another fifteen minutes before the bus pulled up. Darleen wasn't on it.

He dialed her number.

When she answered, he heard the strain in her voice.

"I was about to call you. I missed the bus, but I guess you know that. I thought CS could give me a ride but, well, that didn't work." She'd left her car at Mama's house because information the school sent highly recommended that students in Darleen's program not bring vehicles to campus.

"What if I come pick you up?"

"Are you driving a police car?"

"No, my truck, but I'm still in uniform."

A pause, and then, "I'll wait for you by the main entrance. Let me know when you get close."

Chee had never been to the Institute of American Indian Arts campus before, but he found it easily. The location, away from town and south of a development of new, earth-colored homes, surprised him. He liked the modern look of the campus and, especially, the mountain views that formed its backdrop.

As he pulled up, Darleen wobbled her way toward the passenger door, and he wondered if she had been drinking again. He reached over to open it for her.

"Why don't you take off your sunglasses? You don't need them now."

"Right." She closed the door and then put her sunglasses on her lap. Even in the dim light inside the vehicle, he noticed the tears. He handed her a napkin from the side panel pocket.

"You wanna talk about it?"

When something upset Bernie, his dear wife didn't want to talk about whatever had happened—or at least she didn't want to talk about it right then, and to him. Hours later, she'd matter-of-factly tell him someone she knew had been diagnosed with a terrible disease, or lost her job, or that she had rearrested a suspect she thought had cleaned up his act. The only variation in the way Bernie handled bad news came if the problem was something she thought he could help with. In that case, he'd watch her put emotions aside, activate her logical brain, and enlist him to work with her to resolve the issue. By then she had usually conjured up an assortment of possible solutions, and she'd listen to his opinion on each one. He loved her take-charge attitude, but sometimes he wished she could be a little more vulnerable, more open to sharing.

Her sister was as different from Bernie as he could imagine. Darleen, always a talker, went into overdrive when she was angry or sad or discouraged. Most Navajo people he knew believed that words should be used sparingly and selected them with care to say only what was meant in the clearest way possible. Despite Mama's best teaching, Darleen subscribed to the more-is-better approach. Chee steadied himself for an evening of serious listening.

"Let's go for a ride." Darleen reached for her seat belt, revealing a large blue bruise on her arm.

"Sure. Do you want something to eat?"

"I don't know."

He pulled away from the school entrance onto a quiet paved street. The Institute of American Indian Arts, or IAIA, wasn't convenient to anything, and that, in his opinion, added to its appeal when it came to Darleen. Kids without cars had to settle for on-campus distractions, minimizing the chance for chaos.

"You remember CS?" She squeaked out the name. "He told me to take this program, even helped me with the paperwork. But now he totally ignores me, like I'm a big inconvenience. When I suggest that we do something, he's too busy. And when his friends are around, he blows me off. Like he's embarrassed. I don't see him hardly at all because he's working all the time, like tonight. I asked him if he wanted to come with me to dinner but no. No. No. He always *says* he's working."

She underlined *says* with the tone of her voice.

Complaining seemed to invigorate Darleen. She recited a litany of complaints against her boyfriend as Chee drove past houses in various shades of brown, large but clustered together despite all the open land here. He knew Darleen didn't expect him to interrupt her monologue.

"And when I try to tell him how I feel? He says I should focus on the program, work on my drawings, not think about him so much. And now when I asked him for a ride because I missed the bus, he told me he couldn't do it because of the stupid videos and because his friend was coming to the studio. I'd like to know who this *friend* is."

Chee drove along, minding the speed limit, passing a woman walking a dog on a leash, kids riding bikes. He found a turnout with a view of the mountains to the northwest, parked, and turned off the engine, breathing in the spectacular panorama of a spectacular evening. The fading glow of sunset danced against the flanks of the Jemez range, and he could see the flicker of the faraway lights of Los Alamos, a city created to build the atomic bomb.

Darleen stopped talking and looked out the window.

After a while, Chee broke the silence. "I don't know much about CS. Where is he from?"

Darleen rattled off his mother's born-to clan and his father's born-for clan and those of his grandparents on both sides. "We're not related. He's not even related to you, Cheeseburger. Not that I'm thinking of marrying the big jerk."

"I ran into him today at a restaurant, but he pretended not to recognize me, and I didn't immediately remember where I had seen him before." He told her about the encounter. "Do you know a man named Clyde Herbert?"

She glanced up at him. "What does he look like?"

Chee described him.

"I think I sort of met him, but CS didn't tell me who he was. CS and I drove over to his house. The guy was, like, in the driveway waiting for us, and he walked up to the car and stared at me, like he was surprised I was there or something. Then he told CS he couldn't do it until tomorrow, whatever that meant. Does he have a tattoo on his neck?"

"That's him. He was with CS at lunch. The guy has a real attitude."

She shrugged. "All I know is that when we drove away from Herbert's place, CS said he was working with that guy, and then CS is like, 'Oh, I don't wanna tell you because it's not firmed up yet.'"

Chee heard the anger in her voice. He gathered his thoughts. "I've arrested Herbert a couple times for drugs and aggravated battery. He went to prison, and I thought he was still there."

"Battery? Was he stealing batteries? What's up with that?"

"No. Battery is hitting somebody. I think you—" He stopped. Darleen absolutely resented anyone telling her what to do. "I mentioned Herbert because he's a convicted felon. I want to make sure you're safe, especially if CS is hanging with him. Are they friends?"

"I don't know." Chee could tell by the tone of her voice she was annoyed, but was it with him or CS? He'd try getting the truth from her over dinner, he thought, and he started the engine.

They reached a thoroughfare that took them past the Santa Fe Community College and eventually to a busier street. Darleen told him to turn right and directed him to Harry's Roadhouse, a few minutes east of town. They ordered pizza, roasted chicken with green chile, and sat at a window table waiting for it. Chee had a coffee and Darleen ordered water and a side salad. In the years Chee had known Bernie, beginning when she was a rookie cop and he was her boss, she had never ordered a salad at a restaurant. Now that they were married, she never made one at home, although she politely had a bite or two of the ones he created if he included iceberg lettuce and she could eat around the other vegetables. She liked green chile with pinto beans and chicken but would never have considered either of them on a pizza. Only pepperoni for her. He missed her already.

Darleen ignored him, preoccupied with eating the

salad, checking her phone, and texting. He enjoyed the smell of baking pizza and the diner-like feel of the place. The decor reminded him of Blue Moon, one of his favorite stops in Farmington, except that Blue Moon had no pizza and Harry's had no milkshakes.

When the pizza arrived, Darleen looked up. "You know, even though CS is acting like a big fool, I'm glad I came to the school here. The program is awesome. The drawing teacher comes from, you know, one of those tribes up in Canada where they live by the ocean. He has us walking around drawing stuff, quick sketches. He does some, too, and then we all talk about the drawings, but he only lets us say what we like about the other people's work. In the first class he asked us to do this really cool assignment." Darleen smiled for the first time that evening and talked on.

If it hadn't been for the uneasy feeling he had about her boyfriend associating with a thug, Chee would have let Darleen's stream of consciousness roam free. Instead, he corralled it with a question when she paused for breath.

"This pizza is good. Do you and CS come here?"

"Yeah. We have the veggie because he doesn't eat chicken or sausage or anything."

"Does he live with relatives here?"

Darleen picked up the pizza slice and took a bite. "He's using his friend's apartment."

"What's it like?" A safer question, Chee figured, than *Have you been there?*

"It's little." She slipped off her sweater, revealing the discoloration on her arm beneath the sleeve of her T-shirt.

"That's quite a bruise. What happened?"

"An accident." She tugged her sleeve down. "Do you remember that cool movie we made of the grandmother out by Coal Mine Canyon who wanted to talk to the president, you know, the Navajo president, and bring her sheep along?"

"I know you guys went out there to chat with her about the situation. I haven't seen the video."

"He says he's still working on it." Her skepticism rang in the words.

"You know, just like you don't believe him, I don't believe that bruise was an accident."

She took a sip of water. "Are you going to eat that last piece?"

He moved the pan away from her. "You can have it if you tell me what happened to your arm."

"It's nothing. Forget about it."

"Remember I said the reason Herbert went to prison is that he hit someone? It was a woman he lived with.

He broke her ribs. It bothered me to see CS with him, and it bothers me that CS pretended we'd never met."

"Maybe he didn't recognize you. He wouldn't have expected to see you in Santa Fe."

"Herbert knew who I was, and I hadn't seen him since his trial."

Darleen put the last slice of pizza on her plate. "CS isn't mean like that. No way."

"Then why won't you tell me what happened?"

The words hung between then as the server cleared the plates and offered dessert, which they declined. Chee went to the cashier and paid the bill.

When he returned, Darleen stood and slipped on her jacket. "Don't tell Bernie about Herbert and CS. Please. She's got enough on her mind helping Mama while I'm taking this class."

"I won't say anything for now. But you need to tell me the truth about that bruise."

"It was an accident, OK?" Tears pooled in her eyes. "Leave me alone. You don't have to take me back to campus. There's a bus stop right at the corner."

"I don't mind."

"I'm a big girl." She snapped out the words. "I really can take care of myself."

When he couldn't talk her out of it, Chee left Darleen there and drove back to his motel. He changed out of his uniform into soft jeans and a plaid shirt. Then he phoned Lieutenant Leaphorn. When he thought he'd have to call back, Louisa Bourbonette, Leaphorn's housemate, answered.

"Sergeant Chee, how nice to hear from you."

"Good evening. You seem a little hoarse."

"It's nothing."

They chatted a moment, and then she said, "I bet you want to talk to Joe. I'll give him the phone."

"Yá'át'ééh." Leaphorn's voice sounded clear and strong. "Chee, how are you tonight?" He spoke in Navajo, the language that came to him more easily than English.

"I'm fine, sir. How are you?"

Leaphorn said he was feeling fine and added that he had accepted a set of new assignments and was enjoying the work.

Chee never much enjoyed talking on the phone, unless it was to Bernie. And even in person, face-to-face, he felt awkward making small talk. This was doubly true in conversations with the Lieutenant, the man who had been both his mentor and his biggest critic. "Captain Largo sent me to Santa Fe for some training, so that's where I am." He described the classes and some of the old-timers Leaphorn might know. All that took about a minute. Then Chee steeled himself and got to the point.

"I could use some help, sir. Do you remember Herbert Clyde from Fort Defiance?"

"No."

Chee paused. Leaphorn, at least before a crazy woman shot him in the head, never forgot a name or a face.

"He's a stocky guy, sir. He used to rodeo until he got into meth. Mean. He had a wife in Shiprock. I arrested him a few times, once in connection with that drug trafficking case we were helping the feds with. The rest was domestic violence."

"I don't know any Herbert Clyde, but if you're talking about Clyde Herbert, of course I remember him. He beat his wife with a Smirnov bottle, broke her bones. Why do you ask?"

Chee, who prided himself on his own excellent memory, felt his face warm with embarrassment. He plodded on. "I just saw him in Santa Fe. This dude's associating with Bernie's sister's new boyfriend. I thought you might be able to help me fill in the blanks."

He heard Leaphorn sigh. "This is the girl with the blue hair who got arrested. Darleen."

"Yes, sir, but the blue is gone and she has green streaks now. She's up here in Santa Fe, too, for a week in a special art program. I'm concerned that this guy she's hanging with might be trouble. She said the boyfriend and Herbert are working on a project together. But she didn't know what the project was."

Chee paused, but when Leaphorn didn't say anything, he continued. "I can't check on the boyfriend while I'm here in Santa Fe, but I'm wondering if he's been in some trouble, too. I haven't mentioned any of this to Bernie. I didn't want to bother her with it, at least not until I know what's going on."

Leaphorn might not want to do him a favor, but Chee knew the old lieutenant was fond of Bernie.

"What's this boyfriend's name?"

Chee told him and gave him CS's approximate age and physical description.

"*Aoo*'. I'll check on Clyde Herbert, too, and I'll e-mail you what I find out. And Chee?"

"Yes, sir?"

"It's a very bad idea to try to keep a secret from your wife. It never works out well, even if your intentions are good."

Before Chee figured out how to respond, Leaphorn had hung up.

5

Jim Chee had just turned on the TV when his phone beeped with a text. Darleen had left her sunglasses in his truck. Could be drop them off for her at school on his way to his own class? She told him what dorm she was in and said he could leave them for her at the desk.

No, he thought. He had to be at the police academy early, and her campus wasn't on the way to anywhere. He'd drive them out to her tonight. He felt uneasy and the drive might help him relax. Besides, he wanted to check on her after seeing that bruise.

He drove down Cerrillos Road to Rodeo Road, then south on Richards Avenue, once again past the community college and into the foothills until he reached Darleen's school. It pleased him to see a security guard at the campus gate. He explained his mission, and she found Darleen's name in the student directory, told him how to get to the dorm, and waved him through.

At the front desk, he learned that Darleen had signed out for a movie required for class. He left her sunglasses with the attendant, a young woman in her early thirties with black-framed glasses who was engrossed in reading something on her laptop.

"One more question. Where is the studio for videos?"

"That's the next building over. If you want to talk to somebody about using the lab, you should come back tomorrow. I don't think anyone's there now except maybe some students."

He walked to the building anyway, in the hope that maybe he'd run into CS and could have a little chat with him about his felon friend. The building looked dark and empty, and there was only one vehicle outside—an old minivan idling at the loading dock. He heard roughness from the engine. If his truck sounded that bad, he would be worried.

A gray-haired woman stood outside the van by the side door, fumbling with the latch.

"Ma'am, do you need some help?" He felt for the small flashlight in his pocket.

She looked up and stepped away from him.

"You scared me, sneaking up like that. Who are you?" She was a small woman with a loud, authoritarian voice. Probably a teacher, Chee guessed.

He didn't move any closer. "It looks like you could use a hand there."

She inched toward the van and stared at him. "Who are you, and what are you doing here?"

The fear in her voice surprised him.

"I'm Jim Chee, Navajo Police, the brother-in-law of one of the bridge program students." He switched the flashlight to his left hand, pulled out his ID, and shone the light on it as he held it toward her.

"OK, Sergeant Jim. I'm Beverly Lomasi. Hopi and Laguna Pueblo. I teach here. Bring over that flashlight, and help me slide this door closed."

He walked to the minivan, noticing that even though her hair was gray, she was not elderly. Perhaps in her forties. He discovered that the side door needed to be fully reopened and closed again with a firm push.

"Now, shine that light on the building's back door here so I can get my key in. I forgot my laptop inside."

"Do you work in this building?"

"I'm glad you're suspicious." She reached inside her jacket and pulled out a strap with her college ID card. He aimed his light toward it. Same woman.

She let the card dangle on the cord. "Like it says,

I'm the assistant director of media arts and this is the media arts building. Who's your student?"

Chee told her.

Mrs. Lomasi said, "Shine your light down a little. This lock is tricky."

He did as directed.

"I work with the bridge program. I can't place Darleen."

"She has green in her hair. A Navajo who likes to draw."

"Oh, right." Mrs. Lomasi fiddled with the lock. "She sketched a picture of me while I was teaching. Not bad."

"Do you know a guy named Clayton Secody? He goes by CS."

"CS? I see him in the studio and around campus. He's working on a video project so he can finally graduate. Why do you ask?"

"Darleen is hanging out with him. I'm curious."

She finally got the door to open and flicked on the switch inside the entrance. "CS, huh? Tell Darleen she needs to—oh, never mind. Kids don't want advice from anybody except their friends." She turned away from him.

"Do you know if CS is here tonight?"

"He was here, and I'm sure he'll be back. He's doing a lot of editing."

Chee said, "Would you like me to wait and walk back to the van?"

Mrs. Lomasi laughed. "Nope, but thanks for the offer. Tell Darleen she needs to turn in her homework."

He returned to his truck for the drive back to the motel. Somewhere in the distance he heard a coyote and a few dogs barking in response. Mostly, what Chee listened to was the welcome silence he had been missing. Santa Fe's cacophony of traffic noise, car radios, and the occasional siren made him a little edgy. Combined with Darleen's stonewalling when it came to her bruise and the day's steady bombardment of strangers, including the prickly Mrs. Lomasi, the noise left him out of sorts and off balance.

He parked in the motel lot, noticing the city noise again. He wondered if Darleen appreciated the quiet of the campus.

Bernie had given him a book last week and he'd packed it in his suitcase. It was by a fellow Shiprock person, Luci Tapahonso, the Navajo Nation's first poet laureate. He thought it an interesting gift. He liked to read, but he stayed with nonfiction, especially history. He'd brought Luci's book with him to make Bernie happy but it was whittling away his prejudice against poetry. He'd read a little more after he called her. He sat in the chair next to the bed and dialed.

When Bernie's phone and the landline both went straight to voice mail, Chee called her mother's house. In the old days, sons-in-law and mothers-in-law kept their distance. Times had changed, and it didn't make sense to pretend Bernie's mama wasn't part of their lives. He treated the elderly woman with respect and reserve.

He listened to six rings and then remembered that Mama and Mrs. Bigman, her weaving student, were planning to go to the Crownpoint rug auction. Mama was probably off somewhere, getting ready. When Bernie told him about the trip, he'd heard something unusual in her voice. Regret? His wife had started a rug but hadn't made much progress. She had talked to Mama about teaching her again, but Mama said she should practice first to get her hands and her brain working to remember what she knew already.

He picked up his book again but couldn't focus on it, his mind wandering back to the scene at Tesuque Pueblo. From Caitlyn's mother's reaction to seeing him, he doubted that son-in-law George was at the old house. He imagined Mrs. Vigil made the man's life miserable.

And back in Navajoland, it sounded like Mrs. Curley took every opportunity she could find to irritate Caitlyn, her daughter-in-law. Both elderly ladies wasting precious energy on something that was not their business. It made him appreciate Bernie's mama and, yes, even Darleen.

Chee's class notes were in his truck. It wouldn't hurt to look them over before the next day's session, and a little fresh air would calm his spirit. He took the stairs down to the lobby two at a time. The stairway door opened onto the hallway a few steps from the business center—the euphemism for a room just big enough to hold a desk with a computer, a printer, a chair, and a wastebasket. The hotel arranged the system for guests to conveniently print airline boarding passes, but Chee had figured out how to check his e-mail. The Lieutenant had already sent him something, an attachment with a terse note: Here's what I have so far. Odd. Still checking.

He opened the file and saw a state of New Mexico death certificate for Clayton Secody.

6

Bernadette Manuelito had had an interesting day.

As Manzanares predicted, the search and rescue effort began to roll into place. The incident commander arrived, and volunteers followed. They set up a communication center in the parking lot with computers, supplies for the search teams, and more. The searchers included retirees and young folks, men and women. Some were "ground pounders" trained to work in the backcountry. They did the physical searching. Others were support and logistics crew. All volunteers taking time from their regular lives to help a stranger.

Bernie gave the incident commander, a sturdy-looking fiftysomething woman named Beverly Katz, the detailed description Cooper had written.

Katz read the note. "She even included the reflective

trim on his jacket. But she doesn't mention any relatives. We could use that information. I know this isn't your problem, Officer, but since you've already been in contact with"—Katz looked at the note again—"with Rose Cooper, I'd appreciate it if you could give me a name or two. Just in case."

"I told Mrs. Cooper I'd call her when the search started, so I can ask about that."

"I'm hopeful that it won't take long to find him." Katz zipped her jacket against the afternoon breeze. "Can you show me where the base camp was before you leave?" She talked as Bernie led the way. "It sounds like Cruz is experienced in the out-of-doors and knows this particular landscape. If he is injured badly enough that he can't get back here, he'll stay put. He won't panic. He knows that the people he was with would call for help." Katz looked at the sky. "The weather seems to be cooperating for now, but I saw that a big storm is on the way."

The sandy path to the group gathering place on the mesa was easier than the hike with Mayfair. Like Mayfair, Katz moved quickly and stayed on Bernie's heels. Bernie tossed out a question. "You mentioned one scenario where Cruz waits by a trail to be found. But what else could happen?"

"Well, we keep in mind the possibility that he suffered an injury that could create some confusion. Lots of trails cross through the lava or lead from here into the sandstone cliffs. Even without an injury, anyone can get disoriented. Or maybe Mr. Cruz met someone who was hurt and is helping that person. This area is popular with hikers."

"I hadn't thought of that. The Wings and Roots van was the only vehicle in the lot when I got here."

"Sometimes hikers have friends drop them off and pick them up," Katz said. "And there are several other trailheads. We haven't had any other missing person reports, but it's always a possibility, especially when people hike alone and forget to tell anyone where they're headed."

The path widened, and Katz moved beside her and glanced across the mesa top and out to the highway and the lava beyond. "As a police officer, you're probably aware of this already, but sometimes people go off by themselves to have some space to think, especially if they are feeling overwhelmed by life. Was that true of this man?"

"I asked. His coworker mentioned that he was about to get a promotion, and also was the chief fund-raiser for the organization. That can't be an easy job for any nonprofit. The director denies that he would ever con-

CAVE OF BONES · 113

sider suicide. Neither of them used the word *depressed* when speaking of him."

Katz nodded. "When we talk to the family of the missing person, we always ask them about state of mind and if they have any information that might be helpful for the search. Anything else I should know?"

"Rose Cooper left Cruz's sleeping bag here, in case you need a scent for dogs."

"Good."

When they got to the group assembly area, Katz showed Bernie the map the searchers worked with and how each area the teams had checked would be marked off as the search continued. The highest probability for finding a lost hiker like Cruz, she said, lay in about a four-mile radius of the last spot where he was seen. That was where the search focused.

Finally, Bernie told Katz about the cave with the old bones and, using the map, gave her a rough idea of the location.

The search commander thanked her. "I'll ensure that's undisturbed. We want to find a living man, not the ancient dead."

Bernie made her way off the mesa, walking more slowly, enjoying the view. Even though she had never meet Cruz, she felt like she would recognize him if she saw him hiking toward her. She agreed with Katz's assessment that he could be injured and hoped the search would find him alive. If not, she hoped that at least his body would be recovered so his family would have some peace.

The afternoon had grown cooler and a small herd of clouds gathered to the west. The year would be over in a few more weeks. What changes and possibilities would the new year hold?

Bernie had parked her unit at the edge of the parking lot, facing the highway. But first things first. As she hiked to the outhouse, she nearly stepped on a cell phone on the ground. She picked it up. From the glittery pink case, it looked like something that might have belonged to one of the teenage girls. The screen was cracked but still usable. She pushed the on button. No power.

She asked the members of the search crew about it, and none of them had lost a phone. They didn't look the type for glitter, but you never know.

Bernie left her card at search headquarters in case anyone asked about the phone and slipped the device into her backpack. Before she left, she checked the time. The program's van and the campers should be in Grants. She called, and Cooper answered.

"Bernie! Did Dom make it back?"

"No. The search crew arrived, and they're getting started."

"I'm waiting for the last few parents to arrive. I was hoping to give the girls some good news." From the sound of her voice, Cooper could use some good news herself.

"How was the drive? I was surprised you had to stop in Grants. Isn't the program based in Shiprock?"

"It is, but this was an excursion for teens in Cibola County, with a few Shiprock girls added to give us a full group." She heard Cooper's long exhalation. "The kids were quieter than usual, worried about Mr. Cruz. Annie kept to herself and didn't say a word, a big change from her complaining the whole way. She got really sick, and I had to call an ambulance for her. It was here when we arrived."

"That sounds serious. What was wrong with her?"

"She was hallucinating. That girl. I think she might have had some drugs stashed somewhere. Mayfair called her mother."

Bernie leaned against her SUV. "The incident commander asked me for a list of Mr. Cruz's relatives to inform about the search. She doesn't want them to see this first on TV or read about it. The state police officer who came out told me Cruz's sister married his cousin. Does she still live out here?"

"Yes, she's in Grants. Merilee Cruz. I have her information at the office because she's on the Wings and Roots board of directors. She works as a psychotherapist."

Bernie waited, but Cooper didn't mention any other names. "Anyone else?"

Cooper sighed. "Those of us who work with him are as much family as he has. Cruz isn't married. He never talks much about his relatives, and I never ask. He lives with a roommate. Merilee will know more. I'll text you her information as soon as the kids get picked up."

Bernie heard commotion in the background. Cooper said, "Anything else? I've got to go."

"Did one of the girls mention losing a pink phone?"

Cooper laughed. "No way. Those girls are tied to their phones. If someone had lost it, you would have heard her wailing all the way to Grants."

After Cooper hung up, Bernie climbed into her unit and put on her seat belt. Should she call Mama, or should she talk to Chee first? As she was thinking, Largo came on the radio. He got right to the point.

"Things are slow here, and you don't hear me say that often. Finish whatever you need to do out there. You can check in at the office and handle the paperwork in the morning."

"Thanks, I appreciate it."

"Any news on the lost guy?"

"Not yet. They only started searching for him."

"He's Navajo, right?"

"Right."

"That means he's tough. He'll be OK. Did you tell them about the cave?"

"Yes, sir. The incident commander is a veteran with search and rescue, and she's from around here. She understood. They have a whole lot of ground to cover without bothering with that place."

"Since the search borders on the reservation, there's a chance those bones could be Navajo. I'll put a call in to the state police in Santa Fe, to the overall search and rescue director—I know him—and mention the cultural site issues to be on the safe side." Largo ended the call.

Bernie knew the captain didn't like talking about old bones any more than she did. And the Pueblos felt as strongly about the right of their dead to be left in peace. She shifted her thoughts to something more pleasant. Chee. She smiled as she pictured him. He liked going to Santa Fe for the trainings more than she did and didn't mind getting up in department meetings afterward to share what he had learned.

She was glad she didn't have to head back to the office. She decided to take the long way home and detoured off the freeway to NM 53, the road that skirted the other edge of the Malpais and headed toward the Zuni Mountains. Driving calmed her, especially driving beautiful empty roads like this one. It had been a good day, and she was encouraged by the incident commander's optimism about finding Mr. Cruz. She'd give the number for Cruz's sister to the incident commander when she got it.

She called Chee from the car and left a message when he didn't answer. Sometimes, she thought, a message from him, a quick reminder that she was loved, was enough.

She saw the signs for El Morro, a national monument preserving historic graffiti, signatures of the Spanish and American explorers, soldiers, and settlers who had come this way. The visitors had carved their names into the sandstone face. An abandoned pueblo sat on top of the butte, also open to visitors as part of the monument. Maybe their little store had a book about plants of the area, something that fascinated her. She pulled into the parking lot, noticing one other vehicle—a dusty white Toyota 4Runner with an El Morro National Monument bumper sticker. She walked the trail to the visitor center.

The ranger, a bright-eyed, gray-haired man, was alone.

"What brings you out this way, Officer? I'm Larry Hoffman."

"Bernadette Manuelito. I was in the Malpais and I got curious about the plants there. Do you have any books about them?"

"Not exactly, only some general guides to botany of the desert and the Southwest. On the top shelf over there by the window. Take a look and see what you think. You'd have better luck at the bookstore at the El Malpais visitor center, the big place off Highway 117."

The monument phone rang. "Excuse me."

She heard him answer as she walked toward the bookshelves. The plant books were interesting but not specific to this section of New Mexico or to species that thrived on lava. But she spotted something a few shelves down that caught her attention—a compilation of stories about the formation of the southwestern landscape. A large, beautiful volume with color photos, it included a version of the Diné story of the Monster Slayer and his brother, Born of Water, killing Ye'iitsoh.

Unlike the version Bernie knew, in this variation the monster hid his heart and other vital organs in a cave, and when a lightning bolt from Monster Slayer killed him, the blood flowed from the cave entrance and finally solidified into the lava beds. The book had stories from other tribes and included the science of volcanoes and photos of volcanic eruptions and different types of lava from around the world.

Chee had been less than excited when she'd given him a poetry collection for his birthday, even though the poems were by the first Navajo poet laureate. This might be more to his liking, but it was expensive. She put it back on the shelf for now.

"That's a lovely book, isn't it?" Hoffman said. "I was surprised that the tribes around here have such similar stories about the lava."

"I wonder what the Spanish and the Americans who came through here thought about all the lava. Had they seen anything like it before?"

"I haven't had the opportunity to study up on that yet. Ask me next time you're out this way, and you can see what a good student I am."

His attitude reminded Bernie of Leaphorn, the way the Lieutenant relished an interesting question. "Where were you before El Morro?"

"The Grand Canyon. I was one of the people who got to answer visitor questions." Hoffman changed the tone of his voice. " 'How old is the canyon?' 'Why is it here?' 'Can I bring my dog on the trails?' 'How hot is it at the bottom?' 'Is there an ATM?' And my favorite, 'Where is the restroom?' " He chuckled. "I was there five years until moving out here. The pace of this place is a lot easier on my bad back. I can keep my pain under better control. Are you working out of Ramah, Officer?"

"Please call me Bernie. I was helping a friend, an officer at Ramah, with a special request and got involved in a search out in the Malpais."

"Somebody lost, huh? On Navajo land?"

"Well, hard to say. Part of the lava flow extends onto the Ramah section of the reservation, but the person who is lost was last seen on the other side of the Malpais."

"There are some private ranches there, right?"

"That's right. It's a mix of jurisdictions, and when you're out that way you don't see any demarcations. The lava has oases of vegetation, caves, stone tubes, cinder cones, lots of lichens you don't find elsewhere. It's really interesting."

"Interesting and complicated, like so much of New Mexico. I thought maybe you were out here looking into the vandalism."

"I hadn't heard about that. Here at the visitor center?"

"No. Several people who've stopped here said they had seen cars that someone had broken into, vehicles parked at the pullouts for the Malpais trails. I guess the sheriff or the state police investigate such things. Is that how it works?"

"Yes, usually. Those kinds of incidents are hard to solve unless there are security cameras that capture the scene, and the folks responsible can be ID'd."

Hoffman nodded. "We have cameras in here, but we're fortunate. This monument is relatively small, and people watch out for each other. And the only cars here overnight are in the campground. It seems pretty peaceful, as far as I've seen."

Bernie agreed. "What crime there is usually involves family violence and burglaries related to drug or alcohol problems. The car break-ins are something new."

He smiled at her. "So, you like that geology book. It's beautiful, isn't it?"

"I think my husband would enjoy it. Is it available in paperback?"

"I wish. I could sell one or two of those a day." He took the book off the shelf and inspected it. "Tell you what, it's kind of shopworn. You can have it for ten dollars."

"Wow. Thanks." It didn't look shopworn to her. "I'll owe you a favor."

As she was paying for it, she discovered another

twenty-dollar bill in the coin compartment of her wallet and offered it to Hoffman.

"No. A deal's a deal. You can do me that favor some time."

A young couple came in. Instead of looking at the exhibits, they went right to the ranger.

The man said, "We have been thinking of that wonderful jug you showed us."

The woman said, "He means the olla, is that how you say it? The Zuni pot."

They both spoke with accents. Maybe French, Bernie thought.

Hoffman seemed uncomfortable. "Wait a minute, please. I'll be right with you. Why don't you take a look at the movie?"

The couple walked into the other room, where a film about El Morro was playing.

Hoffman opened the cash drawer and handed Bernie her change and the book.

She put the book in her backpack. "I didn't see any pottery for sale in here."

Hoffman hesitated. "I have a friend who asked me to help dispose of some Indian stuff. That couple is lucky. I'm not doing it anymore after this pot."

"Why not?"

He shrugged. "Let's say my friend and I had a philosophical difference of opinion."

Bernie drove toward the quiet junction for Indian Route 125, marked by the yellow "See the Wolves" sign. The road led to Mountain View and the Ramah Navajo Chapter House as well as the band's school and jail and to the non-Navajo Candy Kitchen Trading Post and Wild Spirit Wolf Sanctuary. The Ramah Navajo Indian Reservation didn't abut the vast Navajo Nation land but rather overlapped two New Mexico counties, west-central Cibola and southern McKinley, and adjoined an edge of the Zuni Indian Reservation to the west. It was separated from the Nation by private non-Indian holdings, national forest, state land, and an interstate highway. The folks who lived here spoke Diné with a slightly different accent than their non-Ramah relatives.

She stopped at the Ramah police station to say hello. Officers David Bluestone and Filbert Nakai had staffed the substation for the past few years. She told them about the search for Cruz. "A woman named Katz is the incident commander."

"Good. She's a smart one," Bluestone said. "You sure got a surprise when you agreed to do Cheryl a favor."

Nakai raised his eyebrows. "It seems strange that

Cruz would get lost. He's been working out there for years. He'd stop by sometimes to chat. Usually had his camera with him. Did the state police . . . I mean, Manzanares . . . show up?"

"Yes, but it seemed to take a while to get things rolling."

The Ramah officers looked at each other. Bernie figured she had company in her assessment of the man. "What's new with you two?" she said.

"The usual." Nakai smiled. "I stopped a guy for crossing the center line—twice, right in front of my unit. A woman was next to him—practically on top of him—and I think there was some hanky-panky going on. He acted embarrassed, so I gave him a warning and told her to keep her seat belt on."

"What were they driving?"

"A new black Jaguar, one of those big sedans, with Oklahoma plates."

"That car passed me. It looked like they were speeding, too."

Bluestone said, "Based on my experience, I think they had a body in the trunk. Probably her husband or his wife."

Nakai chuckled. "Manuelito, mention that to your new FBI agent. Push her buttons a little. I heard the bureau sent her because they thought we had a testosterone overload out here." He paused. "How's Chee doin'?"

"He's in Santa Fe for a training."

"Tell him to learn something for us."

Back on 53, Bernie headed toward the little community of Ramah at the edge of the Ramah Navajo Indian Reservation land, a ranching and farming settlement founded by Mormon families, nestled against the backdrop of the Zuni Mountains. To the west lay Zuni Pueblo, at the heart of which an old village of multi-roomed homes enclosed open-air dance plazas. The bones she'd encountered, she thought, could well belong to an ancestor of one of these residents. An ancient trail through the rock, perhaps a trade route, linked the Zuni and Acoma pueblos.

On this day, though, Bernie turned north onto NM 602 instead. The highway passed the low-lying buildings that housed the Zuni eagle sanctuary, home to birds that could no longer fly free but still produced feathers needed for ceremonies. Beginning the scenic climb through the sandstone and shale cliff that edged the Zuni Mountains, she passed the little settlement of Vanderwagen and its trading post, with plywood cutouts of the Zuni gods. She was headed for the south side of Gallup, the last town where travelers on I-40 could conveniently get a meal or spend the night before the Arizona border.

Bernie loved to drive. It gave her a chance to consider things, and on this stretch of familiar highway, she was considering the case of Domingo Cruz. She thought about Annie lying about her mother being dead, but not about the bones. She thought about the cave and the open van and the opportunity to specialize in domestic violence.

She stopped at a convenience store in Gallup for gas, using the department credit card. While the tank filled, her phone rang. The ID screen read BIGMAN, the name of her clan brother's wife and Mama's companion at the auction. Why would the woman be calling? Bernie's heart sank.

7

"Hello?"

Bernie heard Mama's voice. Mama sounded fine, and as usual, she didn't waste time with preliminaries.

"Have you talked to your sister?"

"Not today. I've been busy working out where there's no service. I was surprised to see you calling from Mrs. Bigman's phone. How are you, Mama?"

Mama ignored the question. "I think something's wrong. When I called her before we left for the auction, she didn't sound right to me. That school is too far away."

"You might have caught her at a bad time."

"You talk to her. Maybe you should pick her up and bring her back here."

Bernie knew better than to argue with Mama, especially over the phone. But the "maybe" gave her hope. "My husband is in Santa Fe, and he told me he would go by to see her, make sure she's all right."

"You talk to her."

"I will call her and see if I can find out what the trouble is."

"OK then." Mama's tone of voice said she'd switched to the next subject. "It's good to be in Crownpoint. I'm seeing people I had not talked to in a long time. Some of the ladies are like me, getting too old to weave much. But now their daughters are weaving, helping them. You see all the people here, more than when we used to bring my rugs here. Some of them ask about you and your sister. When I tell them you are a policeman, they say that's a good thing."

Bernie waited for Mama to ask if she had been at the loom, but Mama said, "You call me at home tomorrow when you've talked to your sister. You tell her if she wants to come back, you will pick her up."

And then she was gone.

Bernie went into the convenience store for a Coke, only her second of the day. She looked at the M&M's and the crispy, salty pork skins and then selected a bag of jerky and a small package of brownies, Mama's favorite. She'd save them until she saw her mother next.

The clerk pushed her money away. She smiled at Bernie. "Did anyone ever find out who stole Mr. Harrison's Jeep?"

"Not yet. Is he related to you?"

"My sister's father-in-law. She's glad it hasn't come back."

Bernie remembered the case. The Jeep wasn't worth anything, and the officer who investigated assumed that someone in the family had absconded with it to keep the old man from driving on the wrong side of the road with his lights off.

The girl laughed. "Now that grandfather is riding his horse again and they are both losing weight, we don't care if you guys never find the Jeep."

As Bernie walked back to her car, she caught a flash of motion out of the corner of her eye and stopped. A gray mouse scurried into a pile of dried leaves that had blown up against the building. Except for dogs, Bernie was friendly with most living creatures, but mice spread hantavirus, a disease that, like bubonic plague, arose on Navajo land periodically. Mice outside were part of nature, essential in the diets of hawks and coyotes. Mice inside, sharing living space with humans, caused a nest of problems on the Colorado Plateau. She wondered if avoiding hantavirus—in addition to avoiding contact with the dead—was one of the reasons her people wisely stayed away from the abandoned ruins of the Pueblo ancestors that dotted the reservation. Fear of lingering spirits might be linked to the fact that mice urine and feces carry the deadly virus after the mice and the people had departed.

When she opened the door to the unit, the radio squawked. It was Officer Manzanares.

Bernie said, "Did they find Cruz?"

"Not yet. I'm not calling about that. A Cibola County deputy told me one of the kids in that group got violently ill—a fever, rapid heart, hallucinations. The hospital in Grants was full so she's on her way to Gallup. The sheriff's department notified her parents. But here's the deal. She told the officer on the scene and the ambulance guy that she needed to talk to you because she lied about something."

"Annie Rainsong, right?"

"You got it. The attendant asked me to give you the message. He knew I'd been with a Navajo officer at the search site, so he called to see if I knew how to reach you."

Odd, Bernie thought. "Did the girl mention if what she wasn't truthful about had something to do with Cruz?"

"How would I know? I wasn't there, remember?"

"Are you sure she'll be at the hospital in Gallup, not Grants?"

"Gallup. She's going to Indian Medical Center. That's a good place for a drug overdose."

Bernie gave the Cibola ambulance crew a gold star in her imaginary tally of good public servants, even though Manzanares had delivered the message with attitude. Ambulance medics had plenty to do without conveying a request from a teenager.

When she called the hospital, after getting passed around to several desks she connected with someone who told her Annie was in the emergency room.

Then, as promised, she called her baby sister, putting her phone on speaker as she drove to the hospital. When Darleen didn't answer, Bernie left a brief message. "I talked to Mama. She's all right but wanted me to ask you something. Call me."

At the Gallup hospital, Bernie went directly to the emergency room. The man at the registration desk responded to her uniform with a shift in expression from overwhelmed to interested.

"What is the patient's name again?"

"Annie Rainsong. She came from Grants by ambulance. One of the ambulance medics said she asked me to come to see her. How is she?"

"Give me a minute." He typed something in his computer and then looked up at Bernie. "I'm sorry, Officer. I don't have any information except that Annie arrived about half an hour ago. And—"

"Hey!" A heavyset, frazzled-looking woman walked up to them and grabbed Bernie's arm, trying to stand directly in front of the information window. She wore her hair in a ponytail, and there was a touch of gray at her temples. "Who do you think you are, Ms. Policeman? That girl is none of your business."

Bernie pulled her arm free from the woman's grasp. "Calm down. Go back to your seat."

The man at the desk frowned and leaned toward the opening in the glass. "Ma'am, I'll be with you as soon as—"

"No. Tell me, why is this cop asking about Annie?"

The man pulled back slightly. Bernie read his nervousness and turned to the woman.

"I'm talking to the gentleman here, and then it will be your turn. Relax. I don't want to have to call hospital security."

Instead, Angry Woman grew more belligerent. "Leave that girl alone, you hear me? There's no proof that drugs are involved in this."

Bernie felt her temper rising. "Ma'am, you'll be removed from the waiting area if you keep yelling."

The woman stared at the nameplate on Bernie's uniform shirt. She turned to the man at the desk. "If you dare tell Officer Bernadette Manuelito anything about my daughter, I'll get you fired and then I will sue you."

Knowing Angry Woman was Annie's mom cast the situation in a different light. Bernie felt a pang of compassion for the girl. She gave civility another try. "I got a message from the state police that Annie Rainsong had something to tell me, that's all. I didn't realize you were Annie's mother."

"How dare you accuse my daughter of being a criminal."

"Ma'am, I'm not accusing your daughter of anything. I met Annie at Wings and Roots earlier today. She told the ambulance attendants she wanted to see me."

The woman responded with a laugh filled with bitterness.

"Drop the stories. I know why you're really here. Whatever trouble she's in, it's no surprise. That girl never thinks of how inconvenient all this is for me and her brother. Leave our family alone."

Angry Woman turned to the attendant. "I need to see my daughter now. I've been waiting half an hour, and that is thirty minutes too long."

The man looked pale. "Christine will take you back. She's over there by the big door."

Bernie watched the woman stomp off. Her disappointment at not being able to talk to the girl surprised her even more than the anger that tightened her throat. Maybe Annie did crave attention, but she hadn't made up the story about the cave. What did Annie want to tell her?

She found a vacant waiting room chair next to a man with a sweaty little boy dozing fitfully in his lap. The room was crowded with people. Frail old ones surrounded by relatives, an assortment of drunks, a woman with a bloody face, and a man with a large "Semper Fi" tattooed on his arm and ripped pants showing an oozing leg wound. An elder, his gray hair in braids, sat hunched over, elbows on his knees, head in his hands. A woman just as old sat quietly next to him. A very pregnant woman with a small girl at her side stared straight ahead.

Bernie pulled her notebook and a pen from her backpack and composed a message. She folded the note in half, wrote "Annie Rainsong" on the outside, gathered her pack, and walked back to the desk. She handed the note to the man at the window.

"Could you give this to Annie's nurse to give to her?"

The man looked skeptical.

Bernie said, "Open it if you want. I'm telling her I got her message, giving her my cell and office number, and hoping she feels better soon."

He took the folded paper. "I'll hand this to whoever is assigned to her." He shook his head. "Maybe they can hand it over when her crazy mother isn't around."

Bernie walked back to her unit and began the drive home. She rolled down Nizhoni Boulevard back to NM 602 and drove across the bridge over Interstate 40. From there, the road number changed to US 491. She passed Blake's Lotaburger with its delicious green chile burgers and drove beyond Tohatchi and Naschitti, sharing the four-lane with big trucks with their heavy loads and watching as cars going over the speed limit realized that the vehicle they planned to pass was a police car and slowed down.

As she rolled along, she replayed the encounter with Annie's mother. She was sure she had seen the woman before but couldn't remember exactly where, and the memory lapse gnawed at her. Angry Woman's reference to drugs helped her make sense of Cooper's assumption that Annie had hidden drugs somewhere. Cooper and Mayfair both dismissed the girl as a liar. Drugs and lies went together like warp and weft.

The transition from an assumption that Annie's

problems came from drugs to Darleen's trouble with alcohol was fluid. Her sister had stopped drinking—or said she had, and left no evidence to the contrary. The opportunity to spend a week at the Institute for American Indian Arts enlivened her, and Bernie had encouraged it. The short course would help her decide if she wanted to go to art school and if she felt, well, mature enough to be away from home. Mama had questioned the whole idea, but eventually Darleen's eagerness and good behavior had paid off and Mama approved the idea.

But now Mama was concerned. Was her sister unhappy? Bernie wondered. Or had Mama misread the conversation because, as much as she wanted Darleen to find her own way in the world, she liked having that girl at home?

Bernie remembered her first weeks at the University of New Mexico—the stimulation of the classes, the excitement of being in such a situation with so many distractions, and her miserable loneliness when the campus fell quiet, and how homesick she was, how she missed being home and hearing someone speak to her in Navajo.

Why hadn't Darleen called her? And why hadn't she heard from Chee, who'd promised to check on her sister? Unlike Mama, she assumed her sister was having too good a time to check in with them. When she got home, she'd phone her again.

Her brain returned to Annie and the mystery of Mr. Cruz, who hadn't returned to base camp. What if he wasn't lost? What if someone had done him harm? What if he had decided to run away? But if someone wanted to murder him, following him out to the Malpais and relying on the coincidence of a girl getting lost was an enormously complicated scenario. Why not just shoot him? The Cruz-as-a-runaway plot demanded more consideration. So far, she hadn't talked to anyone who had suggested that he might want to disappear, but because he raised money for the group, he might have been tempted to engage in some funny business.

Bernie's brain had filled with questions by the time she reached the convenience store. If she planned to see Mama, she'd turn onto the Toadlena road here. But now she headed for the Shiprock trailer she and Chee, the one person who loved her as much as Mama did, shared by the winter-tempered San Juan River. Maybe the song of the river would inspire her thinking.

8

Bernie had finished her morning prayers and was getting ready to go for a run, trying to decide whether she needed gloves and a hat to keep out the December chill, when the landline rang. She hoped it was Chee—it was too early in the morning for Darleen, and besides, her sister always called her cell.

But the voice on the other end was Sandra. "The captain needs to talk to you." Her friend sounded stressed.

"He's in early. Did they find Mr. Cruz?"

"No. The captain is in a terrible mood, and it has something to do with the search. How could that man, of all people, get lost out there? I don't understand it."

"It sounds like you know him."

She heard Sandra's change of tone. "One of my clan

sisters went through the Wings and Roots program when she was fourteen. She talked about how Mr. Cruz really helped her. He even stayed in touch with her afterward, now and then, you know, to make sure she was all right. She invited him to the first laugh party when she had her baby. I met him there."

Thinking about the baby lifted Sandra's spirits, and she told Bernie more than she needed to know about the baby and his mother. Someone had described the A'wee Chi'deedloh as a reverse baby shower. The baby, with the help of its parents, gave all who attended a gift of salt to rejuvenate their good character. Although there was more to it, in a nutshell the laugh symbolized the baby's transition into personhood.

Sandra circled back to Mr. Cruz. "He's a valuable man, and that lava, it's a bad place."

Bernie felt sadness roll over her like cold fog. "The search team won't give up on Mr. Cruz. They will keep looking."

"They must have worked all night. That's already too long for them not to find him. It's freezing out there." The longer the search continued, they both knew, the slimmer the chances that a missing person would be found alive.

"It's rugged country," Bernie said. "There are too many places a person could get lost, but there are also spots where someone could find refuge. And Mr. Cruz would know where they are."

"I understand, but . . . Oh, here's the captain."

Bernie heard a moment of quiet and then some clicks.

"Manuelito?"

"Yes, sir."

"Do you know who Elsbeth Walker is?"

"Yes. She's the council delegate from here in Shiprock, right?"

"That's her. She wants an investigation into Wing and Roots for financial malfeasance. The request went to the chief, and he's pulled in our department."

"Sorry, sir. What does that mean exactly?"

"Councilor Walker thinks the Wings and Roots director, or somebody on the staff, misused funds the president's office allocated to subsidize Navajo kids who were in the program. Mrs. Walker heard about the search for Cruz, and now she's sure he's absconded with the money, or the records or something, and there's a conspiracy. She called last night after she talked to the chief and practically chewed my head off."

"You? Sir, why did she think you had something to do with it?" But even before she was done with the question, she knew the answer. It wasn't Largo, personally, it was law enforcement in general.

"She thinks the police are hiding something, in cahoots with Wings and Roots because the group asked one of our officers—that would be you, Manuelito—to talk to the kids."

"That's pretty far out there. How did she even know about that?"

"It's on the program's website and their social media. They have a photo of you with the award you got for helping arrest the person who hurt Lieutenant Leaphorn."

Bernie felt her skin grow hot with embarrassment at the thought of that unwelcome honor for doing her job. She was glad they were talking on the phone and not in his office.

"An unnamed source told her the group is running in the red, despite some anonymous donations," Largo went on. "She thinks someone at the agency is stealing the tribe's money. I asked what her proof is, but she wouldn't tell me because she thinks our substation is part of the conspiracy. The chief wants you to talk to Councilor Walker and try to get at least your part of this mess straightened out. Do that ASAP. Get this gal off my back."

Largo read her Walker's phone number. "Anything else, Manuelito?"

"Sir, something strange happened yesterday. One of the girls on that Wings and Roots trip, the girl who was lost and led to Cruz getting lost . . . anyway, she got sick and told one of the ambulance team she needed to talk to me." She told him about the incident at the hospital with Annie Rainsong's mother.

"I'll be surprised if the girl has much to say that helps with the investigation, but since Walker has raised the question of Cruz's integrity, call the hospital and talk to the girl on the phone. If Walker objects, tell her it's police business."

"Excuse me, sir? Why would Councilor Walker object?"

"Manuelito, Elsbeth Walker is Annie's mother. I wouldn't be surprised if she sent her girl on that trip as a sort of spy mission. It helped that the daughter has her dad's name."

"Then I was wrong when I told you I hadn't met Walker. She didn't confront me about any of this malfeasance or collusion stuff at the hospital, thank goodness."

Largo ended the call.

The phone rang almost immediately. It was the station again, but to her relief the voice on the line was Sandra's.

"Chee called while you were talking to the captain. He said everything is fine, don't worry about him, and he'll catch you later."

"Later?"

"That's all he said."

Bernie said, "If he calls again, please tell him I'll call when I get a chance."

Bernie telephoned the Gallup hospital several times but was never able to connect with Annie. After she explained the situation, the charge nurse told her Annie was lucid and able to have visitors. Bernie dreaded visiting hospitals, but this trip was part of her job.

Annie looked younger and tiny against the bright white bedsheet. She had scrapes on her forehead, an oxygen canulla in her nose, an IV line running from a bag of fluid into her left arm. Amazingly for this busy place, the bed next to her was empty. The shades were pulled, and only a faint glow from outside penetrated the space. The lights were off, as was the television.

Bernie expected to see Councilor Walker there and was relieved not to have to talk to her. As she approached the foot of the bed, Annie opened her eyes.

"How are you feeling? I hope I didn't wake you."

Annie lifted the arm attached to the IV. "OK, except for this thing. They told me I got dehydrated out there because I didn't want to drink water. Who likes to pee in the bushes?"

"What happened? Mrs. Cooper said you started to feel really bad and were acting crazy on the bus."

"I don't know. I got too hot, and my stomach hurt . . . and then the light bothered my eyes, and then, well, I was just totally out of it. I told Cooper to keep the windows closed so I wouldn't float away from the van. I heard strange music from the jungle or something. After that, I don't remember."

"Did the doctor say what caused it?"

"Everyone keeps asking me about drugs, but I'm clean."

"Do you know if any of the girls or any of the adults at the camp came down with this?"

"I don't know. I don't think so." Annie pushed the button to raise the head of the bed. "They want to do more tests, and that stinks. I feel better but still kinda floaty and strange. Did anyone find Mr. Cruz?"

"I haven't heard." Bernie saw the question in the girl's eyes. "The searchers will keep looking for him. Is that what you wanted to talk about?"

Annie stared at the ceiling for a few moments. When she spoke again her voice was softer. "You remember that I told you I didn't see him out there when he came to look for me?"

"I remember."

"Well, I didn't see him, but I heard him. He followed me as I was walking back to the base camp."

Bernie studied the girl. No obvious signs that Annie was lying. "Really?"

"Really."

"If you didn't see him, how do you know it was Mr. Cruz?"

Annie picked at an edge of the tape that kept her IV in place. "Mr. Cruz has this little metal bell on a cord attached to his backpack, and it swings and makes a sound like *bing, bing.* He said up in Alaska people hike with bells on their packs to let the bears know they're coming. He said this was to let us know when he was coming so we could be good. I heard that sound on the trail to the base camp. You know . . . after I left that cave. I know it was him."

"Did you turn around to say hi?"

"No. I waited for him to say something." Annie drew her legs up underneath her and wrapped her arms around herself, looking even smaller. "I thought he would yell at me for leaving my vision spot. When he didn't say anything, I figured he was super mad. You know, too mad to talk or yell or anything." The girl pulled her knees into her chest, and her shoulders tensed.

"What happened next?"

"I kept walking and I got to where I could see the blue tent, so I knew I was in the right place. I didn't hear the bell anymore. Even if he was mad, I felt safer with him behind me, like my guardian spirit or something in case I wasn't headed in the right direction to the main camp."

"Do you know where he went?"

Annie spoke quickly now. "I turned around when I didn't hear him anymore, but I couldn't see him, either."

"Did you mention this to Mrs. Cooper?"

The girl shook her head. "Cooper would say I imagined it or had a vision or something. I figured Mr. Cruz would come back when he was ready."

"Are you sure you didn't imagine hearing Mr. Cruz because you were still upset about the cave thing?"

"I'm sure." She stretched out her legs again under the sheets.

"Were you high then?'

"No." She reinforced it with a couple shakes of her head.

"Thanks for telling me about hearing Mr. Cruz. I'm going to pass this along to the searchers."

Annie smiled ever so slightly. "Do you think that could help find him?"

"It might. Was there anything else you wanted to talk about?"

"Well, sort of. Did you really find that scary cave? Or you just want to make me feel good?"

"I found a cave that matched the description you gave me."

"Mr. Cruz kept telling us to stay away from caves, you know, because they were filled with things that could cause trouble. We used to laugh, but now I believe him. I think the *chindi* followed me. That's what made me go crazy on the van."

Bernie reached in her backpack. "I found something else, too." She extracted the pink phone.

Annie burst into laughter. "You got it!" she said, and then stopped when Bernie handed the phone to her. She pushed herself up to sitting in the hospital bed. "What happened to the screen? It's all broken."

"It was like that when I came across it in the parking lot, near where Cooper parked the van. Maybe somebody ran over it. But I'm surprised that phone is yours. You told me you didn't have one."

Annie didn't miss a beat. "I meant I lost it, but—"

"But what?"

"But I thought I lost it somewhere else."

A woman with a hospital badge on her lanyard motioned Bernie away from the bed.

"The toxicology screen is back. It looks like Annie ingested an alkaloid, something like datura. Her symptoms ought to be gone in another twelve hours or so. You should have a talk with your daughter about experimenting with drugs. If she had consumed more, this could have had a different outcome."

"Thanks for the information, but this young lady is not my daughter."

The woman looked horrified.

Bernie gave her what she hoped was a reassuring smile. "I'm sure her mother will be here soon, and she'll want to know about the lab report."

She walked back to Annie's bed. "One of the tests showed that you had a hallucinogen in your system."

Annie started to yell. "No way! Nobody had drugs out there. Not even weed. No way. That test must be screwed up."

The hospital woman gave Annie a stern look. "Get some rest before your mother comes."

Bernie left Annie and walked past other patient rooms, a cart with food trays, and a patient in her hospital gown holding the IV tree with her right hand as she strolled down the hall. A person in hospital scrubs held on to the thick white belt that circled the woman's waist. Then Bernie saw Annie's mother leaning on the nurses' desk, across from a gray-haired man. From the body language Bernie could tell it was not a pleasant conversation. Walker stopped what she was saying to the nurse and frowned. "This is a private conversation, Officer. Where are your manners?"

"Councilor, I need to talk to you about your complaints against Wings and Roots."

"Well, this obviously is not the place. We'll talk at the police station." Walker turned her back and resumed her harangue of the man at the desk.

Bernie checked her phone for messages, found none, and called Darleen from the lobby, again getting no answer. This time Bernie's message was more direct. I don't like being ignored. Mama is worried about you. Call me ASAP.

A few moments later, her phone beeped with a text message.

In class. Tell Mama I'm OK. UR distracting me!!!

As she left the hospital parking lot, Bernie thought of Joe Leaphorn and the long days she and Chee and Louisa had spent in the hospital with him. She was only an hour from his home in Window Rock now, but she had to get back to work.

She listened to the scanner, hoping for news that

Cruz had been found but hearing nothing about the search. As she began the drive toward Shiprock, she thought of Annie and datura. In the summer, datura grew like the weed it was on parts of the reservation and the entire Southwest—hardy, with beautiful huge white flowers that turned into prickly pods holding thousands of tiny seeds. Ranchers knew it as jimson weed, and kept their animals away from its toxic leaves. During their conversation at camp, Annie hadn't been high, but she was anxious and worried. She'd told the truth about the cave, and her story of hearing Mr. Cruz's bell seemed honest. She'd lied about having a phone and about her mother's death, though, making the girl a less-than-reliable informant.

Cooper thought the girl's hallucinations came from drugs she'd hidden, and the lab test had found something like datura, Annie had another answer: *chindi*, the spirit of the dead one she'd stumbled upon in the cave. Perhaps the bones came from a Spanish rancher or an American homesteader. A centuries-old trail through the lava connected the Zuni and Acoma pueblos, thirty miles apart as the crow flies, and elders in both pueblos knew places with special significance to their people. Their bones had been found here, too.

Bones made her think of Spider Woman. She remembered the old story of how Spider Woman came

for disobedient children, took them up onto the mono-
lith known as Spider Rock, and devoured them in her
nest at the top, where their bones formed a white ring
in the sandstone. She wondered if Councilor Walker
had told Annie that story, and remembered the councilor in conflict with the nurses rather than sitting with
her daughter. She thought about the way Mama worried over her and her sister. Bernie decided she'd sit at
the loom when she got some time off. That, and see if
she could learn a little more about *Datura stramonium*.

She was still in Gallup, stuck in traffic because of a
load of hay that had spilled onto 491, when Largo came
on the radio.

"The search coordinator called here, looking for
you. They are broadening their efforts, and they need
Cruz's next of kin. It won't be long before Cruz's name
goes public."

Bernie remembered that Cooper had promised to
text her with Cruz's sister's info. "He has a sister in
Grants. I'll call Cooper and get the information to the
search team."

"While you're at it, tell her we'd like to see the program's financial reports. If she doesn't want to hand
them over, let her know what Councilor Walker is saying about the program and about you."

"I'm on my way to the station now."

"No. You need to drive back to Grants and talk to Cruz's sister face-to-face. She's on the board of Wings and Roots and may have a different perspective on her brother's disappearance."

"Sir?"

"A person who matched Cruz's description was spotted earlier this morning, hitchhiking along I-40 west near the Fort Wingate exit." She heard a squeak as Largo leaned back in his chair. "It was an odd thing. The driver who saw him is one of the Cibola County search and rescue volunteers and knew the description of the missing person. He had to leave the search crew because his wife was having a baby. They were on the way to the hospital. The similarity didn't register until after the baby arrived. By then, someone had given the man he saw a ride. It might not have been our guy, but an alert went out for him along the interstate. If it was Cruz, Councilor Walker is on to something with her mismanagement claims." Largo took a breath. "Have you met with her yet?"

"No, sir. I tried, but she said she wanted to come to the station. She said she'd call me."

"When you figure out how to reach the sister, see if she thinks this guy is on the run."

"Yes, sir."

"And stay in touch."

"I'll phone Cooper right now."

Cooper's hello sounded distracted. Bernie explained what she needed and put her phone on speaker.

"Sure, I have the information on Merilee Cruz. I'll text it right now. I meant to send it, but it slipped my mind." Cooper's voice cracked. "I guess I forgot because I can't believe that Dom hasn't shown up, wondering why we're making such a fuss."

"I need to come by your office and get copies of those financial reports and board minutes," Bernie said. "Councilor Walker thinks I'm involved in some sort of police cover-up."

"She told me that too. For some reason, that woman seems to hate you."

9

Before he left for class that morning, Chee called the phone number for the New Mexico State Land Office, asked for Caitlyn Vigil, and was transferred and put on hold before a soft voice came on the line.

"This is Caitlyn. How may I help you?"

Chee briefly introduced himself. "I'm calling because one of my coworkers is worried about George Curley. He asked me to see if you could help him reach George."

The line was silent, and when Caitlyn came on the line again, the softness was gone.

"I can't talk about this here. I'll call you when I have a break."

"All right. Here's my number, but I'm in class."

Chee told her she could also try him at the hotel. "But just tell me this. Is George OK?"

"I don't know. I hope so."

"Give me your cell number in case—"

But she'd already hung up.

Every time he came to Santa Fe and the New Mexico Law Enforcement Academy for a training, Chee decided he would have made a terrible teacher. He was patient, but he grew bored quickly. Teaching something once in a while, like tracking, was fine because of the challenge of putting the talk together and figuring out how to get the class involved. But to teach the same material over and over again? No thanks.

He admired Captain Nailor, the woman who was teaching the day's session, "Staying Alive at Traffic Stops." She acted as though there was nothing else in the world she'd rather be doing. In her shoes, he would rather be hunting for elk or deer to stock the freezer for the year or spending time with Bernie or watching football on television or just being outside and enjoying the views. The captain handled everyone's questions with respect, no matter how off-base, misinformed, and repetitious they were. She kept control of the room when someone wanted to talk on and on about an experience he'd had. She even drew out the quiet students, like the serious young Apache woman from the Jicarilla Police Department, without embarrassing them.

The Apache officer's beautiful black hair made him think of Bernie, a lovely distraction. He would have enjoyed his wife's company, but, besides not being able to get off work, she didn't care much for Santa Fe. Jim Chee liked it better than Albuquerque or Phoenix. It was smaller and had less traffic. In addition to the IAIA Darleen was curious about, there was a well-run community college and special schools where people could work on their projects in physics or archaeology, style hair, or study massage. He saw other Navajos here as well as Pueblo people, Hispanics, and an occasional Asian and African American, along with an abundance of gray-haired white folks. He liked the variety of restaurants. He could order spicy New Mexican chile, Chinese egg rolls, Thai dumplings, hummus rich with garlic, a good thick steak, or chicken wings.

Mostly, though, he liked the setting at the base of the Sangre de Cristo, with the Jemez and the hills of Cerrillos, the Ortiz, and the Sandias spread out before him. He could get to a quiet place in the mountains in less than an hour.

The room where this day's training took place had no windows. That made it easier to watch the film Nailor showed after lunch about how law enforcement officers can stay safe and keep things from going wrong at traffic stops. He'd settled in when his phone vibrated. He pulled it out to see a text from Darleen: Wanna see my art? He typed Sure. Details? and slipped the phone back into his pocket as the instructor dimmed the lights.

He ranked the film as average, with some good ideas but too much talking. About halfway through, he felt a hand on his shoulder. It was Captain Nailor. She motioned Chee to follow her, and they moved to the back of the room and then out to the hall.

"Hey, Sergeant, I need a favor." Nailor kept her voice low. "I plan to ask for stories of personal experiences with traffic stops. You look like you might have a few. You know, those times where you trusted your gut and things worked out fine. Would you share them?"

"Sure. Why me?"

"I've been watching you. You've had enough experience that you know most of this stuff, but you're still paying attention."

Chee wasn't used to compliments, especially from state police officers who were women. He didn't know how to respond.

"Raise your hand when I ask the question so I can call on you."

When the opportunity came, he told the story of

Bernie's traffic stop that resulted in the seizure of some endangered cacti, adding enough suspense that the officers in the audience chuckled when the open trunk revealed plants and not drugs.

Then Nailor gave them a recess. Chee checked his phone and saw Darleen's text: CU@art show and then a little thumbs-up symbol.

He responded: Where & when?

This would be a good time to talk to Caitlyn Vigil, he thought, but she hadn't called him. Instead, he checked in with Largo and learned that life at the Shiprock station was rolling along, including the usual surprises.

"Manuelito has her hands full with Councilor Walker. She thinks Bernie is part of a cover-up of misuse of tribal funds that involves Wings and Roots. She took her complaint right to the chief."

"I thought dealing with politicians was up to you and the chief." As soon as he said that, Chee regretted it, but it was the truth.

The captain chuckled and changed the subject. "Did you hear about the search for that missing group leader in the Malpais?"

"Yes, sir." Word traveled fast in law enforcement circles. "Nothing's turned up yet, right?"

"Yeah. What have you found out about George Curley?"

"I learned that his mother-in-law doesn't much care for him. He wasn't home at the pueblo when I stopped by. I called his wife, Caitlyn, at work but she couldn't talk. She said she'd call me back."

"Deborah Curley talked to the rookie again. Her son George still hasn't been in contact with her. He'd promised to take her to Walmart and help her buy paint for her kitchen. She's annoyed with him."

"If Caitlyn doesn't call, I'll try her again before I leave Santa Fe." The crowd in the hall was thinning. "If there's nothing else, Captain, I need to get back to class."

"Listen hard in there today. Don't let any of those guys recruit you."

Nailor dismissed the group an hour later with a reminder about the Amber and Silver Alert program the next day. Chee checked his phone, texted Darleen again, and then headed toward the IAIA campus. Despite her lack of response, he'd find her and her work. While he was out there, he'd look for CS, talk to him about the death certificate, and move on to his choice of an ex-con for a companion.

Chee parked the truck behind the video studios. This time there were a dozen vehicles in the lot, some identifiable rez cars, some newer and in better condition. Probably faculty vehicles, he thought. Mrs. Lomasi's station wagon looked even worse in the daylight. The door he'd helped her with last night was unlocked. He walked down the hall toward an open space in the center of the building, noticing blinking red lights over several studio doors, with signs that read "Production in process. Please do not disturb." The facility was nice but not fancy, busy but not too crowded with students. The hallway led past smaller rooms with desks and computers and into the larger central gathering room. Chee endorsed the idea of Native people telling their own stories, and he thought video, TV, and movies were great ways to do it.

Darleen might fit right in on this campus. She was good at drawing. Maybe she could make sketches for animation. He'd talk to CS about that, melt the ice a little before he delivered the news that CS was officially dead.

Chee walked over to a pair of young men doing something on their laptops.

"Hi. Do you guys know if CS is here?"

One of them looked up. "He practically lives here, man. He hangs in studio four. You can knock when the light turns off." He went back to his computer.

Chee found a chair with a view of the studio doors. This part of the building, unlike the state police class-room, had windows and skylights. Above him, a cloud drifted by in the darkening December sky. He picked up a magazine, something called *Local Flavor*, and was reading a story about the renovation of an old hotel when he heard the door to a studio open.

A tall, beefy Navajo man in his forties emerged. His nose had that off-kilter angle that came from being on the receiving end of too many fights. He glanced at Chee's uniform and looked away.

"Yá'át'ééh, bro," Chee called to him. "Clyde Herbert, we meet again."

The man turned back. "What you doing here, man? Got lost on the way back to the rez?"

"My sister-in-law thinks she might want to go to school here. I'm looking for CS. You a student in the video department?"

"Student of life, dude."

Chee heard the door open again.

"Here's the man. Ask him about me, Mr. Law and Order."

As CS came out of the room, Herbert strode down the hall and away.

"Yá'át'ééh. What brings you to my studio?" CS seemed even thinner than when Chee had last seen him.

"Darleen told me you were working here. I wanted to say hello, check in, talk a minute."

"Have you seen Darleen's new drawings yet?"

"Not yet. I stopped by to catch you first and ran into your buddy Herbert again."

CS looked as if he were going to say something in response but instead changed the subject. "I haven't seen the pictures in this show, but that girl has mad skills. I'm planning to walk over to the exhibit."

"I'll go with you."

CS went into the studio and emerged a moment later with his jacket. Chee saw him glance at his phone and then slip it in his pocket.

Chee opened the door and motioned CS to go ahead of him. "Darleen and I went out for pizza last night. She was hoping you'd come with us."

"I know. I hated to disappoint her, but I had to stay in the studio. I can feel the hot breath of that deadline on my neck."

"Are you working on something with Herbert?"

"Yeah." CS zipped his jacket against the cold. "Do you remember the video D helped me with?"

"You mean the grandmother who wanted to introduce her sheep to the Navajo president?"

"Well, that project ate up a lot of weeks, but I'm almost finished. The editing was tricky. I realize now I should have shot more scenery and less of the sheep.

D did a great job with the interview. Have you been out here to the campus before?"

CS had deflected the conversation neatly away from the big Navajo, Chee thought. "I came yesterday to pick up Darleen for dinner," he said. "Did you see that bruise on her arm?"

"Yeah."

"Do you know how she got it?"

CS didn't answer right away. "Yeah."

"How?"

"You'll have to ask her."

"I'm asking you. Darleen was upset last night, and it sounded like you two had been arguing."

"I didn't give her that bruise, understand? And everyone argues. What about you and the cop you're married to? That must be tough. I mean, you both come home fried or pumped up from dealing with people and then you have to deal with each other."

Chee stopped walking. "Don't change the subject. Do you know the law about domestic violence?"

CS turned toward him. "Yeah, firsthand, actually. My mom and dad were the king and queen of DV. The cops, guys like you, came to the house and scared the bejeezus out of me."

"Do you know that Clyde Herbert, your pal, beat up a woman? He hit her so hard he broke her ribs."

CS clenched his teeth. "There's more than one side to a story."

"Oh, right." Chee stepped close enough to CS to smell the cigarette smoke that clung to his jacket. "I forgot the part about how he was selling drugs out of their car, and when I pulled his wife over for speeding, I found the meth and the pills and arrested her. She denied being involved in the drug business, but the kids ended up with protective services before it got straightened out."

"Clyde kept all that secret from her to protect her and the kids. His old lady was drinking. She was no angel." CS spoke faster now. "Why is my friend your business? You don't know who he is since he got out of prison."

"I know he was acting like a badass when I saw him at the restaurant out by the police headquarters. And you pretended not to know me, remember?"

CS exhaled. "Sorry about that. I didn't recognize you right away. I wasn't expecting to see you in Santa Fe, dude. And then, when I hadn't said anything and Clyde started giving you grief, I got embarrassed."

Chee flinched at the excuse, and they walked in silence for a few minutes. He reassessed CS. "I don't respect men who hurt women. I hope you aren't someone like that."

"Herbert isn't a stereotype. There's more to him than a criminal record. The situation isn't as simple as you make it sound. People change."

"From my perspective, it's pretty simple." Chee stopped walking and used his fingers to dramatize the points. "A man loses his cool, probably because he's been drinking. He hurts his lady. Maybe he hurts their kids. The process repeats itself until the cops get involved and he goes to the joint or she figures out how to get away from him, or until he kills her. The only thing complicated is the excuses they come up with. The way they spin the situation is to say it was the wife or the girlfriend's own fault, how she provoked them into breaking her arm or choking her." Chee put his hand back in his pocket. "Getting the woman to agree that she deserves better, that can be a challenge, and sometimes the case falls through the cracks. But DV itself? Simple. Simple and disgusting."

Chee took a breath, checked his anger. "I know what I'm talking about because I've seen too many guys like Herbert. I'm sick of it. You need to keep Darleen away from him."

"You're wrong about Herbert." CS started down the sidewalk again ahead of Chee. "And don't worry about D, man. No one will hurt her while I'm around, if I can help it. But, you know, she's so strong-willed she's her own worst enemy."

Chee caught up to him in a few steps. "There's something else I wanted to talk to you about. An investigator friend of mine discovered that your death certificate is on file with the state of New Mexico. What gives?"

CS tugged his cap down tighter against the December chill. "Oh. Strange how that . . ." He stopped talking and pulled his phone from his pocket. "I've got to take this. Darleen's art is in the show in that building with the green roof ahead to the left. I'll catch up."

If he'd been on duty, Chee would have pursued it. But he knew Darleen would be expecting him and that he would have another chance to talk to CS. He found the building for the art show without difficulty.

The fierce Mrs. Lomasi was seated inside the front doors at the gallery entrance at a table with a small stack of flyers that told the visitors about the exhibit and the student artists. She offered one to Chee.

"Welcome. Glad you could make it." He could tell that she didn't recognize him. Probably because of his uniform.

"I'm looking for Darleen Manuelito's drawings."

"You'll find her work over there by . . . oh, you're her uncle. Thanks again for helping me last night."

"Brother-in-law. You're welcome."

"Her drawings are by the big red sculpture."

He took the information sheet. "Do you know if Darleen is here?"

"All the students were asked to stay until the show closes at six, another half an hour."

"How's Darleen doing?"

"Well, she's an interesting young woman with a lot of talent. Take a look at what she's done here."

"Do you think this is the right place for her?"

Mrs. Lomasi straightened the pile of papers. "We'll see. She's got some growing up to do, but that's true for many of our younger students."

The visitors at the exhibition were mostly twenty-somethings, probably fellow students, with a few parent-age folks in the mix. Clusters of students, probably the artists, and a handful of other people were studying the artworks. Although the show consisted of a variety of art, each individual's work had its own space. Chee found Darleen's drawings grouped near the center of the small gallery.

Darleen's work stood out for its intricate detail, and because she worked mostly in black and white, with just a bit of red here and there. Other students who were into drawing used vivid colors. Some of them had dozens of pieces; Darleen had only four, each highly complex. He'd be the first to admit that he didn't have the vocabulary for describing art, but two of them depicted beautiful, surreal-looking creatures that reminded Chee of wolves or maybe coyotes, with a supernatural, graphic-novel-type edge to them. The other two were dreamy landscapes, one that he thought was Ship Rock. They had some swirling parts, as though the land were being created or perhaps destroyed. He'd have to ask her what they meant.

He scanned the gallery for Darleen and watched other visitors come by and study her work. Her drawings seemed to attract a bigger crowd than many of the other installations and displays, and he heard comments that they were interesting and well done, especially for a beginning student.

Chee strolled around the room, stopping to look at photographs of horses and a large bright painting of lines converging in the center of the canvas. Arrows at a target? A maze of highways? It made him feel old to be around so many young people, but energized, too. One group of students seemed to have an assignment to write about the show because they were moving from section to section, taking notes. They spent longer looking at Darleen's work than most of the other artists'. As he watched them, he realized that some of the older folks were students, too.

Finally he spotted Darleen talking with a small cluster of girls. One put her cup of punch on a table and reached in her suitcase-size purse for something—was it a liquor bottle? Her back was toward him, so he couldn't tell for sure. He wondered if Mrs. Lomasi had noticed.

Darleen saw him and left her group to greet him.

"You came. Cool. I forgot to text you back. Did you see my stuff over there?" She waved her arm toward the wall behind the big sculpture. The bruise had changed from solid deep plum to include accents of yellow and green.

"I saw them. Nice."

"Do you really think so?"

"I like your drawings a lot," he said. "They look good in here."

"Which one do you like best?"

Chee's automatic response was to say *All of them*, but he thought harder. "I think the one you called *Secrets*, the one that has something that looks like Tsé Bit'a'í in the lower right corner. How about you?"

She smiled. "I like different ones on different days, but today I like them all the same. I did more, but they weren't good enough for the show. I've been working like crazy to get ready."

"I saw you talking with those girls. Are they in the program with you?"

"Some are."

She looked about the room, then back at Chee.

"Are you waiting for somebody?"

"Well, CS said he would come by." She shook her head. "He's probably mad at me or something."

Chee changed the subject. "Are most of the people here students?"

"Everyone in our class had to come. Before you got here, we each had to stand by our work and introduce ourselves and talk about why we did what we did."

"I wish I had been here for that."

"No, you don't. That's why I didn't tell you about the talking part. One girl started to cry, and that made everybody screw up. I was terrible."

He searched for something reassuring to say and came up short.

Darleen looked toward the group of girls again. "Did you notice the person with the turquoise bag over there?"

"Hard to miss that suitcase. I think she has a liquor bottle in there. Was she the one who cried?"

"No. She makes those bags. Nice, huh? She's my roommate."

"Your mother and your sister both asked about you. Let me take a picture of you with your drawings."

Darleen stood by her exhibit, and Chee snapped photos with his phone. She handed him her phone. "Take another picture of me. They say we need to document our exhibits for our portfolio. This will be the first photo. Don't get your thumb in it."

As she posed, he noticed a blank space on the wall behind her, as if one of her pieces was missing. "Did you have another drawing here?"

Darleen grinned. "Yeah, but somebody really liked it, so I gave it to him."

Chee gave her a look that he hoped said *Go on.*

Darleen laughed. "It was my picture, OK? And I gave it to somebody, OK? Don't worry so much."

He wasn't worried. He was proud of her generosity.

Three of the people Darleen had been with earlier walked to where she and Chee stood. Two looked like they might have relatives at one of the pueblos that stretch in several directions from Santa Fe along the Rio Grande. The other one, the girl with the big handbag, could have been Navajo, or from a Northwest tribe, or maybe had Cherokee blood. Or even a non-native, Chee thought. The school accepted a range of students.

Darleen introduced her friends, first names only. Purse Girl was called London. "This is Jim Chee," she told them. "He's married to my sister." She left out the part about him being a cop, maybe because he was in uniform. Then she handed her phone to London. "Would you take a picture of both of us?"

London snapped several shots and handed the phone back. "Hey, did you actually give your drawing of the Grand Canyon to that guy?"

"He really liked it. He said he would have bought it if he had money and if this was a real gallery."

London shook her head. "That guy is a player."

"He's a friend of CS."

Chee gave Darleen a hard look. "Was it Clyde Herbert?"

She shrugged away her response.

"I hope you at least took a picture of it for your portfolio," London said. "Did CS even get to see it?"

"He saw it when I was working on it. I didn't finish it until right before I had to turn it in for the show."

London handed Darleen's phone back. "If CS wants to see the show, he better hurry. The gallery closes in fifteen. He told me he wanted to look at my purses. I'm annoyed with that man."

But before she'd finished speaking, Chee saw CS at the gallery entrance table, picking up the brochure from Lomasi. He looked sheepish. Maybe it was his late arrival, or perhaps the question about his death certificate, but whatever happened, it had shaken the man's confidence. His mojo clearly was on the wane. Chee waited to see what would happen next.

CS gave Darleen a brotherly hug. "So these are the drawings?" He walked closer to them and studied each of the four. "Nice, D. I love the way that coyote seems to be waiting to pounce on something."

"My stuff is over there," London said. "Come see it before they close up the place." She turned to Chee. "You, too."

London's exhibit was a collection of handbags similar in size and shape to the one she carried but finished with different fabrics and hardware for the handles. They were beautiful and sophisticated, he thought. He knew even less about purses than he did about drawings, but he liked them.

The crowd at the gallery had thinned to small clusters of students. The lights flickered, and Lomasi said "We're closing in five minutes. Thanks to the artists and to the people who showed up to support them. All of you who had work in the show, remember that we're meeting in the classroom for a debriefing in fifteen minutes."

"Debriefing? Like we're spies or something?" Darleen said. "I don't get it."

"Mrs. Lomasi has to analyze everything," London said. "Don't tell her you gave away that drawing, or we'll be here another half an hour."

CS caught Chee's eye. "I need to talk to you about a couple things. Sorry I blew you off before, man. Let's walk back to the studio building."

Darleen said, "I'll meet you in the studio after I'm done here, OK?"

Before CS could answer, Chee said, "Take your time."

As Darleen and London walked away together, Chee took a step toward CS. "My part of the conversation won't take long. Only one comment to start with."

"Tell me now."

Chee lowered his voice. "That death certificate is serious trouble, man."

It was quieter in the studio building now, a lull, Chee imagined, between the school day and evening classes, assignments, and practice sessions. Dinner would be a good thing, he thought. Depending on what he learned, he might invite CS to join him and Darleen and her roommate London. Or he might not. He might use the meal to try to talk some sense into his headstrong sister-in-law.

CS sat on one of the couches and motioned to Chee to do the same. "Give me a minute to check these texts, and then we'll—"

"No."

CS scowled and put his phone aside. Chee stood over him.

"Sit down, man. You don't have to play that bad cop game with me."

"Tell me why the state of New Mexico has a death certificate on file for you."

"The short version is . . . my parents made a mistake, OK?"

"They thought you were dead?"

"Why is my name any of your business, and why did you have someone check up on me? That's creepy."

Chee frowned. "Do you have a sister? A sister-in-law?"

"No."

"That's why you don't get it. My wife asked me to keep an eye on her sister while I was here. I asked a friend to do a background check on you—don't get bent out of shape. He found your death certificate. After you explain that, tell me again why you're hanging with an ex-con jerk."

CS's voice was tinged with anger. "The people I associate with are none of your business or D's, for that matter. It's a professional relationship, and that's all you need to know. Back off."

"Darleen is my responsibility—"

CS interrupted. "No, Darleen is a grown-up. She has a right to make her own choices. And lighten up on Herbert, man. You're too full of judgments on something you don't know a thing about."

"What are the two of you—I mean you and Herbert—doing together?"

"It's got nothing to do with you, OK? Drop it."

"I've seen a lot of bad guys, and the ones who beat up on women usually are involved with booze or drugs or both. Is that it? Are the two of you in business together?"

CS stared at him in response.

"All right, then. How did Darleen get that bruise on her arm?"

"Ask her."

"I did." Chee felt his irritation rising. "Now I'm asking you."

"What did D tell you?"

"What Darleen may have told me is not the question. Stop avoiding the answer."

CS rose to his feet. "Don't you have something else to do besides badgering me? I've got to get to work."

Chee kept his temper in check. If this were a case he

was handling, he'd get tough with CS, but none of this was official, and his sister-in-law liked the guy. At least for now, he'd give CS a pass.

While he waited for Darleen at the studio door, Chee called Caitlyn Vigil's office number again and wasn't surprised to get a recorded message that the office was closed. He punched the right numbers to leave a message.

The Pantry, the family-owned diner close to downtown Santa Fe where he and Darleen were supposed to eat the night before, was Jim Chee's kind of place. Darleen had the stuffed sopaipilla, and London ordered chicken-fried steak. Chee asked for the steak and enchilada plate. While they waited for the food to arrive, Darleen, usually talkative, drank her water and looked out the window. London carried the conversation.

"What's it like to be a cop?"

The question caught Chee off guard. "I really enjoy it, at least most shifts, most days. It's a chance to help make the world a little better. And it's how I met Bernie, the sister of your roommate here, the gal I married."

"My dad was in the Marines. He said he was glad he served, but I think being in the military, or being a cop, would be kinda scary. One of those guys who hangs with CS, Herbert something, he told me he was in the Marines, too, like my dad. He seems mean."

Darleen said, "You're saying that because they wouldn't buy you any wine."

"No, I'm not."

The waitress came with the food. The girls ate with gusto, and Chee savored the first delicious bites. Then his phone rang. He didn't recognize the number, but he hoped it was Caitlyn.

"Excuse me a minute. I have to take this." He walked away from the table.

"Sergeant Chee? I'm sorry if I sounded rude at the office, but I have to keep my personal life, well, personal. Have you heard from George?"

"No." He explained again why he was calling.

"Oh, I thought you had some news for me." Her voice lost its cheerfulness. "George left the pueblo about three weeks ago for a ranch job someplace out in the boonies with no phone service. The boss told him he had enough work for a couple weeks solid, and we can use the money. After that, George told me he was going to his mother's house—he hadn't seen her for a while—and that he'd call when he got a chance. He hasn't called, and I'm worried."

She took a breath. Chee could practically hear her thinking.

"I assumed he was still working or . . . or that he decided to stay with his mother and didn't have the guts to tell me."

She didn't offer anything else. Chee said, "His mother told my coworker she hadn't seen him. She thought he was with you. She told him you two had separated."

"Separated? You mean like getting a divorce? That's a joke. I'm not the easiest person to get along with, and then there's my mother. But Curley is sweet, patient, funny. He's not the most ambitious guy on the planet, but he has a big heart."

"Do you know where he's working?"

"Not exactly."

"When did you last see him?"

"He left early the day after our feast day dances." She gave him the date. "You know about that?"

"A little. I'm Navajo, too."

"I figured you were. Anyway, Curley helped with the feast day meal. He made the grocery run, set up all the extra tables, and even cleaned up afterward."

"Was that the last you saw him?"

"Yes. My mother told me she scolded him about not working hard enough that night, and they had a big argument. Curley had planned to leave in the morning, but he jumped in the truck and drove off. I know he's busy, but I'm worried. And now the police are involved." She stopped talking, and he heard a muffled sob.

"If you can give me the name of the place he went to work, I'll get someone to find out if George Curley is still out there." The rookie, Chee thought, can do the research.

"All I remember is that he said it was west of here. Maybe out by El Morro."

"Did he mention the name of the man who hired him?"

"I don't remember. I don't think so."

Why, Chee wondered, did a job that should have been easy turn out to be full of complications?

He waited for Caitlyn to end the call, but instead she said something that surprised him. "George's mother resents me because I'm not Navajo," she said. "I think she's using you Navajo cops to get my goat. I think George might be with her, and she's talked him into leaving me. Not only that, he's got our new truck. I made last month's payment on it, and now it's his turn.

"Why don't you ask his mother if he's there?"

"I don't have her number. And even if I did, she won't talk to me."

"So you don't know where George is working, is that right?"

"All I know is that he was hired to do a ranch job out in Cibola County or somewhere like that."

"Has he left without staying in touch before?"

"No. Never. Not even when my mother told him to get out. He still telephoned."

"I think it's time to do a missing person report. I'm going to ask you some questions. Let's start with what he looks like."

"He's thirty-six. About five foot five with his boots on, one-thirty. Black hair cut short and a scar on his right forearm from getting burned. Kind of ordinary except for his great smile. I've got some photos."

"We might want that. Was he on any medication?

"No. An aspirin once in a while."

"Any jewelry he might have on?"

"He wears a gold wedding band with our initials on the inside."

"What is he driving?"

"Our new Ford pickup. White."

Chee asked her to call friends who might have seen him and start spreading the news that George was missing. "Ma'am, when I learn anything about him, I'll get back to you. Will you do the same?"

She answered before he even finished speaking. "Call my cell or text me. If I'm at work, I'll slip away and call you back." She gave him the number. "George

CAVE OF BONES · 183

and I had our differences, but I know he loved me. Even if his mother coerced him into going back to Shiprock, he'd call and tell me he was all right. He's not that much of a coward."

Chee returned to the table and picked up his fork. He felt the girls watching him."Don't worry about it. I'm doing a favor for a friend."

He hadn't thought of the rookie as a friend, but he must be because, in a pinch, he knew the guy would have his back.

They enjoyed dinner, and the girls ordered dessert and chattered about school. Chee was glad Darleen had made a friend, but he couldn't get CS and Herbert out of his mind. He pushed the last of his food away and looked at London. "Do you know why Herbert is at the studio with CS?"

"No." London reached for a sopaipilla.

Chee turned to Darleen. "Did CS talk to you about any of this?"

"He said he only has use of the studio until the end of the week and that Herbert is helping him. It's the video about the lady and sheep, remember? I'm doing some extra shots too, some transitions."

"Your arm looks better. How did you get that bruise?"

"It was an accident. I don't want to talk about it."

"She told me the same thing," London said. "I noticed it after she went to that party."

"Shut up about that."

"What party?"

"Just a party." Chee hoped the pressure of two people wanting an answer would stir Darleen to say more, but she focused on the last of her flan.

Before they left for the drive back to campus, Chee called the substation in Shiprock and told Wilson Sam about his conversation with George Curley's wife.

"Caitlyn says George Curley isn't with her. She hasn't seen him for about three weeks, but they aren't legally separated. She thinks George's mother knows more than she told you and that she's just using the police to get her goat. Ask Mrs. Curley if she knows the name of the place where he went to work so Caitlyn can talk to him."

The rookie chuckled. "I'll ask her. She's a feisty one. She reminds me of an older version of Bernie. She swears George is at the pueblo and Caitlyn won't let the guy call back to Navajoland out of pure meanness."

"He's a grown man, isn't he?" But even as he said it, Chee felt a little sympathy for George Curley.

10

Bernie pushed Merilee Cruz's doorbell and waited. When she wasn't able to reach Merilee on the phone, she'd hoped that Largo would decide that someone on the search team or other law enforcement in the area could tell Ms. Cruz that her brother was missing. But mostly because Merilee served on the Wings and Roots board of directors and therefore was part of the Walker problem, Largo ordered Bernie to go to Grants to do the job. Cooper supplied the address and the information that the woman worked at home.

Bernie hated delivering bad news; while this wasn't the worst news, it was far from the best.

An attractive fortyish woman came to the door. She was wearing a dress that hugged her curves without being overtly sexy and a necklace of green turquoise, old and expensive.

"Are you Ms. Cruz?"

"Yes."

"My name is Officer Bernadette Manuelito. I'm with the Navajo Police. I need to talk to you about Domingo Cruz."

"Oh my god! Did something happen?" The woman stepped back from the open door. "Come in, please."

The door opened onto an elegant entry hall, furnished with a small marble table and a large framed black-and-white photograph of petroglyphs. In the living room beyond, Bernie saw contemporary leather couches, graceful lamps and end tables, several more petroglyph photos, and a Storm Pattern Navajo rug on top of white carpet. The house looked neat, comfortable, and expensive, more so than Bernie would have expected from the modest exterior. She felt as if she was inside one of those home living magazines.

"Sit down." The woman waved Bernie to an upholstered chair and sat across from her. "What happened? Is he dead?"

"Ms. Cruz, take a breath. Your brother is missing, and New Mexico Search and Rescue has volunteers out now looking for him. They are good at what they do. Domingo is your brother, correct?"

"Yes, my twin. What happened?"

"He was working with a Wings and Roots group in El Malpais. He went out to find a young woman who hadn't returned from her solo, and he never came back to base camp."

"I don't understand."

Bernie eased forward on the couch to place her feet firmly on the floor. "Do you know about his work?"

"Yes, of course. I'm on the program's board of directors. I mean, I don't understand how this happened. Dom loved—I mean, loves—that part of New Mexico, and he knows it well. He wouldn't get lost. What happened to the girl? Is she lost too?"

"Luckily, the girl made her way back to camp. She's fine."

Merilee leaned forward toward Bernie, elbows on her knees. "I'm shocked. Dom is so good outdoors."

"The incident commander was wondering if you had any information about your brother that might help them find him."

"Have they talked to that Cooper woman, the program coordinator? She usually goes with the groups."

Bernie nodded. "Mrs. Cooper mentioned that your brother seemed preoccupied on this trip, worried about something. I decided I should talk to you in person rather than try to discuss this over the phone."

Merilee settled back into her chair. "How can I help?"

"Was your brother depressed?"

"You mean suicidal? You've got to be kidding! If Dom had something on his mind, so what? It hasn't been easy for him the last few years. He's totally committed to the program, and Wings and Roots has shown marvelous results. That man has changed lives." She studied her hands for a moment and then looked back at Bernie. "He's also our main fund-raiser, and that's taking up more of his time. After their initial enthusiasm, many of our funders seem to have moved on. Begging for money is hard, and Dom told me he was ready to do something else. But he'd never kill himself."

"I have to ask because the search protocol for finding a person at risk of taking his own life is different. Can you think of anything else that could relate to Mr. Cruz's disappearance?" Bernie heard an electronic sound that resembled a bird call. Merilee glanced at her phone and silenced it.

"Well, he likes to take photographs out there, but he never does it on company time. Did Cooper mention whether he had his camera with him?"

"I'd have to check my notes." Bernie remembered Councilor Walker's rant. "Tell me more about the fund-raising."

"The board is finding a contractor to do an audit in preparation for Cooper's pending retirement." Bernie heard the bird call again. Merilee paused, pulled her phone from her pocket, and switched it off. "Sorry. Did Mrs. Cooper mention that she planned to retire?"

"Not directly, but I heard that she recommended your brother for the job."

"That's right. That was on his mind. In addition to the audit, another agency will conduct a comprehensive follow-up study to see what's become of the students we worked with in terms of completing high school and further education, their living situation, contacts with the criminal justice system, employment, and other criteria. We have a lot of anecdotal evidence that the program helps participants with decision making and resisting peer pressure, but the empirical study will help juice up our fund-raising." Talking about the study seemed to animate the woman more than discussing the search for her brother.

Merilee stood. "I need a glass of water and an aspirin. I'll be right back. There are some cookies on the counter in the kitchen and some bottled water there, too. Please help yourself."

She disappeared down the hall.

Like the rest of the house, the immaculate kitchen looked like something out of a design magazine. It had a sparkling stainless steel stove with a built-in grill in the center, a refrigerator taller than Bernie, countertops that looked like pale green marble with veins of mica or something shiny, and a smooth wooden block with slots for knives. Pans of all sizes and functions were neatly arranged on an overhead rack. A bright red ceramic jug filled with big spoons, spatulas, and utensils Bernie didn't recognize sat on the counter. She examined the little pots of fresh herbs—chives, thyme, tarragon, oregano, parsley, and even sage—arranged on a decorative stand.

Sage. The sage in the pot had the same name as the wild plant that grew prolifically in New Mexico, on the Navajo Nation and throughout the Southwest. She knew the culinary sage in the kitchen was cousin to peppermint, catnip, and oregano—all characterized by square stems and aromatic leaves. The sagebrush outside had daisies, asters, and ragweed in its close family ties. Same name, but different genetics. Then she thought of the new FBI person, Sage Johnson. Were her parents thinking of sagebrush or cooking when they named her? Or did she expect that she'd be a wise woman, a different sort of sage. The name made her curious.

For a person who liked to cook, someone like Chee, this kitchen with its fresh herbs and fancy equipment would be paradise. Mama enjoyed fixing meals, too, but Bernie couldn't imagine her in such fancy and complicated surroundings. Mama had her favorite pot, her special knifes, and a temperamental old stove that did the job just fine.

Merilee's cookies, shaped like hearts, sat on a plate with "Eat Up" scrolled in designer script around its edge. Bernie took one. It looked like a sugar cookie, but it had little purple bits inside. She tried a bite. The unusual taste reminded her of something her husband might take a fancy to. She needed a napkin, and opened a drawer beneath the counter. They were there, along with some coffee pods, those fancy little capsules that only made one cup of coffee at a time, and a small plastic bag filled with seeds. Bernie had little bags like that in her house, too. Waiting for spring so she could plant them and see if whatever wildflower had caught her fancy would grow in her yard along the river.

The large photographs in the living room drew Bernie's attention. As she walked toward them, she heard Merilee's voice from the back of the house, raised in anger. "This isn't the time to talk about that. Dom is missing." A pause, and then, "Oh, for god's sake, give it a rest."

The house fell silent.

The photos captured an assortment of images carved or pecked into black rock that looked like lava. Bernie recognized Kokopelli, the water sprinkler and fertility symbol. She saw spirals in another photo, in perfect light to make them pop against the dark textured background. A misshapen tree in the background reminded her of the piñon Annie had used as a landmark.

The dining-room table held a stack of books, illustrated nonfiction volumes on southwestern archaeology, Indian pottery from various tribes, and rock art of the desert, and an auction house catalog with a Plains Indian parfleche on the cover. Bernie picked up the catalog and was thumbing through it when Merilee returned.

"Your brother is a wonderful photographer," Bernie said. "He could be in a book."

"That's what I think, too. A man I know offered to fund a book project in exchange for using Dom's photos on his website. He always wanted to know exactly where the picture was taken, and Dom kept records so the places could be protected. We were moving along, and then after about a year, Dom told me he didn't want his photos up there on the website. That funding fell through, but I'm committed to the project."

"Why didn't Dom want to be part of it anymore?"

Merilee studied her hands. "He went back to a spot he'd photographed earlier for more shots of the spiral in different light. He told me that someone had been digging near there, disturbing what might have been a burial cave. I tried to talk him out of being so angry, to explain that it might just be coincidence."

She motioned Bernie to the couch as before and sat back down in the chair. "I'm worried about Dom. He knows that country. I'm afraid something bad has happened to him. He may have fallen in the lava and hurt himself and gotten trapped, or been attacked by an animal or had a heart attack. I thought of something else, too. I hope you won't think I'm nutty."

"Go ahead."

"I wonder if somebody was after him because they wanted the program to fail, and they ambushed him out there."

"Who would want the program to fail?"

"There are the campers who got kicked out for breaking the rules. Staff who were fired, rejected job applicants. There's a woman on the Navajo Nation Council who wants to shut us down." She took a swallow of water from a glass she'd brought from the bedroom. "Maybe even other nonprofits who offer similar programs. If we go under, they get our clients and our funding. People think that way."

"Back up a little. You said fund-raising had become more of a challenge. Is the program in financial trouble?"

Merilee shifted in the chair. "I can't talk about that. None of this may be relevant to why Dom is missing. And getting back to your earlier question, even if the program were bankrupt, he wouldn't kill himself. He never took the easy way out."

"Do you know Elsbeth Walker?"

"Only by reputation. She's making some unfounded accusations against us."

Bernie hoped Merilee would elaborate, but she didn't. "You mentioned some financial issues," she said after a few moments. "Are they what Councilor Walker is asking about?"

Merilee focused on the spotless white carpet. "It's complicated. Our lawyer or the board treasurer would be the people to talk to about that."

She rose and strode into the kitchen with long steps. Bernie followed. Merilee opened a drawer, extracted paper and a pen, and jotted something down. "You can ask Mayfair for the phone numbers." She handed the list to Bernie.

"I noticed your little bag of seeds. I do that, too, with wildflowers."

"Those are brugs."

"Brugs?"

"Brugmansias."

Bernie tried to remember. "Big flowers, right?"

"That's right. They bloom in a lot of great colors, and they love the warmth and humidity of the greenhouse. I'll give you some seeds if you'd like to try growing some. Do you want to see them?"

"Not today. I'd love to take a look at your plants sometime, but I have another piece of business to discuss. Are there other relatives I should notify about Dom?"

"No."

"No?" Most Navajos had a directory full of relatives.

"Dom and I were adopted, raised off the reservation. I think because we were twins. You've heard some of those old stories?"

"I have." One popular belief among the People was that twins bring good luck—after all, the Hero Twins born to Changing Woman made the world safe for people. However, Bernie had also heard that twins were shameful, caused by a woman having intercourse with two men. And, apart from any traditional views, having two babies to care for certainly added to a family's stress.

Merilee picked up a photo in a silver frame of two preteen Navajo children and showed it to Bernie. "We went separate ways after high school, like a lot of kids do. Our adoptive parents died a couple of years ago, and Dom and I started rebuilding our relationship. I took the lead, partly because I went through a program similar to Wings and Roots but for adults, you know. It helped me get my head on straight after my husband died. That was why I wanted to help Wings and Roots when Dom told me about it."

She put the photo back on the table. "You asked about people to notify that he's missing? There's Michael Franklin, the guy he lives with in Shiprock. Franklin has a little house outside Grants in San Rafael, but I don't think he's there much. I'm sure he already knows, but I'll give you his number." She jotted it down on a slip of paper as she spoke. "The kids in the program are Dom's real family. Before my husband Roger died, Dom was always after me to make him an uncle."

She handed Bernie the number. "How long will they continue to search?"

"I can't answer that. They look until they decide there are no more places to search."

"And then what?"

Bernie sighed. "Then there's nothing much to do except wait."

"Wait?"

"For the person to show up, for some new information, or for the body to be found."

"Do you think my brother is alive out there?"

"They say he knows the area better than anyone. He has wilderness training. Someone on the search will call you when they find him."

"Even if he doesn't survive?"

Bernie nodded. "Even if it's bad news. At least you'll know."

Merilee rose from the couch. "I have a client in fifteen minutes. Thanks for stopping by to tell me about Dom in person."

Bernie stood too. "What do you do?"

"I'm a psychologist. I started my practice after Roger died, so it's still in its infancy. I also sell art on the Internet, mostly Dom's photos."

"Could I take a picture of that photo of the spiral petroglyph?" Bernie removed her cell phone from her pack. "It's beautiful, and I'd like to show my husband."

"That's one of my favorites, too. I have an extra print. You can have it. My gift. What's your address?"

"You can send it to the station. That would be great." Bernie took a business card from her backpack, jotted something on the back, and gave it to the woman. "I wrote my cell number on there, and the number for the search team. Please call if you hear from your brother or if you think of something that would help with finding him. And thanks again for the photograph—and the cookie."

"Lacy Mayfair, one of the people Dom works with, made them. She's interested in herbs and I showed her some plants I'm cultivating in the greenhouse. She added some lavender to these as an experiment. Dom adored them. Last time he was here, he gobbled them up. That man loves homemade cookies."

Bernie felt the cool air on her skin as she walked to her unit, wondering why people had to experiment with something already good, like cookies. Before she climbed into the car she took the cookie out of her pocket and crumbled it onto the frozen ground for the birds. Then she radioed into the station to let Sandra know she was on her way back.

"Councilor Walker has called twice for you. And the captain wants you to talk to this guy Michael Franklin ASAP. The search coordinator referred Franklin to us because he was so upset when he called them. He started talking to those *bilagáanas* in Navajo, and then he started crying over the phone."

Bernie called Franklin from her car. "Mr. Franklin, this is Officer Bernadette Manuelito."

"Oh thank the Lord. They found him."

"No, sir. But the search is continuing."

"I've been worried sick when he didn't come home, didn't call. I remembered those folks who just disap-

peared out there, and then years later their bodies . . ."
He trailed off. "Dom sees snakes, coyotes, bears. I told
him a million times that he worked too hard, didn't take
care of himself. But did he listen? No, he thinks he's
indispensable, indestructible, some kind of superman.
This time, he scared me so badly I called his boss, and
she told me he was lost. Lost. Out there somewhere in
the lava."

"He went out to find a girl who he thought might be
in trouble. I'm sure he didn't mean to do anything to
upset you."

She heard a long exhale over the phone line and then
Franklin's voice, softer this time. "I know. I'm scared
for him. Can I do something to help? I could answer
the phone, bring food. Anything?"

"Well, sir, why don't you contact the incident commander? Maybe she needs a volunteer. They're set
up at the Narrows campground, the place where the
Wings and Roots crew had camped."

"The Narrows? Where is that?"

"Just off NM 117 on the edge of the Malpais, south-
east of Grants. Sir, do you know if Mr. Cruz was depressed or upset about anything when he left on this
trip?"

A pause and then, "No more than usual these days.

Poor Dom. The program is having money problems and the board wants him to become the director. That sister of his is always asking for just one more photo for the book. He's hard on himself—such a perfectionist. That one more photo becomes a huge production. And he stays in touch with some of the kids in the program. If they fail, he feels like he has failed, too. He used to love that job, but I think he was ready for a change." Franklin gasped. "I mean, he is ready."

As Bernie crossed the McKinley County line, she thought about what Michael Franklin had said about Cruz's sister. Merilee must share her brother's fondness for the wild black landscape of the Malpais. In a house kept simple, his photos had a place of honor. Thinking of sisters brought her own sister to mind.

Darleen answered after five rings. "Hey. What's up?"

"Hey there, glad I caught you."

"Sorry I haven't called . . . it's been crazy busy."

"How's the program going?"

"It's fun, but it's kind of hard." Darleen sounded distracted.

"Mama has been trying to reach you."

"You said that in your text. She called me at six a.m., for goodness' sakes, and acted hurt that I didn't have much to say to her when I was barely awake. I've talked to her every day I've been here. What's up with her?"

"Are you sure?"

Darleen laughed. "She says the same thing every conversation. 'Do you have enough to eat there?' and 'When are you coming home?' She never wants to talk long, but she's always been like that on the phone. I wonder why she doesn't remember?"

Bernie looked at the long train headed west on the tracks to the right and the stair steps of red mesas behind them.

"How are your teachers?"

"One of them is great. One is good. And the last one, well, she talks too much, but she's OK. Better than anybody I had in high school."

"How's CS?"

"He's fine, except he's always working." Darleen sounded as if she were going to say something else, but instead she asked, "How are you?"

"Fine, working as usual."

"Did the Cheeseburger send you the photos of my drawings?"

"Not yet."

"He better, or I'll have to punch him."

Bernie ended the call with more questions than answers, as was often the case in conversations with Darleen. Turning away mentally from the drama, she focused on the scenery. She was crossing the Continental Divide, the point at which water sheds on one side to the east, toward the Atlantic Ocean, and on the other to the west, flowing into the Pacific. She passed an elk crossing sign, refineries, and the exit for Iyanbito, the little Navajo town at the base of the red sandstone cliffs.

She decided to call Lieutenant Leaphorn next. She tried his cell phone first, and when that went instantly to message, she dialed the landline. A woman's voice answered.

"Hi, Louisa, it's Bernie." She liked Leaphorn's housemate, but she never quite knew what to say to her. Now that Louisa had resumed the research she had set aside to help the Lieutenant recover, conversation might be easier. "How are you?"

"I'm OK." She heard the fatigue in Louisa's voice. "How are you?"

"Fine."

"You sound a little distracted."

"Well, I'm driving west on I-40, and the traffic is starting to pick up. It's been a crazy day."

"Be careful out there. Is your mother well?"

"Yes. She always asks about you and the Lieutenant." Mama's questions amounted to *Is Lieutenant Leaphorn still living with that bilagáana?* followed by a click of her tongue. Mama might forget that she'd talked to Darleen, but she remembered Louisa.

Before Bernie could switch the topic to Louisa herself or the Lieutenant, Louisa said, "And how's Darleen? I hope she's staying out of trouble."

"My sister is in Santa Fe this week. She enrolled in a sort of trial program at that art school she thinks she might be interested in. I spoke with her and she's enjoying it."

"So what's bothering you?"

When Bernie first met Louisa, she'd been disturbed by the woman's, well, call it forthrightness. Now, she took it in stride. "I called about a situation I'm dealing with at work. Is the Lieutenant home?"

"Joe was taking a nap. I'll see if he's awake. Hold on."

"Please don't wake him."

Louisa put the phone down with a thunk, a sound you couldn't get on a cell phone. Had she done it again? Hurt Louisa's feelings?

Joe Leaphorn's deep voice came on the phone. "Yá'át'ééh."

"Yá'át'ééh."

"Good to hear from you." The Lieutenant spoke fluently in Navajo, but the brain injury still affected his English. The irony made Bernie smile. She'd been told that Navajo was much harder to master—but obviously not if it was the language you'd learned as a child. The Lieutenant had made remarkable progress and now walked without a cane. Still, whenever she spoke with him, she remembered the awful day when she'd cradled his bleeding head in her lap.

She started to share some office news involving a promotion and a retirement, but Leaphorn cut her off. "Manuelito, you don't call to chat. What can I do for you?"

"Well, sir, I was out in the Malpais. The New Mexico Search and Rescue folks have an operation under way, and I remember hearing about another search out there, a few years before I came on the force. Were you involved in that?"

"A little."

"Would you tell me about it?"

"Why?"

"The current situation bothers me, and I'm wondering if there's more to the story than a man getting lost."

The phone went silent as Leaphorn gathered his thoughts. "A *bilagáana* family disappeared. No, wait. Not the whole family, only a father and daughter. They told the rest of the group they were going for a walk—only a half mile. A National Park Service archaeological team saw them that afternoon as they were leaving the parking lot, headed to the Big Tubes area. They never came back. SAR sent ground pounders, dogs, even a plane. As I recall, some two hundred and fifty searchers worked the incident. Nothing. It was as if they had evaporated.

"Navajo PD got involved when a team discovered some old burial sites. My job was to check the restricted area to make sure the missing people hadn't come that way."

He paused. Unlike Chee and herself, she knew Leaphorn didn't believe in *chindis*, the restless spirits of the dead who could cause trouble for the living. His skepticism, Bernie thought, made him the perfect officer for that assignment. "These were old burials, what we used to call Anasazi, and may have dated from the Chaco Canyon era. I didn't find the people, but I saw some of the most beautiful petroglyphs I've ever seen. I took photos of the art and some of the pottery preserved there."

Leaphorn talked on, describing the petroglyphs and the pottery in detail, and noting that the FBI had recently requested the old photos for a case they were working on.

"Eight years later, a Natural Resources survey crew came across some bones that looked human, scattered in a rough part of the monument, five miles away from where the father and daughter told the family they were headed. Turned out, they were the remains of those long missing hikers. The two seemed to have followed an old trail and evidently got disoriented. No one knows for sure why they were so far from where they'd planned to go. It's rugged out there. They made some unfortunate decisions and suffered the consequences."

Leaphorn paused, indicating that the story was done. "Are you involved in something, Manuelito, or only curious?"

"Oh, some of each. I'm puzzled about a man who is missing out there now from a Wings and Roots program—you know, one of those deals where they send young people into the wilderness to get their heads on straight. He is an experienced wilderness guide. I have trouble believing he would somehow lose his way. I'm wondering if he doesn't want to be found and why that might be. Or if he's out there at all. I can't make sense of it."

"This sounds like something Chee would be nosing around in, not you."

Bernie remembered how critical the Lieutenant was of Chee's propensity to follow his gut rather than department rules. "I got involved a little because I talked to a girl who turned out to be the last person to see the missing man. It's a long story with some politics mixed in."

"Office politics?"

"Even worse. Tribal. The girl is the daughter of a member of the Navajo Tribal Council who wants to investigate Wings and Roots for misuse of Navajo funds. Domingo Cruz, the missing man, was . . . is the associate director of this group and the one in charge of their fund-raising. Because I happened to be out there, the councilor thinks I'm involved in a cover-up."

"Is this councilor named Elsbeth Walker?"

Bernie said, "Yes, sir."

"I've known her since she was a kid. She's like a porcupine, prickly on the outside."

Bernie laughed. "I've felt her spines, and I have to talk to her again soon about her charges against Wings and Roots."

"I'll look in my files and send you some background information I should have on her. It might help you to get along with her a little better. I'll see what I can learn about the missing man, too."

"*Ahéhee'.* She and I got off on the wrong foot."

"You know what they say about politicians?"

"What do they say?" Bernie heard some clatter in the background.

"Just a minute."

She heard more noise and then muffled sounds, as though Leaphorn had put his hand over the receiver. After a few moments, he was back.

"I'll e-mail the information about Walker. Anything else?" His voice was now strictly business.

"I appreciate your help. Everything OK there?"

"Louisa says to tell you and Chee something." He paused. "Come and see us." He said the last four words in English.

"I will, sir."

Because Leaphorn had not said everything was OK, she assumed it wasn't. Maybe the problem was nothing much, but she made a mental note to call again soon—or better yet, stop by.

11

After dinner, Jim Chee drove Darleen and London back to campus, stopping at the same overlook where he and Darleen had watched the city lights flicker the night before. Darleen sat next to him on the bench seat and London by the door.

"What's up?" London said. "Why are we stopped here?"

"It's cool. He wants to give me another lecture." Darleen turned to Chee. "Why do you keep badgering me about CS? I thought you liked him."

"I don't like the secrecy, the bad company, not to mention the parties and the drinking. I tried to talk to CS about something important, and he blew me off."

"He's trying to finish that video. He's super stressed.

What's the big deal, Cheeseburger? Give the dude a chance."

London chimed in. "Don't be so hard on CS. He's sensitive about his name. Just because he wanted to keep something a secret doesn't mean it's something bad."

Darleen nodded. "You're as bad as Mama and Sister. Maybe worse. I'm thinking of going to school, away from Navajo, so I won't have a million people bugging me. Stop being Sergeant Chee for once in your life."

"This isn't about being a cop." Even as he said it he realized that wasn't true. "I mean, this isn't *all* about being a cop. Some of it, most of it, is about being a relative who cares about you. That's all."

Darleen's tone mellowed. "The video is all CS has left to finish before he can get his degree. You're only here because of me, so if you do something that gets him kicked out, it would be my fault, too. He probably hates me anyway because of your bugging him."

"Or because of what happened last night?" London didn't wait for Darleen to answer. "That can happen to anybody. He'll get over it."

"What happened?" Chee waited.

The girls looked at each other.

Chee waited some more.

"Can we go?" London shifted in her seat. "I've got an assignment I need to do for tomorrow."

Chee gave Darleen a gentle nudge with his elbow. "What happened?" He felt her shrug off the question.

They sat a while longer. Chee felt the cold seep in and figured the temperature would work in his favor.

Darleen sighed. "OK. I asked CS to take me to this party I heard about from one of the girls in class. He didn't want to because he said he had to work. But Herbert said he'd drive me. A few people had too many drinks, and things got crazy, and Herbert drove me back to the dorm."

"Were you drinking?"

"At first just a Coke, but then someone put some rum in it."

"What else happened?"

"She threw up and had a headache in the morning," London said. "It's cold in here. Can we go now?"

"What else happened?" Chee asked again.

London shifted in her seat. "My auntie always said girls are entitled to have a few secrets."

"That depends on what the secret is."

Darleen pulled her coat around her more tightly. "Herbert drove me to the dorm and told me I was stupid to drink so much. Let's go."

Chee started the engine and turned onto the road that led to the school entrance. "I can tell you're ashamed and embarrassed about what happened last night. Believe it or not, you'll feel better when you tell me about the bruise, too."

The campus dorm hadn't been restricted by the architectural regulations that govern the old neighborhoods of Santa Fe. Its open, modern look fit well with the site. From the outside, it reminded him of a modestly upscale hotel.

A motley assortment of beater cars, little sedans, and old trucks filled the parking places closest to the dorm's entrance, with a few more expensive vehicles intermixed sporadically. Chee found a spot in the rear, a place darker than he liked, and walked with the girls to the door.

Darleen had said nothing for most of the ride to campus, but now she took his arm. "Why don't you come in and take a look at where we live?"

"I thought you'd never ask."

He heard the bing of a text message and pulled out his phone. It was from the rookie.

Call me re Curley

"Is that from Sister?"

Chee turned off the phone. "No. A guy I work with who thinks he's more important than he really is."

They checked him in at the front desk and entered

a large furnished room with windows that looked out onto a courtyard.

Darleen ran her hand along the back of a large tan sofa. "We call this the living room. It's a great place to hang out." The muted television was tuned to an old black-and-white movie, but as far as Chee could tell no one seemed to be watching. A few students sat at desks with their laptops open, and two boys played chess. He heard a phone chirp. In the kitchen area, a pretty, dark-haired girl with silver earrings stood by the microwave as the smell of fresh popcorn filled the room. A boy quietly strummed a guitar in a corner.

"Nice place."

"I just remembered I left my clothes in the dryer." London turned toward a hallway leading away from the common space. "I'll catch up with you."

They climbed the stairs to the second level, the girls' floor. "I have more room here than at Mama's." Darleen headed down the hall. "Our room is this way."

Chee followed her. "So, what's it like having a roommate?"

"It's awesome. London's nice, and she has a lot of friends in Santa Fe."

"Do you think you'd like to be a regular student here, studying art?"

Darleen hesitated. "I like living in the dorm, but I

miss Mama. I miss her cooking. The way she makes the coffee too strong. I even miss her bossing me around. But I like most of my classes, and well . . ."

A young man emerged from one of the rooms. He stared at his shoes and walked quickly in the opposite direction.

"I thought this was a girls' floor."

"Oh, that's just Charlie. He and his roommate live on the next floor. They are part of a band. Cool, huh? Loretta lives there. She's a singer with them." Darleen paused at a door about halfway down the hall. "Give me a minute to make sure I don't have a pile of undies on the floor."

"Don't worry about it." He walked in behind her before she could protest.

The room had a large window, two beds, and two desks. Unlike Darleen's space at Mama's house, it was surprisingly neat. It had nothing in common with the cramped quarters he had shared in the old dorms at the University of New Mexico. A collection of empty beer cans in a cardboard box sat at the foot of one of the beds.

"Tell me about the beer."

"Oh, we save all that for recycling." She tried to shove the box under the bed, but it collided with the bed frame and made a racket.

"After you drink the beer?"

"They don't allow drinking in the dorms. Did they when you were in college?"

"Nope." Chee remembered that hadn't stopped anyone who wanted to drink. "Back when I was at the university, boys and girls had separate dorms, too."

London had walked up behind them. "No kidding? How retro."

"Some people tried to sneak in their dates." He turned to look at her. "Where's your laundry?"

"The towels weren't dry. Why did the dorms operate like that back in the old days?"

The old days? Chee winced. "Oh, lots of reasons. Making it harder for guys and girls to get together, for starters."

"Mama told me that when she was a little kid, everybody slept together on the floor of the hogan, girls on one side and boys on the other." Darleen smiled at the story. "Instead of beds, they used cozy sheepskins."

Chee felt his phone vibrate, and it reminded him to call Bernie. "You girls behave. I've got to go. Study hard."

"Don't worry so much about me, Cheeseburger. I'm really OK. Thanks for dinner."

London smiled at Chee, and he realized she was pretty. "Yeah, thanks. Nice to meet you."

"You, too."

He trotted back down the stairway to the main lobby. He found a chair in a quiet corner and looked at missed calls. Not Bernie, but one from the rookie and another from CS. Wilson Sam answered on the third ring.

"I just got off the phone with Mrs. Curley. She didn't know the name of the ranch, but she said it was out by Ramah country. She said her son came by just once while he was employed there, and that was the last time she saw him."

"When was that?"

"About two weeks ago. Anyway, he told her his wife's mother had called him a lazy freeloader, and that was one reason he took the job. She thinks he went back to his wife to tell her he was leaving. And whammo."

"Whammo?"

"Mrs. Curley thinks the wife lost it and killed him. Or maybe the mother-in-law did him in."

"Does she have any proof?"

"He'd got a new pickup and bragged to her that he never missed a payment. The bill comes to her house, even though he pays online. She said they sent an overdue notice. And there's something else."

Chee heard the chime of an incoming text message and ignored it.

The rookie cleared his throat. "The mother said Curley seemed spooked by something, but he didn't want to talk about it. She thinks the wife and that Pueblo mother-in-law are behind all this. She wants me to take her to the pueblo so she can talk to those women, find out where they are hiding him, and drag him back here."

"Other than missing the payment, does she have any other reason to think he's dead?"

"He always calls her on Sunday mornings unless he forgets or his phone is lost or something, and he hasn't called for two weeks." Wilson Sam cleared his throat. "Hey, Chee?"

"Yeah?"

"Mrs. Curley was the reason I made it through high school. I owe her. She may be a little off, but, hey, who isn't? It's odd to think of her as somebody's mother."

"Why?"

"Don't tell anybody, but I had a crush on her in the ninth grade."

"See what you can find out about the ranch where Curley was working. I'll ask his wife about it, too."

After he disconnected, he called Bernie. She answered right way.

"Hi, sweetheart. I miss you."

"I miss you, too." She sounded tired, he thought.

She told him a little about Domingo Cruz and Wings and Roots.

"Yeah, the captain told me Elsbeth Walker has been hounding you. There's a lot on your plate."

He heard her sigh. "Have you ever dealt with a councilor?"

"No. Do you think I need one?"

Her laughter made him smile.

Chee said, "I've met Walker, and I remember the Lieutenant worked with her on something. He might have a suggestion for you."

"I've talked to him, and he said he'd e-mail me some information."

"You're a step ahead of me. I recall now that I arrested a San Juan County commissioner's son once for DUI. He thought the kid was being unjustly persecuted, called to complain about me. Does that count as dealing with a councilor?"

"Nope."

"Well, it gave me all the experience in that area I need, thank you very much."

"Have you seen Darleen?"

"Yes, I just got back from dinner with her and her roommate."

"How's she doing?"

Chee thought about how to answer. "Her work in

the art show was beautiful, and she likes the girl she shares a room with."

"You know what I mean . . ."

"She's Darleen, but basically fine. Don't worry."

"Mama wants me to drive to Santa Fe and bring her back here."

"Tell her if I get a feeling that this isn't the right place for her, I'll bring her back with me tomorrow."

After the phone call, he checked and found an e-mail, something from Leaphorn with the subject line "not much," and an attachment. Based on the less-than-promising preview, he'd open it later, back at the hotel. He envisioned the rest of his evening. After he read the Lieutenant's attachment, he'd spend a few minutes reviewing the notes from the training. And before any of that, a warm shower and a cup of fresh coffee from the little in-room coffeemaker.

Santa Fe's high desert air greeted him with a frigid blast as he walked back to his truck. He shoved his hands in his pockets. Before opening the door to climb into the cab, he circled the vehicle, as was his habit. The rear tire on the passenger side was flat. He squatted down and used his flashlight to examine it, looking for a nail in the tread. No nail, but the cap was off the valve stem. It was no accident—someone had jammed something in it to let the air escape.

He straightened up and wiped his hands on his jeans, instantly creating a short list of suspects: CS and Herbert. If he'd been a man who swore, he would have had some choice words for the situation. He thought about changing the tire. No, he decided, he'd make the jerk who gave him the flat take care of it.

Unlike Bernie, Chee didn't run as a regular pastime. He felt the exertion in the burning of his leg muscles and challenge to his lungs as he headed for the studio. There were no vehicles on the road; the campus was quiet. Emergency lights and call stations glowed in the darkness to help a student who got in trouble. The jog worked off some of his anger.

He thought about CS. He had liked the guy, admired the passion he had for using video to make the world a little better. He appreciated the way he included Darleen in his project about an old woman and her sheep. He remembered CS driving Darleen's car. Did that mean that CS had to be in the driver's seat in their relationship? And now CS was associating with a jerk who had been imprisoned for domestic violence. He had steered away from Chee's question about the bad bruise on Darleen's arm, an injury that could have been caused by a man squeezing too hard. He recalled Darleen's tears the first night he'd talked to her about it, and the way she tried to hide the bruise. If it really were an accident, as she claimed, why would she be ashamed of it?

As he neared the studio building, he saw a car heading toward him. It moved more and more slowly as it approached, and was nearly across from him before he recognized it as Mrs. Lomasi's vintage station wagon. She lowered the window and stopped. He stopped too.

"Officer Chee?"

"Yes, ma'am?"

"Do you need a ride?"

"No, thank you." He bent at the waist, catching his breath. "Is CS in the studio?"

"Yes. Always. Why are you jogging without a flashlight? It's dark out here, you know."

"My truck has a flat tire, and I want to talk to CS about that."

"I have Triple A," she said. "I can call somebody for you. CS is awfully busy."

"Oh, he'll make time for me."

"Maybe that big guy in the studio with him can help you."

"The Navajo man?"

"Right. He looks strong to me."

He was glad to hear that Herbert was there, too. And glad his service weapon was with him in its holster.

"You have to use the keypad to get in," Mrs. Lomasi

said. "They can't hear the bell from the studio. Sound-proofing, you know." She gave him the code to unlock the door before she drove off.

There were five vehicles in the studio lot, including the banged-up truck he'd noticed at the restaurant the first day he saw Clyde Herbert. Chee used the moon-light to negotiate the keypad and opened the door.

It was dark inside except for a flashing red bea-con pulsing down the hall over the entrance to Studio Four. As he felt along the cool wall for a light switch, the flashing stopped and he heard a door open. The glow from the studio backlit the large person walking toward him and shone through the brown glass of the beer bottle in his right hand.

Chee's fingers found the light switch, and he turned it on. Then his hand moved toward his weapon.

Clyde Herbert stopped. "Jim Chee? You're like a bad case of the trots, man. You keep coming back. Don't you have some cop friends to hang with?"

"I got a flat in the parking lot at Darleen's dorm. I was thinking you and CS might know something about that."

"Yeah, I've had some flats, blowouts. Tires go bad, dude, even off the rez. Even for cops. CS probably don't know much about it." Herbert made a chortling sound. "I think he rides a bike."

Chee looked at Herbert's hand. "What's with the bottle?"

Herbert's attitude changed. "Nothin'. It's empty. Don't worry 'bout it."

"You know, I am worried. My wife's sister is taking a class here, and she's got a big bruise she won't talk about and went to a party where things got out of hand. And she says you were there."

Herbert laughed. "Dude, that girl handles herself better than you think. Why are you hassling me, man? Quit blocking the hallway. I gotta go to the john."

Chee moved aside to let Herbert pass and walked toward CS's studio.

Herbert's voice bellowed after him. "Do not open that unless you need CS to kick your behind all the way back to Shiprock."

Before Chee could answer, a long buzzing sound interrupted his thoughts, followed by a loud knock from outside the building door.

12

Captain Largo rolled his chair back slightly from the desk. Bernie smelled a hint of his Old Spice.

"Manuelito, how cozy are you with Rose Cooper?"

"I barely know her. I've spoken to her a couple times on the phone and talked to her in person when I went out to meet with the Wings and Roots group. That's it."

"And Domingo Cruz?"

"I never met him."

Largo sipped his coffee, then put the cup down. "That's what I thought. Well, Councilor Walker will be here in an hour. The chief's office called me about her again. She's still insisting you're part of some conspiracy with Cooper and Cruz to divert tribal funds—or maybe to cover up their misdeeds. She wants your head, and the chief wants you to talk her down so he doesn't have to deal with this."

"I don't understand why she thinks I'm part of some conspiracy. I mean—"

Largo dismissed the argument with a wave of his hand. "Talk to her. Make her go away."

Bernie got some coffee and then sifted through her messages, but she couldn't focus. Checking her e-mail, she found the promised note from Leaphorn about Councilor Walker:

I met Walker years ago when she accused the public safety department of collusion with the contractor the council hired to build the police headquarters (see attachments). She turned out to be a valuable ally once I realized how to stay on her good side. She has the most passion for issues that affect youth and about fiscal responsibility.

Great, Bernie thought, with Wings and Roots she has both of those, and she thinks I'm a bad guy.

She sent back a quick note thanking the Lieutenant. Any clues for how to get her to step back?

Sandra's voice came over the intercom. "Annie Rainsong on the phone for you."

"Put her through."

A moment later, the phone rang. "Hello? Officer Bernie?"

"Hey, Annie. What can I do for you?"

"Uhm. Well, Mom is still really, really mad at me, and she's going to make me come with her to see you. Could you do me a favor and not tell her about the cave and the old bones?"

"Why don't you want me to mention the cave? I saw it too."

"Because Mom already thinks I'm a total loser, and when she finds out I broke the rules and hiked out into the lava at night by myself she will lose it. Again. She knows enough of my screwups already. She doesn't need more reasons to hate me."

"I'll consider your request on one condition. Annie. Tell me if what you said about your last encounter with Mr. Cruz was the truth. The searchers are focusing their efforts beginning from the place you mentioned."

Annie's voice took on a ring of defiance. "What I said was what I remembered."

Bernie softened her tone. "When we talked about Mr. Cruz, you'd only come back from your solo. You were tired and scared. You could have said something you didn't really mean. Or you might have thought of something else."

"That's what happened. I was confused."

"About Mr. Cruz?"

"No, not him or about the cave. That's all true. But about something else, the phone you found in the parking lot."

Bernie hid her surprise. "Go on. Just the truth."

"We were supposed to put them in the box so they would be locked in the van, but I hid it in my sleeping bag, and I lost it. It fell out or something. I told Mom I left it home like she told me and didn't take it on the trip. and then my brother broke it by accident." Annie's words flowed out in a torrent. "But I'm sure I didn't lose it in the parking lot because I had it in my tent for the solo. That's not a lie, either."

Councilor Walker arrived promptly. Annie stood next to her, shifting from one foot to the other, showing none of the assertiveness she'd had on the phone.

Bernie took them into the station's old conference room. She sat on one side of the table, and mother and daughter sat where officers usually placed the suspects.

The councilor waved off the pleasantries and asked the first question. "Tell me why you were giving Cooper money."

"What are you talking about?"

"Annie saw it as the girls were getting on the bus

and told me. Was that to keep her quiet about your involvement in the cover-up?"

Bernie shook her head. "I loaned her some money for gas for the van."

"Oh really?"

"Mr. Cruz had the business credit card in his wallet, and the rental company wanted the van full when it was returned. She agreed to pay me back. What else are you concerned about?"

"Corrupt cops, especially when they have access to children."

"I gave her twenty dollars." Bernie pushed a stray strand of hair behind her ear. "If I wanted to bribe someone, I don't think twenty dollars would get me very far."

She hadn't meant to be funny, but Walker laughed. "You're right about that. It was too little money, even for a group as cash-strapped as that one. And too obvious an exchange. I guess you just lack the experience to understand how these crooks work."

Bernie bit back her response. Breathe in calm, she told herself. Breathe out trouble. "If you have charges to make against me, I'm happy to respond. That's why I'm here."

"I came down here to look you in the eye. If you're really not on the take, you can prove it by finding out what's going on with Wings and Roots and the money the tribe gave them. Come up with something definite, and I won't pursue any charges against you or the department." Walker wiggled her middle and index fingers. "You tell me whatever you find. Since you already loaned her money, she'll trust you."

"Councilor, you know that request is totally inappropriate." Bernie studied the desktop, expecting an argument from Walker but getting none. "I understand that you know a friend of mine, Lieutenant Joe Leaphorn."

"That's one smart man."

"I will look into Wings and Roots and how the program spends its money, and I will ask the Lieutenant to help. If we find everything on the up and up, I need a promise from you."

"What might that be?"

"That you will work for a bill to give them more tribal money to keep going."

"You're trying to negotiate with me? You're a pushy one, aren't you?"

"I know that program helps kids, and there are more kids who could use it than they have money to serve." Kids like Annie, she thought, who need to develop more confidence. "You're in a powerful position to do good, to serve as a role model for these youngsters."

Walker picked up her briefcase—or maybe it was a purse that looked like a briefcase—and pushed her chair back, motioning to Annie with a jut of her chin. "Don't lecture me about doing good. You find the money that guy ran off with. That new FBI woman told me she didn't think tribal police would have the interest to get involved. Or maybe she said *integrity*." Walker emphasized the word with her tone of voice.

Annie looked up from her pink phone like a turtle rising for air. "Officer Bernie, did they find Mr. Cruz?"

"I haven't heard anything new about the search."

"At first, I blamed Cooper, but now I think Cruz is behind all this." Walker stood. "He's not lost. He arranged for someone to pick him up, and he's in Hawaii or somewhere with the money. That's what you'll find out as soon as you start digging behind the scenes. I hope Leaphorn will help you. I trust him. I'm going to talk to your captain next."

Bernie opened the door, and the councilor stomped out with Annie sulking along behind.

Bernie took a few deep breaths, regaining her equilibrium. If Largo thought she'd overstepped her responsibilities, so be it. She warmed her coffee, chatting with Officer Bigman for a few minutes about his wife and her mother and their joint expedition to Crown-point. She had barely returned to her cubbyhole that served as an office when Sandra buzzed her. "The captain needs to see you. And Rose Cooper wants you to call her. Do you need the number?"

"No, I have it."

Largo sat behind his big desk, a pile of papers before him, his computer open to several screens. "So, Walker told me how Cruz's disappearance is tied to a big embezzlement scheme. And how our office might be wrapped up in all this and how, after she talked to you, she decided you can solve it and that I need to release you from all your other assignments. I told her we needed a place to start if we were going to look into Cruz as a runaway embezzler."

He stopped.

"Did you really say runaway embezzler?"

"No." Largo grinned at her. "Councilor Walker asked me—told me, actually—to give you the assignment to look into a connection between Cruz's disappearance and Wings and Roots' money problems."

"So, first she thinks I'm on the take, and now she wants me to be her flunky or something. Do I have that right?"

Largo chuckled. "She told me, and I quote, 'She's

the smartest one of your sorry bunch.' Do you want a minute to think about it?"

"No. I'll do it." She wasn't used to the captain giving her a choice of assignments.

He handed her a slim folder on the top of the pile. "Walker left this information for you. It shouldn't be that complicated to match it up with the reports from Cooper. Talk to Cooper about the tribal funds, how much they get and the way the program accounts for the money. Ask if there was any problem receiving the money or spending it, if the funding has increased over the . . . is it five years they've been operating?"

"I think that's right." Realizing that she should have been taking notes, Bernie extracted her notebook and a pen from her backpack. She put Walker's folder inside.

The captain waited until she stopped writing. "You should be able to tell from Cooper's attitude if she's got something to hide. If this stinks like a real problem and not a councilwoman's ranting, we'll kick it up to the chief's office and the feds. If it's nothing, we'll say that and get Walker out of our hair until she comes up with another scandal. You sure you don't want a minute to think about it?"

"No, I'll do it." She said it with conviction. "Will you really give me the leeway to just focus on this?"

"Sure. Take the next twenty-four hours."

"You know, sir, I'm not an expert when it comes to numbers."

"You'll do fine, Manuelito. Ask for help if you need it."

She mentioned her idea to involve Leaphorn if he were available on short notice, and Largo agreed. "We can pay him on his regular contract."

"So the councilor called us a sorry bunch, is that right, sir?"

"I've been known to call you guys worse than that on a bad day."

Back in her office, she finished her coffee and called Mama.

"We were talking about you yesterday." Mama's voice sounded strong and clear. "The woman I am teaching to weave says you are lucky to have a mother close by."

"And she is correct about that. How is Mrs. Bigman doing with her weaving?"

"She's coming along. Are you using that loom?"

"A little. I've been busy with my job."

She waited for Mama to scold her, but Mama changed the subject. "Daughter, I need groceries. We can go after your work."

"I am sorry, Mama, but I can't help you today. We talked about this earlier, remember?"

"I have a list of what I need. We will go to that City Market. I will go in, too, because I might see something else."

"I can't help you tonight, Mama. Maybe Mrs. Darkwater can loan you what you need."

"I need to get coffee and paper for the bathroom and . . . Hold on."

She heard Mama set the phone on the counter. She waited a few moments, studying the ever-present memos Sandra had placed on her desk. Nothing earth-shaking.

Mama was back. "The lady is here to pick me up, and we have to go to the senior center now." Mama sounded surprised by the turn of events. The senior center had a loom that Mama used to teach Mrs. Bigman. The staff left her weaving up, partly to encourage others to learn to weave and mostly because no one else needed the loom at the moment. Bernie had gone to the center once to watch Mama and Mrs. Bigman, and was surprised to see a crowd of other ladies watching, too. Mama had been patient with Mrs. Bigman's mistakes, more patient than she had ever been with her own daughter.

"Don't worry about being too late. The store is open until ten." Mama hung up.

Bernie looked at her cell phone. She'd asked Darleen to make sure Mama had plenty of what she needed before she went to Santa Fe. Darleen had assured her everything was under control, that Mama had plenty of food to get by while she was taking the class. But had she asked about toilet paper or coffee?

Bernie collected her thoughts, and picked up the office phone. She thought about calling Chee to complain about his lack of attention, but instead called Cooper and explained that she needed to talk to her about the program's use of tribal appropriations.

"Seriously? I admit that we're not in the best financial shape," Cooper said, "but we haven't done anything illegal with the tribal grant or any other funding. How come you got stuck with this?"

"It doesn't matter. Can I come to the office and take a look at the paperwork?"

"Sure, whenever you want. I'll be happy to show you any files, bank records, whatever, but all this seems a distraction from finding Mr. Cruz."

"The searchers are out there doing their job."

"How come it took so long to get going?" Cooper's voice flared with anger.

Manzanares was a short-timer; maybe he'd done a few errands before coming to meet her and get the search going, Bernie thought. She kept her speculation private. "I don't know, but they are working hard now."

"Come on over and I'll give you some tea. Poor, poor Dom."

Before heading out to see Cooper, Bernie called Beverly Katz, the incident commander, for a progress report. Unfortunately, it was exactly what she'd expected.

"No clues, no news, no sign that anyone named Domingo Cruz has ever been in or near the Malpais." Katz sounded wired and worried. "We've exhausted most of the possibilities, and the weather's changing. It looks like a front is coming in overnight. Our next step might be a thermal imaging device, one of those cool machines that can pick up a person's heat signature. The colder it gets, the better that thing works. And then maybe the K9s. I'll have to talk to the trainer about how well their feet will hold up to the sharp lava or how they can handle the snow."

"That's tough." Bernie remembered the challenges of hiking in the lava. "I really admire those volunteers."

"Did you send a guy named Michael Franklin out here?"

"Well, I guess so. He's a friend of Mr. Cruz and

wanted to do something. I hope he didn't cause a problem."

"Not at all. He's a great help. Thanks for referring him."

Cooper worked near the Shiprock hospital, a neighborhood Bernie hadn't visited very often in her role as a police officer, in a converted garage separate from the main house. She opened the door to Bernie's knock, and offered her a seat in one of two padded rolling desk chairs.

The office was neat except for the desk, where papers in uneven piles covered the surface. Cooper noticed Bernie's glance. "That's my filing system," she said. "Those farthest away are the bills. The smaller stacks are the donors I need to acknowledge. And the middle stuff is, well, miscellaneous." She sat down in the chair next to Bernie and turned to face her. "So, have they found Dom? Is he dead? Is that why you're really here?"

"No, no, no. Like I told you, I'm here to talk about the financial reports."

"As long as they haven't found his body, that means hope is out there, on the prowl." She gave Bernie a weak smile. "That's what we tell the kids, you know.

That hope, grace, whatever you want to call it, waits for us all like a lifeline. We just have to believe in ourselves enough to reach for it."

Cooper got up, filled a mug with water, and put it in the microwave. "Do you want some tea?"

"No, thank you." Unless the person offering was a Navajo grandmother, she declined tea. Her experience with Louisa's herbal blend had left her ever wary.

"I've got some instant coffee, too."

"No, thanks. As I mentioned, Councilor Walker thinks there's some malfeasance going on with the agency and its use of Navajo Nation funding. She thinks Cruz was involved in it, and that's why he disappeared."

"That's crazy."

Bernie watched Cooper take a box down from the cabinet above the microwave, open it, and take out a tea bag. "If we get a donation, Cruz records it and deposits it, and then I or Cruz or Mayfair draft a thank-you. All our audits have been clean except for some minor discrepancies."

"What were those about?" For the first time, Bernie wondered if Councilor Walker might be onto something.

Cooper sat down again. "Oh, a balancing issue between our records and some new bookkeeping software the board talked us into. Somebody got the software as a donation."

"With some groups, the main job of the board is to raise money."

"You're right, and that's part of the problem here. The board is supposed to connect us with donors, make donations themselves. or come up with ideas for fund-raising that they take ownership of. But instead of that, sometimes board members really want to run the programs themselves, or meddle with them, or try to get their relatives hired." The microwave beeped; Cooper removed the cup and added the tea bag. "When someone new comes on the board who actually cares about the kids and really wants to help, that person may try to change the culture, but often they get frustrated and resign, or stop speaking up."

The aroma from the tea drifted over to Bernie. It was some sort of mint. It might possibly taste as good as it smelled, she thought, but more likely it didn't. "I'd like to see your records of grants from the Navajo Nation and how the money was used."

"Sure. The information about tribal funds and the way we use them is in the annual report. I have last year's in the computer and paper copies of the more recent ones over there in the file. Bank deposits and expenditure statements are there, too. If you have any questions, I can answer them or find someone who can. I wish Walker had come by and asked us for an accounting instead of assuming things were out of balance here."

"What about this year's donations?"

Cooper put her mug down. "Dom is working on that. If he doesn't come back, I guess I'll have to have Mayfair do it. She knows the numbers, but she's not much of a writer."

"I might need to look at those in the next few days."

"I'll do my best. You may have to help me go through his stuff." She glanced at a second desk on the other side of the room. The top was covered with shoe-box-size containers that seemed to be filled with papers.

Bernie looked at the papers on Cruz's desk and then shifted her gaze to Cooper. "Why do you think Walker is after Wings and Roots?"

Cooper sighed. "It's a personnel matter. I can't talk about it."

"You have to. If I understand her motivation, it will help resolve things." Bernie paused. "Walker told my boss there's collusion between you and me involving the program's funding. I'd like to clear my name and be done with this as soon as I can, and I'm sure you would, too. The more I know, the better job I can do."

"This can't get back to her, agreed?"

Bernie nodded and watched Cooper consider what to say next. "Councilor Walker's brother worked for the program a few years ago. I had to fire him. She and I have never met, but she's been after me and Wings and Roots ever since."

"What did he do wrong?"

Cooper hesitated. "I'll only say it was a personnel matter. I offered him a chance to resign, but he told me to fire him so he could collect unemployment. His termination didn't have anything to do with tribal money. The councilor called me and wanted the details. I told her I couldn't talk about it. She was angry and still is."

"I heard that Dom is your choice to be the new director."

"It's up to the board . . . but I'd be honored if he would be the one to replace me." Cooper stood. "If you don't have any more questions, I'll get those reports for you."

Bernie looked more closely at the art on the wall behind Cooper's desk. It was a photograph of a curving line, a representation of a snake or a lightning bolt, or maybe both, incised in the lava.

"I really like this photo."

"Me, too. It's a famous petroglyph. Vandals destroyed it a few years ago."

"Where did you get the picture?"

"Dom gave it to me for my birthday. I was thrilled."

"It's beautiful. Is it in New Mexico?"

"Yes, actually somewhere out in the Malpais. He told me it was a challenge to get there, but worth every step."

"So Mr. Cruz took the picture?"

"That's another thing that makes it special to me."

Cooper opened the file drawer and extracted a three-ring binder. She handed it to Bernie. "You'll find board minutes and staff reports for the past five years in here, and copies of bank records, too. I'd like this back when you're done."

"No problem. I'll copy whatever I need to hold on to." Bernie pulled her notebook and a pen from the backpack, and jotted down a little receipt for the reports.

Cooper looked at it. "You don't need to give me that. I trust you."

"I trust you, too, but I need to keep everything official."

Bernie drove back to the office, with the binder on the front seat of her unit. One more step in this assignment and then, she thought, she could get back to police work in the field. She radioed to tell Sandra she was on her way in. "The captain wants to talk to you. He told me to tell you to stay off your cell."

Her phone buzzed a minute later. "Manuelito, we

have received a report of a culturally sensitive discovery at the search site. The incident commander, Mrs. Katz, called the Cultural Preservation Office, and the director is on vacation. When she talked to the staff, they said they can't get out there today. She mentioned that you'd alerted them to a cave with bones, and they referred her to the chief, who passed the ball to us. Since you're already familiar with the players, I want you to get over there."

She waited for the important information.

"The searchers think they saw human bones and, from their descriptions, what might be a *jish*."

A *jish*, Bernie knew, was the sacred bundle a *hataali*, a healer, used to help his patient get well.

"Manuelito, you just need to make sure this is legitimate, and then it can be off limits until the Cultural Preservation folks get out there."

"Sir, is this the cave I mentioned to the searchers earlier?"

"I don't think so. But it sounds as though it has been looted, just like the one you saw."

"You know I'm not an expert in this."

"Anything else, Manuelito?"

"What about Cruz?"

"No word yet. Did you pick up anything from your interview with Cooper?"

Bernie had been thinking about it ever since she'd left Cooper's office. "Sir, she was almost too cooperative. It was as if she anticipated my questions. She seemed to have been expecting me to ask about the money. Nothing she said made me think there was any funny business going on. She seemed eager to give me the reports and have us check for problems."

"That Wings and Roots stuff is crucial to get Walker off our backs. Make it your priority as soon as you're done in the Malpais." Largo didn't need to say more.

"I will. I'm on my way. Anything else I should know about the old bones?"

"Probably, but you already know as much as I do."

With that, she climbed back into her unit and headed to the Malpais, wishing Chee, the man who had trained to be a *haatali* and knew more about the world of the sacred, was with her.

13

Chee heard the knock at the studio building door again, only more insistent. "Who's there?"

"Who the hell do you think? I'm freezing my girls off out here. Quit messin' with me, Clyde."

Chee didn't recognize the voice, but he knew what trouble sounded like. He thought about it for a split second and opened the door. A hefty woman rushed in, stomping her feet against the cold, then raising her gaze.

She took a step back from Chee and grinned at him, revealing a missing bottom front tooth. "S'up, man? What you doin' here? Who called the cops on me?"

"I had a flat tire, and I came to talk to CS about it. Why are you here?"

"It's not your business, but I came to check on my man, Clyde Herbert. You seen him?"

Chee stayed silent.

"A big cop like you needs help changing a tire?" When the woman chortled, she smelled of beer. "You think my man or CS did it on purpose, right? You cops are paranoid, dude. At least nobody stole your ride."

Chee felt his temper rising. "I'm Jim Chee. What's your name, ma'am?"

"Juanita's good enough."

Chee heard steps behind him, and turned to see Clyde Herbert, who was frowning at Juanita. "What you doing here?"

"I tracked you down like a coyote on a rabbit." Her laugh was a cackle. "You been avoiding me. Are you seeing somebody else?"

"Like I told you, I'm working. CS and I are making a movie."

"Oh right. You an expert on that?" She laughed again.

"I'm clean now, and I'm staying that way. You can't be here. I've got work to do."

"I'll just watch. Then we can play."

Herbert rubbed his thumb and middle finger together nervously. "CS doesn't like an audience."

"Well, who put that stick up his rear end? He doesn't

own this building." Juanita grabbed the big man's arm. "He's down here, right?" She shoved Herbert down the hall. "He can deal with me."

The leather heels of their boots echoed off the hard floor. Chee followed. "He can deal with me now, too."

Herbert stopped and stared at Chee. "I don't know what's eating you, man, but this is not the night to mess with CS."

"What's so special about tonight?"

"It's the last night he has the studio, and he's got three nights of work to do."

The three stopped outside the studio door. The light was off. Herbert rapped his knuckles against the door frame. His hands looked like they'd done some work, Chee thought.

CS opened the door and took a step back in surprise. "Jim Chee! I didn't expect to see you here."

"Hard to travel with a bad tire. I thought you might know something about that."

"A flat, huh?" CS shifted his weight from one foot to the other as the three stood in silence. "Juanita. Wow."

Chee nodded. "She was outside doing something, like letting the air out of my tire."

Juanita's eyes lit with anger, and she took a step toward Chee. "You son of a—"

Herbert touched her arm. "Stop it. You'll get your-self in trouble."

CS turned to Herbert. "Wait out in the lobby a min-ute. Sergeant Chee and I have something private to discuss." He pointed to Juanita with his lips. "You need to be out of here by the time I come back."

He motioned Chee into the studio and closed the door. Chee took in the scene: a green notebook, an open laptop computer, headphones, and a six-pack of beer bottles. He saw a baggie of white powder, a college catalog, a stack of unopened bills, a pistol, and the dis-tinctive bottles of miniature liquor, some full and some empty.

"What's all this?"

"Props. I'm expanding the video to talk a little about the disruptions to families when they are forced off their ancestral land. Have a seat." CS picked up the gun on the table.

Chee instinctively reached for his weapon, but CS set the gun down on top of the pile of bills and shoved the catalogs toward the middle of the desk. He perched on the edge of the desk, waving Chee to the chair.

Chee didn't move.

"I know you're leaving tomorrow," CS said. "I wanted to clear up whatever's going on with you and me."

"Good idea." Chee worked to keep the anger out of

his voice. "Your death certificate. Tell me the story. That's a reasonable place to start. And then you can move on to why you gave me a flat tire."

"That death certificate." CS rested his back against the wall. "My mother had a baby before I was born, a little boy. He passed away when he was about a week old. She gave me the same name."

Chee felt his eyes widen with shock. In the world in which he had grown up, the names of the dead were buried with them. In the *bilagáana* society, children might be named for dead relatives, but traditional Navajo families didn't operate that way. He waited for CS to explain.

"Mom worked in the oil company office out in Farmington, and the white people pitched in to give her a big savings bond the first time she was pregnant, and they put the name of her baby on it, you know, the little one who died. She decided that I should be given that name, so when I got old enough I could have the money for school. Her relatives were horrified and my father's family advised against it, but she didn't listen. I mean, giving a baby the name of a dead child has to be bad. I use CS or a nickname or sometimes my private name, you know?"

Chee nodded. He had his secret Navajo name that no one used except Blue Woman, the beloved wife of the deceased uncle who had begun to teach him the prayers, songs, and sand paintings of a *haatali*. And now, Bernie.

CS leaned forward. "That name . . . it freaks me out. No one ever called me that until I went to school, and then the teachers needed a birth certificate. They used it until I got them to stop. CS fits me, and it doesn't have to do with the negative. What your investigator thought was my death certificate was for that baby. I wasn't trying to get away with anything, OK?" He stood. "If you don't believe me, ask my mother. What's with all your suspicion, anyway?"

"Well, besides the death certificate, there's the way you pretended not to know me at the barbecue restaurant. The fact that you're associating with a guy I arrested for assaulting a woman. The black-and-blue place on Darleen's arm." Chee looked around the studio again, at the gun, the beer and liquor, what could have been drugs. "I think it comes down to trusting that a person is who he says he is. What's going on in this studio?"

"We'll get there, but I have a question for you first. Why are you so tough on Herbert?"

Chee shifted his weight from heel to toe. "We've talked about that already, and my answer is the same. I have no respect for men who beat up on women. Is he the one who flattened my tire?"

"No. I did that so you'd come over here to talk to me. And yeah, you're right. Herbert did some time for domestic violence. But he is less angry now. He learned how to get out of tough situations at home without using violence." CS motioned to the gun, the baggie with the white powder, the beer, the empty liquor bottles. "You're probably wondering about this stuff, right?"

"Right."

"Like I said, these are all props for the video. Here." He handed the gun to Chee.

Chee took it and looked at it. It was unloaded.

CS picked up the little zip-lock bag. "This? It looks like meth, right? But it's salt a friend gave me from Zuni Salt Lake. It's a blessing to have it here." He handed it to Chee. "Taste it if you don't believe me."

Chee opened the bag. The contents did look like salt, but he wasn't about to taste it. He closed it and offered it to CS.

"We're done with it. Take it."

Chee put the bag of salt in his pocket. "Tell me about the bruise on Darleen's arm, and then we'll talk about my tire."

CS glanced at the big digital clock over the door.

"Better than that. D will be here soon. She can tell you herself."

"No, I left her and London at the dorm. They said they had to study."

"I told D there were too many secrets around here and that I was going to tell you about my name. She said she was ready to tell you about what happened to her arm."

"How did she know I'd be here?"

"I told her."

"You knew because of the flat tire?"

He nodded. "I figured giving you a flat meant you'd come here and blame it on me or Herbert."

"You're right about that."

"And then we'd talk, and you'd understand and give us some help."

"Help? With what?"

"With whom, actually. With Juanita."

14

Joe Leaphorn left the Window Rock offices of the Navajo Tribal Police Department in a mood that matched the heavy overcast sky. He argued with the weather: *Come on, snow, if you are going to. Enough of this pointless cold gray.*

He stopped at Bashas' for some cough medicine for Louisa and a copy of the *Navajo Times*, and on impulse picked up a box of Navajo Tea bags, the kind some entrepreneur made that saved grandmothers the trouble of gathering the plants and enabled Navajo families living in Pittsburgh and Boston to have a reminder of home. He could certainly have asked one of the secretaries at the station for some of the herbs and had enough to make a gallon for free. But he didn't like to receive favors unless he knew he could repay the kindness, and the office staff seemed different every time he visited.

That's why he enjoyed helping Chee and Bernie. When he was busy as a private investigator, they had gathered information for him that as a civilian he didn't have rapid access to. He happily returned the good deed when he could.

Chee had come across an ex-con who might have it in for him, another questionable character, and a man alive despite a death certificate. Thinking of Chee, Leaphorn remembered how a cat had saved the man's life by alerting him to an intruder. That triggered another memory, the crucial thing he'd come to the store for: cat food.

Leaphorn held firm to the opinion that cats should support themselves by ridding the house and surrounding landscape of mice, but neither Louisa nor the cat agreed. Looking at the bags and cans of cat food with their pictures of big-eyed felines, well nourished and stress free, lifted his spirits. He smiled at himself, an old man cheered up by illustrations on cat food containers.

He selected a bag with a cat that looked like his—or was it Louisa's?—and headed home.

Louisa had warmed some soup for them. She always

added crackers and sometimes cheese or peanut butter to their weekday lunch, but she hadn't done it this time, so Leaphorn filled in. He set the table with spoons and a rectangle of sturdy paper towel he preferred to her little napkins. She sat in her regular place looking out the window, not reading, not asking him yet about the meeting and his new assignments. A sign, along with the neglected lunch additions, that she must feel terrible.

He gave her the medicine. He thought the tea deserved an explanation.

"My grandmother offered a tea like that to us kids every winter, so I hope you will try some. She told us it strengthened us for the cold weather. She sweetened it with a little honey when we had some."

Louisa looked at the box. "This has *Thelesperma* in it. That's good." She put the box down and examined the package of cough syrup. "This stuff is guaranteed to put me to sleep."

"Try them both. A little sleep might do you good." Leaphorn spoke as he served the soup, using a measuring cup to transfer it into the bowls since he could not find the ladle Louisa hid somewhere.

"Sleep would be good for you, too. I bet my coughing kept you awake all night."

"No, no." He was glad she had said "all night" because he had slept periodically between her coughing jags.

"How was your police meeting?"

"Fine, I guess. They want me to check on a couple of cold cases. Both of them have some interest to me: the suspected murder of a boy who died mysteriously at boarding school and a woman who walked away from her family and disappeared."

"They sound like they will keep you busy." She coughed.

After the soup, Leaphorn fixed Louisa the Navajo tea and put it on the table.

She had a swallow. "Good, even without the honey."

He realized he had forgotten the honey and taken her spoon with her half-eaten soup. He placed a spoon on the table for her, on top of the paper towel next to the honey plate. He watched as she added and stirred.

"You worry too much, Joe. I'll be fine. It's only a cold or maybe a touch of flu."

He leaned toward her. "Sit in my big chair in the living room. You'll be more comfortable. Leave your cup, and I'll bring it for you."

She rose without argument and settled into the recliner. She pulled his throw with the Navajo Department of Public Safety logo over her legs. The cat curled onto her lap.

"I got the *Times* at Bashas'. Do you want to read the paper?"

"No, you look at it first."

Leaphorn handed her the cup, and she took another little drink. "Thank you. Don't fret over me. I know you have things to do. I might take a little nap right here in this chair. Go. Do your work."

The cat usually followed him to the oversize stuffed chair in the office, but today it stayed with Louisa.

Before he started on his new assignments from the meeting, Leaphorn decided to finish distilling Chee's information. Clyde Herbert's background had been easy to find, but the man hadn't left much of a trail since prison. That meant he'd either stayed out of trouble or become more competent at covering his tracks.

He looked at his notes and realized he could do more digging. But maybe he'd take a nap first. A gray December day, the image of Louisa snoozing peacefully with a warm cat on her legs, the soup and crackers, all inspired a move toward the comfortable chair in his office, the one that gave him pleasant dreams. He'd stretch out for a few minutes and then . . .

An electronic sound woke him. His cell phone. He

didn't use it very often this time of year because he stayed home more, and the land line was more reliable. He saw that it was Bernie. "Yá'át'ééh."

"Yá'át'ééh, Lieutenant." Speaking in Navajo, Bernie made polite conversation for a few moments, and then got down to business. "I could use your advice on how to deal with Councilor Walker. I know you said she's a *dahsáni*, but so far I'm only seeing this porcupine's quills, not her soft side. She suspects that I'm involved in some sort of corruption cover-up, and Largo told me to change her mind. She's taking over my working life."

"You know what animals eat the *dahsáni*?"

"Well, sir, out here it's bobcats and mountain lions."

"Do you know how they get around the quills?"

"Not exactly, but they must figure out how to reach the porcupine's stomach. That's the only area not protected."

"Correct." Bernie could figure out the rest, he thought.

"Sir, I need another favor. It's a big one this time, and Largo says the department will pay you." He listened as Bernie mentioned the three-ring binder of information on Wings and Roots from Cooper and the slim folder of papers from Councilor Walker.

"I can look at Walker's information if you can get it to me soon. The folks at headquarters gave me some assignments today. The binder will have to wait until next week."

"I appreciate it, sir. I can scan the folder's pages and e-mail them."

"It would be better if you could make a copy and drop it by."

"I can't take the time today to drive to Window Rock. Could you meet me somewhere in Gallup?"

"How about T&R?" T&R was an all-purpose rural shopping mecca—a truck stop, feed store, grocery, pawnshop, and snack bar a few miles west of the junction of the road into Arizona and the road to Shiprock.

"That works, sir. I'm leaving the office now. Will Louisa be with you?"

"No, she isn't feeling well."

After the Lieutenant's injury, Louisa had done all the driving. Now he had recovered enough to drive, and that freedom seemed to have further stirred his brain into more recovery.

"Let me know if you have any tips on getting Councilor Walker to stop shaking her quills at me. And how to find her soft spot."

"Any leads on the lost man you were involved with?"

"There's a little article about him today in the *Na-vajo Times*. There may have been a sighting of him hitchhiking on the interstate."

He'd brought the newspaper into his office, and Leaphorn quickly scanned the two paragraphs about Cruz, thankful that his ability to read English outpaced his ability to speak it. Then he noticed an announcement that the Navajo Tribal Council's Law and Order Committee was meeting that afternoon, chaired by Councilor Elsbeth Walker. He'd stop by to talk to her before he met with Bernie.

He didn't mean to wake Louisa, but she glanced up when he entered the room to get his truck keys and his jacket. "How are you doing on all that research?"

"I'm almost done with Chee's request. I realized that, in his case, no news was good news." He told Louisa about the odd death certificate and the ex-con. "Bernie wanted some information about how to deal with the councilor I know who is giving her a little trouble. The woman thinks Bernie is involved in something underhanded."

Louisa chuckled. "Bernie? That's crazy."

"I'm going to the council chamber for the Law and Order Committee meeting, and then to the T&R to pick up some work from Bernie. I shouldn't be long."

Louisa coughed and sipped what was left of her tea.

"I'm glad you and Bernie get along. I never know what to say to her on the phone. I think I always talk too much."

"You have interesting things to say. Are you feeling better?"

"A bit. The rest helps."

Outside, what might have been a snowflake drifting past the window, and a few minutes later, a couple more of them. Good, Leaphorn thought. They could use the moisture, and the gloomy day would have meant something. He turned to Louisa to see if she had noticed the snow, but her eyes were closed. He gently pulled the throw a bit higher.

The committee usually met at the Law and Order Building, officially the Navajo Department of Public Safety police headquarters. But the heat was out over there, as he had learned from his appointment that morning. The chief had mentioned that the committee would use the larger Navajo Nation Council Chamber. "It's warm there already," he had said. "The heat is on because some movie people are making a documentary on WPA art. They want to include the Gerald Nailor Sr. stuff over there. A bunch of bigwigs were roaming around all morning, taking pictures of the murals and shooting video."

Leaphorn parked his truck close to the exit, as was

his habit, and walked to the large east-facing entrance door in the red sandstone wall. He hardly used his cane anymore, despite Louisa's urging. He had been inside the hogan-shaped meeting room a few times, always to share a personal story about why the public safety department needed more of everything. He looked around for Councilor Walker, seeing half a dozen Navajo men talking in clusters and two women standing alone together. One of them he recognized as Elsbeth Walker, a few pounds heavier, perhaps, and still a handsome woman.

The councilor looked over at him and smiled. "Lieutenant Joe Leaphorn. It has been a long, long time. Yá'át'ééh." Walker introduced the woman with her, a councilor from Kayenta who left them alone to talk. "What brings you here, Lieutenant?"

Walker hadn't changed, he thought. She was never one for excessive pleasantries. "Councilor, I have a colleague. A woman you know, too, Officer Bernadette Manuelito from Shiprock."

Walker frowned. "I remember that she said she was going to talk to you about some problems with an agency in Shiprock. I can't discuss it."

Leaphorn waited until he was sure that she meant what she said.

"I respect you as a councilor. You take the job seriously, and you spend more time on tribal business than other councilors I've met. I remember when you thought there was something wrong with the police administration here, how you stuck with it until you uncovered the truth." Leaphorn didn't add that the truth exonerated the department. "Once you found it, you helped us get more funding."

She smiled faintly. It wasn't appropriate to be too proud of oneself, but she obviously recalled her success. He switched the topic back to Bernie.

"Officer Manuelito reminds me of you in that way. She doesn't give up on something until she has it figured out. When someone shot me, she was the one who discovered who had done it and why. She will be the same with the fraud case and the missing man."

Walker drummed her fingers on the desktop, but Leaphorn had seen the porcupine's restlessness before.

"You know, people like us, you as a public official and me when I worked full-time, we hear a lot of things. Sometimes the person telling the story only has half the information, or leaves out something important. Sometimes they lie. That happened to me quite a few times, and it made the investigation more difficult."

She stopped drumming. "Lieutenant, get on with it. Say what you want to say."

"Officer Manuelito has a fine career of service ahead

of her. She's young, but she's smart and resourceful. And honest. Just like you."

Walker laughed, "Like me, except for the young part. Joe Leaphorn, let's have a cup of coffee next time I'm here for council. I want to know what it's like to almost die."

"No one has asked about that. I'll have to think on it."

"Think on it. I'll call you. Now I have to get to work."

15

Verifying a burial cave was not Bernie's job of choice. But the assignment gave her a work-related reason to do what she'd been craving—go back to the Malpais and check on the progress of the search.

But before that, she had an appointment to keep.

She pulled her unit alongside the convenience store and passed the gas pumps. No one was buying fuel, but there were three other vehicles there: Leaphorn's white pickup, a brown minivan with Arizona plates, and a sedan with thick plastic taped to the hole where the front passenger window would have been.

Inside, the smell of cleaning solution and food under heat lamps greeted her. She saw the Lieutenant seated near the window, the expected cup of coffee on the tabletop. Bernie stood at the empty place across from him.

Leaphorn acknowledged her with a nod. "You made good time, Officer. Have a seat."

"I will, but first, I'm going to get a Coke out of the machine and a hot dog. Do you want something?"

"No, thanks."

When she looked at the franks spinning under the heat lamp, she decided on a bag of peanuts instead. She waited for a little girl filling her cup with a splash of each soda the machine offered. It seemed like only yesterday her sister had been that young, and now she was thinking of going to a school hours away.

When she returned to the table, Leaphorn was holding a large tan envelope.

"I think this missing man, Domingo Cruz, is an interesting person. Complicated. I didn't find anything criminal, although he has some activist tendencies. He was involved with AIM and spent two weeks at the Dakota pipeline protest. But no arrests. I guess that goes without saying for a guy who is a top dog at an agency that works with kids, but these days, you never know."

Leaphorn opened the envelope and extracted some printed sheets of white paper. He put the first one on the table facing Bernie. "What do you notice about it?"

She looked. "Most petroglyphs I've seen are on sandstone or softer rock, not pecked into lava."

"Anything else?"

"The design itself. The spiral is larger than most I've seen. It must have taken someone a long time to carve it." She put the picture down. "I saw this image in Cruz's sister's house. When I commented on it, she said her brother had taken the photograph and given it to her for her birthday."

"Interesting. Now look at this." He moved the first picture aside and showed her another.

Bernie picked it up. Cruz's photograph, or one very similar, formed a backdrop for a website that sold Indian artifacts. She couldn't tell from the tiny images on the sheet if the pots, arrowheads, and spear points were old or reproductions. But the large text said GENUINE ANCIENT NATIVE ARTIFACTS FROM PRIVATE LAND. PRICELESS! The rest of the type was too small to read.

She set the sheet of paper back down. "Did you click on any of these items to see if there was more description or a price?"

He took a taste of his coffee. "They are all expensive and not well described. The website address is there, so you can look yourself. In the meantime, this might help."

He handed her an old-fashioned magnifying glass. She held it over the tiny type. The text credited the objects to archaeological sites near a historic trail running through the lava that connected the Zuni and Acoma pueblos.

"This thing makes me feel like Sherlock Holmes." She started to hand the magnifier back to him. "What do you think?"

"Keep it. You'll need it for this." Leaphorn passed her another printout. "I took it from that same website. Take another look."

"There's a credit line." She read it out loud: " 'Background photo by Domingo Cruz from the collection of Merilee Cruz. Original photography for sale.' "

Bernie enjoyed her Coke. "I talked to Cruz's twin sister, Merilee, and she told me she sold art on the Internet but not Indian artifacts. When I admired the petroglyph photo, she told me she had an extra print."

He put the pages back in the folder and handed it to her. "Technology is not my strong point. But the appearance of Domingo Cruz's photo on that site makes me wonder what Cruz might have been doing out in that lava besides working with Wings and Roots."

"He doesn't seem like the kind of guy who would steal from the dead." Bernie stirred her Coke with the straw. "He told the girls to stay away from the caves."

"Earlier, you said you had seen this photograph in

the home of Cruz's sister. Are you sure it was the same picture?"

"Yes."

Leaphorn reached into the breast pocket of his shirt and took out the small spiral notebook he always carried. He thumbed through it. "I discovered that they were adopted by a family in Utah. I didn't do any specific checking on her. Only on Domingo."

"Merilee told me she and Cruz went different directions after high school."

"That's right, as far as I can tell." He took another sip of coffee. "You better get on the road, Manuelito. I will do a little more checking into the Cruz family. I'll let you know if I find anything else interesting."

He slid the envelope toward her. "And I think you have something for me."

She put her backpack on a chair, pulled out the folder from Walker, and extracted some papers held together with a staple. "Here's a copy of what the councilor gave us."

Leaphorn glanced at what he had been handed. "Drive carefully," he said. "I hear a big storm is on the way."

At the search headquarters, the mood was subdued, a contrast to the adrenaline-filled scene she'd encountered on her first visit. Katz, the incident commander, looked older than when they had met a few days ago.

"I'm glad you're the one representing Navajo out here. It's always easier to work with a person who already knows the lay of the land. Are you ready for a hike?"

"Sure. Give me a minute to put on my hiking boots." Bernie regretted leaving the boots in the trunk of her unit, where they had soaked in the cold. She pulled her warmest hat over her ears, grabbed her gloves, and added an extra energy bar to her backpack. She moved the three-ring binder to the trunk.

Katz introduced a young man with a mustache. "This is Ted. He found the cave, and he can take you to it."

"Thank you. How far?"

"Oh, about three miles, if we don't get lost." He grinned. "Don't worry. I know exactly where it is. The last thing we need is another lost or injured person."

The hike took Bernie to an area of the Malpais she hadn't seen before, beautiful and treacherous. Ted set a fast pace, and she pushed herself to keep up. After about twenty minutes, she felt more assured on the uneven terrain. The exertion of climbing boulders, hiking up stone ridges, and balancing along a ropey snake of solid stone warmed her, and she shoved her hat into her coat pocket.

There was no trail, only common sense and the memory of navigation guiding them. Ted took the lead. The thousands of years of erosion since volcanic activity had laid down this stone jungle had melted a few of the sharpest edges and brought some vegetation, but the rocks were still treacherous. The mix of sizes and the crevices between the stones forced Bernie to keep her eyes down rather than look up at the clouds building in the turquoise winter sky. Islands of trees and shrubs had formed where the mechanics of geography allowed for the creation of soil and retention of water. Periodically Ted stopped and checked his compass and the GPS to make sure they were headed in the right direction.

When they paused for water, Bernie said, "Why does the lava look so different from place to place? I mean, this area where we've been walking isn't much like what I saw with Wings and Roots."

Ted glanced up from his GPS. "Several different volcanic eruptions created this area. The McCartys lava flow is only three thousand years old, one of the newest in the United States—excepting Mount St. Helens and Hawaii, of course."

They hiked on. Bernie enjoyed the cool fresh air, the rhythm of the trail, the good luck of being out of the car and out of the office on a semi-mild December day. She told herself to focus on that and not what lay at the end of the hike.

About the time she was seriously considering a drink from her water bottle, Ted paused, studying the rocks ahead. His voice had a deeper degree of confidence. "I remember that ridge with all the lichens. We don't have far now."

They stopped again a few minutes later, and he motioned Bernie up next to him. "You see where that juniper is growing up against the lava?"

She nodded.

"Look up at the top of the tree, and then take a straight line to the right. Follow that ridgeline."

"Is that the cave?"

"Yes. Ready to see what's in there?"

"In a minute. I want to ask you some questions."

Ted lowered himself onto a relatively flat piece of rock and nodded. "Ask away."

Bernie sat across from him. "Give me an idea of what to expect."

He twirled the end of his mustache with one hand and told her about what he assumed were rib bones and some human vertebrae. "Whatever or whoever is up there predates our version of the southwest by a long, long time. It felt, I don't know how to describe it . . . Creepy, I guess. Uncomfortable. And I've been in a lot of caves."

"Did you touch anything?"

He cleared his throat. "No way."

"The incident commander told my boss that you noticed something in the cave besides the bones."

"It looked like dried buckskin, maybe an old bag. To be honest, I didn't spend a lot of time looking. I figured it might have some spiritual significance, and I knew it wasn't any of my business." He spoke with an intensity that surprised her.

Bernie looked toward the cave. "Thank you. I'll take a look now."

"Do you need an extra flashlight?"

"I'm fine." She had double-checked to make sure hers worked.

He slipped off his backpack, unzipped the big pocket, and handed her a pair of rubber kneepads. "You'll need these. Do you want me to go with you?"

"No. I won't be long."

"Do you have your gloves?"

"I think so."

Bernie took the pads and hiked to the entrance, saying a prayer for protection as she approached. As in the cave Annie had found, the lava boulders someone had placed to block access had been shoved away—another confirmation that this might be a burial and, worse, a burial that had been looted. She climbed over the last of the rocks and paused to stare into the darkness.

She took off her backpack, removed the flashlight from her duty belt, and put on the kneepads and her gloves. She inhaled deeply, feeling the cold air at the tip of her nose, and looked up at the sky, now filled with towering gray storm clouds. Then she squatted down and slowly let the beam of light explore the cave's interior as her eyes adjusted to the darkness.

At first, she saw nothing except the dark rock she'd expected. She moved the light slowly, and then the beam glanced off something lighter in color. She focused on it but couldn't be sure what she was seeing.

Bernie lowered herself to her hands and knees and began to inch inside, shining the light directly in front of her, looking for relatively smooth places on the lava to spare her hands. She moved forward a little more, stopping to shine the light into the darkness. The roof of the cave seemed to get closer, the space tighter. Her chest tightened too. She crawled deeper inside.

And then she saw something. A bone, varnished to a deep yellow with the patina of age. It did, indeed, look human. She adjusted to squatting, the top of her head brushing the cold roof of the cave. Slowly she ran the light along the shaft of the bone, discovering another bone and then a small grouping, like part of an assembly-required, life-size skeleton puzzle. A cluster of small turquoise beads lay next to the bones, probably from jewelry buried with this poor soul. She continued on the same trajectory, stopping when her light found fragments of broken pottery. Perhaps the looter had dropped the bowl, or one of the old ones might have broken it years before when they respectfully interred the body. Whatever ceremonial jars, fiber mats, or other artifacts had been placed here to help the deceased on the final journey were long gone.

Pushing aside the clenching in her stomach and the rapid pounding of her heart, she crawled closer to the old bones, searching thoroughly. There, next to what could be part of a human pelvis, she saw what Ted had described. The strand of what looked like leather and the gray feathers might indicate that the person buried here was a *hataali*, but Bernie's intuition said otherwise. Whoever this skeleton had once been, she deduced, probably wore those items as part of the burial garb.

Exhaling to calm herself, she turned around and put the flashlight to work on a final scan before she left this sad, desecrated place. The stone floor of the cave kept its secrets, but she noticed some pockets of sand and another broken bead, one that could be shell. Then the beam reflected off a jawbone, clearly a human mandible, yellowed with age.

Bernie dropped the flashlight, which rolled away from her, toward the mouth of the cave. She followed on hands and knees, oblivious now to the rough stones that penetrated the leather on her gloves. As she grabbed for the flashlight, she realized that the cold had stiffened her fingers to near uselessness. Pushing herself to sitting, she pressed her frozen hands between her thighs. Finally her fingers regained their flexibility, and she crawled back toward the skull. Even though it bothered her, she had to finish the job. She pulled her phone from the jacket pocket and took off her gloves so she could turn on the camera flash. She needed pictures of everything here—the other bones, the beads, and the leather and feathers—to show the Cultural Preservation Office staff.

Finally, she started back down the slope to where Ted waited.

He stood when he saw her approach. "I was about to go up and holler for you. That took a while."

"I needed photos. There's no doubt in my mind that you found human bones. Old bones. I'll tell the Cultural Preservation Office about this."

The wind made a noise in the trees, and she looked

up. On the rocks above the cave, she saw something skitter. Smiling at her own hyperattentiveness, she was about to turn away when she noticed something else: a spiral pecked into the rock.

Ted was starting to put his pack back on, but Bernie motioned for him to stop. "Could you help me with something?"

"Sure."

"We need to do some hauling."

"I'm not following you."

"Someone removed the rocks that protected the entrance, the boulders the old ones had piled up to keep the burial private."

"I'll do it."

Normally, she would have argued, but she'd already spent enough time in the presence of the dead. "Thanks. I appreciate it."

After he'd finished moving the rocks, Ted led the way back to the search base camp.

"Do you spend much time out in the lava?" she asked as they walked.

"I did as a kid. My uncle had a ranch near here. The Manzanares spread. Maybe you've heard of it."

"I met an officer named Manzanares. He works for the New Mexico State Police out of Grants. At least for a little while longer. He's getting ready to retire."

"I know who you mean. He's my cousin. He looks after the place now. I haven't been back to the ranch since he's been in charge." The tone in his voice said that it wasn't for lack of interest.

"Why not?"

"Let's just say I don't feel welcome."

Ted's radio squawked, the transmission loud enough for Bernie to overhear. "The vultures Fred and Liz spotted were enjoying a deer," Katz said. "Mr. Cruz is still missing. The search will resume at dawn, depending on the weather. Head on in, everyone, and thank you."

Ted turned his radio to broadcast. "Officer Manuelito verifies ancient human remains. We blocked the cave, and I will give you the coordinates. No sign of Mr. Cruz. Save me some dinner."

Bernie thought the hike back seemed faster, perhaps because her anxiety about viewing the body was gone now. At base camp, she reported to Katz, stressing that the site needed to remain off limits to the search teams. The cook invited her to join the rest of the crew to finish a stew they had made for the volunteers' lunch.

She took a bowl and found a quiet spot to eat before her drive home. She was nearly done when a slim Navajo man with black-framed glasses came over to her. "Are you Officer Manuelito?"

"That's me."

"I'm Franklin. The one you talked to on the phone about Dom."

He looked like a well-dressed cowboy, complete with a handsome leather jacket—not the image she'd created to go with the understated voice on the phone. He was slim in the hips, broad of shoulder. The same build as Chee.

He switched to Navajo and gave her his clans. Bernie reciprocated. They weren't related, but he was related to Chee through the paternal grandmother's elder brother.

"Have you heard anything from Dom?" she asked.

"I wish. I check my messages whenever I can, thinking maybe this is only a mistake, and now that he's had a chance to think things over, he's on his way home. If he's still alive, I think he would at least want me to know he's safe. I mean, if he *is* safe." Franklin turned away. When he turned back, his emotions were under control. "I wanted to thank you for caring."

She thought about saying she was only doing her job, but she realized he was correct. She did care.

Franklin had started to walk away. When she called after him, he turned to face her, the fringe on his jacket swaying like the mane of a well-groomed horse. She motioned to him to sit with her. "Join me here a minute, and tell me about Dom."

He sat next to her, and she breathed in the faint fragrance of his hair gel. "Domingo is the nicest man in the whole world. You know about all the work he does with kids—giving them hope, building them up, changing their lives?"

Bernie nodded.

"Well, he likes to cook for us and does the shopping, too. This situation, him disappearing—it's terrifying." Franklin clenched his long finger together, then straightened them again. "I'm so worried I can't think straight."

"It is terrifying. Do you know of anyone who might want to hurt him?" Bernie waited, but Franklin seemed to need prompting. "Did he have any enemies?"

"Dom gets along with everybody. That's how he can put up with me, I guess." He chuckled, and she thought he was about to add something, but he changed the subject. "He loves his sister, but she drives him crazy—telling him what to do, where to be, how to act, rubbing it in that she's his big sister because she's a few minutes older. But he's still sweet to her. You know that they're twins?"

"I know."

"I think she's jealous of me, of what Dom and I have together. Maybe she's still upset because she ended up as a widow. Of course, everyone knows that Roger wanted to divorce her. If that had happened, she probably would be living in a tent somewhere, not in that nice house."

"I heard she planned to divorce him."

Franklin stood. "It doesn't matter now. I shouldn't gossip. I've got to help clean up. Thank you for suggesting that I volunteer out here. It sure is better than pacing around our place. I was useless at work, but this helps."

Franklin headed off. Bernie took her stew bowl to the washstand and walked to her unit, thinking about what Franklin had said. If Dom had met with foul play, those closest to him would be the obvious suspects. He'd wanted to say something else about their relationship, and then he'd pulled back.

She slid across the icy seat of her unit, started the engine, and as soon as the temperature gauge moved a micron off the C, switched on the heater. She'd seen enough old bones these past few days to last a lifetime.

She thought again about Franklin. Maybe he was worth another conversation if Dom wasn't found soon.

16

Jim Chee considered himself a patient man. But even his patience had its limits, and the women in his life seemed to know exactly how far to stretch those boundaries.

Take his sweet Bernie, too busy to answer his calls. At least she sent an I love you text. But he wanted more.

Or Darleen, not usually the silent type, adamantly refusing to tell him how she got that large ugly bruise on her arm.

And now he was growing frustrated because of four other women: George Curley's mother Deborah and his wife Caitlyn, who seemed nice but not very assertive; Mrs. Vigil, who was more worried about the new truck than her wandering son-in-law; and the mysterious Juanita, who was sitting in the studio in stony silence.

Dealing with a flat tire, an ex-con, a husband on the lam, and a suspicious character who should be dead was easier by far.

After their discussion about his birth certificate and the bona fides of his associate, Chee had more questions for CS but decided to hold them; several might be better answered with Darleen there, too. So he sat, first listening to CS explain, at considerable length, why the music from the band Herbert's nephew played in would not be right for the video, how music provides texture for a video but should not dominate unless the subject is the music itself. Or something like that. Herbert countered with "But he's family, man. . . . He needs a break. He can use the money."

Chee texted Darleen twice and got a thumbs-up and a smiley face in response. He enjoyed the lazy warmth of the studio building and the cozy chair. A nap wouldn't be bad. A little snooze. He closed his eyes and tuned out CS's lecture, but his brain began to churn up what he had to do before he could really call it a day.

After he dealt with CS and Darleen, he needed to walk back to the dorm, change the tire on his truck, drive to the motel, and pack up so he could head home to Shiprock and his—no, their—trailer.

He'd ask if the Cibola County deputy in the class knew anything about George Curley, an unlikely possibility, or about a rancher out there hiring workers in November. Then he'd call Caitlyn once more to see if she'd heard from George or had any other ideas about where he could be. It would be wonderful to listen to the song of the San Juan River. And to hear Bernie's gentle breathing in place of rap music.

He had almost given in to grogginess when his phone buzzed with a call. He looked at the number and turned to CS. "I have to take this. It's Bernie." He stood up and walked to the far end of the room.

"We'll be in the studio."

Juanita stood, too, but Herbert blocked her. "You're not welcome here. Go home. You know it's over between us."

"You found someone else? You stinkin' . . ."

Chee turned away from the rant. "Sweetheart?"

"Hi. Glad I found you."

"It's great to hear your voice. But you sound tired."

"Oh, it's work."

"What's happening with the search in the Malpais?"

"Cruz is still out there somewhere. The weather is predicted to change for the worse." She told him about the second cave. "I want to hear about Santa Fe and the training." Her tone of voice changed. "But first, have you seen my sister tonight?"

"I have. We had dinner with her roommate, and I

took them both back to the dorm, and she gave me a tour. I'm waiting for her now at CS's studio." He didn't bother Bernie with the beer cans and the bruise. "Want me to ask her to call you?"

"No, but would you call me and then hand the phone to her?"

"You sound aggravated."

"You must be psychic." The sound of her laughter lit up his day for a moment. "I have some loose ends to tie up here, but I can't wait to head home. Don't forget to call when Sister gets there. Use my cell number."

"Sure thing. It's good to hear your voice. I thought you were mad at me or something."

"Only too busy. I miss you." And she ended the call.

A loud knock distracted him, and he turned toward the sound. "I'll get it."

Darleen rushed in, her cheeks red with cold. Chee spoke softly. "Wait here a minute. I need to tell you something."

Darleen kept her voice low too. "What now?"

"Bernie is upset about something. She asked me to call her and then put you on the line."

"Fine. Don't stress over it. Give me a minute." Darleen unbuttoned her coat. "Who's Herbert arguing with?"

"A woman named Juanita."

"Juanita?"

"You know her? Thirtysomething, on the hefty side."

"I haven't met her but he's been talking about her like she's seriously evil. Holy smokes. Juanita came looking for him!" Darleen sighed. "I'm ready. Go ahead and call Sister."

Bernie picked up on the first ring this time. "She's there?"

"Hi, sweetheart. I'm with Darleen."

"You're special, Jim Chee. Let me talk to her."

He handed the phone to Darleen, who rolled her eyes. "Hello. What's up?" After that, she seemed to be listening.

Chee left the sisters to figure out whatever they needed to figure out.

The signature aroma of marijuana drifted toward him as he walked to the studio, and he heard a racket from the open door. Juanita's voice dominated: ". . . that little creep . . . made you God?"

"I don't make the rules," CS said, "but you can't smoke in the building, and you especially can't smoke weed in here."

"I've got a medical card. Wanna hit?"

Well, Chee thought, I need to step in and be the bad guy. But then he heard Herbert's voice.

"Baby, put that joint out and pay attention. We're done, you and me. You bully me, you don't listen, you've got an attitude, and you won't help me stay straight. That guy, the tall Navajo? Well, he's a *real* cop, not an actor in the movie."

Juanita laughed. "Is that right?"

"Right." Chee walked into the room as he spoke and grabbed the joint from her hand. He extinguished it with a pinch before she could protest and dropped it on the floor. "Leave now before I detain you, call security, and you end up in jail."

The woman put her hands on her broad hips. She gave CS a dark look, Chee a darker one, and stared at Herbert a long moment. Then she bent down, picked up the smashed joint, pulled a plastic bag out of her pocket, and stowed it there. "You ain't done with me, Clyde Herbert. You'll see." She turned and stomped toward the door.

CS said, "As soon as Darleen gets here, we'll start. I'll make sure—"

"I'm here." Darleen approached from the hall, her voice strained, and handed Chee his phone.

Chee noticed that she'd been crying, and that she noticed him noticing. She reached into her purse for a tissue, wiped her eyes, and put the tissue in her pocket.

"CS, he wants to hear about my arm. I'd like to tell him now, and then Chee can leave, and we can work."

CS nodded. "Do you want to talk in private?"

"No, you and Herbert are part of the story." She turned to Chee. "Let's sit over there." She twisted a lock of her hair. "After I tell you, will you tell Mama?"

"It depends."

"How about Sister? Will you tell her?"

Chee nodded yes. "I don't think secrets are good for a relationship. Do you?"

"It depends. Sometimes a secret keeps somebody from a broken heart."

He thought about that, remembering Leaphorn's advice. "If the person finds out later, and they usually do, the heartbreak is twice as bad. Keeping a secret means you don't trust or love somebody enough to tell them the truth."

He saw her blinking back the tears and felt a wave of sympathy for her. "Just tell me, and I'll decide after that."

Darleen rolled up her sleeve. The bruise had turned dull yellow at the edges, but still resembled nothing more closely than the grip of a hand.

"CS did grab me, just like you guessed. But he had to. He and me and London and Herbert went to a party, and there was beer, the high-octane kind, in the cooler. CS brought me a Sprite or something in one of those sleeve things. I poured it out and helped myself to a beer and then two or three more using that sleeve thing, you know, so no one would be on my case about it. It was only beer, bro."

She stopped. Chee watched her fidget.

"Tell me the rest."

"Well, I was acting real cool, talking to some other kids in the program, and then CS came over and said he had to get back to work. He smelled the beer on me and got all bent out of shape. He told me . . ." She swallowed, and Chee saw her struggle to control her emotions.

"What did he tell you?"

"He said I was immature, that I'd never be a real artist because I didn't have any discipline. I told him he was a stupid, controlling jackass. And then . . ." He saw the corners of her mouth slope down, and her bottom lip begin to tremble.

"And then CS hurt you?"

"No. Not at all. Then Herbert came over and put his arm around CS and took him into the other room. I was crying, and then I decided that I hated both those jerks, and I was going to just get out of there." She stopped talking.

Darleen twisted a different lock of hair.

"Well, instead of leaving, I thought I'd have another beer to calm myself down. After that, I was acting crazy like, dancing around. Maybe half an hour went by, and CS found me again and wanted to get me out of there. There were some steps, and I was yelling at him to leave me alone and I missed a step, or maybe two or . . . I don't exactly remember. He caught my arm right before I fell. He had to grab hard."

Darleen looked down at her shoes. "Herbert helped me get into the car. He told me to behave myself."

Chee let her story sit for a moment. "What do you think about all that?"

"I drank too much, and then I acted like a jerk. CS and Herbert were good to me."

Chee thought he should say something wise, give her some advice about turning her life around, but he'd already said it, already told her. As she repeatedly reminded him, she was old enough to make her own choices and deal with the consequences.

Darleen looked at him. "You know I like drinking because it makes me feel free, not like a dumb girl. But then I act like a dumb girl." Chee saw the tears now. "I only want to be happy and do my art. And for people to trust me. But when they do, when they give me a chance, like Mama and Sister did, I screw up."

Herbert had been sitting next to the studio door, listening and, Chee knew, observing him and Darleen. Now he stood and walked toward them. He looked at Chee. "Mind if I give this lady some advice?"

"Go ahead."

Herbert squatted next to her. "Honey, you don't want to end up like Juanita. You've got a lot of talent. Don't let booze get in the way. You know that drawing you gave me?"

"Yes."

"Every time I look at it, I'm gonna think of you as an artist. You'll go far if you put your energy there. Don't get sidetracked with partying, or you won't be able to be an artist."

Chee said, "Thanks for telling me the truth. I won't lie to Bernie, but I won't mention this to her unless she asks or unless you want me to tell her."

"Really?" Darleen was crying now. "But tell her I fixed your flat, OK? I could do that because of what she taught me about cars."

"You fixed it? For real?"

"Exactly. That's why I was so late."

17

Officer Bernadette Manuelito drove out of the search and rescue base camp parking area, headed back to NM 117 and then to the interstate and, ultimately, home to Shiprock. She enjoyed this highway, with the acres of dark lava on one side and the wind-carved sandstone cliffs on the other. A respite before she hit the truck traffic on the interstate. She needed time to think about Cruz, the spirals, and how this all fit with Councilor Walker's suspicions.

As she slowed for three does bounding across the highway, she spotted a vehicle that had run off the road and into a fence post or guardrail. The rear end rose from the incline of the shoulder, and exhaust from the running engine created a cloud of gray. Because of the angle of the embankment, she couldn't see the front of the car.

Pulling to the side of the road behind the vehicle, she parked and turned on her light bar, took her first aid kit out of the trunk, and zipped her jacket. She jogged to the car, passing several miniature liquor bottles strewn along the shoulder. Another drunk-driving crash? Or were they older debris from passing motorists?

As she got closer, she recognized the El Morro bumper sticker. This car belonged to Larry Hoffman, the ranger she'd spoken to about the lava stories. Peering in the back, she saw a figure slouched over the steering wheel. She scrambled down the rock slope and rapped on the driver's-side window. The bloodied man behind the steering wheel opened his eyes and looked up at her without recognition. The airbag had deployed, probably on impact with the guardrail. Hoffman was wearing his seat belt. He was the only person in the car.

"Turn off the engine, Larry!" she yelled,

He fumbled with the switches and eventually lowered the passenger's-side window. She walked around the rear of the car, down the slope, and reached in to turn off the engine. Except for a nose bleed, she didn't see any other injuries, and he seemed to be breathing without difficulty.

"Hey. I know you. You're that Navajo cop. Bernalito Manuel, right?"

She didn't hear the telltale slur that came with too much to drink, but something was wrong. "Cop is right. I'm Bernadette Manuelito."

"Burn-a-debt. Hey. That's it." When he chuckled, she sniffed for the sweet, chemical smell of alcohol. There was none. No marijuana aroma either. "Help me out of the car, OK, honey? There are too many ants in here."

She called 911 from her cell phone and gave the dispatcher the closest mile marker sign to the accident. "My unit is on the shoulder with the lights on. The car is to the right of that. The driver is the only injury. He's conscious and not complaining of pain, but he has a nosebleed and is hallucinating."

She leaned in closer to Larry. She didn't see any liquor bottles or drugs. No ants, either. "Sit tight. An ambulance is on the way. I'll stay here with you until it gets here."

"Where'd all this blood come from?"

"The airbag whacked you in the face when it went off."

"Wow. It felt like a frozen cloud. Debbie, be careful leaning on the car. You don't want the ants to get on you. They've been friendly so far. Some of them are singing to me. The ones that are by my ear. Don't let them crawl in, OK?" He attempted a grin, but it transformed into a grimace.

She looked at both his ears. No ants. Not that she had expected to see any in December. Had he taken some sort of hallucinogenic drug? "Try to stay still, sir," she said. "Have you had a beer or something else alcoholic to drink?"

"Only a little. I've always been a little trippy. But not on purpose, Debalito." His laugh ended in a wince. "My back was giving me fits. A swig or two makes the painkillers work better. But now I can't see very well."

"Your glasses broke, that's part of the trouble." The impact had smashed Larry's glasses and, from the looks of it, fractured his nose. "Why did you crash down here?"

"Craaaashed?" He roared out the word, then stopped and looked at her as if he'd completed the sentence. "The phone figured out who called when the road swerved. Can you get me outta here?"

Far down the highway, Bernie could see the lights of the approaching ambulance. "I can't, so just try to relax. The medics will be here soon, and they'll help you. They can do it without making anything hurt worse."

"My right arm doesn't wanna go anywhere."

She glanced at his right shoulder, which sat at the odd angle that usually meant a dislocation. "Does it hurt?"

"Not unless I try to move it." He demonstrated, grimacing with pain. "You're nice to stop to help me. Ms. Officer, could you do me a favor?"

"What is it?" She hoped it didn't involve the imaginary ants.

He swiveled his upper body, trying to look toward the back seat. "Youch. My wings are crushed."

"Your wings?"

"Yeah. Can you see if anything broke in the back seat?"

A brown box sealed with tape lay on the floor behind the front seat. "The carton slipped off onto the floor, but it doesn't look damaged. What's in it?"

"A beautiful pot." He motioned toward the floor of the passenger seat with his left hand. "Could you use that? I called her when I left the office, so push that little wart, and there you have it."

She walked around the car again and opened the passenger's-side door, looking for a phone. By lifting the floor mat, she finally found it, wedged between the mat and the door frame. She replaced the mat smoothly on the clean floor beneath it and then checked the last call. "Merilee Cruz?"

"Good-looking woman, huh? I told her I'd bring back her pot, but I can't leave the ants. Could you tell her what happened?"

"I'll dial, and then you can talk."

Bernie punched the green button to place the call, put the phone on speaker, and held it near Hoffman's mouth.

Merilee didn't even say hello. "Where are you? I've got a million things to do besides wait around for your lazy carcass."

The man didn't respond.

"You agreed to have it here in half an hour."

"I'm trapped in my car, and there's a problem with blood."

"What? Larry, you're scaring me. What's going on out there?"

You talk, he mouthed to Bernie, and turned his head away.

"Merilee, it's Officer Manuelito. Ranger Hoffman had a car accident. I'm here with him now, waiting for the ambulance."

The phone went quiet for a long moment. When Merilee spoke again, her voice had changed. "Oh dear. How bad is he?"

"I don't know. I can hear the ambulance rolling toward us now." Let the paramedics examine him, she thought, and then Hoffman can tell her his condition if he wants to.

"Good. Is Manzanares there, too?"

An odd question, Bernie thought. "No, ma'am." She looked toward the white pickup as it rolled to a stop.

Merilee hung up without a good-bye.

Bernie offered the phone to Hoffman, and he tossed it toward the passenger seat. He didn't react when the phone bounced from the seat onto the floor.

"So will you?" he said.

"Will I what?"

"That box?" She could see him struggle to find the words. "If my house rolls away, something might happen, you know?"

"You mean, when your car is towed, the box might disappear?"

Hoffman pointed over his shoulder into the back seat. "For Mamarilee. My flavor please. Remember?"

She recalled the book he'd sold her at a bargain price. The gift still sat in the trunk of her unit, awaiting Chee's return and their reunion.

She took out her phone and took a picture of the box as it rested on the back-seat floor, and a close-up that showed the address on it, that of Merilee Cruz. Then she lifted it out of the back seat, put it in the trunk of her unit, took another picture, and came back to keep an eye on Hoffman.

Some minutes later the ambulance crew members jumped out, unloaded their stretcher, and headed toward the car. Bernie felt relief course through her. Hoffman would be in good hands. Two attendants began helping Hoffman while the third spoke to her.

"Did you see what happened?" he asked.

"No. I noticed the car as I was driving by." She paused as a pickup pulled off on the shoulder and parked in front of her unit. "His right shoulder looks like it might be dislocated, and his nose is at a funny angle and bleeding. He's hallucinating, and his glasses broke."

"Is he drunk?"

"He told me he'd had a drink and some painkillers. He isn't combative."

"Anything else?"

"His name is Larry Hoffman, and he's a ranger at El Morro."

The medic thanked her. As she headed back toward her unit, she saw Manzanares, out of uniform, walking down the slope from the pickup white, toward the accident.

He stopped when he reached her. "What happened?"

"Hoffman said a phone call distracted him, and he ran off the road."

He nodded. "Clear road. No traffic. How badly injured is he?"

"You'll have to ask the ambulance crew. It looks to me like a broken nose and a dislocated shoulder. I don't know what else."

"At least he didn't hurt anybody else. If you hadn't been out here, it would have taken a while for someone to find him. Especially now that it's getting dark." Manzanares sighed. "Dumb bastard. Why are you here?"

She resented the attitude that went with the question. "I was checking out some old bones at the rescue site, and I saw a car off the road." She'd used the wrong word, she realized; Cruz had not been rescued yet. "Have you heard how much longer the search will go on?"

"I don't know, but the team is running out of places to look, and a big storm is on the way."

"Why did it take so long for the search to get started?"

"What do you mean?"

"You showed up and made the call, and then at least two hours before anything happened, before Katz arrived and got things moving."

"You know how ladies are."

"I do. Efficient and professional. Katz said she was on the road within fifteen minutes of getting the call."

"Well, then, it's a mystery, isn't it? Kind of like Cruz disappearing out here in the first place." Manzanares turned his back on her and started down the hill.

As Bernie climbed up the slope to her police car, she glared at the Dallas Cowboys bumper sticker on his truck. Another point against the man. She liked the Broncos. She started the engine and, finally, headed for Shiprock.

The highway was dark now, and only one vehicle passed her. She enjoyed this ride in the daytime, but now, especially after the hike to see the bones and the excitement of Larry's accident, she wanted to be home. Snow fell lightly now and she turned on the wipers.

At the junction with I-40, she hesitated, deciding that she had enough fuel to wait until the truck stop west of Grants. She would stretch and get some coffee, shake off the weariness she felt. From there it was about two hours to Shiprock. She heard her phone vibrate. Chee? No, it was Manzanares.

"Larry Hoffman is in the intensive care unit. Did he talk to you about a box that was in the back seat?"

"Yes. He said it was an old pot and asked me to take it to Merilee Cruz for him. I said I would because he was so concerned about it disappearing when his car was towed."

"He played you. Bad move. I found pills in a baggie under the front passenger's-side floor mat. I don't think there is a pot in that box. Or if there is, it's probably packed with drugs. What were you thinking, sweetheart?"

His condescending attitude made her bristle.

"Are you sure about the baggie?" Bernie remembered lifting the mat and replacing it. It had fit snugly, with nothing hidden beneath it.

"Of course I'm sure." Manzanares spoke with a sneer. "I didn't find a phone in the car or on him. Did you take that, too?"

"I saw him try to toss it on the passenger seat. It bounced to the floor."

"Well, don't worry about the phone. It's not your case or your jurisdiction, and I know you've got plenty to do. I'll talk to Merilee Cruz about the box and handle this." And he ended the call.

She drove on, her earlier sluggishness evaporated in the heat of Manzanares's lies. Her brain, which had been puzzling over Cruz's disappearance ever since she received Cooper's worried call, grasped some rough edges that gave her purchase on the problem at hand. She hadn't missed the drugs; they hadn't been there when she searched. That could only mean one thing. Manzanares had planted them for some reason.

Her next stop was Merilee's house. She would open the box in the woman's presence. If there were drugs in it, she'd take photos. If not, she'd ask some questions about how the pot was acquired and exactly what the Internet art business was, and see where the conversation went from there.

Hoffman had referred to the pot as "her" pot. Did that mean Merilee had purchased it from the museum shop? What if, instead, he'd had the pot on consignment there from Merilee?

By all accounts, Domingo Cruz knew the Malpais, and he hiked with his camera. What if he'd stumbled across some burials, caves of bones such as Annie had found, but with grave goods intact? It would be easy for him to photograph them as he found them, and then Merilee could market them on the Internet. Or Larry Hoffman could sell them under the counter at the monument store, preferably to visitors like the French people she met or others who didn't know or care enough about the antiquities law protecting cultural resources to ask how they happened to be at the gift shop.

The more she thought about the pot in the trunk of her unit, the more questions she had.

No lights were on in Merilee's house, and there was

304 • ANNE HILLERMAN

no vehicle in the driveway. She rang the doorbell, and when there was no answer, rapped with the big metal knocker. As she waited in the dark, snow began to fall in earnest, melting as it touched the ground. The temperature had dropped, too.

Her mind scrolled back to her encounter with Manzanares at the accident scene. He hadn't asked her to give him the box, or even to leave it at the police station for him. That reinforced her idea that the issue wasn't drugs in the box with the pot, but the pot itself. One of the searchers had mentioned that the Manzanares family ranch bordered public land. Had Dom taken the pot from the ranch? An old pot found on private land could be legally resold if it wasn't associated with a burial. One from the Malpais, with its collection of federal agency jurisdictions, was off limits, as was anything associated with the dead.

Did any of this explain why Domingo Cruz was missing? Was Merilee propping up Wings and Roots with her Internet sales?

Bernie rapped again and called for Merilee, then took an official Navajo Police business card out of her backpack. On the blank side, she wrote "Call me about Larry's box."

As she walked back to her unit, she looked over at the

greenhouse, a building about the size of a two-car garage. The lights were on, creating a warm glow. Maybe Merilee was there. Bernie opened the waist-high garden gate and walked toward the greenhouse along a path illuminated with small solar lights. Heat and moisture had steamed up the glass, but she could discern treelike shapes, faintly green through the opaqueness.

She rapped on the door. "Merilee, it's Bernie Manuelito. Are you in here?" She waited, then tried the doorknob. It turned, and she entered.

It took a minute for the loamy perfume to reach her and for her to feel the warmth and humidity. The raised beds were empty, their dark soil resting from whatever crop they had held. Large pots held rosemary and small trees bearing aromatic white blossoms and small little oranges among the shiny leaves.

Some ficus trees had yellow leaves along with the green, as she would have expected in December. Sticklike dormant plants waited for the welcome warmth and light of spring. On the wall was a timer, evidently the device that controlled the watering and the light system for the greenhouse. But no Merilee.

A heady fragrance drew her to the brugmansia. One plant, its showy yellow trumpet flowers as big as soup bowls, was fully in bloom, giving off a rich, deep perfume. Rubber gloves lay next to the plant's pot, a reminder that, like many beautiful things that grow in gardens and greenhouses, brugmansia are potentially toxic. Bernie looked around once more, and then went back into the chilly night air, closing the greenhouse door tightly against animal intruders and the cold before she hurried down the lit path to her unit. The fresh air cleared her brain after the heavy scent of the beautiful brugs.

As she drove out of the neighborhood, a dark vehicle passed her, headed in the opposite direction. She slowed, thinking it might be Merilee, but it wasn't the Mercedes she'd seen in the driveway on her first visit, but an older truck. As she watched the vehicle in her rearview mirror, it made a U-turn. The driver flashed the headlights at her and honked. She pulled to the side of the road, and the other driver stopped next to her and lowered the window.

She lowered hers, too. "Franklin. What are you doing out here?"

"Officer Manuelito, hi. I was looking for Merilee, same as you, I guess. I heard some terrible news, and I thought, well, if she didn't know, I'd break it to her."

"What?"

He brushed the snow off the truck's window frame.

"These flakes are the forerunners of a huge storm. If things are as bad as the weather service predicts, they'll be calling off the search tomorrow."

"I'm sorry to hear that."

"I thought Merilee might be able to do something since she's a blood relative. It's not right, you know." His voice began to crack. "It's just not."

Bernie turned her heater up a notch. "I was out there today with the searchers, and they looked exhausted. A break might give them more energy and ideas."

Franklin pulled a blue knit cap tighter over his ears. "I guess I can't blame them. I mean, they don't even know Dom, and they are leaving their own families at home to help find him, and the weather will make all of it more dangerous. But I hate to think of him out there in the cold, in the snow. I mean, if he's conscious, if he's still alive somehow. Or even if he's dead, his poor body . . ." He stopped and sighed. "I'm babbling. I wasn't prepared . . . I wasn't expecting—"

"I could use something to eat before I drive home," Bernie broke in. "I don't know Grants very well." She thought about suggesting a fast food place—they'd have burgers for sure—but the generic anonymity did not seem an appropriate setting in which to deal with fresh grief. She mentioned the only place she'd tried that wasn't fast food—First Street Cafe, with its view of the mountains.

Franklin nodded. "I like that place, but they don't serve dinner. I know a good family-run New Mexican spot. El Cafecito."

"Do they have hamburgers?"

"Probably so. Dom and I always get the New Mexican specials."

The restaurant featured whimsical metal lizards on the walls and smelled of simmering chile sauce. Despite Franklin's enthusiastic recommendation of chile rellenos and sopaipillas, Bernie ordered a Coke and a burger and bought coffee for Franklin, who protested that he wasn't hungry. He added three sugars to his cup but barely touched it. Under the restaurant's bright lights, his nails looked ragged, and there were dark circles under his eyes.

"Have you slept since Dom disappeared?"

He shook his head. "Every time I'm about to nod off, I think of him, and I wonder if he's cold, if he's hungry, desperate for water, you know."

"I wish I had met him. Tell me about him."

Franklin talked as she ate. He reinforced what she already knew: Domingo Cruz was both nervous and excited about the opportunity to become director of the Wings and Roots, but he hadn't made a firm decision yet. If he took the job, Franklin explained, he'd miss the direct work with the kids, but he wanted to make sure the organization continued. "I believe he'll stay because he thinks the best way to solve the problem is to become the director."

"What's the problem?"

"Dom didn't talk specifics, but I know they need money. Every nonprofit group in the country is hurting because of the economy. Dom always pushed for Wings and Roots to work with all the students who need the help, not only the ones whose parents can afford the price. Sometimes, if a student wanted to be part of the program and her relatives couldn't pay, he'd contribute to the tuition. All quietly, of course. He didn't want any attention." Franklin shifted onto one hip and pulled a handkerchief out of his back pocket to blow his nose. "I told him he couldn't afford to do it, but he said he'd get by. And he always did."

"How much does he give?"

"He put in three hundred dollars once." Franklin chuckled. "We ate a lot of beans that month."

Bernie put her burger down. "I saw some of his photos at Merilee's house. They are beautiful."

"He got interested in photography as part of a teacher training program he took at the New Mexico State University branch college here. He uses a camera, not a cell phone, to take photos. He's excited about the book he and his sister are working on, a collection of some of his pictures. Even though he was exhausted, he'd stay behind after every trip to the Malpais to get some shots. When Merilee told him she was having trouble coming up with money for publication, he stopped for a while and fell into a funk. He went back to taking photographs this fall, and it seemed to lift his spirits."

"Does he specialize in petroglyphs?"

"No, but he likes to take pictures of them. He said it was interesting to see how they almost disappeared, depending on the light. He said the idea of standing where the ancient ones had stood when they made the drawings gave him a great appreciation for the past."

"Did he ever mention anything about graves?"

"No. Not to me. We don't talk about that kinda stuff. I think the dead should be left alone."

"Agreed." Bernie sipped her Coke. "Did Dom share that view?"

"Dom doesn't spend much energy thinking about the ones who have left us; he focuses on the future. That's why he loves working with kids. When we'd argue about something, he used to say that the past is the past, and we can't change it. If we want a better future, we have to work with the present." Franklin looked at his coffee cup. "He always tells me to make each day count and consider it a gift. I had to remind him of that when he was feeling down about the agency and all the debt."

Watching Franklin's throat vibrate as he swallowed, she gave him time to rein in his emotions. "Do you think Dom could have been mixed up in something dangerous?"

"Dangerous? Just being out there was dangerous. Other than that, no."

"I'm just trying to consider all possibilities."

Bernie took the last bite of her burger. They sat quietly, like old friends, and she watched the waitress clear a table across the room. The restaurant was nearly empty. Closing time.

Franklin broke the silence. "When Dom and I first met, he took me for a hike out there in the lava field. It was late April. He showed me some petroglyphs and said they had probably been left by the relatives of someone from Acoma or Zuni. We ate lunch and listened to the wind. He told me that was his special place, where he always felt peaceful. I felt safe with him. Wherever he was, when I was with him, it was my special place. We'd come out here on weekends and stay in my little house in San Rafael. Without him, if he's gone, I don't have a safe place. They can't stop the search and leave him out there tonight." Franklin bolted to standing.

Bernie put her hand on his arm. "I can call Katz right now, and you can tell her what you know about how to find that place. If they haven't already looked there, they—"

Franklin pulled away. With one quick motion he zipped his jacket and tossed a five-dollar bill on the table.

"Wait for me to pay and—"

Bernie stopped. He'd already run to the door and disappeared into the night.

18

Bernie hurried into her coat, leaving her last twenty for the meal and the tip; she couldn't wait for change. By the time she reached the parking lot, Franklin was gone, the taillights of his truck red beacons growing smaller in the falling snow. As she ran for her unit, she watched him turn left onto Grants' main street, toward the on-ramps to Interstate 40 and, beyond that, the eastern side of the Malpais.

As she put her backpack on the seat, Bernie felt her cell phone vibrate. Mama, Darleen, Leaphorn, even Chee—whoever it was would have to wait. She clicked on her seat belt, started the engine, and radioed the local law enforcement that she was in pursuit of a distraught Navajo man driving a black Ford pickup.

"You're aware of the weather conditions?"

"Yes, that's part of my concern." She gave the dispatcher Franklin's name and description.

"You know about the ongoing search out there for the missing person?"

"Yes."

"Be careful. Make sure they don't end up looking for you, too."

Her first judgment call came as she neared the freeway entrance. She could get on I-40 West here, head toward Gallup, and then get off at the San Rafael exit, which accessed the west side of the Malpais and also was closer to the house Franklin and Cruz shared in San Rafael on weekends. But her instincts told her to keep going straight toward the badlands, straight to the area where the search for Cruz was based.

The bridge over the freeway had started to ice, but it wasn't slick yet. Traffic on the interstate was surprisingly heavy; the storm must have caught the truckers off guard. Snow had accumulated on the edges of the highway, but the paved roadway was wet, not icy, at least not yet. She experimented with increasing her speed until she found the right level, as fast as possible without undue risk. The wipers set a steady rhythm for her thoughts and did a decent job of clearing the swirl of rapidly falling snow.

She should never have mentioned suicide to Franklin. He was partially unglued already, judging not only by his unkempt looks but by his tears and impulsiveness. His mental stability had been hanging by a thread, and her questions might have taken him to a dark place.

She'd spent too many nights talking to cops, she decided. She knew that words had consequences; that was why the Holy People had taught the Navajo to use them wisely and with restraint. Talking about the negative, as she had done, brought it into the forefront, like inviting evil into the hogan, into your living room. She was only talking, not thinking. Talking too much, a little too proud, a little too full of herself. All behaviors the Holy People warned against.

The snow came down more heavily now, fast enough that her wipers struggled to keep the windshield clean. A slick spot on the highway slid her unit across the yellow shoulder line. She automatically took her foot off the gas, eased back into the proper lane, and focused her full attention on driving. The wall of falling snow in front of her made it hard to see the directional signs indicating curves and switchbacks and intersecting roads until she was on top of them, but she had driven this way often enough recently to know when to slow down. She peered through the windshield, looking for Franklin's taillights, seeing only a moving curtain of white.

She watched for the junctions. Seeing no tracks at the road that went to the closed BLM ranger station or to the Sandstone Bluffs entrance a few miles farther south, she continued toward La Ventana Natural Arch, looking for Franklin's truck beside the road. The snow made it harder to see if another vehicle had come this way, or if she was driving through a layer that was undisturbed.

Franklin hadn't had that much of a head start. If he were driving much faster than she, she would have seen his truck—or its tracks—in a skid off the highway. She looked at the clock on the dashboard and decided she'd give the road another ten minutes, unless she got to the arch parking area first. If she didn't spot him there or before, she would admit that she'd made the wrong call and he was on the road to San Rafael, the highway on the west side of the badlands. In that case, he had too much of a head start for her to find him, and she'd quit worrying and head home.

The snow was falling even more heavily now, sparkling white. Headlights approached from the south, hopefully in the opposite lane. The distance between them closed. It was a big truck pulling a trailer, moving cautiously through the storm and staying in its own lane.

She pulled into the Ventana parking lot to turn around, finding no tracks, only beautiful unbroken snow. On another night, if the moon were shining and the blizzard had ended, she would have climbed out to see the sandstone arch covered with snow. She turned the unit around to head back toward Grants, disappointment weighing on her. Franklin must have gone the other way. Maybe he'd done the smart thing and gone home to bed. When her phone buzzed, and she saw it was Mama, she stayed in the parking lot, put the unit in park, and took the call.

"Daughter, I'm waiting for you to take me to the grocery store."

Bernie sucked in her breath. She knew she had told Mama she couldn't help her tonight. "Oh, I'm sorry. I've had some crises at work. Those things soaked up my time, and I forgot to call you." She didn't get into the specifics of Franklin's despondency or Larry's accident. "We will go as soon as I can. Did you have something for dinner, Mama?"

"I don't know."

"Are you hungry?"

"No. Mrs. Darkwater came over, and we watched that show on TV, you know, where people try to guess words and spin the big wheel. She brought some applesauce, and we had that too, for dessert. It was good, but not as good as those brownies I like."

Mrs. Darkwater, Mama's closest neighbor, had become a friend to her and an auntie for Bernie. Mama usually didn't like talking on the phone, but tonight was different. Bernie turned up the heater a notch, put the phone on speaker, and shifted into drive.

Mama chatted on, telling her about Mrs. Darkwater's grandson and how he was making a volcano for his science project. Then she talked again about her weaving student and her slow but steady progress. Bernie drove faster now, pushing the unit against the storm, convinced that Franklin had taken a different route.

Mama finished bragging on her student and told Bernie again about the applesauce and the TV show. Then, "Did you talk to your sister?"

"Yes. Her program is over on Friday. A few more days, that's all, and then she'll be home."

"I miss her." Mama paused. "You sound far away. Where are you?"

"I put you on the speakerphone, Mama, that's why I sound different. I'm out by Grants, but I'm heading back to Shiprock now."

"That is a long drive, daughter. Be careful. I saw on TV that a storm is coming. I think it is good that we did not go shopping tonight. Will your husband be home soon?"

"I hope so."

Mama ended the call. Bernie felt a pang of anxiety about the conversation, but she filed it away to consider later.

The snow continued with a vengeance. New Mexico needed the moisture, a beautiful gift, but she wished it had waited until she could snuggle warmly in bed. She turned her wipers on to high and slowed down a little more. Her earlier tire tracks had disappeared, along with the center line. She used the reflectors along the side of the road to navigate.

Keeping the interstate highway open during a storm took precedence, so she hoped that a plow and sand truck had already been out to scrape the asphalt. Less-traveled roads like the one she was on now were a lower priority. On the Navajo Nation, most roads were un-paved, and snow removal usually consisted of neighbors with plows on their trucks or, more often, the emergence of the sun and warmer days. That created another problem. Every year she rescued people whose vehicles had gotten stuck in cold, deep mud.

Except for the truck and trailer she'd encountered,

no vehicle had passed her in either direction. Even though she was almost sure Franklin had taken the other road—the one she wasn't on—she watched for a vehicle parked off the road. She slowed down as she reached the turnoff for the Acoma-Zuni trailhead, remembering that this was where the trailer had passed her. If Franklin had parked here, she would have missed him. She looked closely as she drove past. Did she see a vehicle, or was it only a reflection from the snow?

She tapped the brakes, feeling the unit slide before the tires found traction. She backed up until her headlights caught the entrance road. A set of tracks was faintly visible in the snow: someone had turned here. She drove in. Her headlights reflected off a glint of glass and chrome—a snow-covered truck. Franklin had parked his dark vehicle behind a cluster of piñon trees at the spot closest to the trailhead and farthest from the highway. She pulled in next to it.

The hood of the truck was still warm, and the driver's door was locked. Bernie shined her flashlight inside. Franklin wasn't there, but the winter jacket he had been wearing earlier was on the seat. His hat and gloves were on the floor. She studied the snow with her flashlight until she found the smooth prints of his cowboy boot soles, then called in the situation to local law enforcement, put the space blanket from her trunk in her backpack, and pulled on her knit cap and her gloves, all the while envisioning Franklin out in the blizzard, cold but safe.

The trail, a single track in the dirt, was marked by rock cairns. It would have been a challenge to follow in any circumstances. Now, about six inches of snow had accumulated, and even with her boots the flat stretch at the beginning held some challenge. Using her flashlight to hunt for Franklin's footprints and for obstacles now buried beneath the relentless snow, she followed his faint tracks, thankful that he stayed on what must be the narrow path of the trail.

She remembered hiking this way once with Chee in the spring, and how the trail started out heading toward the lava, then made a surprising turn to the right and edged along the flow before climbing through the rugged black rock. That had been several years before, and in the daylight, but she hoped the route had wedged itself in her memory, to be accessed if needed.

The snow had begun to settle in little drifts against the base of rocks and trees. After about ten minutes of walking, she called to Franklin. There was no response from the darkness. Then she saw a place where someone, probably Franklin, had slipped.

The snowflakes melted against Bernie's cheeks,

tickled her eyelashes. Her hands and toes were cold, and the wind pushed the frigid air through her jacket. She nearly tripped over a log made invisible by the snow, and as she waited to catch her breath, she noticed another disruption in the snow's surface. Franklin had fallen here. She walked faster, hoping that if he collapsed somewhere, she could find him in the blizzard. The dark night and the intensity of the snowfall were disorienting, conditions that made it easy to get lost in a dangerous place. She was glad she'd left the emergency lights flashing on her unit, a beacon to guide her back.

Now, when she scanned the snow for Franklin's boot prints, she couldn't see them, only the way the snow had drifted over the trail. She walked on. Still nothing.

"Franklin? Franklin! It's Bernie. Are you out here?"

She continued, using the snow-covered rock piles as guides, but his prints didn't reappear. Either the blizzard had buried them or he had turned off the trail somewhere, and she'd missed the place. She called again, listened. The wind stopped, and her chilled bones rejoiced, but the only thing she heard was silence. She called again, listened to the hush of the flakes landing on piñon needles, sage, and lava rock.

Her face was numb now, and her toes barely responded when she tried to wiggle them. She couldn't risk becoming another job for the search team. Saying a silent prayer for Franklin, she turned back; she'd pay more attention to the sides of the trail now, for places he could have headed off into the lava. She had walked only a few minutes when she noticed faint depressions in the snow away from the trail to the west. An animal? Maybe. She looked at the prints more closely, and then for landmarks to help her find the spot to connect back to the parking lot trail, spotting a lone snow-covered tree that leaned to the right. Not much, but it would have to do.

She remembered how he'd been dressed at the restaurant, only a long-sleeve denim shirt and jeans under the jacket she'd spotted in his truck. If she felt chilled now, as warmly dressed as she was, he must be close to frozen.

She called again as she set out, stepping in the indents that might be his tracks. Adrenaline energized her, and she forgot her cold feet and hands, focusing closely on the rapidly disappearing path she hoped Franklin had made. The deepening snow crept over the top of her hiking boots and sifted in to melt against her socks.

At first, it sounded like an animal, maybe a rabbit in distress or a fox. The sound wasn't exactly anything she'd heard before. It stirred ancestral memories of shape-shifting creatures that roamed the earth at night, causing trouble. She stopped, her heart racing. It came again, and this time it sounded human.

"Franklin?"

She heard the sound a third time, and then something heartbreaking, muffled by the snow. It could have been her own name.

19

Bernie nearly stumbled over him, sprawled in the snow-covered lava, his arms folded over his chest.

"You're not dying tonight," she told him. "You're coming with me."

She supported Franklin to a sitting position and then slowly to standing, the emergency blanket from her pack wrapped around his shoulders. His soaked clothing had already started to stiffen. It wouldn't have been long before hypothermia set in. She put her warm hat over his icy ears and assisted him on the cold, slick walk to her unit. The challenge and the stress helped her forget about her numb toes and frozen hands.

When they finally reached the parking area, she asked Franklin about the keys to his truck so she could unlock the vehicle and extract his coat, hat, and gloves.

He stared at her without responding. She felt his pockets but didn't find the keys.

She opened the trunk to get the extra blankets and energy bars she kept in case of emergencies, pushing aside the cardboard box the ranger had entrusted to her. That encounter seemed like weeks ago, not just that afternoon.

After helping Franklin in, Bernie started the engine and waited what seemed like forever for the orange needle to float up to the C and then a touch beyond it. Finally she cranked up the heat to maximum as Franklin shivered in the seat next to her.

"Sit on your hands to help warm them up," she said. His face was ashen, but a warmer shade of gray than when she had discovered him, partly covered in snow with the big flakes melting on the bare skin of his face and neck.

"I wanted to da-da-die there." The bone-deep cold made his teeth chatter. "Ba-ba-but when I heard you calling, I had taaaa-to answer."

When the unit grew warmer, she persuaded him to remove his soaked shirt and gave him one of the soft, warm blankets for his bare shoulders. She poured some lukewarm coffee from her thermos into a cup and held it while he drank so his shaking hands wouldn't spill it.

"That tastes terrible."

She laughed. "Did your grandmother forget to teach you any manners?"

"My *shimásání* is gone. Dom must be dead, too."

Everything she could think of saying in response sounded clichéd. She changed the subject. "Do you know where the keys are to your truck?"

"I dropped them in the snow. I left my coat in the car so it would be dry for Dom if I found him. My hat and gloves, too. I thought he would need . . ." Franklin left the thought suspended in the winter air, and they sat with the pain, raw and deep.

After a while she offered him an energy bar. "Eat this. You could use the calories. Then try to relax. We need to go before the roads get any worse. Would you like me to take you to the hospital?"

"No. I'll be fine. I want to go home. You're ca-ca-cold too, aren't you? Here, take your hat back."

"I'm OK. I'll drive, you rest. You don't need to talk. Think of a warm, safe place."

Franklin wrapped the blanket more tightly around his bare shoulders.

"I always feel safe with Dom. He's my anchor, you know, strong, smart, kind. And now . . ." Bernie heard a choked sob.

"Franklin, you weren't meant to die out there. That's the reason I found you."

She stopped talking to give driving her total focus. In the long minutes she had spent finding Franklin and getting him to her unit, NM 117 had accumulated enough snow to force her to slow down even more drastically. The blizzard made each curve a driving test, and the gusty wind created periodic whiteouts. She could see only as far as the place ahead where her headlights penetrated the wall of falling snow.

From the corner of her eye, she watched Franklin tug the blanket around himself. "If I'm cold sitting in this car with the heat on and wearing your hat and everything, imagine how Dom must feel. I hope he's dead. That's better than suffering." He let out a low sob. "No, no, I don't mean that."

"Shhhh. Rest." She drove with both hands on the wheel, using the reflectors along the roadside to make sure her unit stayed on the pavement, headed in the right direction.

After what seemed like forever, she came to the overpass that led to the interstate. She relaxed a tiny bit when she saw that the highway department had not erected the road-closed barriers—not yet. She expected the bridge to be slick, and it was. She stayed in the center and then eased onto the four-lane highway heading west to Grants. Her passenger sat up straight, staring unblinkingly ahead, watching the storm and the trucks that crept along. She appreciated his silence.

She heard the radio squawk, and Franklin flinched.

"Manuelito, where are you?" It was the rookie, Officer Wilson Sam.

He chuckled when she told him. "No kidding? The interstate is closed west of Grants because of the storm. A truck overturned, and it's blocking both lanes. You won't make it back tonight."

"I guess not. Is the captain there?"

"No. He told me to check with you before he went home, but I just got around to it. How bad is it out there?"

"It's snowing hard. The wind was fierce earlier, but it's calmer now, only occasional gusts." She didn't think of weather as good or bad. Storms were an expected component of winter at 6,000 feet on the Colorado Plateau, and blizzards came with the territory. Wind, slush, mud, drought, rain—it all had a purpose in the way the Holy People had designed Dinétah, the Navajo universe.

"No snow here in Shiprock yet. Any news on the lost guy? You know that sighting of somebody who might have been your man Cruz? Turned out he was somebody else."

"They suspended the search because of weather. A friend of Mr. Cruz was out searching tonight and ran into some trouble. He's in the unit with me now." She talked on, not offering the rookie the opportunity to say anything critical of Franklin or Cruz or the searchers. "Tell the captain I'll be back as soon as the highway reopens. I'll check in when I leave Grants."

"I'll let him know." The rookie laughed. "I don't know what you did to attract Councilor Walker's attention, but she acts like you're her new best friend. She called for you several times and wouldn't leave a message and doesn't want to talk to me or anybody except you and the captain."

"That's interesting." Both the captain and Sandra knew her cell number and used cautious judgment in deciding who to release it to. Obviously Councilor Walker's behavior had not met their high standards. "Anything else I should know?"

"The new FBI came by. She looks like a California surfer girl wearing a business suit. She was asking about that car bomb that killed that dude at the high school, so I filled her in. She was happy to have the information."

Bernie remembered, with residual annoyance, the way the rookie had second-guessed her commands that night when the two of them had to handle crowd control and protect the crime scene until backup arrived.

She turned the heater down a notch. It felt as warm in the car as in Merilee's greenhouse.

"And Largo asked me to look over that budget stuff you picked up from Cooper, remember that?" He didn't wait for her to respond. "He looked on your desk, in the vertical files, everywhere he could think of, but it was nowhere, and he was ticked off. So I guess that job boomerangs back to you."

She knew exactly where the files were. In her trunk. She hadn't had time to leave them at the office, and Largo should have remembered that. "Is that it?"

"Good luck finding a room out there. I heard the hotels in Grants are full, and they're putting people up at the high school gym until the interstate reopens. Lucky you're short. You can sleep in the unit."

She exhaled, breathing out her irritation. Sandra, Officer Bigman, even Captain Largo, would have offered to make some calls to find her a motel room at the discounted law enforcement rate. The rookie reminded her of the annoying little brother she was glad she never had. She shook her head once to get rid of the frustration and focused on driving.

Truckers heading west to Gallup, Flagstaff, Kingman, and beyond took I-40 through New Mexico's red rocks and lava as their preferred route. Tonight, the big trucks moved at a glacial pace toward the exits. Passenger vehicles, buses, pickups pulling horse trailers, and drivers who seemed to have never encountered snow before added to the confusion. Her unit's wipers handled the test fairly well, although ice had begun to accumulate on the blade on the passenger side. She leaned toward the windshield for a better view as she passed a car on the shoulder with its emergency flashers on, the driver scraping her windshield and thumping the wiper blades against the glass to clear the ice.

Bernie was concentrating so hard on the other drivers, the weather, and the challenges of the road that Franklin's voice startled her.

"I'm sorry for all the trouble. I didn't expect you to follow me. I mean, you really don't even know me. You could have gotten hurt out there in the lava."

"I was concerned about you because of the way you rushed out of the restaurant."

"You know, Dom did the same to me. We had an argument right before he left on the Wings and Roots trip. I said some things I shouldn't have, but he was working himself to death. I told him he should only focus on photography—that was what he loved—and work with kids as a volunteer or something."

"And what did he say?"

"Nothing. He just stormed away from the house without a good-bye." Franklin looked out the window at the snow. "Earlier he said his photography had led to problems, and he wished I hadn't even brought it up."

"What problems?"

"I don't know." Franklin sighed. "I was so angry I didn't even ask."

"The only pictures of his I've seen are of petroglyphs. Does he do other things?"

"Oh, yes. All kinds of photos. Landscapes intrigue him the most."

"I'd like to see them sometime. But for now, could you do me a favor?"

"If I can."

"My phone is in my backpack, on the floor behind you. Can you make a call for me?"

Franklin pulled the backpack into the front seat.

"It's in the side pocket."

She saw the flash of light as the phone came on.

"All set. Now what?"

"Go to contacts, and you'll see Chee."

He scrolled through the list. "Got him."

"He's my husband. He knows I'm working out here, and he always watches the news and the weather reports—"

She stopped, her attention caught by the steady beat of taillights on emergency flash reflected in the snow on the shoulder, where a small sedan sat beside the interstate at an odd angle. She turned on her own light bar and pulled in behind it. "I'll be right back."

Franklin lifted her jacket off his lap. "You'll need this." His fingers felt cool but not ice cold, as he handed it to her. "Would you like your cap now?"

"You keep it." She zipped up her jacket and climbed out into the night. She stretched her back a moment before she put on gloves, grabbed her flashlight, and closed the unit's door. It felt good to be standing. The frigid air sharpened her brain.

The snow hid the ice on the road, and she nearly lost her balance as she hurried to the stranded car. Snow covered the windows, enough to tell her it had been parked for a while. She knocked on the driver's side and yelled, "Anyone in there? You OK?" No answer.

She brushed off the snow and shone the light into the little sedan. The car was empty.

She said a little prayer of gratitude as she cautiously made her way back to the unit.

Fastening her seat belt, she noticed that Franklin had set her phone down on the car seat and had his own up to his ear.

". . . cold and embarrassed, but I'm here." A pause and then, "I'm with Officer Manuelito, you know, the Navajo cop." He stopped to listen. "I'll ask her."

He put the phone in his lap. "Merilee wants us to come by. She says the storm is supposed to keep up until after midnight. She's inviting us to stay with her."

"Put your phone on speaker so I can talk to her."

He pushed on the screen and then held it closer to her mouth.

"Merilee, tell me about the pot."

The voice on the phone sounded far away. "Bernie, you two should sleep at my house tonight. All the motels are full because of the interstate being closed, and Franklin's road will be a disaster. And you can drop off the box."

"Tell me about the pot and your connection to Hoffman." Bernie put more steel into the request.

The phone was silent for a moment. "I asked him to sell it on consignment for me, but then I changed my mind. He was on his way to return it to me when you . . ." Static interupted her. ". . . him . . ."

"Merilee?" Bernie waited for a response until the distinctive fade-away chimes came on to mark a lost signal. She pushed the phone back toward Franklin.

He squirmed to slip it back in his pants pocket. "If

the weather was better, you could stay at my place tonight but it's way out Cholla Road, and with all this snow we'd never make it. Merilee has a lot of room."

"I'll drop you off there. I need to give her the pot, and there are some other things I need to talk to her about."

She drove through the curtain of snow, inching along with visibility no farther than the end of her headlights.

Franklin adjusted the heater vents. "Do you still want me to call your husband?"

"No, by now he would have made some calls, and he'll know how bad the roads are. I'll catch him later." Or, she thought, he'd gone to bed blissfully unaware of the blizzard.

Bernie followed a line of trucks to ease her unit off the interstate at the next exit and took Franklin's directions to Merilee's house, the unit sliding and slipping. Maybe luck would be with her, Bernie thought, and the interstate would reopen by the time she had talked to Merilee about the pot and the website with Cruz's photo. She didn't mind driving in the snow, but she was tired.

"Did you and Cruz visit Merilee often?"

"No. Not at all. The two of them are friendly, but not cordial. Dom is thoughtful, analytical. Merilee jumps in with both feet and then tries to figure out what's next. I think not knowing what their clans are or why they were put up for adoption has left some, you know, issues for both of them."

"How did you meet?"

"I met Domingo through his sister. I'd done some carpentry work for her back before her husband died, custom cabinets she'd seen in a magazine. She introduced me to Dom. She asked her brother to come by and give her some ideas for the kitchen while I was there. And, well, one thing led to another." She heard the smile in his voice. "Merilee is a powerful woman. I always tease Dom that she got the energy and the good looks and he got the brains and the big heart."

The streets of Grants were deserted. Families would be hunkering down in the face of the ongoing storm—parents watching the news, wondering if schools would be closed the next day. It took Bernie longer to reach Merilee's house than she'd expected. This time, even from a distance she could see warm light shining from the windows.

"Watch it!" Franklin yelled at the same time she saw the big coyote lope directly in front of the unit. She just tapped the brakes, but even the small change in momentum put the unit into a skid. She tried to correct, to steer and cajole it back to the street, but conditions worked against her; the snow was too deep and the angle too sharp. The car slid off the road at the edge of Merilee's driveway and skidded down a short embankment. The coyote stopped, watched, and then disappeared into the blizzard.

After a few futile tries, Bernie realized that the vehicle couldn't extricate itself and radioed for help. The dispatcher sympathized and told her what she already knew: all available tow trucks and wreckers were in use, but they'd get to her as soon as they could. She gave Bernie the direct phone number of the service they used.

Franklin, unlike many men she knew, sat quietly while she struggled to get the unit unstuck, only speaking after she'd radioed in her problem.

"Well, I guess you'll have to leave the police car here for now." He pushed the blanket from his bare shoulders and reached for his shirt. "I'm glad we made it this far. Let's go."

"Wait. Put that back on. You don't have a coat, remember? And your shirt will still be soaked."

"I feel like a fool in this thing." But he kept the blanket.

They walked past the Range Rover in the driveway, crowned with at least six inches of sparkling snow. Before Bernie could ring the bell, Merilee opened the front door.

"Michael Franklin! You could be a refugee or home-less. What in the world happened to you?"

"Oh, I went for a hike in the snow and we just slid off the road because of the blizzard, but I'm fine. Thanks to Bernie here."

"Come on in, you two. Warm up. Would you like tea, soup, coffee, something hot?"

"Sure, whatever—some of everything." Franklin pulled the blanket around him. "I'm chilled to the soul."

"Thanks," Bernie said. "I have some questions for you."

"I know you do. Warm up a bit. It's brutal out there. Is your car damaged?"

"No, but I had to call for a tow."

Franklin followed Merilee down the hall to the kitchen, leaving sloshy footprints. Bernie knocked the snow off her boots on the welcome mat, took off her coat and gloves, and put them on a bench by the front door. The petroglyph picture in the entryway was gone now. In its place Merilee had hung a large color pho-tograph of magpies, their wings glowing blue-black and their ebony heads shiny in the sunlight. One of the birds sat on a wire fence, and the others looked as though they had just taken flight. The hogback forma-tion near Farmington towered in the background.

As Bernie entered the kitchen, Merilee motioned her to a seat at the counter next to Franklin. She put a red teakettle on her black stovetop and turned on the heat beneath it, took a plate with cheese and grapes out of the refrigerator, and found some napkins in a drawer. Then she returned and stood in front on Bernie.

"Do you want to talk now, or warm up and relax a little first? You both look like you've had a long day."

Franklin reached for a grape. "I don't want to think about anything right now."

Bernie looked down. Residual snow from her hiking boots had fallen onto Merilee's sparking floor and begun to melt. "Let's talk now. I'd like to get business out of the way, so if the tow truck comes, I can head back to Shiprock when the roads open. By the way, what happened to Dom's photo that you had in the entrance hall?"

"Oh, I took it down. I took them all down. I like to rotate the art. These that replaced them are his work, too."

"I saw one of your brother's photos on an Indian antiquities website. Tell me—"

Merilee picked up the thread. "Oh yeah, that was a failed experiment."

Bernie shifted a little on the stool. "There's a Navajo Nation Council member who thinks something fishy is going on with the Wings and Roots funding. Dom is her main suspect because he works as the organization's fund-raiser. She isn't convinced his getting lost before he was scheduled to become the program director is coincidence."

"That's crazy talk." Merilee turned to Franklin. "Right?"

Franklin nodded. "Dom would never do anything to hurt the program. He put some of his savings in to keep it going."

"The board was looking forward to having him as the director." Merilee sounded angry. "I couldn't have voted on his appointment, of course, because of the nepotism rules, but I know all my colleagues thought he would do a fine job. That councilor is flat wrong. Dom would never—"

The shrill whistle of the teakettle interrupted her, and she turned to the stove. When she spoke again, she'd regained her composure. "I've got tea, hot chocolate, instant coffee, and decaf." She phrased it like a question.

"I'll have some hot chocolate." Franklin shifted on the stool. "Dom loves the program. He likes working with kids, but he was ready for a change. Being director would be easier in some ways. He and Cooper get along great, and she told him she'd help with the transition."

"Bernie, how about you? A cup of tea?"

Tea? She shivered at the thought. "Oh, no thanks, only some water for now."

Merilee filled a glass and gave the water to Bernie. She took a swallow before she spoke. "I have another question for you. How much progress had you and Dom made on that book of his photographs?"

"I'm exploring it, but as fine a photographer as he is, he's an unknown. We created a prototype, and I've been showing it to publishers, but no luck. I would have to pay for the book myself. That's expensive. I'm still looking into options, but I need money to do it."

Franklin glanced up, his voice tinged with surprise. "Dom thought the book was still in the works. That's why he kept knocking himself out, going to the Malpais to get more shots, better photos, different lighting, all that. When were you going to tell him about the money?"

Merilee's face clouded. "I kept thinking I could figure out a way to write a grant or something. I hadn't told him about the problem yet because I knew it would be hard for him to swallow. He's got enough on his mind with the Wings and Roots finances."

Bernie broke in. "So, were you selling Native artifacts with fake provenances to help finance the book and to keep Wings and Rocks afloat?"

Merilee shook her head, her dark hair swinging from

side to side. "No. Of course not. All I sold, or tried to sell, through my online art business were Dom's photos. Why did you even ask me that?"

"I'm trying to make sense of Dom's disappearance."

Merilee sighed. "I can't understand it. Are you having any luck?"

"Well, because he's so familiar with the area, I'm thinking he may have disappeared on purpose because of something questionable he got involved with. Or he did something or knew something that made someone angry enough to hurt him." But even as she said that, Bernie dismissed the second option. If someone wanted Cruz dead, there were many easier places to kill him.

Merilee went to the sink, and they sat in silence while she cleaned up, or perhaps collected her thoughts. The little containers that had been on the counter when Bernie first visited were missing. "What happened to the herbs?" she asked.

"I gave them to Mayfair. She wanted them for some recipes."

"They came from your greenhouse, right? I looked for you in there when I stopped by this afternoon to drop off the pot. I saw those white angel trumpets. Impressive. Amazing to see them blooming this time of year."

"I've encouraged them." Merilee wiped a damp spot

off the countertop with a napkin. "I found the card you left in the door. I must have been at the hospital with poor Larry. I've got some apricot trumpets and pink ones that are almost done blooming."

Angel trumpets had been one of Bernie's favorite plants when she was a college student. In the dry, windy Southwest, the big, showy flowers survive best in botanic gardens or in the hands of devoted fans with greenhouses.

"The flowers remind me a little of datura," Franklin said.

"I guess you could call them clan sisters." Bernie readjusted herself on the seat. "But datura is hardier."

Merilee smiled. "Most people aren't that interested in plants."

"I think botany is fascinating. The variety, the adaptability, the beauty, the toughness of some plants and the fragility of others. From those great redwoods in California to the little mountain orchids we have in the Lukachukais. They are amazing."

Franklin held his mug of hot chocolate in both hands. "Ladies, I'm like most people. I'll eat my veggies and smell the roses, but I don't care much about how they grow. As of now, I hardly care about anything except sleep. I'd like to go to bed."

Merilee switched her attention to Franklin as if suddenly remembering he sat there. "You look cold, Michael. What happened to your coat and your shirt?"

"The snow soaked my shirt, and it's out in Bernie's police car, stuck in a snowdrift. I left my coat back in the truck."

"That's inconvenient. You're lucky you didn't get frostbite. Are your fingers and toes alive?"

"My fingers are stiff and cold and tingling a little. My toes ache."

"Take off your shoes, and I'll loan you some warm socks. You can sleep down the hall in the guest room." Merilee smiled at Bernie. "You're welcome to the bed in the office."

"No, I can't stay. I'll just wait for the tow truck."

Merilee shrugged. "Well then, make yourself at home. I'm going to tuck Michael in, close the blinds, and turn on some music for you in the living room. I'll be back, and then I'll show you the pot in the box and answer your questions. If you decide you want something hot, I keep the chocolate packets in that center drawer. There are tea bags and coffee pods in there, too, for the coffeemaker." She indicated the fancy machine near the stove.

Then she padded down the hall, Franklin following, the blanket dragging behind him like an oversize cape. "Tuck him in" sounded like what you say to a child, and poor Franklin looked the part.

Bernie realized that, like Franklin, she was exhausted. She could hear music now, jazz with a lot of drums and timpani. The drums made her remember how her phone had been vibrating when she rushed out to find Franklin. But first she reconsidered Merilee's offer of coffee and found the pods in a drawer, selecting one called Goodnight Mocha Blend—coffee and chocolate. The bag of small dark seeds that had been in there, too, on top of some neatly folded blue dish towels, was gone.

A sound like a bird call came from the back of the house. A few minutes later, the music out of the speakers in the living room grew louder.

The coffee pod slid into the machine without effort. Bernie pressed the button, and the machine went to work with a soft whirring noise. After the coffee, she would go out to the frozen car to retrieve the box, the binder from Cooper at Wings and Roots, and the files Walker had left for review. She would bring in the damp shirt so Franklin would have it, and she could take back her emergency blanket. She would radio for a highway update, although judging from the flakes falling outside Merilee's window, the interstate must still closed. Until the tow truck came, she was stuck in Grants anyway.

That bothered her. Spending the night in a Merilee's house—especially when Merilee might be a suspect in whatever shady business Hoffman had been dishing out—wasn't proper law enforcement procedure. Too bad her top preference, sleeping in her own bed with Chee next to her, wasn't available.

She went to the entryway and brought her phone and backpack into the kitchen. She fished the phone out of her backpack and called Chee.

He sounded groggy. "Hi there. I thought you'd forgotten about me. Where are you? I hope you aren't stuck in the storm somewhere?"

"I'm safe in Grants. Do you want to go back to sleep?"

"Not when I can talk to you. What's going on?"

She filled him in on the road closure, her unit's misadventure, and other crucial details. "I feel uncomfortable staying here when I haven't figured out how Merilee is involved in all this."

"What choice do you have? Relax until the tow truck comes. Just be glad that you found a warm place to wait, and you're not freezing in the blizzard. Your only other option is sleeping in your unit. Promise me you won't do that. Just sit on the couch in that house and wait for the tow, and relax a little. If the truck gets there before morning, you can see if they have a spare bed at the women's prison."

"I don't like this situation."

Chee chuckled. "Do you remember back when we first met, and you were so embarrassed because you slid off the road in the mud and I had to rescue you? You didn't like that much either."

"Don't remind me. Let's talk about something else. What's new with you?"

"Well, did I tell you about George Curley? The poor guy took a landscaping job, and no one has seen him since."

20

As she listened to Chee tell how George Curley's mother-in-law assumed the man had become a Navajo policeman, Bernie heard a noise, the crunch of tires in snow. A tow truck? Could she be that lucky? Lights from outside reflected steadily on the tile floor, indicating that the vehicle had stopped. She built a scenario: the driver wisely assessing the situation from the warmth of his cab, figuring the best angle to park his truck for the tow. She'd go out and talk to him as soon as Chee finished telling her about grumpy old Mrs. Vigil.

But no, the roar of the engine, even with the muffling factor of the snow, wasn't deep enough for a tow truck. It was probably a neighbor inching home, wanting to see if Merilee was in trouble after noticing the police unit stuck near her driveway. Should she leave her cozy car to walk through the deep snow up to the door and check? Or would it be acceptable to mind her own business? The headlights flickered through the stained-glass window in the front door, throwing colored confetti into the room as the driver decided.

Then the lights faded. Mind-your-own business won the evening.

She refocused on the conversation. "Is it snowing in Santa Fe?"

"No. But it's cold. I wish you were here to warm me up."

"Did you learn anything interesting at the training?"

"I did, and I'm looking forward to the Amber and Silver Alert session tomorrow. Largo wants me to fill everyone in at the next staff meeting. But you, my dear, might get a private sneak preview of some specialized maneuvers."

She missed him. There was nothing sexier than a handsome cop with a sense of humor. "I'd like that. Maybe we can work something out, Sergeant."

"That's what I'm hoping. See you soon, sweetheart."

The machine had filled the kitchen with the steamy aroma of coffee and chocolate. She took a tiny sip. Delicious, hot, creamy, not too sweet. Yum. She liked the way the machine made each beverage fresh and that people could choose what they wanted. She wondered if Largo would consider one of these for the office. Having grown up on Mama's stovetop version of campfire coffee, she wasn't a coffee snob, but this drink got a gold star.

She savored each sweet mouthful, grateful that her day was nearly done, that she wasn't driving, wasn't talking anyone out of suicide by exposure, wasn't listening to the rookie's inane comments, wasn't giving her sister advice she never listened to or listening to Mama's advice for her. For a few minutes, she could just be Bernie.

She finished the mocha, walked to the entryway, grabbed her keys, zipped up her coat, and opened the door, checking to make sure she hadn't locked herself out. On Navajo, most families didn't lock their homes, but in the city it was a different situation.

No tow truck in sight, but the snowfall had lessened. Larger flakes, as light as the air itself, danced silently on their descent to join their tribe on the ground. The sky was gray from the reflected light of the moon, the air crisp with a hint of moisture.

If the snow stopped, maybe the highway department would reopen the road, the tow truck would come, and she could head on home tonight after getting some answers from Merilee. She would ask about road conditions when she radioed again for a tow truck. She felt better about the situation. Perhaps the mocha, and certainly the thought of Chee's special maneuvers, had revived her.

She stopped fantasizing as she drew closer to her unit. The trunk lid was up, and snow had drifted inside. She jogged up to it, careful of her footing.

The box Hoffman had entrusted to her was gone. She instinctively moved her hand to the gun in her holster, but the only sign of other humans was the soft light seeping through Merilee's window shades into the December evening. The thief must have been in the vehicle she'd heard earlier.

Looking more closely at the trunk, she saw that the latch had been jimmied. She walked to the driver's-side door and tried it. Locked, just as she'd left it. The other door was locked, too, with no signs that someone had tried to get in.

She unlocked the door, climbed inside, and radioed the incident to the local authorities. Then she called the Shiprock substation. The rookie answered the phone, sounding half asleep, but she gave him her location, told him about the theft and the damage to the unit, and said she'd send photos. The perpetrator had broken the latch. She shone her flashlight carefully around the interior of the trunk. Nothing except the pot had been taken.

Then she asked about the roads.

"It's bad out there. No fatals, but three multi-vehicle accidents, one involving a truck hauling cattle. Messy. The state police and the highway department are looking at a long, cold night."

Bernie took pictures of the tire tracks of the vehicle that had parked next to where her patrol unit had slipped off the road, and of the footprints that led from the road to her unit's back bumper and up to the street again. She removed the binder, found wire in the trunk, and fastened the lid well enough to get her back to Shiprock.

Doing something took the edge off her anger and the feeling of violation.

The burglary puzzled her; she knew it wasn't random. Why break into the locked trunk of a police car during a blizzard? Someone knew about the box Hoffman had given her. That person also knew her location, and wanted the pot badly enough to brave the storm.

She could think of only three people who fit that description: Merilee, the intended recipient, who'd been in the house with Franklin at the time of the theft;

Hoffman himself, who was probably still hospitalized; and Officer Manzanares, who had asked about the box and told her it was filled with drugs.

Bernie remembered where she'd heard the bird call before: on Merilee's phone, during her first visit, when the ringtone interrupted their interview. Merilee had disappeared into the back of the house a short while later, allegedly for an aspirin, and then Bernie had overheard one side of a heated conversation. And this time, after she heard the bird call, someone had shown up to break into her unit.

It was past time for a talk. She grabbed Franklin's shirt, charged back to the porch, stomped the snow off her boots, and opened the door to Merilee's house.

21

A wave of warm air with a hint of chocolate greeted Bernie. Her hostess and suspect, seated at the kitchen counter with a mug in her hands, looked up. "What were you doing outside? It's really cold out there."

"Someone broke into my unit." Bernie watched for Merilee's reaction, noted her lack of surprise, and continued. "I went out to get the pot and Franklin's shirt, and the trunk was wide open."

"Wow. Are you sure you didn't leave it that way? You looked really tired when you came in."

"I'm sure."

"That's awful." Merilee put her mug on the counter. "Is anything missing?"

"Yes. The box Hoffman asked me to bring to you."

"Oh dear. Did the break-in do much damage to the car?"

"Some. I took photos."

"I imagine this weather has all the police out dealing with accidents tonight anyway. An auto burglary probably wouldn't have priority." Merilee picked up the mug and moved it toward her lips.

Bernie spread the damp shirt over the seat of a kitchen stool. "This might get more attention than you think. One of the state police officers, a man you know, might be involved."

"Manzanares, right?"

Bernie sat down at the counter next to her. "Right. I was puzzled when you asked if he was at the accident site when Hoffman had me call you. When I said no, you hung up on me. Shortly after that, he arrived."

"Oh, did I? Sorry. I was so worried about Larry. I didn't mean—"

Bernie gave her the shut-up-now look she had cultivated for drunks who tried to flirt their way out of getting arrested. Merilee stopped talking and sat up a bit straighter. "Manzanares hates me. He thinks I killed his cousin—my ex, you know. He thinks I killed Roger myself, or had him killed, and got away with it. He hounds me. Torments me. He's awful."

"Have you reported him?"

She shook her head. "He's careful about all this. And law enforcement is a closed circle, a boys' club. You know that. And I'm a triple outsider—a woman, a Navajo, and I didn't grow up here."

"Well, he messed up this time. I have pictures of his footprints and the tire tracks. And you'll vouch that the box was in my trunk."

Merilee shook her head. "I'm sure you had it if you say you did. But I never saw it. I can't swear to that."

"You're afraid of him. So scared you can't tell the truth."

Merilee stared at the countertop for several long minutes. When she looked up, Bernie saw her tears. "How about some more coffee? I've got decaf." She opened the drawer and pulled out a couple of pods.

Merilee slipped a pod into the machine, but didn't turn it on.

"Why would Manzanares think you'd kill his cousin?"

"You'll have to ask him. Ask him why I'd go to all the trouble of hiring a lawyer and starting divorce proceedings against Roger if I were going to kill the scumbag."

"I heard he wanted to divorce you."

"Toward the end, our animosity was mutual and far-reaching. But Roger wasn't murdered. He drowned in a boating accident at Navajo Lake. Manzanares knew our marriage was rocky. He even asked me out, but I told him no. After that, he had it in for me. He was part of the investigation, and the drowning gave him a reason to get back at me, especially when I didn't want an autopsy."

"You know that decision made you look suspicious."

"I knew. I didn't care." Merilee's voice flared with anger. "Even though we were ending our marriage, I didn't want his body violated. Would you? But they did it anyway. They told me they found alcohol and also something they called 'unknown substances' in his body. I'm sure those were herbs we were taking for allergies. I used dried leaves from the brugs to make a little weak tea for both of us. No, I didn't kill my husband, but I wasn't sorry when he died."

Merilee stood, and walked with her cup to the sink. "I have to work in the morning, assuming the roads are open so my clients can get here to talk about their problems. I need to get to bed. Let me show you where you can sleep."

"I don't plan on spending the night. I'll just stay until the tow truck comes."

Merilee shrugged. "Suit yourself, then."

"I've got a couple more questions. Manzanares thought the box might be full of drugs. Was it?"

"How would I know?" Merilee put both hands on the counter and leaned toward Bernie. "I think you're right about Manzanares being behind this. I can picture him driving over here to steal my pot out of sheer meanness."

"How did he know I'd be here?"

"Maybe he's stalking me, saw your car, and went crazy."

"Maybe he called you when you had the music up loud and I was on the phone with my husband."

Merilee stared at her hands. "Don't be ridiculous."

"Why did Larry Hoffman have your pot?"

Merilee looked up. "Things have been tight financially for me ever since Roger died. I left it on consignment, hoping some tourist might come into the monument shop and be interested."

"How did you get that pot?"

"Roger gave it to me as a wedding present."

"Did he say where it came from?"

"Not exactly. He said he bought it from a collector."

"Did he tell you who?" Bernie thought she knew the answer.

"No. I didn't ask."

"But you think he got it from Manzanares, and that Manzanares acquired it illegally. And now he's stolen it to cover his tracks."

Merilee nodded. "It wouldn't surprise me. Roger was handsome as a fat coyote, and as deceitful, too. After he died, Manzanares asked me to give the pot to him as a reminder of Roger. Enough for tonight."

"Not quite. One more question. Why did you help him steal it?"

Merilee shook her head. "I think the long day has affected your thinking. I can't stand that man."

"But you called him to tell him I was here."

"I, I . . ." Merilee open both hand, extended her fingers as if she were giving up.

"What kind of a pot is it?"

"It was an old seed pot from Acoma Pueblo, with crosshatching and a parrot design."

Bernie knew the type. They had a tiny opening in the top to keep the start of next year's crops stored safe from mice and other critters. Not a practical choice for hiding drugs.

"I forgot to ask, how was Larry?"

"Larry?"

Bernie made a mental note of the stumble.

"Oh, you mean in the hospital." Merilee ran her index finger across her jaw line. "I, ah, didn't get to talk to him. He was sleeping. I'm going to bed now, too. I'll answer your questions in the morning. Based on the weather, none of us are leaving anytime soon."

After watching Merilee disappear down the hall, Bernie extracted her cell phone, called the tow company again, and got a recording. She took her phone charger from her backpack and plugged it into an outlet in the living room, near a chair from which she could see both the front door and the hallway that led to Merilee's bedroom.

The *bing* of incoming e-mail reminded her of Leaphorn's promise to do some investigation into the Cruz family. She'd see if he'd sent something—she hadn't checked all day. While she was at it, she'd look at the highway conditions and the weather forecast for the morning.

Leaphorn's messages added to her wakefulness. They had come in when she was looking at the old bones, and both had the subject line "Merilee Cruz." The first one had two attachments—tricky to open on her phone—so she looked at the second message first.

Just as he always did face-to-face, the Lieutenant got right to the point.

Here's what you need to know:

1. Merilee's husband, Roger Bateson, an experienced boater, died at Navajo Lake under suspicious circumstances. The widow, who was not at the

scene and reported him missing, tried to block an autopsy on Navajo cultural grounds. Because the man was non-Navajo, her request was denied.

2. The autopsy found some anomalies, as you can read in the attachment, but confirmed that drowning was the cause of death. The police report showed that he was not wearing a life preserver, hit a rock, and was thrown from the boat.

3. Although one of the husband's relatives, a state policeman, pushed for a murder investigation because of animosity between the couple, the case was closed.

She clicked on the first attachment, and after some churning, the police report opened in a new screen. She squinted to read the small print on the face of her phone, but finally gave up and opened the autopsy attachment. It was even worse, a bad scan of a photocopy that might have been blurred to start with. She put her phone down and rubbed her temples.

She went to her backpack and grabbed the Wings and Roots binder and Walker's folder. The annual reports Cooper had given her included financial summaries, board minutes, and other material. These, plus the information Councilor Walker provided, seemed like the perfect way to use this extra work time: pages of numbers and official-sounding jargon.

She opened Cooper's blue binder to the budget sheets, wishing she had paid more attention to book-keeping in school. She started with January and found the line item accounting of the tribe's grant to the pro-gram noted as income. In the narrative summary, she read how the money was spent: "funding the program for Navajo youth." She thumbed through the rest of the summaries. The grant money was always listed and accounted for: how much the tribe had initially given Wings and Roots, how much had been spent that month, and the total amount remaining. It looked legit-imate. She'd double-check the expenditure pages next. If everything jibed, she could tell Councilor Walker to worry about something else, like her daughter Annie.

But another entry caught her attention, a pattern of donations: $25,000 every three months. She went back to the January summary where she'd seen it first. She moved on to February, March, and April. Over that period, the group's income from fund-raising and grants declined to only a few hundred dollars. There were adjustments in expenses, but the income-to-outgo gap widened. Then came the anonymous gift, and the program was back in the black.

She double-checked to make sure that the tribal grant, earmarked for the program, hadn't been somehow diverted into this unnamed donor fund. That money was secure, as far as she could tell, and devoted to subsidizing Navajo students for adventures in the outdoors. Who was behind the $25,000 donations? The wealthy grandparents of a child the program had helped? She didn't know any Navajos who had that kind of money, but the program helped non-Navajos, too. Maybe a former student who appreciated what she'd learned and used it for a successful career was pitching in.

She left the budget summaries and turned to Cooper's compilation of the minutes from the monthly board meetings. Her director's report was high on the agenda. In January, Cooper explained that the budget deficit was caused by a problem with an anticipated grant from a foundation that had agreed to support new, nonpaying students. The announcement had generated great publicity and a deluge of applications. The foundation reneged on its commitment, Cooper had written, but the agency had already accepted some of the new non-paying students, mostly teenagers from what she called difficult situations. The board agreed to honor its commitment to the teens already accepted. Cooper said she had alerted the staff that, if the budget situation did not resolve itself, the program would have to be cut and group leaders laid off. She stressed the role of fund-raising to fill the gap.

In February, Cooper told the board that $25,000 the previous month from an anonymous donor had put the group back in the black: "We received a cashier's check in the mail made out to Wings and Roots with a note that said the money was to be spent as needed." She wrote that she was "exploring all options" to find another underwriter to cover the unbudgeted increase in enrollment and to reduce expenses. The pattern repeated with another donation for the same amount arriving in April, July, and then quarterly. The money didn't cover the entire deficit, but Cooper made enough other cuts to keep the group from going under. From what Bernie read, the board hadn't questioned the source of the donation, at least not as a group where minutes were taken. Had Domingo Cruz made the appeal to Mr. and Mrs. Anonymous? Was this somehow connected to his disappearance?

She wondered if this could be the money Franklin had mentioned that Dom himself gave. Could he be involved in the illegal pottery business with Manzanares? She thought about the lucrative market for ancient Indian pottery, and filed the thought away.

In the minutes of the July meeting, she read, "As they discussed the budget, Cooper reminded the board that she had not had a raise in the five years she had been director. She said that Cruz, Mayfair, and some of the other staff volunteered to work extra hours to help with the budget situation." The budget summary showed Cruz and Mayfair donating their overtime salaries with the hours recorded as if they were cash. She didn't know enough about accounting to know if this was standard procedure, but at least the group was transparent about it.

The tribe's money, to Bernie's eyes, seemed properly documented. She wondered if the board had praised Cooper for securing the $25,000 gifts, or blamed her for letting the funds drop so low. The minutes were silent about that.

Putting the report aside, she skimmed the paperwork from Councilor Walker, copies of what she'd read in the Wings and Roots minutes and clippings from the *Navajo Times*, mostly bad news. The newspaper articles quoted Walker as saying she thought there was something questionable about the way the agency operated. One of the stories confirmed what Cooper had told her about Walker's relative who worked for the program and had been fired. The reporter quoted Walker as saying that the man had been a whistle-blower, and that was why he'd lost his job.

More awake than ever, Bernie thought about going to the kitchen for a cup of hot chocolate but decided against it. Setting down the reports next to her backpack, she walked to the window. The storm had tapered off to a light flurry. At this rate, snowplows and sand trucks would do their magic, and she'd be able to get back to Shiprock as soon as the tow truck liberated her unit.

A patch of light reflected off the snow. It came from the other side of the house, the wing where Merilee's guest room was. Maybe Franklin was having trouble sleeping. If he was awake, she could retrieve her blanket and ask some questions about Dom, Merilee, and Manzanares. She wondered if he had heard Dom talk about the generous but mysterious donor. It would save her some steps in the morning and the hassle of a follow-up call.

She stepped into the hallway, triggering a motion-activated night light that made it easy to find her way. Heading quietly toward the guest room, she saw that the door to what must be Merilee's bedroom stood open. The rumpled bed was empty. As she moved farther down the hallway, she realized she didn't have to worry about being quiet. The sobbing coming from the guest room would have drowned out any noise she might have made. She moved a few steps closer and saw the two of them, their arms around each other as if forming a circle of protection.

Her brain was packed with questions, but she understood the power of grief. She went back to the chair and thought about how nice it would be to be home again.

When the phone woke her, it was beginning to get light outside. She spoke to Captain Largo, then called the tow company again and learned she was next on their list. She dressed and walked into the cold, bright new morning to clear her thinking and get her bearings for the challenge ahead. Snow had filled last night's tracks and sparkled on the trees and power lines in the predawn glow. She didn't go for her usual run, but she sang morning prayers, brushed off her unit, and scraped the windshield.

Then, knowing he was an early riser, she called the Lieutenant to see what he had learned from reviewing the Wings and Roots files. Perhaps, as often happened, his insights and his connections would surprise her.

Leaphorn answered on the first ring, his voice

strong. After some pleasantries he asked, "So, did you have any questions about what I sent you?"

"I couldn't read the attachments clearly, sir, but I assume your summary covered it."

"That's right. I looked at the material you gave me from Councilor Walker. She has a reputation as a watchdog of tribal money, and those anonymous donations that keep the Wings and Roots rolling along got my attention, too. I'm going to do some additional checking. So far, I don't see any problem with misuse of Navajo funds. Any questions on that?"

The rhythm of footsteps drew her attention to the hallway. Merilee, dressed in a dark skirt and red turtleneck sweater with a large turquoise necklace and matching earrings, nodded to her and headed to the kitchen.

"No questions as of now, sir. I looked at the agency's minutes and financial reports for a few years. I'm not an expert, but it seemed to me that all the Navajo money was appropriately used. I puzzled over those donations, too. I appreciate your looking into that."

"I heard that a blizzard closed the interstate last night. Did you get caught up in that?"

"Yes, sir. That's why I had time to review the financial documents Mrs. Cooper gave me."

She ended the call and joined Merilee. The aroma of dark coffee dripping into the mug stirred her brain to pleasant, professional wakefulness. "Good morning. The coffee smells good."

Merilee gently pushed the cup that had just brewed across the countertop toward her. "I heard that the interstate is open. Local school and government offices have a two-hour delay. I hope that doesn't include your tow truck or my clients for this morning. I saw you on the phone. Is there news about Dom?"

Bernie held the steaming cup of coffee in both hands.

"No. The captain called to tell me that Larry Hoffman died early this morning."

"Poor man. Those injuries must have been worse than they seemed."

"It looks like the cause of death was a drug overdose."

"I know he had trouble with his back. Maybe he took too many painkillers. I liked Larry. It's a shock to hear that he's dead. I didn't think he was in bad shape physically, except for the shoulder and the broken nose. His death—"

"Hold on," Bernie interrupted, hearing a noise outside the house. "I think the tow truck is here."

The driver had climbed out of the truck to study the

situation. It looked as though he'd put in a full night's work. "Sorry," he said, "I couldn't get here sooner. This will just take a minute or two."

When he smiled, Bernie noticed his dimples. "I appreciate you coming," she said.

"I could have been here last night except for the big mess on the interstate. I just finished with that and stopped for breakfast."

He attached a chain, pulled the unit up the snowy embankment, and was on his way in twenty minutes.

Back in the kitchen, Merilee was stirring sugar into her mug.

"We were talking about Larry and his accident," Bernie said, picking up the thread again. "You need to tell me about Manzanares's role in all this and your involvement with him."

Merilee sighed. "I will. It's complicated. I offered to show you the greenhouse. Why don't we talk out there for a few minutes?" She opened the connecting door. The snow had slipped off the steep glass roof, and the sun shone in warmly.

"It's lovely in here, isn't it?" Merilee closed the door behind them. "You know, I marvel at the amazing plants that thrive out there in nature, kind of like the girls we work with in the program. But these hothouse beauties are my passion. Unlike Manzanares, they are just what they seem to be. Beautiful without deceit. I could kick myself for getting tied in to him."

Bernie gazed through the greenhouse glass at the blue sky as she inhaled the irresistible sweetness of orange blossoms, a fragrance she remembered from her days at the University of New Mexico, when she would head to the biology department's greenhouse to study. One of the things that made her proud to be Navajo was the way her creation story honored plants as well as the Insect People and the Animal People.

Merilee motioned her to a bench near a vivid purple-and-red fuchsia.

"Tell me more about Manzanares's connection to you and your brother," she said.

"He hates me, bullies me, does whatever he can to make me miserable. But like I said, you need to ask him. He hasn't spoken to Dom more than two or three times that I know of."

"What about the girl who went to the hospital. Do you know about that?"

Merilee grimaced. "I heard about her. She couldn't have come across datura growing out there in the winter, that's for sure. I don't think you'd find it in the Malpais, anyway. As a cop, you know more about teens and drugs than I do, and how some kids think that what comes from a plant can't harm them. But the incident gives Councilor Walker another reason to try to shut down our program. Worrying about that woman keeps me awake at night."

"Speaking of that, I heard Franklin crying last night. And I thought I heard your voice, too."

For the first time since Bernie had met her, Merilee seemed uneasy. Embarrassed. "Oh . . . sorry. I couldn't sleep because I kept thinking about Dom. I heard Michael weeping, and I thought maybe some of the tools I use as a counselor might help. Maybe they did. Maybe he helped me more than I helped him. We grieved together."

"When I first talked to you about people to be notified about Dom, you didn't even mention Franklin. Why?"

"You asked about relatives, remember? Franklin's not related to us." Merilee twisted a ring on the middle finger of her right hand. "Since Franklin and Dom live together, I figured he already knew Dom was gone. Franklin worried that all the arguing they'd done recently about Dom becoming the program director had distracted my brother and caused him to have an accident."

Bernie nodded. "Tell me what you know about Dom's financial situation. Franklin intimated that he didn't have a lot of money but was making contributions to the program. The books show large anonymous donations."

"You mean the twenty-five thousand? My brother lives from hand to mouth, just like I'm doing now without Roger. That was one reason I wanted to sell his photographs, or try to, in my online art store."

"A person showed me one of Dom's petroglyph photos as the background for a site on the Internet that's selling Indian artifacts. The merchandise looks suspicious, and—"

"I told him to take those down. I begged him. I can't believe—"

Bernie jumped in. "Told who?"

Merilee clenched her hands together, fingers overlapping. "I didn't mean for any of this to happen. I only wanted to save Wings and Roots and help Dom sell his photos. And Larry? I don't understand how he could be dead."

"Told who?" Bernie's voice had more force this time. "Manzanares?"

"He thought I'd poisoned Roger because of some herbal supplements I gave him, but Roger liked to get high. He lost control of the boat because of booze, not because of anything herbal. I'd never use plants to hurt someone. Manzanares kept threatening me with re-opening the investigation, but he said he'd forget about it if I would let him use the petroglyph photos on his website and tell him where certain ones were taken. He said he wanted to work with us to keep the graves safe. What a liar." She spat out the words.

At the creak of the door to the greenhouse opening, they both swung around. Franklin walked toward them. He wore the shirt Bernie had brought in from the car, and there was a bulge in his pants pocket. "Hey, ladies," he said. "What's up? You look too serious for such a bright morning."

"I was asking Merilee about some photos Dom took. His work seems to be linked to a website that's selling Indian pottery."

Franklin took a step closer. "Why are you worried about that? Dom would never involve himself in anything that was questionable. There are mountains of pottery out there, new and old, legitimate stuff."

"And then there are the old, old pieces, some of them stolen from public land. From the looted caves I saw in the Malpais. Those pots go for a lot of money, enough to keep Wings and Roots in business."

"But you don't think Dom . . . He would never even consider doing anything like that. How dare you imply . . . ." Franklin's voice rose with anger.

Bernie turned to Merilee. "You need to tell me

what's up with the photographs you've been selling and the pottery, and what Manzanares's role here is." She looked up at Franklin. "And I'm curious about if and how you, Mr. Franklin, tie into all this."

Bernie saw the look on Franklin's face even before his hand quickly moved to his pocket. She pushed Merilee off the bench to the ground, fell on top of her to shield her body, and hoped the man was a bad shot.

The bullet crashed through the glass behind them. Bernie scrambled to her feet as she watched Franklin sprint out the door toward the driveway. She looked at Merilee. "You OK?"

"Yeah. He's running for my car."

By the time Bernie got outside, all she could see was the back bumper of the black SUV speeding down the snow-covered street.

22

Jim Chee got to the classroom for the morning's training a few minutes early, hoping to encounter the deputy he knew from the Cibola County Sheriff's Department. He was in luck. After some small talk, Chee got to the point. "I'm trying to find a rancher out your way who might have hired a guy whose family is worried about him. They can't remember or never knew where he was working, except that it was a ranch in Cibola County. He hasn't come back or contacted them."

The officer smiled. "What a bad boy. Well, at least they know the county where he's supposed to be. The best person to talk to would be Cris Manzanares. Maybe you've met him?"

"I've heard the name. My wife worked with him a

little on the search that's under way out in the Malpais."

"Yeah, he lives outside of Grants, and his family has run cattle there for years. He might be able to help you. Most ranchers aren't hiring in the winter. Hold on. I'll give you his cell."

The deputy pulled out his phone and hit a few buttons. "Ready for his number?"

"Thanks. This is convenient."

"He's my poker buddy."

Chee checked the time and then walked out into the hall to make the call. When Manzanares answered, Chee explained the situation about George Curley.

"That's an easy question. George worked on the ranch for me, oh, it must have been for a couple weeks, and then said he was leaving for home. That was the last I saw of him."

"When did the job end?"

"Oh, probably mid-November."

"What was he doing for you?"

"I've been selling some lava rock for landscaping. He was helping with that."

"So your place is in the Malpais?"

"My family has been there for years. Why all the questions?" Manzanares chuckled. "Don't tell me. Curley got himself in some kinda jam."

"Could be." Chee thought about it. "When Curley said he was going home, did he say back to his wife or back to his mother?"

"He didn't say. He wasn't much of a talker."

"His mother and his wife are both worried about him."

"Too bad. I wish I could be of more help."

The hallway had started to clear when Chee ended the call, but he had one more piece of business to take care of before class. It was time to ask Caitlyn for the photo. George Curley should have been home by now. He sent her a text. He'd need the photos when he took the next step and notified area law enforcement to activate the missing person network.

When the class ended at noon, Chee felt inspired and motivated to do all he could to help find missing kids and elders. He silently thanked Largo for sending him. He saw a text from Caitlyn with instructions for picking up her husband's photo—a crucial part of locating the man if he actually was a missing person.

He had arranged to meet Darleen for coffee before he drove back to Mama's house, and he found her at the IAIA cafeteria. She sat with a glass of water, fiddling with her phone. He got some coffee and a sandwich and joined her.

"Hi." Darleen said, smiling at him. Last night's drama seemed to have happened in a parallel universe. "How was your class?"

"Great, but I'm eager to get home." He unwrapped his sandwich. "Want half?"

"No, thanks. Save it for the trip. Guess what?" She didn't pause for him to speculate. "We made good progress on the video last night. It looks terrific, and Herbert added some cool stuff to the narration on his own. I wish you could have stayed and watched. CS will start the final edits tonight. They agreed to give him more time in the studio. Will you tell Sister I have to stay another day? The dorm people already said it was OK. No charge! I'll talk to her and Mama about this, but if I can't reach them, will you tell her, as a backup? I don't want her to freak."

"Sure. This sounds great. Will CS bring you home?"

"No, he has to hang here a few more days. Herbert said he'd give me a ride first thing tomorrow."

Chee frowned.

"Don't be grumpy, Cheeseburger. The guy is OK. He said he'd buy me lunch, too, because I gave him the drawing." She sipped her water. "I'm glad I told you about the bruise. I was embarrassed, but, well, I'm putting it behind me and moving on with my art. It feels good to not have that secret."

Chee sipped his coffee and realized that, except for the question of what had happened to George Curley, he felt good, too. Darleen talked on about the drawings she was planning, about London, about other people she'd met, and more. The Darleen he knew was back.

After half an hour, he wrapped up the uneaten half of his sandwich. "I've got to get on the road. Take care and I'll see you soon. Sure you don't want this?"

Darleen took it. "Thanks, Cheeseburger. Be safe out there."

His next stop was Tesuque Pueblo. Caitlyn had texted that her mother would leave a photo of Curley for him in a brown envelope under the doormat. Instead, the old woman handed the envelope to him. She wasted no energy on civility.

"I gave you the picture in here because it shows the truck." She tapped the envelope with her index finger. "Find that truck for my daughter. We need it, and she's the one who makes the payments."

"Thank you for the photo. We'll do what we can."

She made a snorting sound and closed the door.

He opened the envelope, prepared to ask Mrs. Vigil for another photograph if the one she'd handed him was too much truck and not enough Curley. There were three photos. The largest was color and showed a small, slim Navajo man looking directly at the camera, standing at the back of a white pickup truck. The tailgate was up, and the truck looked new. The yellow-and-red New Mexico license plate and a dark blue bumper sticker showed clearly in the picture. There were also two small shots of the truck, including one that coincidently captured Curley in profile.

Chee put the envelope on the passenger seat of his pickup. He'd let the captain and the rookie deal with this. Maybe the department would issue a BOLO, asking fellow law enforcement to be on the lookout for Curley and the Ford. Maybe Curley would give his wife or his mother a phone call and ease their worry. Maybe he'd come home. Or maybe the department would find his truck on someone's used vehicle lot in Gallup or Farmington or Chinle or Tuba City or even Flagstaff. Whatever. He'd done his part to solve the mystery. Time, finally, to head home.

The storm that had stranded Bernie in Grants was long past, replaced by strikingly blue skies. Snow lay beneath the ponderosas as he crossed onto the Jicarilla Apache Reservation. Beyond that, the sandstone formations were partly buried beneath white caps. He passed the turnoff for Chaco Canyon and Nageezi and was rolling toward the oil and gas country outside of Farmington. He was thinking about Bernie, the wonderful smell of her hair and the delicious smoothness of her skin, and how he'd missed her, when his phone buzzed. He put it on speaker, and Captain Largo's voice filled the truck.

"Where are you?"

Chee told him.

"Good. Take a nap if that appeals to you, and then come on in. I need you to work the late shift."

23

While she drove in the direction she'd seen Franklin take, Bernie called the Cibola County sheriff's department to describe Merilee's stolen car and the man who drove it.

"Too bad the interstate is open. That makes the search tougher. And the plows worked on the local streets last night."

"Franklin might head out to the Malpais." She explained.

"We'll contact the search crew and state police. Thanks for the heads-up. Someone is on his way now to the house to talk to Ms. Cruz."

The Cibola County sheriff's deputy sent to interview Merilee about the incident was still there when Bernie returned. He was young and efficient and helped arrange cardboard over the shattered glass to keep the heat in the greenhouse. She couldn't imagine Wilson Sam doing that.

Bernie filled in some blanks and described Franklin's distraught behavior the previous night. The deputy took notes and then said, "My boss asked me to tell you to check in with your captain."

"Sure thing." Bernie grabbed her belongings and walked to her unit. She called the Shiprock station, expecting to talk to Sandra, but the captain answered. "What about the old bones you hiked to? You never gave me a follow-up."

"Sorry, sir. It looked like another looted gravesite. The incident commander said they won't disturb it since I verified there was no sign of Mr. Cruz. Cultural affairs knows about them. Well, I hope they do. I left a detailed message and sent photos."

"And what about the Wings and Roots problem?"

She told him about the anonymous donations that kept the program afloat, adding "They are having some challenges, but all the tribal money is accounted for."

"I need you back here ASAP to get Walker off my back. Tell the councilor what you learned. Did you find a place to stay last night?"

"Yes, sir, and there are some interesting developments in the story of Mr. Cruz and his disappearance." She explained about the pot stolen from the trunk of her unit, the gunshot, and the stolen car.

"Did you mention your suspicion about the pots to the state police?"

"No, sir." She added the Manzanares component.

Largo was silent a moment. "Interesting. The new FBI agent asked me if we knew anything else about Larry Hoffman, the ranger who died after that car wreck. I'll pass this along to her. She might call you. She's also interested in the looting."

"Yes, sir." Bernie pulled onto the entrance ramp for the interstate. The highway was slushy and red from the mixture of salt and sand used to help clear it. Traffic seemed about normal. The sun was out and added a glimmer to the frosting of snow on the lava beside the highway. Beauty all around her.

Largo intruded on her meditation. "I'll bring Walker into the office now, and you can deal with her."

"Yes, sir."

The councilor's voice came over the phone, crabby as ever. "I've been trying to reach you for more than twenty-four hours, Officer. Thanks a lot for being so responsive."

Bernie let the comment go. "Councilor, I reviewed

the Wings and Roots paperwork, and you're right. It seems that there are some discrepancies."

"I thought so."

"As I read it, the agency should never have agreed to the tribe's arrangement. There was too little money offered for too many students. The program director and her staff and the board lived up to the stipulations of the grant. According to the minutes, they made attempts to notify the tribe that there was trouble with the ground rules, and those notifications were addressed to you and, well, they were all ignored."

"You must be wrong about that." Bernie heard some muffled sounds, as though Walker had put her hand over the receiver. Then the councilor was back. "I was the contact person, and all they ever sent were big envelopes with the minutes and the budget reports."

Bernie thought about the next question. "I know you're busy on the council. Could it be that some of the mail they sent didn't get to you? Or didn't get opened?"

The phone went silent.

Bernie spoke. "Someone made anonymous donations to subsidize the group that the tribe had agreed to fund."

"It was the director's own stupidity that caused the problem."

"You mentioned that if there was no evidence that

Cooper or anyone in the group had done something wrong, you'd lobby for more money for the kids."

"I remember. I need to see the proof, and—" The sound from the phone became muffled again: more mumbling, then Walker's voice, impatient. "Someone says she has to talk to you."

A younger female voice came on the line. "Officer Manuelito, it's Annie."

"Hi, Annie. Go ahead."

"I need to tell you something important. Not on the phone. Can we please meet somewhere?"

"What do you want to talk about?" Bernie heard Walker in the background, yelling something at Annie.

"It's about Mr. Cruz."

"Just tell me now."

"I can't because it's about . . . oh, Mom, wait." The background noise sounded louder, and then she heard Walker say "Cruz?" and the rumble of Largo's voice. Then Walker was shouting something she couldn't decipher.

"Annie, are you there?"

After some silence, Largo came on the phone. "You still there, Manuelito?"

The background noise had evaporated. "Are we still on speaker?"

"Yes, but Walker and Annie left. The mom wasn't expecting that sort of conversation. I told them to wait outside, calm down."

"I knew that girl wasn't telling me the whole truth about Cruz. Maybe she knows something we can pass along to the search team. Can you put her back on the phone? I'd like to talk to her again."

"And I'd like to lose ten pounds by Késhmish. I'll check back with Walker when she cools off, but don't hold your breath. I doubt that the girl really has anything important to say, but if she does, we need Walker there as a witness. I'll work on persuading her."

"Thanks, Captain. Christmas is still a few weeks away, you know."

"If Walker agrees to let you talk to Annie, maybe you can take her out for a burger or something. You'll get more information outside the station, even with her mother hanging over her like a bear with her cub. I'll talk to Walker about it. Tell her you'll have to record it. I'll have Sandra call you if she says yes. You need to do this ASAP."

"Yes, sir."

Two hours later, the three of them—Annie, Councilor Walker, and Bernie in her uniform—squeezed around a table at That's A Burger. Bernie ordered hamburgers and Cokes for everyone, charging it to the office.

Walker offered her a five-dollar bill, but Bernie waved it away. "I don't want you to think you can bribe me."

Stone-faced, Walker slipped the money back in her pocket. They sat silently until the food came and they'd had a few bites. Annie looked nervous. Councilor Walker seemed annoyed, as usual. Bernie focused on the food. Then she took her notebook and a pen from the backpack, turned on the recorder, and started the session with time of day, place, and those present.

"Annie, you told me on the phone that you needed to tell me something more about Mr. Cruz. Because I think what you have to say might be important, I'm recording this session and taking notes. Is that all right with you and your mom?"

"Fine." Walker's voice was hard. "Get it over with."

Annie fiddled with the straw and then looked up. "Does my mother have to be here?"

"Yes, I have to be here, but Officer Manuelito is in charge and I'm not going to say anything. Pretend I'm back home."

The girl fidgeted some more, then glanced out the window.

Bernie leaned toward her. "I'm listening. You said that you wanted to tell me something important about Mr. Cruz. You can start whenever you're ready."

Annie put the straw down. "So, do you remember how I told you that I heard Mr. Cruz walking behind me, and then I didn't hear him, and when I turned around he was gone?"

"Yes. You said he had a bell on his pack, and that's how you knew he was there. Is that right?"

"Yes. Yeah. Well, I forgot to say that we were on a tricky part of the trail."

"Tricky? Can you tell me what you mean?"

"Get on with it, Annie." Walker's voice dripped with impatience. "You—"

Bernie gave the councilor the behave-yourself look she'd practiced on misbehaving teens. The attitude might bring repercussions later, but it worked to stop the interruption.

Annie moved the index finger of her right hand to stroke each little gold ball in her ear. "Tricky, you know, like dangerous or something. Part of it, I mean the lava, was real sharp, and there were cracks you could fall into, and some of it was slick because of the ice in the shade. So I kept looking down. I asked Mr. Cruz if I should go back and get my tent and my other stuff, and he said no, he would take care of it. He said that place where I was, that cave, was sacred, and I wasn't supposed to be there. He said I should walk back to camp as quickly and carefully as I could." Bernie heard her voice begin to grow tight, but Annie kept talking. "He said he was glad I wasn't hurt."

She stopped and took a gulp of her Coke.

Annie's mother shifted in her chair, as if she wanted to inject something. Bernie gave her The Look again and turned her focus to the girl.

"What happened next?"

"Mr. Cruz told me to go first so the pace would be what I could handle. He said he wanted to see if I could find the way back without his help. I didn't tell you that already, did I?"

"No, you didn't mention that."

She sat without moving, staring straight ahead. "So we were walking. I heard that little bell, like I said, and I kept going, thinking about how mad Cooper would be. The bell didn't ring all the time, I guess because of the way he had it tied onto the pack."

She stopped talking, fingering her earrings again. "Then I heard something different. A strange kind of noise. Like I told you, I was ahead of him, so I turned around, but I couldn't see him. I yelled, 'Hey, Mr. Cruz, are you there?' but he didn't answer."

"And then what happened?" Bernie saw Annie's

eyes grow shiny and then the tears on her cheeks. "Go ahead. It's OK."

"I ran back to camp, and Cooper was all over me about breaking the rules, so I made up a story that I hadn't seen him so she'd shut up. And I kept waiting for Mr. Cruz to come back. But he didn't. I thought he would be OK. He said he was testing me, and I thought that was it."

Annie twisted a strand of hair between her thumb and forefinger and stopped talking.

"Do you remember any landmarks out there that could help someone find that spot?"

"Landmarks?"

"Anything like a tree struck by lightning, an unusual rock formation, a broken fence?"

"We were following the Karens, you know?" Annie sucked on her lower lip for a few moments. "Why did they name those piles of rocks after a girl?"

Bernie smiled. "It sounds like the girl's name, Karen, but it's spelled differently. C-A-I-R-N-S. So was one of those rock piles unusual?"

Annie nodded. "On one of the ones I saw right before I didn't hear Mr. Cruz's bell, there was a piece of lava on top with a hole you could see through."

Bernie held her notepad out to Annie. "Could you draw it for me?"

Councilor Walker slammed her hands on the table. "Oh, for heaven's sakes. This is ridiculous."

"It's fine, Mom." Annie looked at Bernie.

"Go ahead."

The girl put pen to paper, then handed the little book back. "It was kind of like that, but about as big as, as . . ." She stretched out her fingers and moved her hands apart parallel to each other.

"Like a volleyball?"

"A flat one, maybe."

Bernie added some words to the base of the drawing.

"Could you find the place where you think Mr. Cruz fell?"

"I don't want to go back there ever. No way."

Walker stood up behind Annie's chair. "Can you shut up with the questions now? We have to go."

"No, Councilor. Please sit down. I have a few more things to ask her."

Bernie waited until Annie stopped crying. Walker glared at them both from her seat across the table.

"You told me about seeing the bones in that cave. Now that you've had a while to think about it, do you have anything else to say about that?"

The girl looked at her fingernails on the tabletop. Bernie hoped that meant she was framing the truth, not conjuring a lie.

"I, well, I wasn't as brave as I made myself sound. I was crying a lot."

Walker bolted up. "I never should have sent you on that trip."

"Mom, I knew I should have stayed at my solo site. I wasn't supposed to be in that cave. I just wanted to get on the van and come home. I was so scared out there."

Walker's face softened. "Scared of what?"

"Everything. The noises, being by myself with no friends, without you and my brother. I thought Mr. Cruz could lose his job because I'd gone where I shouldn't have, and so he had to go there, too. He told me not to worry. He said he knew I could get back to the base camp, but if I got confused he would help."

Bernie took a drink of her Coke, waiting to see if Annie had more to say.

The girl looked toward the restaurant door and frowned. A curly-haired woman had come in, holding a briefcase. She made a beeline for their table. "Hi, Annie. Councilor Walker, I'm Rose Cooper, the director of Wings and Roots." She stood behind the empty chair. "Hello, Officer. If you're done with your interview, this lady and I have some issues to discuss."

24

"Mom," Annie Rainsong said, "Mrs. Cooper is the one who gave me that volunteer job. You know, the one I can do before school? She's really nice, and—"

"I know who she is. Giving you that job was the least she could do after what happened." Walker turned toward Cooper. "You should have been taking better care of my daughter on that camping trip. She could have died from being lost and whatever drugs you let her get into. You—"

Bernie put her hand up to stop the attack. "Save it."

She turned to Cooper. "I'm recording this interview with Annie for follow-up information on Mr. Cruz. I think we're almost done."

Cooper took a few steps back. The other patrons

in the restaurant had put their own conversations on hold and were taking in the show. Walker's face became an angry mask, but at least she remained quiet.

Bernie turned back to the girl. "Did you eat or drink anything with Mr. Cruz?"

"No, but . . . no."

"But what?"

"When he first found me, he offered me a cookie. He had some that somebody had given him in a little sack in his backpack. I took two, but I was too freaked out to be hungry." Annie laughed, for the first time that afternoon. "Mr. Cruz always had cookies. We call him a cookie monster. These were little, so he put a handful in his mouth at once, like popcorn or something, and started chewing. He made a face. He said they tasted odd, bitter, and it was a good thing he was hungry. I knew he hadn't had anything to eat for a while because he said he always fasted with the groups, you know, to stay in sync."

Bernie thought about it. "What did you do with the cookies he gave you?"

"I put them in my coat pocket. I tried one when we were in the parking lot, you know, when Mrs. Cooper was passing out the phones. I only ate half. It tasted awful. I left the rest on the van."

"You said he gave you two. What happened to the other one?"

"I guess it's still in my coat pocket, unless it fell out or something." Annie twisted a lock of hair as she talked. "I found something else out there by the cave, I remember now. A little silvery disk. I put the cookie in the same pocket as that."

"And where is the coat?"

"It's at home."

Bernie glanced at the notes she'd been taking as Annie talked.

"Annie, do you remember when we first met, out on the Malpais?"

She nodded.

"You were scared. And you were exhausted. In those circumstances, people sometimes say things they don't mean or forget to say something important. I want you to think about that for a moment, OK?"

She nodded again. "Can I have some more Coke while I think?"

Before Bernie could answer, Walker snatched up the cup and went to the dispenser. When she returned, Annie had thought of something. "I should have told you that he was a good guy who really cared about us kids, not a phony or a hater. I should have gone back to look for him." Sadness and regret pooled in the girl's dark eyes. "If I had, maybe I could have helped him. I said I didn't want to go back there ever again. But I could do it if it would help find Mr. Cruz."

"Do you want to say anything else?"

When she shook her head, a few tears fell on the table.

Bernie picked up the recorder and spoke into it softly, indicating that the interview with Annie Rainsong was over and that the other voices were Annie's mother, Councilor Elsbeth Walker, and Rose Cooper, the director of Wings and Roots, who had arrived near the end of the session. She clicked it off and put it in her backpack.

Bernie sensed that Councilor Walker's fuming had reached the explosive threshold. But Cooper spoke first. "Councilor, I apologize for what happened to Annie out there. As the program director, I take full responsibility."

"But I was—" Annie interrupted.

Cooper silenced the girl with a look and focused on her mother, speaking quickly.

"I assume you've looked at the budget information you requested. I am seizing this opportunity to go over the figures with you, like I have long wanted to do.

If you have questions, I am prepared to stay as long as necessary to answer them." She took charge of the empty chair and set a folder on the table.

"You inject yourself into a private interview, impose on my time as if I owed it to you. You've got a lot of nerve."

"I do. I'm beyond angry at the way you've been trying to eliminate the program without any basis, without any facts, only your opinion. You haven't even bothered to get the story straight before you start accusing us of misusing tribal funds. I have a lot of nerve because I am appalled that you would attack a good program that helps kids."

Cooper glanced at Annie, who looked as though she wanted to crawl under the table or run out the door. The director put her hand on Bernie's arm. "There is something criminal going on, all right, but it's not on our agency's end of things. Dom had figured out the problem with the tribal grants, and if he hadn't disappeared, all of that would have come out."

Walker bolted to her feet and lurched at Cooper. "You . . . you don't know what you're talking about. How dare you?"

Cooper was standing now, too, eyebrows drawn together, lips narrowed. The other customers in the little restaurant were still staring at them, probably waiting to see who would throw the first punch. Bernie pushed between the women. "Stop it. You two need to act like adults. Especially in front of Annie."

"Mom. Please. Chill out." The girl turned to Cooper. "Do you hate my mom? Is that why you were so tough on me?"

"No, honey. You came into the program with a bad attitude. It had nothing to do with your mom."

"Leave Annie out of this. Manuelito, you set me up." Walker reached for her daughter's hand, but the girl pulled away.

Bernie took a deep breath, exhaling to calm herself. "Listen to me. I didn't know Cooper was coming."

Cooper said, "Captain Largo told me you were here."

Bernie motioned to the empty seats. "You're together now. Cooper has the files, the information you've been saying proves misuse of tribal funds. She's here to answer your questions. Get this worked out, ladies. Talk to each other. Any more fighting, and I'll have to arrest you both for disturbing the peace."

Cooper looked embarrassed. "I didn't mean to yell. But this program is, well, it's my life."

Walker stared at the clock over the restaurant door and then back at Cooper. "I'll give you twenty minutes."

"Mom, can I have some fries while I wait?"

Before Walker could answer, Bernie said, "Annie, you mentioned that Mr. Cruz gave you a cookie and that it was still in your jacket. I want to have our lab look at it in case it made you sick." She turned to Walker. "I'd like to take Annie home so she can get the cookie and give it to me for the lab to check."

"Go ahead. I'd like to know if that was how she got drugged. Leave her home with her brother."

Annie broke in. "But, Mom—"

"Let's go." Bernie put her hand on the girl's shoulder. "Don't argue anymore, OK? Mr. Cruz wouldn't want that."

Annie slid into the passenger seat and started asking about the equipment in the unit. Bernie welcomed the change of subject and lack of conflict.

Annie and her mother lived slightly off US 491 in a manufactured house with a hogan next to it and a few sheep in a corral. A dog approached the car, barking energetically.

"He's friendly." Annie smiled. "He always does that."

"Get out first and tell him to chill."

"Are you scared of dogs?"

"Mostly, yes."

"I didn't think you were scared of anything."

Annie opened the unit's door, and as soon he saw her, the dog stopped barking and began wagging its tail.

"Do you want to come on inside with me while I look for the cookie?"

"I do, but wait a minute." Bernie unzipped her backpack and found a plastic bag. "You can put the cookie in this for the lab."

Bernie climbed out of the unit slowly, keeping an eye on the black-and-brown mongrel and noticing that he kept an eye on her, too. She followed Annie to the house and waited while she climbed up a ramp and unlocked the door.

"Dylan, Dylan." Annie yelled louder the second time. "It's me. I've got a lady with me, too."

Bernie heard a grunt from a back room. "Who's Dylan?"

"He's my brother. He's probably playing video games or something."

"Hi, Dylan. I'm Bernie. Hello back there."

A voice called back, "Hello out there. When is Mom coming?"

Annie took the question. "I don't know. She's talking to Mrs. Cooper."

"Who?"

"Oh, someone you don't know."

"So will you fix us something to eat? Chili dogs?"

"I'll do it in a little while."

Annie opened the door to the closet by the front door. She stared at the coats crowded inside for a moment and then grabbed a blue one and pulled it off the hanger.

Bernie put a hand on her arm. "Stick your hand inside this plastic bag like it's a glove, grab the cookie, and then turn the bag inside out."

Annie's face filled with questions.

Bernie showed her what to do. "The cookie might be tied to what happened to Mr. Cruz or to why you had to go to the hospital."

Annie patted the big pocket on the right side of the jacket and then the one on the left. "It's not here."

"Are there other pockets?"

"Yeah. Wait a minute." Annie slipped the coat on and ran her hands over the front, stopping to unzip zippers and pull open Velcro. She found some tissues, a quarter, a nickel, and a piece of candy. She frowned. "I guess I was wrong. Sorry."

"Are you sure this was the coat you wore?"

"It's my winter coat." Then Bernie saw her face light up. "I remember. I used Mom's old jacket because she was afraid this one might get ripped or something."

"Do you know where it is?"

Annie pressed her lips together, thinking. "Yeah. It's in the other closet, across from Dylan's room."

Bernie walked with her a few steps to the back of the house, thinking about the difference between Merilee's grand home and this small, practical space shared by three people.

"Hey, brother, company coming your way."

Bernie heard a squeaky sound and then saw a thin young man in a wheelchair.

"Whoa. You're a cop. What did my sister do now?"

Bernie squatted down so she could talk to the man at eye level. "Nothing. In fact, she's helping me get to the bottom of a big puzzle."

"That's good. Are you a friend of Mom's?"

"I respect your mom and her commitment to the people." Bernie guessed that the young man was about her sister's age. "Dylan, are you going to school?"

"Some online courses. We have to get a van that can handle the wheelchair."

Behind her Bernie heard the sound of hangers moving over metal, and then Annie was back, empty-handed.

"I can't find it."

Dylan rolled to face her. "What are you looking for?"

"That old green jacket of Mom's that I wore to camp."

"Look in the dirty clothes pile, silly."

Annie's grin brightened the hallway. "Good idea. I'll get it. Come on."

Annie led Bernie back to the front closet. On the floor in a plastic hamper, the girl found a green parka. Bernie remembered Annie wearing it, remembered thinking it was too big for her and probably let in the cold.

Annie lightly patted the front pockets. "I found the cookie." She used the bag to pick it up, sealed it, and handed it to Bernie. "There's something else, too." And before Bernie could caution the girl, Annie reached her bare hand into the pocket.

"I forgot about this. I found it right outside the cave with the . . . you know." Anne opened her hand, and Bernie saw a small oval disc with a figure on it and a ring of metal at the top for hanging it from a chain. "Officer Bernie, would you like it?"

Bernie looked at it more closely. Writing around the edge of the medallion read "St. Christopher Protect Us." It stirred a memory. "Let me borrow it." She slipped the medal into her pocket.

"Did someone say cookie? Do we have cookies?" The voice from the back room had a comic lilt to it. "You better save me one."

"No cookies. Sorry, bro."

"I heard you say cookie."

"I was teasing." Bernie gave Annie a look. "It was an old thing leftover from camping. It might be why I had to go to the hospital."

"Then, no thank you. Can you help me change my shirt?"

Bernie looked down the hallway toward the sound of the voice and back at Annie. "Are you two all right here until your mother comes home?"

"Sure. Mom leaves me in charge in the evenings, on the weekends, when she has to go to meetings, stuff like that. Dylan helps me with my homework. He reads me recipes when I cook."

"I can get dressed by myself," the voice said, "but it's easier if somebody does the buttons for me."

Bernie raised her voice a little. "Dylan, I have some brownies in my car. Would your mom mind if you and Annie had some?"

"As long as it doesn't have nuts. I don't like those."

"No nuts. They're chocolate."

"Great."

Bernie closed the door, and she and the girl walked down the ramp and to her car. "How old is your brother?"

"He's twenty." Annie looked down at her polished fingernails. "He got screwed up in a motorcycle wreck. But he's still pretty cool."

Bernie unwired the trunk and gave Annie the box of brownies she'd planned to take to Mama, and the girl went back inside. Bernie watched the front door shut behind her, and then labeled the bag with Cruz's cookie in it, looking at the cookie more closely. It was small and dotted with little bits of brown that looked like chocolate.

She started back to the office and put her phone on speaker. Time to call Darleen and tell her she was proud of her.

But before she could do that, Sandra came on the radio.

"The captain needs you."

Largo's gruff voice filled the unit. "Manuelito, are you done at the restaurant?"

"Yes, sir. I left Cooper and Walker talking. It looked like they might work it out." She told him about Annie and the cookie.

"Good work."

"There's something else." Bernie told Largo about the information from Annie concerning Cruz's last whereabouts.

"I'll pass it on to SAR."

"Sir, Annie said she thought she could find the place."

"I doubt that they'd want her out there, but I'll mention it."

Bernie hesitated before asking the next question.

"Have you heard anything more about Michael Franklin, the guy who took a shot at me and stole Merilee Cruz's car?"

"No, I haven't. He's still out there somewhere. Why do you think he shot at you?"

"I don't know, sir."

She heard some muffled noise. Then he was back. "Two more things. The toxicology on Larry Hoffman shows that he died from an opioid overdose compounded by alcohol. And the new FBI agent needs to interview you about a lead on a case she's working that somehow ties into all this."

"Me? Did she say why?" A fatal one-car accident with drugs and alcohol as a factor was usually not a matter for the FBI. Such things, unfortunately, happened regularly in New Mexico.

"She's following up on the lead about Manzanares— remember him, the state cop?" Largo didn't wait for an answer. "He told the investigators that you were first on the Hoffman scene and removed potential drug evidence that has now disappeared."

Bernie couldn't help herself. "Disappeared? Disappeared! No. He stole it out of my trunk during a blizzard. My guess is that Manzanares is into something, well, something off the books, and it stinks. So when does the FBI want to talk?"

"She's on her way now. You should be, too."

25

Bernie understood the value of making a good first impression, and she realized she was failing miserably as she sat in the tiny conference room at the Shiprock substation with FBI agent Sage Johnson across the table. For starters, watching this blonde—about her age, maybe a touch older—look through her notes before she started asking the questions didn't sit well with Bernie. Her time was valuable, and this woman didn't mind wasting it.

And why hadn't the agent started out friendlier? After all, they'd be colleagues in law enforcement until this manicured white girl got a ticket off the reservation. Johnson offered her name and a handshake but didn't follow up with any pleasantries. No "How are you?" or "I look forward to working with you." Nothing.

As she waited for the interview to start, Bernie considered what else she needed to do. She hadn't even seen Chee since he'd come back from Santa Fe. She had put off talking to Darleen and that circled back to her lack of time with her husband. Then came the problems of the missing Mr. Cruz, the stolen pot, Annie's lie, Annie's retraction of the lie, Annie's cookie, Ranger Hoffman's death, the heartfelt connection between Merilee and Franklin, and Franklin's firing a pistol and then becoming a car thief. Questions spun in her brain like planets on a wobbling orbit.

She hadn't had an opportunity to read the autopsy summary or the police report Leaphorn had sent on Merilee's husband's death. The Lieutenant would never have sent these if he didn't think they contained something important. And now she had to wait for someone who should have had it together to get organized.

Finally Johnson looked up from her notes at Bernie. "Officer Manuelito, I've reviewed Officer Manzanares's notes about the accident that resulted in Mr. Hoffman's hospitalization and death. He wrote that you were the first responder. Is that correct?"

"Yes."

"Did you speak to Mr. Hoffman at the scene?"

"Yes."

"Tell me about the conversation in detail. Everything you remember."

"Really? You want to know all the wacky, delusional things he said to me?"

Johnson smiled, revealing perfect teeth. "There's no reason to be combative, Officer. We're on the same side here."

Bernie drew in a calming breath. Play nice, she told herself. Get this done. "Ah. He told me he recognized me and made a joke about my name."

"Is Bernie short for Bernadine?"

"No. Bernadette."

"Go on, please."

Bernie regathered her thoughts. "He asked me to help him out of the car because there were too many ants in there."

"Aunts? As in women?"

"Ants. As in the little bugs. I told him he had to wait for the ambulance people to help him."

"Wait. When did you call an ambulance?"

"I called 911 to report the accident, and I said a man was injured."

Johnson made a note. "Tell me more about the conversation."

"He asked me where the blood came from. I told

him it was from his nose colliding with the airbag. He said the airbag was a cloud of ice and to be careful about touching the car so the ants wouldn't climb on me. He told me the ants were friendly." Bernie paused. "Are you sure you need to hear all this?"

"Please continue."

"He told me he couldn't see very well, and I explained that he had broken his glasses in the accident. I said I was surprised he would be drinking or doing drugs while he was driving. He told me he never drinks while he's driving, and that the only drug he takes is pain medicine for his back."

"Did he say how much?"

Bernie thought about it. "I don't remember. I may have it in my notes."

Johnson frowned. "Go on."

Bernie added every trivial detail she remembered, including the ants singing in his ear and the crushed wings, and Johnson kept asking for clarification. Bernie had to admit that most of the agent's questions were good ones.

"Tell me more about the phone call he said caused the accident. Did he say who was calling?"

"No."

"When he asked you to call someone and tell her that he had been delayed, did he give you the name?"

"No."

Johnson frowned again. "You can volunteer information. If you are more helpful, we can both be done with this, Officer."

"I saw that the call was to Merilee Cruz." Bernie explained about the green wart and offered more details. "When I called her, she seemed to be expecting someone else and asked if Manzanares was there."

Agent Johnson interrupted. "Did she say Cris Manzanares?"

Bernie thought about it. "No, she only used his last name."

"What did you say?"

" 'No, he's not,' or something like that."

"Did Ms. Cruz say anything else about Manzanares?"

"No. She hung up without saying good-bye."

"Why did you remove the box?"

"Hoffman asked me to take the box to Merilee Cruz. He said he was afraid something might happen to it. He talked about his house rolling away."

"Enough with the hallucinations. Did you do as he asked?"

"Yes. I put it in the trunk of my unit."

"Did you have any misgivings about doing that?"

"Yes. That's why I took photos." Bernie paused and

then brought up the conversation about owing Hoffman a favor because of the good price on the book.

Johnson nodded once. "Did you have any contact with Officer Manzanares at the accident site?"

Bernie relayed their conversation about the accident and the pot. "I asked Manzanares why it had taken him so long to reach the Wings and Roots campground to activate the search. He didn't give me a straight answer."

"You mentioned that you put the pot in your unit. Where is it now?"

"I don't know."

"Why not?"

"Someone broke into my trunk and removed it."

She thought she saw the whisper of a smile on the agent's face, an expression that said *Don't give me this line of nonsense.* But Johnson only said, "Did you mention this to Merilee Cruz?"

"Yes. She said she couldn't verify that I'd actually had the box intended for her because she hadn't seen it."

Johnson jotted down another word or two and closed her notebook. "We're done here for now. Thank you, Officer."

"I have something to ask you. Is the FBI just interested in a possible problem with pot hunters, or do you think this has something to do with the man who disappeared out there in the Malpais?"

Johnson smiled, this time flashing her perfectly straight teeth. "That's a great question. Have a good day."

Bernie went outside to calm down before she called Chee. Just like Mama, he had an uncanny way of sensing her moods. She paced around the parked cars and trucks, organizing her thoughts about Hoffman's death, Domingo Cruz's photographs, her suspicion that Manzanares took the pot from her trunk, and Annie's cookie.

Lately, parking lots had been bad luck for her. There'd been the car bomb at the Shiprock High School lot, where she was the first law enforcement person on the scene, and before that, witnessing Lieutenant Leaphorn take a bullet next to his truck in a Window Rock lot. Thinking of the Lieutenant reminded her again of the autopsy report on Merilee's husband and the police report about the drowning. She'd read those things next and then talk to the Lieutenant again to see if he'd had any more insights about the Wings and Roots donor.

She kept moving, breathing in the crisp December air, consciously shifting her thoughts to the positive until she had cooled off enough to call her husband.

Just when she felt ready to call him, there was Chee's well-used pickup pulling into a parking spot.

She walked over. He lowered the window and was talking before she even reached him. "Hey, beautiful. Aren't you cold out here without your jacket?"

"No, the new FBI agent got me steamed up. I'm better now."

Chee shut off the engine and unfastened his seat belt. "You've been hard to get a hold of. I've missed you."

"I've missed you, too. Did you take Darleen back to Mama's house?"

Chee hesitated. "She made other plans. We need to talk."

She watched him climb out of the truck, swinging his long legs onto the ground with grace and strength. "The captain has you working tonight. You're really early for your shift."

"I know. I planned it that way. With the hours you've been working, I figured I might find you here catching up on paperwork."

As they approached, the door to the station opened, and Agent Johnson emerged with her briefcase. She gave them a questioning look before walking briskly to a new steel-gray SUV.

Chee squeezed Bernie's hand. "Is that her?"

Bernie nodded. "She's investigating a fatal auto accident that I was first responder to. She just spent half an hour interviewing me."

"That's odd. What aren't you telling me?"

"Oh, I owed the guy a little favor so I made a phone call for him and took something he wanted delivered because he knew his car would be towed. He was only a loopy guy with a dislocated shoulder and some interesting hallucinations. I don't know how a traffic accident turned into a federal case. I hope she knows what she's doing."

Chee opened the door and motioned her to go ahead of him.

Bernie smiled at him. "What's going on with Darleen?'

"Let's get some coffee, and I'll tell you. And then you can tell me what you said that made her cry."

"OK."

Chee shook his head. "Don't look so worried. It's not as terrible as you probably think."

She laughed. "Right. It's probably worse."

26

Chee poured them both some break room coffee. From the way it smelled, it had been sitting for a while, but he'd been well trained not to let anything go to waste.

He sat across from her. "Where shall I start?"

"Start at the end. Darleen's program is over, but she didn't come back with you. What's up?"

"She's helping CS finish the video of the lady with sheep, and they are working on it tonight. She traded a drawing for a ride home and lunch with someone who is helping with the taping."

"Oh. Another person in the program?"

"Ah, no. A man with a rich, deep voice. CS asked him to help with the narration."

Chee stopped at that. If Bernie had more questions, he'd give her the expanded version.

"So tell me about CS and the death certificate and then weave in the parts about Darleen and what you think of the school."

"You know, when the Lieutenant told me about how he discovered that Clayton Secody was dead, I thought I'd misread CS, and that he was some kind of fraudster. But I was wrong. Can you believe it?"

She could tell from the twinkle in his eye that a major story awaited her, but he stopped talking.

Captain Largo walked into the break room and right to their table. He acknowledged Chee with a quick jut of his chin and focused on Bernie. "Manuelito, you're not answering your phone. Or the radio, obviously. Agent Johnson needs to talk to you again."

"Thanks. I'll call her."

"No. You need to go now. And put on your vest."

"Where? Why the protective gear?"

"She's working a hostage situation outside the Wings and Roots office." Largo narrowed his eyebrows. "It's that Franklin guy you found in the Malpais."

"He's a hostage?"

"No. He's the one with the gun."

Chee stood.

Largo looked at him. "Sit down, Sergeant. The feds are on this. And the rookie is already there. I've got a backlog of assignments for you when your shift starts, and if you want to get going early, that's fine."

Bernie found Wilson Sam waiting by his unit, parked across the road from the Wings and Roots office to block further access. His excitement was palpable. He started talking before she got out of the car.

"I responded to a 911 call that came in from a neighbor who said a man with a gun was acting crazy, pacing outside the agency's office, talking to himself, maybe drunk or on drugs or something. When I drove up, I saw the dude open the door and go inside the building."

Bernie looked toward the office and the cluster of houses and outbuildings nearby, picturing the scene. A San Juan County sheriff's car and several unmarked FBI units were pulled up close to the office.

"So I walked up to the door. I knocked, but nobody answered, so then I yelled in and asked him why he was walking around crazy-like."

She pictured a neighbor, probably some older person or a woman home with a baby, peeking out at the pacing man, thinking it was odd. Looking again and again and then seeing the gun and calling the police. She could see the rookie arriving, lights flashing, blustering his way into the situation. "When did you get here?"

"About an hour ago."

"What did the man say when you asked him what he was doing?"

"The guy said everything was really messed up, and it was all because of Wings and Roots. So I'm standing outside there, and I'm getting cold. I heard, like, an argument, and somebody else, a high voice—a girl or a woman—screaming 'Don't hurt me,' stuff like that. I tried the door, but the dude must have locked it." The rookie paced as he talked. "I told him to leave that person alone and come out or let me in so we could talk better. That was when he yelled at me to go away or he'd shoot her. And if I stayed, he'd shoot me, too." He scowled at Bernie. "He told me to get the FBI because what he had to say was bigger than federal, state, and Navajo together. He said he would not hurt the hostage if the FBI would listen to him. So I said, 'What's the hostage got to do with this? Why don't you send her out? She sounds scared.' "

Obviously that tactic hadn't worked, but Bernie played along. "What did he say?"

"He said, 'No, she's probably in on it.' And I said 'In on what?' like they do on TV. He said something like 'All the problems that weighed on Tom.' "

"Tom or Dom?" Bernie asked.

The rookie shrugged. "Something like that." He gave her a cocky smile. "Now here comes the good part. I told him before I could do that, I needed to know who he was, his name, you know, because the FBI would ask me that. And I needed to know what he wanted."

"That was smart." Bernie made a quick thumbs-up.

"So he told me his name, Michael Franklin, and I radioed Largo. He called the FBI. The new FBI agent got here real quick, and when she saw what was up, she asked me to call Largo and get you."

"I've got to find Agent Johnson."

The rookie pointed toward the group of black cars with a turn of his head. "She's over there. So you know this Franklin dude?"

"I do."

She had to give the rookie credit. He'd done what was required, hadn't made things worse, and no one was hurt. She pictured Cooper at her desk, Franklin pacing outside, building the courage to open the office door and talk to her, perhaps hoping to have her words ease his soul. Of all the people she'd interviewed about Domingo Cruz, Cooper and Franklin cared about him the most.

Bernie kept her gaze on Agent Johnson as she approached the huddle of officers. A pickup blocked the other end of the street. A blue sedan she recognized as Cooper's car was parked beyond it. Why would her car be there, so far from the Wings and Roots office?

Johnson caught her eye and motioned her into the group of officers. Sam followed. The agent introduced her to the others—FBI agents and a San Juan County sheriff's deputy. Manzanares was the only one she knew except Johnson, and he didn't acknowledge her.

"I guess you heard why you're here."

"Sam said that Franklin wants to talk to me. I'm surprised that Rose Cooper hasn't already solved this herself."

"Cooper? Who is that?"

Bernie took a step back. "She's the director of the Wings and Roots program."

"You mean the older woman over there?" Johnson pointed an index finger with a neatly shaped nail to Cooper, who was standing in the sun, far from the action.

"Do you know who the hostage is?"

"A Navajo teenager working as a volunteer for the program."

"What's her name?"

"Anna Rainsalot."

Bernie sucked in a breath. "Do you mean Annie Rainsong?"

Johnson gave her a sour look, rechecked her notes. "Yes, that's right."

The rookie was talking now. "What is that kid doing there? I mean, shouldn't she be in school? Maybe it's already winter break. Or maybe she's a senior or something and gets credit for volunteering?"

As he jabbered on, Bernie gathered her thoughts. She didn't understand why Franklin needed to speak to her, but she knew that hostage situations often turned out badly for both the hostage taker and the hostage. She didn't want either of them to get hurt.

Johnson finally interrupted the rookie. "Officer Sam, the girl is a hostage because she was in the wrong place at the wrong time. Our mutual goal is to resolve the situation as quickly and safely as possible."

"I didn't mean—"

She cut him off. "Go back to your unit. We don't want any civilians here who could get hurt, so make sure no one comes in unless it's law enforcement or an ambulance."

"I'll watch the back of the building," Manzanares said, and walked away. Johnson motioned to a pair of other agents, and they headed that way, too.

Agent Johnson handed Bernie a bullhorn. "Tell Franklin you're here. Ask him what he wants. Don't promise him anything. I'll coach you."

Bernie couldn't help herself. "How many hostage situations have you dealt with? I heard that this is your first posting."

She watched Johnson's eyes go hard. "I trained at the academy with hostage negotiation as one of my specialties."

"Well, welcome to Navajo, where incidents like this are probably different than what you learned. More personal, usually involving alcohol. Family matters that escalate out of control."

Johnson tapped the speaker. "You know how to turn this on?"

Bernie flipped the switch and walked out from the group to face the house.

"Mr. Franklin, it's me, Bernie."

She had never talked through a bullhorn before, and it made her voice sound tinny and too loud. "They said you wanted to talk to me. Why don't you come outside so I can hear what you have to say?"

The front door opened. "I'm staying in here with Annie," Franklin yelled. "Put that noisy thing down, and come on over and talk to me. Bring Cooper and the FBI woman, too." The door closed.

"Tell him nothing happens until he frees the girl," Johnson said. "Tell him taking a hostage is a federal offense. The backups here are ready to go in after him."

Bernie put the bullhorn down and pulled her phone from her backpack.

"What are you doing?"

"I'm calling Annie."

"What?" Johnson shoved the megaphone toward her. Bernie pushed in the numbers.

"You're . . . oh . . . Put her on speaker."

"I did."

The girl's voice sounded small and scared.

"Annie, it's Officer Bernie. Could Mr. Franklin please use your phone to talk to me?"

Silence and then a businesslike "Hello."

"Mr. Franklin, I'm worried about you. I have you on speakerphone so the FBI can hear too. What's going on?"

"I tried to tell that FBI woman, but she couldn't even get Dom's name right. That's why I wanted you. You understand."

"Have you been drinking?"

"No. Just coffee. Too much, I guess."

"Mr. Franklin, FBI agent Johnson is here, and she asked me to figure out what the problem is and why you have that gun in there with Annie. She sounds terrified. You aren't the kind of man who makes a young girl afraid."

"Oh, Bernie, it got messed up, like when I shot at you this morning. All I wanted was to talk to Mrs. Cooper, to clear Dom's name if she thinks he was stealing money from the program or something, and to tell her that his photos were just photos and had nothing to do with those looted caves. But Cooper wasn't here, only this volunteer girl, and . . . and . . ."

She heard his voice crack. "Take a breath, Mr. Franklin. There's no hurry. I've got all the time you need."

"It's freezing out here," Johnson said. "What's he talking about?"

Bernie muffled the phone against her jacket. "Give him a minute."

When Franklin spoke again, he sounded more composed. "Here's what I want. I want somebody to look at the agency's financial records and clear Dom's name. I want the FBI, or whoever does this, to make sure everyone knows that Dom wasn't involved in any funny stuff with the old pottery sites, with the Internet, with diverting tribal funds. I want everyone to understand he's a good guy. That's it. They can take me to jail as long as they promise to tell me when Dom comes back. Even, you know, even if it's bad news."

Johnson grabbed Bernie's hand with the phone. "Agent Sage Johnson here," The agent's voice rose to a shout. "Before I agree to anything, I need to make sure the girl is safe. You admitted shooting at someone already this morning. Send your hostage out now."

"Annie doesn't want to leave. She thinks she's the reason Dom is probably dead."

"Tom, Tom, Tom! Tom who?"

Bernie cringed, and Franklin was silent.

They heard Annie's voice. "Dom Cruz. Mr. Domingo Cruz. Don't you know anything?"

Bernie pulled the phone free from Johnson's grip. "Mr. Franklin, I'm going to explain to the FBI agent who Dom is. I think that will help her understand what you want."

Johnson scowled and gave her a double thumbs-down.

"Go ahead, Bernie." She could hear Franklin, or maybe it was Annie, weeping. "Do it over the phone so we can hear you, too."

"Go ahead, for God's sake," Johnson whispered. "Let's get this done."

But Bernie took her time. She knew words had power, and Franklin's Navajo parents, and surely his grandparents, had taught him that, too. She said a silent prayer and hoped that adrenaline would buoy her if the words ran low.

"The first thing I have to say is that Domingo Cruz is a good man, a valuable man whom I hope to meet one day. From what they say, he spends his life helping to make Wings and Roots a strong organization to give girls and boys who need some extra guidance tools they can use to grow up to be people who honor their relatives and make a good difference in the world. From what people tell me, he would never do anything to harm the program, his relatives, or the young people who hold him in high regard."

She talked on, intermixing English with Navajo for those ideas in which only Navajo captured the complexity of the concepts, such as kinship and the duty that came with being Navajo. She talked about how warmly Mrs. Cooper and the girls in the camp spoke of Mr. Cruz, how much they valued his leadership and his generosity. She talked about how his sister and Franklin honored and respected him.

As she spoke, Bernie realized that, except for some comments that the man sometimes seemed preoccupied, the only person she had ever heard speak against Cruz was Mayfair. She filed that bit of information away.

When she finished, she asked Franklin if he had something to add.

"Agent Johnson, do you understand?"

Johnson put the megaphone to her mouth. "Yes. I think you should let Annie come on out right now. Mr. Cruz devoted his life to helping young people like her. What would he have said about you holding her hostage?"

Bernie frowned at Johnson's use of the past tense.

Franklin's voice had more energy now, and more anger. "Annie is fine. Dom would be pleased that I am trying to clear his name, whether he returns or not." He stopped talking and then said, "What the—"

They heard Franklin yell something else and the phone clattered away, about the same time as Bernie heard the gunshot.

Things happened fast after that. The shot was followed by a scream and then another shot. The door of the Wings and Roots office swung open, and Annie raced into the road, her dark hair flowing behind her. Cooper appeared from somewhere behind Bernie and Johnson, running toward Annie, catching her in a fierce embrace and then pulling her farther away from the place where the shots had come from.

Bernie ran toward the house, Johnson keeping pace beside her, followed by another agent. By the time they got there, one of the two agents whom Bernie had seen moving toward the rear entrance was standing next to Manzanares, who held his hands over his left knee.

Blood oozed between his fingers, and his gun lay on the floor in front of him. He looked up at Johnson and then at Bernie with questions in his eyes.

Before he could speak, Johnson said, "Cristóbal Manzanares, should I arrest you now, or wait until you're indicted? Either way, you can kiss that juicy retirement good-bye."

Manzanares uttered an obscenity.

Bernie saw the agent smile.

Johnson put her gun in her holster. "You made our job a whole lot easier today by adding attempted murder to your résumé."

Manzanares turned his head to the left. "Attempted? You mean I didn't kill that rat bastard over there?"

"You're a lousy cop and a lousy shot."

The agent who was attending to Franklin radioed for an ambulance. ". . . leg wound," Bernie heard him say. "A second victim shot in the shoulder. Both conscious . . ."

She walked up to the agent. "I can keep an eye on Franklin while you deal with Manzanares. I know Franklin."

The agent nodded once and walked to the other side of the room. Bernie squatted down next to Franklin. "Just stay still."

"Where's Annie? Is the girl hurt?"

"She ran outside. She didn't get shot."

"Thank God. Where's Manzanares?"

Bernie explained, all the while applying pressure to his shoulder wound.

He listened, shaking his head in disbelief. "He came in the back door. Surprised me."

"It looks like he wanted to kill you."

Franklin gave her a quick nod. She thought he looked pale.

Bernie released the pressure a bit, checked the bleeding, and pressed again.

"He didn't want to kill me. Manzanares wanted to kill the girl because of something she'd seen in the cave. He was after Annie, not me. When he drew his gun, I stood in front so she could run. He thought she had found something of his that tied him to that place. I don't get it. Too many crazies around here." His voice was a whisper. "Officer, can I tell you something in confidence?"

Bernie readjusted her position, She left his question unanswered.Franklin squeezed his lips together. "Annie had the idea that I pretend she was a hostage. She feels bad about Dom—she calls him Mr. Cruz. She thought that if we did that, someone would listen and she could help the searchers find him." He breathed deeply. "She wanted to help me and she could have left anytime. I should have made her go." He shifted toward Bernie with a painful grunt. "Tell that girl I'm so, so sorry she got mixed up in all this. I only wanted to do some good for Dom, and I've caused more trouble." Franklin grimaced as he raised himself to a seated position. The movement restarted the bleeding.

Two of the other agents were standing with Johnson, men Bernie had worked with on occasion and men both she and Chee respected. Old hands in the Four Corners. Maybe they were giving Agent Johnson some tips. One was saying, ". . . arrest him, and that means someone has to stay in the hospital with him. My daughter's concert . . ."

Agent Johnson left the group and walked toward Bernie and Franklin.

Franklin seemed weaker now, but he kept talking. "I just needed someone to listen."

"I'm listening," the agent snapped at him. "Give me the quick version of why you did this, in case you bleed to death. Start with you bringing a gun to the Wings and Roots office."

Bernie would have used a softer tone, and left out the part about bleeding to death, but Johnson was in charge here.

"The gun? I always have a gun. I came to tell Cooper that Dom told me that Mayfair, the one who did the bookkeeping, really made some mistakes, and that she should check into that. Not to blame him. The girl said Cooper wasn't here, so I went outside, pacing to stay warm, thinking, talking to myself like I do. Then that young cop drove up. I thought he might be coming to arrest me because of the shot I fired at Merilee's house."

"You shot at a residence?" Johnson's perfect crescent eyebrows moved toward her hairline.

"Well, not exactly. It was a greenhouse."

"We can come back to that. Go on."

"When that cop started hassling me, I went inside the office. The girl and I started talking, and that's when I found out she was the last one to see Dom before he disappeared. She told me that she'd seen a skeleton in a cave." Franklin shuddered. "We were both crying."

Agent Johnson looked puzzled.

Bernie tried to simplify. "The girl, Annie, didn't stay where she was supposed to, and Cruz disappeared when he went out to find her. Besides working directly with the kids, he also is the group's fund-raiser." She paused. "Why are you involved?"

"Besides the hostage situation, the other agents and I are here because Manzanares has been the subject of an ongoing investigation," Johnson said. "It seems he was creating fake provenances for Indian artifacts and selling them to European and Asian clients on the Internet as part of an organized crime network."

"Agent, ask him why he wanted to kill Annie." Franklin's voice had softened with exhaustion and blood loss. "She's just a kid."

"I can't talk about that."

Bernie turned to Johnson. "Is there a connection between Cruz's photos and the illegal pot business?"

Johnson looked surprised. "I'm not at liberty to say."

"Dom took pictures of petroglyphs and landscapes, for Merilee's book. That's it," Franklin said. "Why all the secrets?"

Johnson finally crouched down to Franklin's level. "Did he ever show you any pots or artifacts that he collected out there?"

"Never *ever* would he even touch that stuff." Franklin grimaced. "You wouldn't ask that if you knew him. Those things are grave offerings, and no one who follows the Navajo way wants anything to do with it."

Bernie could hear an ambulance siren now, faintly. She hoped Johnson would stop the attendants from putting Franklin and the man who tried to kill him in the same vehicle.

"Dom is a good man, and that's why I came here. To make sure people knew that." Franklin closed his eyes but kept talking. "Merilee asked Dom to keep track of possible burial caves so they could make sure they were protected. He was careful to document them. They were going to share all of that with the National Parks and Wilderness Conservation people."

The siren grew louder, and then, with a crunch of tires on the dirt road, the wailing stopped. Bernie heard doors opening and closing. She put her hand lightly on Franklin's arm. "The ambulance guys are here. Rest a moment. Save your energy. They'll need to ask you questions."

She turned to Johnson. "What led you to arrest Manzanares today?"

"The agency was tracking Larry Hoffman, a ranger with some links to a group that sold illegal Native American artifacts online and then used the pots for moving drugs. That's what brought us to Manzanares. It looked like he was providing false provenances for the pots this guy fenced, saying they came from his ranch. We were investigating Manzanares when I was notified that Hoffman was in a one-car accident, and that Manzanares had arrived on the scene and insisted on interviewing Hoffman, who later died of what we're told was a bad combination of alcohol and prescription opioids. The attendants suspected that Manzanares had given him something that killed him."

Johnson broke away to talk to the ambulance driver while a medic began to examine Franklin. Bernie stood to leave, and Franklin reached for her hand. "Please don't let them give up on finding Dom. Tell Merilee I never meant to hurt her. I was out of my mind when I took a shot at her. How could I help but love her? When I look in her eyes, I see her brother, too."

27

Bernie stood outside the Roots and Wings office and watched the ambulance leave. She noticed Cooper and Annie. They looked shocked and cold, as if they'd been standing there for a while.

Annie ran toward Bernie. "Were those gunshots? Is Mr. Franklin dead?"

"No. He got hit in the shoulder, but he'll be all right. He said to tell you he's sorry that you got tangled up in all this."

"The whole dumb thing was my idea."

Cooper frowned. "Let's go inside and warm up. You can call your mom and tell her you're OK."

Bernie heard a car door shut, and then Mayfair bounced over to them. "What were the federal agents doing here?"

CAVE OF BONES • 441

"Agent Johnson didn't exactly say, but it had something do to with Officer Manzanares," Bernie said, and then summarized what had happened.

Mayfair raised an eyebrow. "Do you think the FBI involvement has anything to do with Wings and Roots and our money problems?"

Before Bernie could answer, Cooper stepped in. "Councilor Walker and I got that worked out."

"What do you mean?"

"I mean, I convinced her that the money from the Navajo Nation was accounted for. Well, *I* didn't really convince her—it was the bookkeeping. I showed her the reports Cruz had prepared."

"Dom took the credit, as usual, but I did the work." Mayfair moved her hands to her slim hips. "There was never any problem with the tribal funds. The problem was the loss of the other grants and private money . . . and Dom's inability to raise enough money. If it hadn't been for that anonymous gift, we would have gone under."

"Do you know who the donor is?" Bernie asked.

"No. If I did, I would have pressed that person for more money in exchange for keeping his or her name confidential. Dom was too laid-back. He didn't have enough passion for raising money. He just wanted to go hiking with the kids. If I'd been the director, I would have hired a real fund-raiser, and put the old man out to pasture."

"Dom never said anything negative about you." Bernie heard anger in Cooper's voice. "I'm going to be relying on you even more. You'll need to step in as fund-raiser, but you have to be more respectful."

"I have a better idea." Mayfair's grin, combined with her braids, made her look like a teenager. "Why don't you work as our volunteer fund-raiser in your retirement? Everyone knows you. I'll be the director and hire some interns to help with the trips. I'll supervise you, for a change."

Cooper's eyes widened. "You know I love this organization, but, after the board put me on notice, I doubt that I have any credibility. Besides, I'm another of the old coots you'd like to put out to pasture."

"We could raise money with a bake sale, and Ms. Mayfair could make the cookies," Annie broke in. "But don't make any like those little ones you gave Mr. Cruz. The one he gave me tasted funny. Kind of bitter."

Bernie heard the shock in Mayfair's voice. "You ate one?"

"No offense, Ms. Mayfair, but I couldn't even eat it. Officer Bernie thinks it might have made me sick."

"Those were the same cookies I always make," Mayfair said tightly. "Peanut butter."

But Annie held her ground. "I love peanut butter, but the one I tried was like a yucky sugar cookie with something brown in it."

"You're wrong about that, Annie," Mayfair said.

Bernie frowned. The girl had described the cookie she'd seen in Annie's pocket perfectly.

Annie's voice softened. "It's OK to screw up, even with cookies. Everybody can make a mistake, right, Officer Bernie?"

"Right." Bernie looked at Mayfair. "Did you give anyone else any of those cookies?"

"No, I baked them especially for Mr. Cruz."

Cooper motioned them to start walking toward the office, talking as she moved. "Why? You usually made cookies for all of us."

"They were a gift, to show I didn't have any hard feelings about him being picked for the director job." Mayfair moved next to Annie now, Bernie and Cooper trailing behind.

Bernie felt the cold seeping through her socks. She spoke quietly to Cooper. "The FBI thinks Cruz and his sister have something to do with the illegal artifacts business Manzanares was involved with. What do you think?"

"Never." Cooper opened the office door and then turned toward Bernie. "Dom is committed to preserving the Malpais, and that included any burials out there."

Mayfair pushed her braids behind her shoulders and stood straighter. She smiled at Bernie. "You know, he always stayed after our trips. He said it was to take photos, but maybe there was more to it. Will the FBI check on that?"

"I'm sure they will." Bernie shoved her hands in her pockets. She needed to check with the lab to see what they'd found in that cookie.

Cooper looked at the truck that was blocking the road. "Why is that vehicle still there?"

"It belongs to Manzanares," Bernie said, " I'll call for a tow."

"Wait," Mayfair said. "Maybe the keys are in it, and I can move it out of the way."

Bernie watched her climb inside, heard the engine start, and saw her park it along the road. She handed the keys to Bernie. "Nice ride. I never took that guy for a Cowboys fan."

"What you do mean?'

"The sticker on the bumper. I'm a Patriots girl myself."

Bernie got home late. She called Mama and spoke to her only long enough to learn that Darleen had phoned and told her she'd be home the next day. Mama had asked the man who gave her a ride to stay and eat with them.

Chee served fried bologna sandwiches and tomato soup. Bernie ate like a starving person and then had seconds.

Chee cleared the table. "All right, tell me about Manzanares getting arrested."

"It's complicated." She summarized while Chee did dishes.

"Now, tell me what you said to Darleen when I called you in Santa Fe and handed the phone to her. What made her cry?"

Bernie grabbed a towel and started to dry the silverware. "Mama kept saying that Sister was ignoring her and hadn't called or stocked the house with food and essentials like I'd asked. But when I talked to Sister, she said she had talked to Mama every day, and every day our mother scolded her for not calling. She said that Mama didn't remember." Bernie's words rushed out. "She told me they had driven to the grocery store and come home with food, toilet tissue, all the essentials. Plenty for Sister to have been gone an extra week. Something's going on with Mama. We were both crying by the end of that call. I'm glad I'm off tomorrow morning. I'm driving there to see what I can find out."

"That's tough, sweetheart. I encountered a lady at Tesuque Pueblo who makes me appreciate how lucky I am that your mama is part of my life." Chee told her about Mrs. Vigil and George Curley, finding the humor in it and making Bernie smile. "Curley did some work on a ranch out here and said he was going home. He's still missing, and I helped his wife file the missing person report. The photo Mrs. Vigil gave me to use had Curley in the background. It was mostly a picture of the new truck he and his wife had just got. The picture even had the Cowboys bumper sticker and the numbers on the license plate. Mrs. Vigil didn't care about Curley, but she wanted that truck back."

Chee rubbed a knuckle over his chin. "You know, he's lucky he's not working for Manzanares anymore. He'd probably never get paid."

Bernie looked at him. "Did the truck turn up?"

"I haven't heard that it did."

"What did it look like?"

Chee paused. "A new Ford pickup. Hold on. I took a picture of the photo I left at the Santa Fe County Sherrif office." He pulled out his phone and scrolled until he came to it. He stood and passed the phone to Bernie.

She studied the picture and sat up a little taller. "I think Manzanares was driving it. What work was Curley doing for him?"

"Cris said he was selling lava rock for landscaping, and Curley helped with the hauling. I thought that was funny because Curley is a little guy, about the same size as Manzanares. Five foot five at the most."

"Just the right size to crawl into a cave to remove some grave goods."

Chee sat down. "His mother said that something spooked him, and he'd talked to her about a ceremony but never came home to make the arrangements. Why didn't he follow through?"

"I know why." She sighed. "Let's get to bed early. We'll have a long day tomorrow. I'd like you to go out to the lava flow with me."

They called the station and then left for the Malpais before first light, arriving just as the search and rescue team was setting up coffee. Bernie gave the commander on duty information about where they were headed, and she and Chee set off.

She led them to the entrance to Annie's cave through a combination of memory, logic, and good luck. It seemed undisturbed since her last visit.

"I can take a look inside if you'd rather not," Chee said. "You've already been in there once."

Bernie shook her head. "Come on. Let's get this over with."

They hiked up to the ledge, where Chee squatted next to her as they peered into the darkness. The cave looked just as it had when she'd first found it, although it was smaller than she remembered.

Chee stood up. "That space is really tight. I don't think I can get very far inside."

"That's right. But George Curley could have maneuvered in here. Like you said, he was a little guy—five-five, just slightly bigger than me."

"Was?" Chee sniffed the air. "Oh."

"And after Curley said no to looting graves, Manzanares would have fit inside, too. Would you shine your light to the rear of the cave?"

He watched the beam against the lava. "What's that? The stone on that back wall looks different."

"That's what I thought. I believe I know why it looks that way now." She brought up her own beam to match his and then turned it off. "I'm climbing back there."

She quickly put on the gloves and knee pads she'd brought. "Can you give me as much light as possible?"

Chee shone his flashlight ahead of her. "Take your time. It could be treacherous."

Bernie inched her way through the tight entrance with as much respect for the old bones as she could manage, using her own flashlight to help avoid contact. Then she moved to the larger space, the area of the cave she hadn't explored before. She could stand up if she hunched forward.

She shone her light along what had looked like smooth lava as she approached, breath by breath, step by cautious step. It wasn't rock. It was black plastic. Her light reflected off a large bag, the kind a restaurant might use to line an extra-large garbage can.

She turned away from the stench toward the cave opening. "Can you give me more light back here?"

"I'll try." He did. Bernie moved to the end of the bag. Someone had tied it in a knot. She propped her flashlight against a rock and used both hands to rip through the plastic, then grabbed the flashlight again. Before she could think about what she'd see, she moved the beam to shine inside the bag.

Bernie turned her face toward the mouth of the cave. "I think I've found the man you were asking about at the pueblo."

"Get out of there now!" Chee yelled back to her. "Follow my light, and be careful. We need to call OMI."

When Bernie reached the mouth of the cave, she watched the worry in Chee's face turn to relief. She'd never been so happy to see the sunlight. The office of the medical investigator would handle the body, but they knew the man in the bag must be Mr. Curley.

They walked silently for a few minutes before Chee spoke again. "Why would Manzanares risk everything he'd worked for to loot graves? He had the ranch. He had a good retirement on top of that."

Bernie let the question hang unanswered in the cold air over the lava trail.

"You know," Chee said, "if he'd figured out how to get the new truck back to Mrs. Vigil, Manzanares might have gotten away with it."

"I think you're right. That, and if Annie hadn't told the truth about the cave of bones."

At the search base camp, while Chee called the medical investigator's office and talked to the state police about the scene, Bernie told Katz about the body.

"I'm a deputized officer, and I've dealt with body retrieval, crime scenes, and OMI many times. Too many times." Katz gave Bernie a sad smile. "You two go on home. I'll make sure they keep you in the loop."

"Thanks." Bernie shook hands with Katz. "And let me know when you find Mr. Cruz."

"Of course."

Chee offered to drive. Bernie watched the scenery and thought about George Curley and his wife and mother, thought about how death sometimes came unexpectedly. She thought about Mama. She wondered if shifting to specialize in domestic violence would be a transition she'd feel comfortable with. As they approached Shiprock, Chee radioed the office with the news of what Bernie had found and told Sandra they were heading home.

He drove straight to their trailer, and they went inside. "Are you still planning to visit your mother?" Chee asked. "Since your sister will be home soon, she can check things out and save you a trip."

Bernie nodded. "You're right. So, tell me about Darleen and the IAIA and that video."

Chee filled her in on the school, the dorm situation, Clyde Herbert's evident rehabilitation, and the video. "The whole experience gave me new respect for CS."

"What about Sister and drinking?"

Chee stayed silent.

"Did you give her a lecture?"

"I talked to her about it, yeah. She told me she's going to focus on her art. You would have been proud of her, the way her work looked in that show. She has talent."

"So what about—" Bernie gave him the wait-a-minute sign and reached in her pocket for her phone. She looked at the ID and answered.

"Sure, go ahead. This is great. I've been waiting to hear test results." She listened, nodding occasionally, as if the person on the other end could see her agreement.

"You mean, like fraternal twins?"

She listened some more.

"Can you send me an official copy of that, and one to Agent Johnson?"

She smiled. "Thanks. I really appreciate it."

She put her phone down. "The lab found high levels of a poisonous alkaloid in the cookie Annie had saved in her coat pocket."

He didn't even have to ask.

"That means eating some of that could have been the cause of her hallucinations. Probably was. But the substance wasn't datura, as the hospital assumed, but some botanical cousin."

"I heard you say fraternal twins, and that made me think of Dom and Merilee."

Bernie nodded. "That's right, but the report referrs to another member of the brugmansia family, another plant that can cause trouble if people aren't careful. In addition to hallucinations, the alkaloid leads to heart failure, respiratory problems, and even death."

"So Annie was lucky that she was on the van when that happened," Chee said. "If a person ingests that stuff by accident and starts hallucinating, she thinks she's going crazy."

Bernie nodded. "Cruz gave the girl that cookie. If he ate some too, that explains how he could have lost his way in familiar territory."

"Where did the cookies come from?"

"A coworker made them and offered them to him as gift. I'm going to call Agent Johnson and tell her to expect the lab report." Bernie put her hand on his. "It's been a long morning, and we have to go to work in a few hours. How about a nap?"

"Wait a minute. Darleen asked me to give you something." He reached in his shirt pocket and pulled out a pair of heart-shaped earrings with red stones, earrings he'd given Bernie as a speical gift. Earrings she had reluctantly loaned her sister for the video and never really expected to see again.

He placed them in Bernie's upraised palm. "She asked me to tell you she's sorry she kept them so long."

28

The search team discovered the body of Domingo Cruz a week later, right around Christmas, in a deep, snow-filled crevice far from the Wings and Roots base camp. The victim's skull had fractured in numerous places, and exposure compounded the deadly situation. They found no signs of struggle, indicating that he had died on impact.

By then Larry Hoffman's death had been ruled a prescription-opioid overdose, enhanced by the alcohol in his system. The death raised the question of accidental overdose, but in Bernie's mind there was no doubt that Manzanares had given Hoffman the fatal drug.

The autopsy confirmed that George Curley died of gunshot wounds, including one to the heart. He had been dead approximately a month when Chee and Bernie discovered him in the cave. The murder weapon matched the gun with which Manzanares had shot Franklin.

Bernie was surprised when Merilee called her a few hours after she'd learned that Dom's body had been recovered. "I'm glad they found him," she said. "But even though I assumed he was dead, it's tough."

"I'm so sorry."

"At least I'm not worried about him now."

"I heard that the FBI came to see you." Bernie tried to be tactful. "Did Agent Johnson ask about your brother's photos?"

"Right. I think we worked it out, but I may need a lawyer. Manzanares is claiming that I knew he was raiding the graves and colluded with him to raise that anonymous money for Wings and Roots. I could kick myself for having gotten involved with him and, even worse, involving Dom."

"I'm sorry I never met your brother."

"You would have liked him. Franklin and I are helping each other get through this. I'm grateful and lucky to have his friendship."

"How is Franklin?"

"Sad, relieved, stunned. About like me." She paused. "There's something I'd like to give you. I'll drop it off at the substation when I get a chance."

"I noticed that the bag of brugmansia seeds you were saving was gone. Did you give them to someone?"

"I think Mayfair has them. Maybe she thought I said she could take them when I offered her the herbs."

As soon as Merilee hung up, Bernie called Wings and Roots. She expected Mayfair to answer, but it was Cooper.

"Mayfair's gone," she said. "She left before I could fire her."

"Why?"

Cooper rushed to answer. "Those anonymous donations didn't sit right with me. I tracked them down through a friend who works at a branch of the same brokerage house that issued the cashier's check. My friend could get fired over telling me this, but it turns out the money came from a foundation set up by Mayfair's family."

Bernie recalled their conversation in the Malpais, Mayfair saying her parents were glad she'd moved away.

"I talked to Mayfair and tried to thank her, but she blew up at me. I'd seen that temper before, when I told her I was recommending Dom for the director's job. I told her to take a walk, get herself under control. Instead, she started swearing. I knew I had to fire her—what if she lost it like that with the kids?"

"Did you?"

"I wanted to dial back my own anger first, so I went outside to shovel the driveway. When I came back, Mayfair had left her key and a letter of resignation, for so-called personal reasons."

Bernie processed the information. "So I guess you aren't retiring."

"I can't leave until I get all that settled. I love this program, and I've got good volunteers and some students who might be interested in working part-time until I can find another professional to train to take my place."

After Cooper hung up, Bernie called Agent Johnson and left a message about the missing seeds and Mayfair's parents. "She told me she'd changed her name when she left home. I'm sure Cooper can fill you in. I know she's responsible for Domingo Cruz's death."

At home that night, Bernie shared what she'd learned with Chee.

"Agent Johnson still thinks Cruz may have been scouting for sites to loot in the wilderness area or the conservation land or even on Ramah. No one who lives the Navajo Way, like the man who took those pictures, would mess with graves. I bet Mr. Curley couldn't do it either once he realized that's what Manzanares wanted. Johnson makes me wish Agent Cordova were still here."

Chee had been removing his boots as he sat on the bed, but he straightened up now. "You know, we're going to have to work with Agent Johnson and make the best of it."

"I know."

"I talked to the Lieutenant today to thank him for helping me figure out CS's death certificate and for the information on Clyde Herbert. He said Agent Johnson had reached out to him for background on Manzanares and the old search in the Malpais he'd been involved in."

"The one where the bodies were found years later?"

"That's right. He mentioned that she told him Manzanares had connections to international Internet fraud."

Bernie brushed her hair from her face. "Wow. I don't get it. People become cops because they want to help, not rip off their neighbors."

"Every profession has a few failures. That goes back to what you said about Mayfair quitting and leaving Cooper with no support. Unprofessional, to say the least. And it sure makes her look guilty of something." Chee went back to his boots. "One more detail and then let's go to bed. The Lieutenant said Larry Hoffman, the guy from El Morro, tied into this because Manzanares got greedy. He asked Hoffman to sell some of the pots locally, always to foreigners who weren't likely to understand the antiquities laws."

Bernie smiled at him. "That reminds me. Wait a minute."

She walked to the living room and came back with a paper bag and a white cardboard tube. She handed him the tube first. "I wanted to show you this. It's a picture Domingo Cruz took out in the Malpais. I admired it, and Merilee gave me a copy. I think I'll give it to the Lieutenant as a thank-you."

He took the cap off the end of the cylinder, pulled out a sheet of paper, and unrolled it to discover the photo of the swirling petroglyph. "This is beautiful. No wonder Merilee wanted to do a book of his work."

Bernie handed him the paper bag. "And this is for you. For believing in me enough to go to the Malpais and find what we found in that cave of bones."

He pulled out a book, the stories about the formation of the southwestern landscape that she'd found at El Morro.

"This is fabulous." He thumbed through it slowly while she watched the smile on his face grow larger.

"You mentioned that you learned something at the training you wanted to show me," she said after a while.

He put his arms around her. "I learned how special you are, and how lucky—"

She put her finger on his lips. "Actions speak louder than words."

29

They had finished dinner and were chatting in the Lieutenant's living room, nursing cups of Louisa Bourbonette's herbal tea. When he extended the invitation, Leaphorn had told Chee and Bernie that Louisa had fully recuperated. As usual, he was right. Louisa had done ninety percent of the talking, as though she had been starving for company.

Now, she started asking her guests questions. "We haven't seen you two for ages. What have you been doing, Bernie?"

"Working as usual. I was out in the Malpais." Bernie explained a little about the looting scam and how the information Chee had gathered in Santa Fe led to the discovery of a dead man.

"How sad for his mother."

"At least she knows what happened to him," said Chee. "A man we work with, Wilson Sam, has been checking on her, spending time with her. I think it's been good for them both."

Louisa shook her head. "I don't know how you two, and Joe, too, manage to handle all this sadness and evil. It would get to me."

Bernie paused, considering. "You know, despite all the human ugliness I've been dealing with, that country near Ramah makes my heart sing. It's beautiful in the winter. Have you seen it?"

"Many times. When I was researching my comparative religion project, I came across one story that said Zuni fetishes were inspired by animals that had been trapped and turned to stone by the volcano."

"Interesting." Bernie listened with half an ear. As she saw it, religion was what the Franciscans, Presbyterians, Methodists, Mennonites, Latter-day Saints, Christian Reformed, and others offered.

Louisa passed Chee the plate of cookies. Some looked like oatmeal; other were probably chocolate chip. "I didn't make them, but they're pretty good."

Chee helped himself without hesitation. "I spent a while in Santa Fe getting some training in the Amber and Silver Alert systems for missing kids and elderlies. It will be a boon to the Navajo Nation."

Louisa passed the plate to Leaphorn. "Would it have helped with that youth worker who got lost?"

Leaphorn took one of each kind of cookie and then spoke. "No. He was in the wilderness. The state search and rescue teams are like the Silver and Amber Alerts on steroids." He broke off a bite from each cookie, chewed, and smiled. "These are good, Louisa."

"The bakery at Bashas'."

Leaphorn passed the plate to Bernie, and she took one out of politeness. After spending so many hours considering poisoned cookies, she would have preferred pie, cake, Jell-O, canned peaches . . . anything else.

Louisa stood up. "I'm going to straighten up a little and call it a day. There's more tea."

Leaphorn put his hand on her arm. "Don't bother about that. I'll do it later. You go on to bed. I'm glad you felt well enough tonight to have company."

"Oh, you worry too much." She patted his hand and headed down the hall. Then Leaphorn turned to Bernie. "What did you think of the information on the anonymous donor and my report on Wings and Roots?"

"I thought you were smart to pass the information along to Mrs. Cooper," Bernie said. "I should have been more suspicious when Mayfair told me she'd changed her name, and that her family was glad to see her go."

"You're still young. Be glad that you're more trusting. How did you and Councilor Walker get along?"

"It worked out. She came around once Cooper explained the books to her. She was still prickly, but she listened. Now she's working with the council to get more funding for the program. Something seemed to have softened her attitude."

Leaphorn grinned. "She wants to buy me a cup of coffee. For a *dasani,* she's not—"

Bernie's ringing phone interrupted him. She looked at the number—the FBI office in Farmington. "Sorry, it's work. I better take this."

Leaphorn nodded, and Chee reached for another cookie.

"Manuelito, Agent Johnson," said the voice on the phone. "I wanted to let you know that the bureau will follow up on Mayfair."

"That's great." But, Bernie thought, news that didn't need to interrupt her off-duty time. "I need to talk to you again about the Manzanares case."

"I'm in the middle of something now, but go ahead." Chee passed her the cookies, and she waved them away.

"That Saint Christopher medal the girl found looks like more evidence that Manzanares murdered Mr. Curley. Good work on that."

"Thank you."

"I was thinking . . ." Johnson's speech slowed. "Maybe we could have coffee tomorrow?"

"I'm working the early shift. If this is an official request, it should go through Captain Largo." And, Bernie thought, you know that.

Johnson said, "It's not official. We got off on the wrong foot. I'd like to start over."

Epilogue

Domingo Cruz had located Annie Rainsong quickly. Now she was on the trail back to camp, not injured, not in danger, and still a disagreeable spoiled girl with an ugly skull tattoo. He followed, moving quietly, until he knew she could see the tents of camp headquarters. It was better for her to come in on her own, without him, so she would at least get the credit for finding her way to offset some of the trouble she'd be in for leaving her solo site. Cooper would deliver a sterner-than-usual version of the standard be-responsible lecture. The fact that she'd found her way back by herself might give Annie's confidence a little boost.

He was glad to see the last of Annie Rainsong. That girl was a pain in the neck. He smiled. Yes, and she was also the very sort of kid Rose Cooper had envisioned when she designed the program. He'd watched as she bounced along the trail in front of him. When the terrain allowed, he stepped behind a large rock, removed the bell from his pack, and slipped it silently into his pocket. Then he made a sound, his best imitation of an injured animal. She didn't turn back. Good girl. She remembered what he had said about testing her.

As he watched her head toward base camp, he had an idea. Rather than return to camp immediately, he'd hike to the parking lot. The Lobos, his favorite team from his days at the University of New Mexico, were playing their in-state rivals, New Mexico State University, the basketball game of the season. Maybe he could quickly get the score from the strong AM station in Albuquerque before he went back to work.

He breathed in the cold air, tinged with a hint of sage and the possibility of snow. He still felt exceedingly strange. He hadn't been sleeping well. Worried about Franklin's growing emotional distance, worried about the challenge of becoming the Wings and Roots director, and worried about Mayfair and the likelihood he'd have to fire her because of her snarly attitude toward him. But mostly he worried about Merilee. His big sister—she was three minutes older and never let him forget it—was involved in something bad, something wrong, something that she wouldn't talk about. She'd always been the impulsive one, the stronger of the two of them, although she didn't look it. She'd bounced back from the death of her terrible husband, even though his cousin, that state cop, blamed her for the accident.

When he reached in his pocket for the key to the group van, he felt Annie's phone. He had picked it up at the cave where she dropped it, where she never should have had it. Cooper had told all the girls to leave their electronics in the van as directed. He'd give it back to her at the campsite with another lecture about following the rules.

He unlocked the door and climbed inside, noticing that he had trouble getting the key in the lock. Low blood sugar, he thought. Those cookies he'd eaten a while ago ought to begin to help with that. Mayfair was usually a good baker, but that batch was terrible. If he hadn't been so hungry, he would have thrown them away.

He couldn't focus on the game because he couldn't adjust the volume: it was either too loud or not loud enough, and the knobs moved away from him as he reached for them. His mouth felt dry. He remembered the extra water bottles in the back of the van. He'd grab one before he hiked back to . . . where was he going?

His stomach churned now, and the world was spinning. Something was wrong. Cruz looked at the gray asphalt that stretched away from the parking area. The road was undulating. He looked at the phone that was somehow back in his hand. It had started to move in his grip like a living thing. He tossed it down onto the asphalt and ran back toward the lava. Something was happening inside him, fascinating and terrifying and totally unexpected.

He thought of the spirals he loved, the swirls he'd photographed on the lava. It was more than an image—it was a force inside him now, pulling him back toward the beautiful blackness. He had no choice but to follow.

At first, he watched for the piles of rocks to show him the way, and then he didn't. He couldn't see very well, but his feet had their own eyes. When he came to the crevice, he realized he could fly.

Acknowledgments

First of all, I would like to thank the many Navajo people who have made it a point to reach out to me—either in person, through e-mail or on social media—to thank me for continuing my father's stories of Joe Leaphorn and Jim Chee. Nothing delights me more at a book signing than to be asked to pose for a photo with a Dine' grandmother, daughter, and granddaughter, and to hear how they love reading about Bernadette Manuelito solving crimes.

While writing is solitary work, research, editing, and brainstorming take a village. I am grateful to more people than I can name here, but special thanks to Rebecca Carrier for her brilliant insights into what makes Bernie tick. Her sharply focused critique of an early version of this book improved the story. Writer and editor Lucy Moore came up with some wonderful questions that deepened and broadened the novel and also saved me from embarrassment.

Big thanks to Kayt Peck for sharing her personal stories of working with search and rescue in New Mexico and to Robert Rodgers, New Mexico State Police search and rescue coordinator, for his time and good advice. New Mexico's chief medical investigator, Kurt B. Nolte, MD, now also a Distinguished Professor at the University of New Mexico, answered my questions about dead bodies in language that made it easy for me and Bernie to understand the process involved in autopsies. David Greenberg helped me grasp the complications involved in state, tribal, and federal law enforcement interaction in a hostage situation. Gail Greenberg's generosity and kindness as I weathered personal challenges in the course of this book helped keep me on target and on deadline (more or less).

Thanks to Scott Hicks for hiking the Malpais with me, and to the staff there for answering questions about critters and lost folks. The staff at Cottonwood Gulch and the Henio Family added to my understanding of Ramah and of programs that get kids outside. Tony Dixon and Misty Blakesley at the Santa Fe Mountain

Center filled in the blanks about the links between wilderness adventures and teen behavior. My writer friends, the Literary Ladies, kindly listened to my complaining and bragging about this book as it took shape, and editing by Jim Wagner of Daddy Wags saved me from considerable embarrassment. I am in your debt.

Using her extensive knowledge of the material available at the Laboratory of Anthropology Library on Santa Fe's Museum Hill, librarian Allison Colborne made it easier for me to discover origin stories of the Malpais lava flow from the Laguna, Acoma, and Zuni people. The staff at the Institute of American Indian Arts allowed me to tag along on a tour for incoming students. I invented the program Darleen joins and readjusted their architecture a bit, but I didn't have to fictionalize the warm spirit at this wonderful arts college.

Huge thanks to my agent, Liz Trupin-Pulli, for her endless kindness and encouragement, and to all the folks at HarperCollins: my editor, Carolyn Marino; her trusty sidekicks, Hannah Robinson and Laura Brown; publicity director Rachel Elinsky; and Tom Hopke, marketing manager. And a warm shout-out to freelance copy editor Miranda Ottewell, whom I also had the honor of working with on *Spiderwoman's Daughter*.

My husband, Don, and children, Brandon, Sean, Carrie, and Kevin, all deserve halos for putting up with me as I focused on writing. You guys mean the world to me.

And, last but not least, who would I have been, as a writer or a person, without Tony Hillerman?